FAENCINA'S HOPE

Rebekah Amman

FAENCINA'S HOPE

HOPE

Water's Maiden

REBEKAH AMAN

Design by Kristen McGregor

Published in the United States of America

ISBN-13: 978-1518742361
ISBN-10: 151874236X

1. Fiction / Fantasy / Epic
2. Juvenile Fiction / Fantasy & Magic
15.10.26

DEDICATION

To my brothers,
Matt, the carefree, playful wave, and
Lamar, the deep, calm waters.

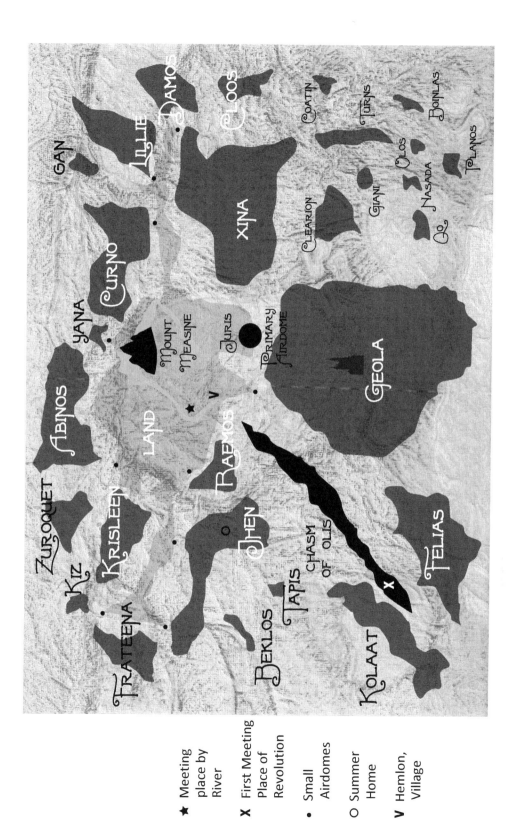

★ Meeting
   place by
   River

X First Meeting
   Place of
   Revolution

• Small
   Airdomes

O Summer
   Home

V Hemlon,
   Village

PROLOGUE

All was peaceful…or so it seemed.

The ocean was not thrashing about; the wind was not chillingly brutal. Instead, the water was serenely lapping along, nearly glass-like, and the breeze was that of a gently loving caress. Beneath the surface, bright and insistent sunbeams dove deep, deeper than might be expected, but even they could not shed light into the deep chasms of the ocean floor. That was precisely why this spot in the Chasm of Olis had been chosen.

"Quiet, all! Settle down, if you will!"

The angry hubbub from the crowd began to dwindle, and once the conch sounded, silence reigned supreme.

"You know why we be here!"

The speaker shot an intense stare into every one of the hundred or so faces before him. These were the leaders of the many districts in this corner of Faencina. They all had problems that had not been addressed by the sovereign ruler, the Prime who governed those both below and above the water. Everyone here believed it was time that something was finally done about their uncaring tyrant.

"We shall take this mistreatment no longer!" he yelled, raising a fist into the air. "The taxes have grown increasingly brutal, our citizens cannot find jobs, murderers and thieves abound…and then there be the children."

Muttering began again. It was not just anger on the faces, not just sadness, but confusion and great worry. Somehow, this most disastrous and all important factor, the one thing that brought everyone together in this mutiny and that started the downfall, did not really seem to be the

Prime's fault. However, someone had to be blamed, and their ruler was an easy target.

The speaker nodded sadly. "We must do something, but we must be smart."

The crowd began nodding with him. His words were so true, and clearly he was a brilliant man. He was old enough to be gifted with wisdom without having lost all of youth's vitality. He had a welcoming and appealing face without being too attractive, and he had dark eyes that could capture your attention without causing any fear or discomfort. This golden speaker could lead them to a revolution that would solve their problems.

"The Prime and Prime-Mate must both be imprisoned and a new leader put into place. We need someone who knows every citizen's needs, has lived beside them, toiled with them, understands them."

Cries of affirmation rang out.

"What do these spoiled royals know? Nothing! So we shall rise up. We shall take our stand and make our needs known!"

More excited shouts of agreement sounded, but above it all came a question.

"How be we able to do such a thing?"

The speaker gave a satisfied smile. "Exactly! This be what you all should ask. There be many obstacles in our path, and if we look to succeed, we cannot be rash. Everyone here must hold their tongues, keep silent, and hide away this secret plan if we wish for revolution. It shall not be quick, but will take a great many months. We shall infiltrate the castle, station our people as servants and guards. Our eyes and ears must surround the royals at all times. When we be ready, a sabotage shall occur on food storage, weaponry, travel. Then we shall attack. The Prime and Prime-Mate shall have no choice but surrender, and we shall lock them away!"

The room roared with the crowd's approval, and it did not die down for some minutes. The meeting was adjourned, and these ambitious district leaders broke into groups to discuss more ideas or left for home to begin the infiltration. One, however, moved to question the speaker.

"Excuse me, sir."

He turned with a raised brow. "Yes?"

"I…um, have a question."

"Certainly," he boomed with a large smile. "Tell me, which district be you from? I seem unable to place you, though I thought I knew all the leaders around these parts."

"Oh, I be not a district leader. I be Luik. I work at the castle."

The speaker's eyes gleamed. "Truly? Ha, ha! We be one step closer then. Already an ally be within the Prime's court."

Luik cleared his throat. "Well, maybe. I agree with you about the happenings…me brother be one of the children…anyway, me question be what you plan to do with the Shoring Water Maiden."

The speaker seemed surprised. The daughter of the royals had not even been given a fleeting thought. "I suppose she shall be imprisoned as well. We may have some use for her, but at this stage, she be unimportant."

"You will do her no harm?"

"I do not plan to harm any of them. Even their prison shall not be a standard prison. They shall reside in their summer home in Jhen but be well guarded."

"You swear it?"

The speaker paused almost imperceptibly. "It be so sworn."

Luik nodded and shook the speaker's hand. "Then I shall be at your service."

"Glad to hear it!"

The speaker's attention was then caught by another discussion nearby, which he enthusiastically joined, and Luik was free to leave. He was quite young, only twenty years, but he was very aware of the fact that the speaker's oath to keep all three royals safe could very easily be broken. As such, he vowed to himself that very night to protect the Shoring Water Maiden in the coming revolution. It seemed wrong somehow for her to be punished for her parents' mistakes, and although she probably would not recognize him or even remember his name, he would do this and thus prove his devotion to her.

CHAPTER 1

"I shan't accept this!" the girl responded, her tail viciously slicing through the water to release some pent up agitation. She instantly realized her mistake, but it was too late to take back her reaction, and she was far too proud to retract the statement. Thus, she merely lifted her chin in challenge as she faced her emotionally distant parents.

"It be decided, and you shall," her mother answered, her mind somewhere other than the troublesome girl before her.

The girl's eyes slid to her father, who sighed as he returned the look. It was the same response she always received from him. She remembered times when he would sneak her treats at the dinner table or play with her outside, but inevitably, her mother would interrupt them to either steal him away or give her some order that she refused to obey. Either way, the father-daughter bonding moment was utterly destroyed, and though her father seemed upset about it, Diahyas was still left alone again. Not once could she remember a time that he was on her side against her mother.

"It be best, Diahyas, if you follow through with little protest," he said.

Her lips tightened as she glared at each of them in turn.

"And I be having no say in this matter?"

Slowly, the Prime turned her head to place frosty eyes on her heir. "None."

Inside, Diahyas felt her heart constrict, her lungs freeze, her stomach tighten with dread. Outwardly, she revealed only anger with another violent swish of her tail.

"It be your duty as Shoring Water Maiden," her father pointed out softly.

Diahyas latched onto that ferociously. "Precisely. I be Shoring Water Maiden to become Prime Water Maiden, the highest position there be for a mermaid. Should I not choose me own mate?"

Her mother's eyes snapped. "You be not Prime Water Maiden yet, and still me rule be absolute. This mating be perfect for the furtherance of me primage."

Diahyas' brows drew together in consternation and confusion. Further her primage? What more could she possibly want? She already ruled everything on Faencina, so to use her only daughter in such a cruel way...her eyes flashed.

"But I be the one to mate with him. Surely no furtherance be worth that?"

"You be questioning me?"

Her mother's tone was dangerous now, a warning. Diahyas felt the eyes of all the servants and guards milling about in the spacious and richly decorated throne room. Although they all must have worked at the castle for years, Diahyas had not a prayer of naming them. Neither did her mother, but that did not mean that the Prime would appreciate her daughter pushing the matter before her subjects.

Diahyas pressed on obstinately. "I be questioning you."

"Insolence!"

Her mother's eyes flared as she swam up from her thrown to tower over Diahyas. Her father quickly dove over to hover nearby, not that Diahyas believed him capable of controlling his wife.

Diahyas scoffed, which went completely against her better judgment. "It be insolence for me to question me future mate?"

All movement in the room stilled.

"It be insolence to question your Prime Water Maiden!" the Prime hissed before turning her head and muttering. "How be it I be cursed with such a daughter?"

The words stung deeply, which wasn't surprising since they were so intertwined with bitterness and venom. Again, Diahyas hid her hurt by lifting her chin and giving her mother a cheeky grin.

"Be it honestly surprising? I be told we be just alike."

There was a gasp from a corner of the room. Diahyas glanced only momentarily in the direction of the sound, noting the young, male servant that seemed vaguely familiar, before focusing all her attention back upon the Prime. A corner of the girl's lips twitched up briefly.

For a moment, she had her mother fuming speechlessly. Then the Prime's arm shot out, her finger pointing imperiously toward the door.

"Out!" she yelled. "Out! Leave until I call again, which may be never."

As Diahyas began to swim from the immaculate throne room filled with the countless servants and guards that had witnessed her humiliating audience with the Prime, she tossed a few dangerous words over her shoulder.

"I hope that be true, for then I shan't mate this stranger after all."

"Who do they think they be?" Diahyas muttered angrily as she swam into her lavish bedchamber, seeing none of the opulence before her.

They be the rulers of all mermaids, she answered herself silently, and all her helplessness in this matter washed over her. She tamped it down.

"Sea-ena, why be you drifting there in the corner when I be needing to change?" she asked without looking in the female's direction.

Her maid, who had watched her grow from such a wee thing, was used to this type of exchange...especially after a visit with the Prime and Prime-Mate. This kindly servant was of average build, average age, and average looks. What was truly lovely about her was the shade of her coloring. Her skin was a pale coral, her short hair a slightly deeper, rosy hue, and her tail glimmered with orange and yellow shooting through the underlying coral. Of all this, her eyes were what truly caught one's attention, though. The deep green was full of kindness and understanding, the latter of which made her the perfect companion for her rather difficult charge.

Diahyas was proud, and each time her parents brought her low, she felt the need to prove her self-worth on all the many subjects beneath her. Sea-ena understood when no one else did, so she merely pitied the girl where others glared their disdain. Only Sea-ena saw the lonely child beneath the façade, the daughter that would cry in her maid's arms each time mother and father swam past without a spare glance. Diahyas didn't have anyone, just Sea-ena, but even their relationship taboo. The

Shoring Water Maiden should not befriend a servant, should never show weakness to her subjects...yes, Diahyas with all her riches and power truly had nothing at all.

"Sea-ena, must I be waiting this day long?" Diahyas grumbled.

"Certainly not." The mermaid swam forward with a smile. "Where be you headed that you be needing a change?"

Diahyas' eyes flashed. "That be no concern of yours."

Sea-ena bowed her head in contrition. "I be asking only to choose the outfit."

"Oh."

Sea-ena looked up just in time to catch the uncertainty and apology in the girl's eyes. Then she straightened, and the momentary lapse was replaced by haughtiness.

"Then you could simply ask me what I wish to wear. Me destination be no concern of yours."

"Of course." Sea-ena bowed again and waited as Diahyas slowly came to realize that she could do nothing until an order was given.

Diahyas floated in indecision, knowing her mistake and not wishing to show it. However, her eyes flickered to sweet Sea-ena. Her maid would not fault her just this once.

She softened with a smile, her genuine self finally being given the freedom to peak forth. "I be having no clue what I should wear, nor what be hiding in me closet."

"Allow me to help?" Sea-ena offered with a gentle, answering smile.

Diahyas nodded in relief. "I be going..."

Her brows drew together in thought. She hadn't decided on a destination yet; she just needed to get far away. Where to go?

"I be going on Land," she decided with a nod, but even that was general.

Where to go on Land? She usually stayed close to shore, walking around the primitive stores and seeing all the land folk that were so fascinating. She had also gone into the woods further inland. That was quite lovely and wonderfully isolated...perhaps she should go there? No, she wanted something new, something different, something to counteract her currently unstable world...where might that be? She closed her eyes and pictured Faencina.

Her world was mainly water, which was good since the majority of the creatures living there were mermaids. Beneath the waves, the ocean's floor was divided into districts with large cities and small communities, but closest to the sole landmass was the capital—the largest city of them all, the home of the ruler of all on Faencina. The Prime Water Maiden was the supreme leader, even over the Yuens on land; it was a job Diahyas would eventually hold.

The capital was Geola, named after the very first Prime Water Maiden, and it was bustling all the time. All creatures came here to sense the best of everything. They had a fantastic system in place to allow the land creatures easy access. At the moment, though, Diahyas didn't care about all under the water; her focus was Land.

The one continent above ground was simply named, but there was no other like it to cause confusion. It had a large port city called Juris that was close to the underwater capital, but everywhere else there were only small towns. In one part of Mid-Land, there was a vast forest with a saltwater river splitting it in two. As one walked further north and to the east, the trees thinned until only parched, dry earth abounded. This was the desert caused by the salt-water lakes and rivers surrounding the lone mountain in its center. Diahyas could think of only one mermaid who had ever gone there, and he had died. The fool had not brought any water with him. Nonetheless, it had served as a warning, so the mountain resting in its very core remained unknown...unknown, yes.

Diahyas perked up. It matched her situation perfectly, and she was in just such a mood to throw caution to the wind.

"I go to Mount Measine," she declared finally.

Sea-ena's eyes widened. "You jest."

Diahyas shook her head. "I jest not."

"But it be suicide," Sea-ena protested. "Surely you jest."

"If anyone can do it, it be me," Diahyas replied confidently. "I have me tiara for transport, and I be the essence of water. If there be any water in this desert, I shall be able to find it."

"I think you ought not go."

"I think it be not your decision."

Sea-ena looked as if she wished to argue, but she held her tongue. Instead she said, "As you wish. I shall retrieve something."

She disappeared into the large closet. "I suppose I can be understanding this desire of yours," came her voice from within. "The ferocious heat be matching the intensity of your anger. The stark isolation from all things living be matching the loneliness of your soul. The thirsty ground helplessly searching for water be the equal to your…"

"How be it you know already of this evil match me parents hath chained me with?" Diahyas asked angrily.

Sea-ena peeked around the door, her face the picture of utter surprise. "A match? This be news to me, but surely it be not too bad."

Out she came with a thin seaweed skirt that would retain moisture and keep her young charge cool. The matching top, quite a small slip of covering, joined the bottom. Seeing as no one would view Diahyas in this desert, propriety need not be kept, and the outfit would do.

"Be not too bad?" Diahyas scoffed. "I know not this male, and based on the words spoken, I believe he be not of this world."

"Not so!" Sea-ena exclaimed in surprise.

Diahyas nodded as Sea-ena began replacing her current clothing with those just chosen. "Me mother said it shall further her primage. All of Faencina be under her control…so where else but another world?"

Sea-ena shook her head vehemently. "She shan't. Faencina need not be compromised with these other creatures, all above water."

"We have our own land creatures."

"Few in number, not a threat," Sea-ena said absently. "Besides, we have not enough land to welcome more."

"Nonetheless, I believe this to be her goal, and I shall be mating with a beast."

Sea-ena shook her head again. "No, I shan't believe it. Even your mother could not be so harsh to a daughter."

Diahyas sighed, her shoulders slumping slightly. "You give her too much credit."

Sea-ena had nothing to say to that.

"I just be needing to get away," Diahyas continued softly.

"But to Mount Measine?" Sea-ena pushed. "You could die. There be no water there, none at all, even for you to find."

"Perhaps it be better that way."

Sea-ena paused as she folded the discarded outfit. "Surely you mean not that!"

Diahyas shrugged, her expression distant and resolved but her eyes full of sadness. "Well, there be no need for an essence of water. What danger be there here? And why need we a Shoring Water Maiden with such a Prime Water Maiden as there be now? She be not willing to step down anytime soon, and she certainly wishes another heir. Perhaps she shall mate with this male she be planning for me and get precisely what she desires."

"Diahyas!" Sea-ena scolded, her surprise and horror quite evident.

Then Diahyas turned with a mischievous gleam in her eye. "You be not thinking that one such as me could contemplate death?"

Relief flooded the maid's face. "You be jesting only, then?"

"Most certainly. One such as me be too great to die." Diahyas winked with a haughty flip of her head.

"You be certain?" Sea-ena asked suspiciously.

"You be questioning me?" Diahyas asked with a raised brow.

"So you be not going to Mount Measine?"

"Oh, no, I definitely be going, but I shall show me mother that I cannot be forced to do things against me will. Even the fierce Mount Measine and its surrounding desert be not able to force me death, so who be she to try to force me mating? I shall survive what no other has, and she shall see."

"Unless you die," Sea-ena pointed out with worried eyes.

Diahyas laughed. "Then she be definitely beaten, see?"

"You must use reason, Diahyas. This be too dangerous, even for you. Reconsider!"

"Tell no one," she ordered with a smirk of anticipation, and then she closed her eyes to focus her being. The gem on her tiara, a beautiful blue sapphire, began to glow brightly. Sea-ena's eyes widened.

"Do not use the portal!" she hissed. "You shall be unable to return for hours. You shall be stuck in the desert."

Her plea fell on deaf ears, and her eyes were soon staring at emptiness as the mermaid transported in a dazzling blue light to the land of no water.

"Must this match truly be made? There be plenty of merfolk that would better suit Diahyas."

The Prime-Mate rarely spoke against his wife's decisions. That was why she usually listened when he did, not that she would ever allow anyone to see this behavior.

"Why say you this, Leeyan?" she asked with a tilted head. "You be implying I decide incorrectly?"

"You have seen this man, Bailena. He be unlike any other creature."

She nodded. "Yes, but that be what we need."

"What *we* need? What about our daughter? What be her needs? Not some unknown male of dubious species."

"He be human. I be sure."

"How? What experience have you?"

She paused. "The same as you, which admittedly be not much."

Leeyan nodded. "Yet I be not certain he be all human. How can you be?"

"I...I suppose I be not certain," she finally admitted. "But there be no humans on Faencina."

Leeyan's forehead creased. "Why must she mate with a human?"

He watched his wife grow quiet. Bailena would go through periods of stony silence, haughty silence, mischievous silence, and even reproving silence. Never had he seen her fall into this form of pensive and worrying quiet. What hadn't she shared with him? He knew all she knew; he was her sounding board. Why would she not tell him something that must be incredibly important?

"What be the matter, Bailena?"

She shook her head and sent a small smile his way. It was meant to be reassuring, he was certain, but it really only heightened his worry.

"Bailena."

She looked down in thought, and he waited as patiently as he could.

With a firm jaw, she finally met his gaze. "It be me wish to expand beyond me primage. This man be able to help me succeed."

Leeyan studied her expression for several minutes.

"If you do not wish to tell me the truth, at least assure me there be a very good reason behind your decision," he finally said.

Bailena almost broke then. He could feel her struggle, but she reigned herself in. "It be the best reason imaginable...and even you could not imagine this."

"Why cannot you tell me? Surely you wish to ease this burden."

She nodded. "This be true, but until things be settled, no one shall know. It be best not to cause panic."

Leeyan was quiet for some time. "Be you sure we should trust this man? I dislike him and feel something be hidden beneath the surface."

Bailena's gaze met his sadly, her agreement with his statement conveyed to him without words. "Do I trust him? No…but for me people, I can make no other decision."

CHAPTER 2

The portal opened several feet above the ground, with just enough space to allow Diahyas to switch from tail to legs and tighten the skirt around her waist as she landed smoothly on the parched ground.

"Hmmm," she said as she looked all around her. It wasn't quite what she had expected. It was really hot, hotter than she had imagined, and everything seemed more dead and lifeless here than she had thought it would. This was nothing like her forest adventure, but she was stuck here for a while, so she might as well explore…nothing. There was literally nothing here.

Her gaze scanned the flat land before her; where was the famous mountain? Surely she had not erred. Then she turned around, smiling as she saw the powerful earthen monument rising up. It was gorgeous, taller than anything she'd ever seen.

She laughed aloud and took a few rushed steps toward it in excitement. There, that was what she wanted to see. She wanted to climb up, be a part of that majesty…not all the way, but maybe there was a lower ledge she could reach. With that in mind, her eyes scrutinized the mountain's surface. Then her brow furrowed. Was that a boat?

She squinted upward and began to climb higher for a closer look. If it was, then it was a long way from home.

Higher and higher she climbed. It was not yet too steep, and she hadn't much farther to go before reaching the rather large ledge that housed the curiosity. As she drew closer, she was even more surprised to hear voices. Who would be out here in the desert?

"How much water do we have?"

"Before or after I finish slurping it down?"

"Fil."

"It's hot out here!"

"Well, it's a desert. Did you expect otherwise?"

"Yes, actually. I was expecting cool water in a fog-filled sea on Randor."

"Stop whining, Fil...and will you take it easy with the water? We have no idea how long we'll be out here."

Fil sighed and took one last swallow before corking the water skin. Eorian glanced over at his cousin from where he lay on a bench.

"It's not all that bad."

"Tell me again why we aren't using that pouch of dust to get back to Randor."

Eorian sat up. "Because I don't know how to use it. We could end up somewhere worse than this."

"You've got to admit, this would be hard to beat. I mean, look around you," Fil said as he gestured at the parched ground. "Everywhere you look, you see..."

He broke off, and Eorian sighed. "I realize, Fil. I'm sorry. We'll start walking when the sun goes down, and maybe we'll find a town before morning. It won't be that bad."

"E...come over here; come look at this."

"I already know we're in the middle of a desert. There's no need to rub it in."

"No, seriously, E, come here. I think I'm seeing a mirage."

Eorian pushed to his feet and sighed in aggravation. "You can't have heat stroke yet. We haven't been here long enough."

However, when he peered over the railing, he understood Fil's words. There was a woman climbing over the edge of the shelf on which they rested. Quickly, he grabbed for a rope to swing to the ground.

"Stay here," he said absently without his eyes ever leaving her, and he swung over the side to land softly before the woman.

She was the strangest thing he'd ever seen – one of the most beautiful, no doubt about it, but definitely the oddest sight his eyes had ever beheld. She sparkled, literally. Her skin was a thin sheen of what looked to be lightly colored sand, a pale blue in color that glistened faintly when the sunlight kissed her with its warmth. It was clearly her skin, though, and not some dusting of glitter or sandy soil, and it was the most intriguing sight. Eorian felt stirring within him an almost overwhelming urge to brush his fingers along her arms...to caress her cheek. He knew it would be soft somehow, despite its grainy appearance, but he fought the temptation down. Surely she was no mirage because he could never imagine a woman like her.

Her eyes were blue like his, but they were lighter, and it almost seemed like they rippled, as if they were moving even while they focused on his face. But most miraculous of all was her hair. It was unlike anything he could possibly describe. It reminded him of water, for it swam around her face even while no wind was present to play with the flowing strands — if indeed it was even made up of strands, and Eorian was beginning to believe that it was not. Her hair too was blue, slightly deeper in tone than her skin, lighter than her eyes, yet it was white as well. It was as if the white and blue swirled together, separate...together...lighter...darker... creating different shades and hues as her hair continued to roll about her in waves — yes, that was it! It reminded him of ocean waves with their white crests and blue troughs — and its length hit just above her waist, her tiny slip of a waist.

Yet as fascinated as he was by her, she seemed equally fascinated with him, her eyes practically glowing with excitement as she drank in his appearance.

She took a step toward him, drawing his gaze to the long expanse of her pale blue, sandy leg. He frowned. She was not wearing nearly enough to be wandering around a desert. Arms exposed, midriff bare, and quite a lot of leg peeking out as well. She was certain to be cooked alive out here. He dragged his gaze back to meet hers and was taken aback by the sound of her voice when she spoke.

"What be you that look so very odd with the smooth, tan skin and strange-appearing hair?"

Eorian could not speak. Her voice made his ears beg to hear more. It was fluid — there was no other word to describe it. It bubbled. It was just like a stream… flowing… rippling… teasing and playing and glorious and smooth, just like everything else about her. Eorian shook his head and tried to keep his reactions and emotions under rigid control as he answered.

"We're humans from Randor, traveling by…well, we were traveling by sea, but as I'm sure you're aware, we are no longer on the water." He made a gesture toward his grounded vessel before running a hand through his hair.

She watched his hair move in fascination, then nodded as she glanced away to peer at his ship. "Certainly, no, this be not water. What be humans? Me ear has not heard such a description, nor me eye seen one of the likes of you."

Eorian thought a moment. "Well, we're…I don't know how else to describe us. We're just human. What are you, if you aren't human?"

The woman reared back as if offended. "I? What be I? I be mermaid. Certainly, you jest, for surely you have heard of me. I be the Shoring Water Maiden, heir to me realm's throne."

Eorian shared a glance with Fil, who returned a slight shrug. "Shoring Water Maiden? Is that like a princess or something?"

The girl rolled her eyes and pushed back a piece of her hair, which sloshed away languidly with a slight rippling sound. "Only Yuens have them a princess, and I be much greater than those. I shore up to the Prime Water Maiden when she be called away from her throne."

"You take over for the queen when she dies?" Eorian asked.

The mermaid nodded. "For the Prime, yes. Me mother has time yet, for me time be not come. She be not willing to give up her power just yet."

Eorian nodded as he waded through her words. She had an odd way of speaking, but it wasn't too difficult to understand once he picked up the flow of it.

"May I ask your name?" he asked politely.

She grinned and glided over to him, her movements just as graceful and fluid as her voice. "I be Diahyas, and be ye who?"

"Eorian, and that be…*is* my cousin, Fil," he replied as he gestured toward his cousin. Diahyas' gaze flickered upward momentarily to examine the other human before Eorian's next question pulled her attention back to him. "Can you tell us where we are?"

"You be on Faencina's shores," she replied, then bit her lip and lightly touched his cheek with one finger, her mouth forming a grin as she felt the rough texture and allowed her other fingers to stroke him as well. "I have you a place, which you cannot refuse to see. Come, and I shall house you travelers from this far off Randor of yours, and you shall be clean and fed and warm and safe."

"It seems you are our only friend on this planet thus far, so yes, we'll definitely come. Lead the way."

Fil dropped down beside him with a bag over his shoulder. "I take back everything I said. I could get used to this place."

Eorian's eyes narrowed. "Forgetting my sister already, Fil?"

"You're kidding, right?" Fil asked with a smirk. "You're stuck with me on that front."

"Your words imply otherwise."

"What?" Fil asked in surprise before realization hit. "Oh, no, I'm just thinking we're in for the royal treatment. A princess…"

The narrowed gaze of their savior hit him full on, and he quickly corrected himself.

"Sorry, a shoring…water maiden?…is offering to take us to her palace. Who wouldn't like that?"

Eorian rolled his eyes before turning to Diahyas. "I apologize on my cousin's behalf."

She eyed Fil up and down with slight distaste.

"He be unusual."

Fil smirked, which pulled a scowl to her mouth, and she turned to Eorian with a gleam in her eyes. "But you be fascinating."

"Thank you?" Eorian replied in discomfort. "Any chance we can head out now? I feel my skin burning."

"That be not possible," Diahyas answered.

"But you said…" Fil began before she cut him off with a look.

"We must wait on me stone to reach full power," she explained as she gently reached up to touch her tiara, bringing their attention to the gem it held.

"I take it walking is out of the question?" Eorian asked with a raised brow.

"It be too far."

"How good are you at using those portals?" Fil asked suddenly.

Diahyas scoffed. "Portals? There be only one such as this."

"On this planet," Fil agreed. "But Eorian has the one from ours. Could you use that?"

"Fil," Eorian chastised. "Not something we tell everyone we meet."

"Why have you this portal?" Diahyas asked suspiciously.

Fil opened his mouth.

"Because I'm a pirate," Eorian jumped in quickly, ignoring Fil's look of exasperation.

"What be a...pirate?" Diahyas tasted the word on her tongue, not particularly liking it.

"Well...I sail the sea and trade things."

"Ah, a merchant." Diahyas nodded in satisfaction.

"Sure."

"And you picked it up in your tradings?" Diahyas asked.

Eorian worded his answer carefully. "It was given to me during one of my dealings, yes."

"Let me see," she ordered as she held out a hand.

Eorian and Fil shared a look.

"I'm not sure..." Eorian began.

"You refuse me?" Diahyas asked, her temper rising.

"No, no," Eorian quickly contradicted, feeling relief sweep over him as she calmed down. At the moment, staying in her good graces was paramount. "Here it is."

He passed her the pouch of diamond dust. She handled it reverently, her eyes bright as she slowly opened the small bag. However, her expression quickly turned to disgust upon viewing the contents.

"This be dirt."

Eorian shook his head. "It's diamond dust."

"It be useless." She tossed him the bag and crossed her arms.

Eorian considered her a moment before sharing an exaggerated frown. "So you can't do it? I would have thought that someone as powerful as you could have managed, but I guess I was wrong. Yes, I'm sure it's too difficult."

Her eyes widened at the affront. "Too difficult! Too difficult for me? No. Give it to me."

Again, her hand shot out in an imperious demand. Eorian complied.

"If you're sure..."

Her eyes narrowed. "You be mine, human. Do not question me."

Eorian didn't have enough time to process the pronouncement, much less question it, before they were all surrounded by light and he again felt that unusual and slightly uncomfortable tugging sensation. At least this time it wasn't as fierce.

Water...everywhere...no air...he was suffocating! That crazy, blue woman was trying to kill them!

Fil's eyes popped open, his arms flailing in the water. Where could he swim? There had to be air somewhere, right? His gaze flicked around him. He saw Eorian's own alarm, although his cousin was handling this a lot better than he was. Then he took in their surroundings...it was a room...a bedroom...a very nice, expensive-looking bedroom with a huge golden-edged, light pink shell filled with cushions and a large mirror hung on the wall before a low table strewn with what appeared to be beauty products. Fil's eyesight began to darken.

He needed to breathe, but he was trapped in a water-filled room. Then he saw that princess swimming...wait, she had a tail now? Yes, she did, and she definitely looked like a mermaid. He had wondered about that when she first said she was a mermaid. He must be delusional. Here he was about to pass out from lack of oxygen, and he was focusing on her blue and purple shimmering tail.

That's when he noticed her popping something onto Eorian's nose. His cousin reared back slightly, but then he seemed to relax, his chest expanding and contracting as if he could now breathe. He grinned at Fil, and then Diahyas snapped the same type of contraption onto his nose. Sweet, blessed air! Fil sucked it in, filling his lungs. Oh, how he needed that.

"There," Diahyas announced, her voice still surprisingly clear through the water. How was that possible?

"What is this?" Eorian asked as he gestured to the life-saving implement on his nose. His voice came out garbled and barely understandable.

Diahyas grew frustrated. "Wait a moment. We have something for this...Sea-ena!"

She whirled around, her eyes jumping from place to place until they finally landed on the middle-aged mermaid that swam into the room. The poor woman looked about to faint from shock upon seeing two male humans in her charge's bedroom.

"Diahyas...where...what...how..."

So many questions filled her wide eyes, so many words fighting one another to tumble from her clogged throat. It was a jam of epic proportions that unfortunately did not have the right audience, for each person in the room was so overcome by the new sensations around them that no humor or even compassion could be found in yet another display of utter confusion.

"Sea-ena," Diahyas snapped. "Be you still and quiet one moment. I be needing two vibrords."

Sea-ena's mouth snapped shut, but her eyes remained glued to the strangers before her that stood on two legs regardless of the water surrounding them.

"Sea-ena!" Diahyas repeated in frustration.

Finally, the woman snapped out of her stasis.

"Yes, highness," she muttered before swimming from the room.

She returned just a minute later, carrying two small items. They were light green and looked a little like seaweed. Sea-ena stopped beside Diahyas, warily eying Eorian and Fil. Diahyas rolled her eyes in consternation.

"Honestly, Sea-ena," she scoffed as she snatched the vibrords from her maid's hand.

Then she swam over to Fil and gently spread one of the slimy things across his throat. Fil was careful not to move, unsure of what was happening...especially when that green seaweed adhered fully to his neck like a second skin. His eyes darted to Eorian, who was staring at the vibrord in curious intensity.

Diahyas swam over to him next, giving him a winning smile as she applied the second one to his throat, lingering this time and again rubbing a finger along his cheek. She also took the opportunity to feel the blond hair that so intrigued her.

"You be able to talk now," she explained with a small smile.

Eorian cleared his throat without thinking, surprising himself at how clear and normal it sounded.

"Interesting," he said with a chuckle as he looked over at Fil. "It's like they knew we were coming."

Fil became alarmed. "Maybe they did. Maybe this is some kind of trap."

His eyes flew to Diahyas with her cocked head and bemused expression.

"Are you going to lock us up? Kill us? How long have you known we were here?" he demanded.

Eorian sighed. "Honestly, Fil, you can be one of the most illogical people. She very clearly has never seen anything like us before, so I doubt that..."

"Then how did she know that we would need air and a way to speak down here?" Fil asked stubbornly.

"We were just on land, Fil. Land. My bet is that they have other creatures that breathe air and would find it difficult to speak underwater."

Diahyas was nodding, completely enraptured with the unusual men before her and ignoring Sea-ena as she pulled on her arm.

"That be correct," Diahyas agreed with Eorian. "There be many land creatures in need of such inventions as you now use. This be the capital of all Faencina, after all. Land creatures have a need to visit as well."

Eorian turned to her. "What are these things anyway? How do they work? You called the one on my throat a...vibird?"

Diahyas giggled, shrugging off Sea-ena's more insistent tugging. "No, it be a vibrord. We have some of the most inspired of scientists here at our capital. I have little interest in such things, but I believe it reacts with the vocal chords in some way so as to enable your speech patterns to mirror the chirps of dolphins...at least, to allow the vibrations to cut through the thickness of the water.

"The other be an oxy...well, that be an abbreviation, but the true word be too long and complex to pronounce." Diahyas smirked. "It be pulling enough oxygen molecules from the water to enable pure breathing, since you landlings possess no gills."

Fil latched onto that. "Gills? I don't see any gills."

Diahyas pushed back her hair and turned to the side. "They be just here, hidden behind me ear. You see?"

Fil grinned. "That's fantastic. So you use your gills when you're underwater and your nose when you're on land?"

Diahyas nodded. "That be correct."

"How is it that you have both a tail and legs?" Eorian asked pensively.

"When me tail becomes dry, the scales receded. When again moisture returns, then me scales return," she said simply with a shrug.

"Diahyas," Sea-ena whispered insistently after realizing that her tugging would continue to be in vain. "What have you done? Your parents shall be displeased if they ever discover these two. Besides, they could be dangerous."

"Dangerous?" Diahyas repeated with a chuckle. "What could they do to me? They clearly be not water beings, and I have absolute control over the water within which they be immersed. However…"

She paused in thought over the other half of her maid's protests. "You be correct about me parents. They be unknowing of these human creatures, and me mother be not the most reasonable with unknown things…"

Eorian and Fil shared a wary glance after noting the worry present in Diahyas. She was gently gnawing her lower lip as she contemplated the situation.

"They also be from another planet, Diahyas," Sea-ena pointed out. "You be knowing how very much the Prime dislikes that sort of thing."

Diahyas scowled and waved a hand at the pesky words. "Yes, yes, I be knowing that. However, she seems to have changed her mind on that of late."

"Look, if you'll just tell us how, I can use my dust to get back to Randor…once it can be used again, that is," Eorian said. "I need to get back anyway."

Diahyas immediately shook her head, her eyes hardening. "You be not leaving."

Eorian straightened. "I'm sorry?"

"You be me pets now, and there be no leaving," she said hotly.

"Pets?" Fil stuttered in surprise.

"Let me make myself perfectly clear, your *highness*," Eorian stressed the title sarcastically. His voice was firm and calm, his eyes slightly mocking. "You will not be keeping us here. One way or another, Fil and I are both going back to Randor, where we are very greatly needed. We are also no less intelligent than you are, so this business of 'pets' is completely inaccurate. We are guests only, and as such, we reserve the right to leave."

"You be defying me?" Diahyas asked in astonishment.

"Come now, you know that edict is unreasonable. You can't honestly expect us to follow it," Eorian said with a frown.

Diahyas' tail whipped back and forth quickly. "This be insolence. This be intolerable insolence. I should have you flogged…drowned…"

For a moment she seemed at a loss for another punishment, but then she relaxed with a small, triumphant smile, and her eyes twinkled her superiority.

"No, there be no need for that," she said softly. "You be unable to leave. You be unknowing of me underwater primage, and even should you step from beneath me protection, you would be captured immediately, for you look nothing as we do."

Eorian scowled before making his point. "We don't need to leave this room. All I have to do is travel through the portal."

A mischievous grin crossed the girl's face. "Though you be knowing not how?"

Eorian took an angry step toward her. "I'll risk it."

Diahyas pulled an exaggerated pout. "You be wanting to leave me already? There be nothing I can say, nothing I can do?"

A slight warning bell sounded in Eorian's mind, but he ignored it. This mermaid was just too aggravating and egotistical for his liking.

"That's right. Nothing."

Diahyas paused for the space of one heartbeat before grinning widely.

"Nothing I can say, perhaps…," she held up Eorian's bag of diamond dust, "…but surely keeping your means of travel be plenty for me to *do*."

Eorian growled and lunged for the pouch, but he found himself swirled up in a tornado of water. Fil gaped in astonishment just before he too was caught up in the strange force. They could not fight it as they were carried away from Diahyas and into another room, and neither of them was fast enough once they were released to stop the door from closing and locking them inside an expansive closet. It looked like Diahyas was going to be able to keep them there after all.

CHAPTER 3

"Diahyas, this be insane," Sea-ena said worriedly as she glanced toward the closet. "You cannot keep them. Allow them to return home. This be no place for them…and I fear what your parents may do."

"Relax," Diahyas said absently as she too looked toward the door. "Now, I cannot be keeping them in there forever. How can I ensure they remain when outside me closet?"

Sea-ena's eyes widened in confused frustration. "You be not listening to me! Diahyas, see reason. Either send them back or give them to your mother."

"I shall do no such thing," Diahyas scoffed. "They be mine and mine only. You be telling no one about them. Understood?"

Diahyas looked her maid fiercely in the eye. There could be no slip-ups here. One whisper of a word and Diahyas' mother would have the newcomers wrapped in chains and thrown into the deepest part of the ocean.

Sea-ena sighed upon seeing the determination in her charge's eyes. "I be telling no one."

"Swear it."

"It be so sworn," Sea-ena agreed sadly.

With a grin, Diahyas turned away to swim about the room. "There now. Not so very hard, be it? Now you shall help divine a way of keeping these two with me."

"Must I?"

"Of course." Diahyas nodded with a grin. "It be much more fun if there be two joined together in this scheme of mine."

Again, Sea-ena sighed. Her life would be so much easier were Diahyas to find friends of her own. Unfortunately, Sea-ena was all she had...which may be the very reason she was so adamant about keeping the two males locked in her closet.

Just then, one of them began banging on the door—a rather ineffective show of frustration and anger when underwater. This was soon realized, and the banging was exchanged for shouting.

"If you don't let us out voluntarily, we'll break the door down."

Diahyas grinned with childish delight. "He be fantastic, do you not think? He be strong and forceful and handsome...he shall be a good servant."

Sea-ena blinked in surprise, wondering how exactly to make Diahyas see the contradictions in her thinking. She opened her mouth, closed it again to ponder some more, then finally she decided upon a slow approach.

"I believe it to be in your best interest to reexamine that last statement," she said carefully, ignoring the shouts of "open this door" coming from behind her.

Diahyas paused a moment.

"You do not believe him to be a good servant?" She shook her head with a laugh. "Of course he shall be. He shall love to do me bidding, for who should not? He shall be quite efficient, I be certain, and attentive."

A very contented smile spread across her face as she imagined a future in which that decidedly authoritative man would gladly answer her every whim. Sea-ena frowned and then started at yet another angry shout.

"This is uncivilized and barbaric. We have not threatened you or harmed you in any way. We just want to go home, and if you don't let us out and give me back my diamond dust, so help me, I will shake you until you do!"

The other man finally spoke through the door. "Not that he means that to sound in any way threatening. Any chance we can get some food?"

"We don't need food, Fil. We need our freedom. Let us out, Diahyas!"

"You honestly think *that*"—Sea-ena gestured toward the door—"will be any good in a subservient capacity?"

Diahyas pursed her lips. "You be right."

Sea-ena sagged in relief. Now her life could go back to normal.

"I shall have to train him," Diahyas continued with a nod. "That be it! The perfect thing! Sea-ena, ensure they stay. I shall be back quite soon."

Without a backward glance, Diahyas flew from the room, leaving a worried and wary Sea-ena to guard two unhappy humans locked in a closet.

"I wonder what they have to eat down here," Fil mused. "It's not like they could have bread… uggg, soggy bread."

"How should I know what they eat?" Eorian answered in frustration as he glared at the door. "If I have my way, we'll be gone before we find out."

"You are really worked up, E," Fil pointed out. "What's eating you?"

Eorian turned to face him. "I would like to know how you can be so calm about all this."

"Honestly, I'm loving it," Fil said with a huge grin. "My unflappable, in-control cousin appears to be having a minor crisis."

"You call being trapped in a closet under the ocean on a foreign planet while your little sister and loyal crew is floating in small rowboats away from a vast fleet of ships led by an insane and evil tyrant bent on killing them a *minor* crisis?"

"Well, considering how not an hour ago you were telling me to relax when there was a very good chance we were going to die in a desert, you can see how your reaction to our current situation seems a little hypocritical."

Eorian scowled and ran a hand through his hair. "It's that…that little, spoiled girl out there. She wants to keep us as pets, *pets*. It's as if she thinks we have no lives except to please her, and unfortunately, she seems to have the power to do whatever she wants."

"I wonder if all mermaids can move water around like that," Fil pondered. "That's a pretty cool trick, something the essence of water would be able to do."

Eorian hung his head with a sigh. "Yeah, I thought about that too."

"We should tell her."

Eorian's brows drew together. "And give her yet another reason to think everyone should worship her? I think not."

"She could come in handy when we're fighting Raef. All she'd have to do is dump a huge wave on his head and drown him."

"You don't honestly think that the little pampered princess would ever consider leaving her cushy palace to fight someone else's war. She might break a nail."

Fil snorted, but he couldn't argue. Then he looked down at his fingers, bringing them up for closer examination.

"E...look at my fingertips." He wiggled them toward his cousin. "They're all prune-y. Should we be getting worried?"

Eorian brought up his own hand and frowned. "I can see how this could be problematic, yes. We need to talk to her."

He turned to the door, readying himself to shout, when it opened. Diahyas swam in.

"Hold out your hand," she ordered primly.

Eorian and Fil shared a glance, wondering how she'd heard them discussing the water's effects on their skin. After a heartbeat, he complied, only to be surprised by the metal bracelet she clamped around his wrist.

"What's this?" he asked.

"You have need of training," she said simply.

"Training?" Eorian repeated as if he'd never heard the word before in his life.

"Yes, you be not servant material yet, and I have fears that you may attempt to run from me. That cannot be allowed, so I gave you a band."

A moment of silence passed.

"E, I think she just gave you the mermaid equivalent of a collar," Fil said as he choked on a chuckle.

Eorian ignored him. "I am *not* your servant, nor will I be. How do I get this thing off?"

He began tugging at the band with little success. It was completely baffling. Diahyas had so quickly and easily snapped it on, but Eorian could see no hinges, no lock...how did this thing work?

Diahyas clicked her tongue in reprisal and shook her head. "Now that be not the correct words of a servant. What you should say be, 'It be a pleasure to serve you.'"

"There is absolutely no way in this underwater deathtrap that I will ever..." he broke off with a startled shout of pain. His wide eyes flew to the band around his wrist as he muttered a curse. "*Ouch*, what was that?"

Diahyas raised her dainty brows. "That be your punishment for not doing me bidding. Now, what do we say...?"

"Did you just shock me?" Eorian asked in growing anger.

Diahyas nodded. "We have brilliant scientists that be able to harness the gift of the eel. We hardly have need for such a band, but it seemed necessary for you."

Eorian closed his eyes and took several deep breaths before holding out his arm to the girl and responding in a very moderated tone. "Take this off my wrist. Now."

Diahyas' eyes grew round in affront. "That be lesson number two. I be the only one giving orders."

"I'm sure you're quite skilled at that," Eorian snapped. "How about you try to learn a new skill today and do something someone else wants for a change? Take. This. Off."

Again, that powerful shock jolted into him. Eorian gritted his teeth and continued to stare angrily at his tormentor. Sure, she was easy on the eyes, but she was so incredibly spoiled that she was destined to be lonely her entire life. Not a soul would willingly put up with her, and Eorian was determined to leave her as soon as possible.

Diahyas stared down at her own band, the one that was enabling her to exact punishment, but it was clearly giving off a very strong voltage. She looked back up at him in confusion.

"Take it off," Eorian shook his wrist at her for emphasis.

Diahyas' chin jutted out obstinately.

"No," she said as she flipped her hair behind her. "You shall learn. But for now, you shall both come with me to your air chamber. Prolonged water be not good for land creatures such as you."

Eorian considered refusing, but fortunately, logic prevailed.

"I don't have to wear one of those bands too, do I?" Fil asked worriedly as they followed Diahyas from the closet.

Diahyas gave him a look over her shoulder. "You be unwilling to leave here without this other one. I see no need to control you with a band as well."

"Good," Fil said with relief.

Just two doors down, Diahyas gestured for them to enter a tiny cube of a room. She shut them inside the small area and locked the door.

"Does she actually think this will work for a room?" Fil whispered.

Eorian had been slightly worried about that himself. There was barely enough space for the both of them to stand in the small chamber. Then the water began to drain. Slowly, it was sucked out through a grate in the floor until there was no water left, and then the wall in front of them slid open.

Eorian and Fil removed the strange items that had enabled them to breathe and speak underwater, examining the beautiful room before them without a word. There were large shell beds in two corners of the room, there were two, beautiful desks against the back wall, an expensive-looking rug took up most of the floor where cushions were strewn about for lounging, and half of one wall was taken up with a floor-to-ceiling waterfall that created a rather large pool at its base. It almost looked like a spacious tub was sunk into the floor.

"Wow," Fil muttered as he finally stepped into the room.

Eorian followed slowly, feeling a little like he was relinquishing his freedom as he did so.

Fil crashed down onto some incredibly soft, colorful cushions with a laugh and huge grin.

"What did I tell you, E? We're in for the royal treatment." His smile shrank a bit, though it didn't disappear, at his next words. "Except for that shock collar she's given you for obedience training, I could really get used to this."

Chapter 4

Diahyas sat in front of her dressing table mirror as Sea-ena removed the various sea creatures used to decorate her flowing tresses—small starfish, a tiny crab in a beautiful conch shell, and her favorite little goldfish. They were to swim free throughout the night while Diahyas slept.

As she patiently waited for her maid to finish, her thoughts again strayed to the strangers held within the air room, often called an airie. She had forced herself many times throughout the day to refrain from visiting them, reminding herself that being held in the room without having the privilege of her presence was Eorian's punishment for failing in his new role as servant. It simply baffled her as to the reason behind his refusal of such a lofty and sought-after position.

It was no matter, though; he would come around. She just had to be a little more patient than she was used to. Humans were odd. Their words, their appearance, and their characters were so very different...although, now that she truly thought about it, there seemed to be something familiar about them as well. It was vague, so very vague.

"There now. All done. You be ready for bed," Sea-ena pronounced.

Diahyas turned slowly, still pondering that hazy image.

"Do you know, Sea-ena, that I believe these humans be not the very first I have seen?"

A laugh escaped before Sea-ena could trap it, and she hastily smothered the remainder of her merriment. "You be jesting with me surely. There be no place for you to have seen them. No humans reside here."

Diahyas shook her head, still deep in thought. "No, not here. You be right…but somewhere. They be not all unfamiliar to me."

"You be getting to bed now. You be tired, that be all. Come on, up with you."

Sea-ena urged the girl to her bed, settling her down amongst the soft sponges and seaweed. Finally, Diahyas seemed to snap out of her reverie.

"Yes," she chuckled slightly. "That must be it."

Sea-ena nodded, content with that response, before swimming from the room, but she could not immediately go home as she so wished. She glanced down at the small slip of coral parchment in her hand. She had recognized the writing immediately, but the message that was penned could be dangerous if seen by the wrong person. She sighed as she swam the corridors in search of her target.

Finally, she located him in a small closet as he put away clean dishes.

"Luik, me boy, you must stop this," she said as she shook the message at him. "Have I not told you already the repercussions should this fall into the wrong hands?"

Her young nephew looked at her pitifully. "But she must know. You tell me I cannot visit her, so I must write. Otherwise she may worry I have faltered in me affections."

Sea-ena closed her eyes. She hadn't the heart to tell Luik that Diahyas had received only one of his many notes…that the girl's furious response to a love letter left by a mere servant had Sea-ena worry for the boy's life. She had quickly hidden all the others and tried to reason with Luik, but the boy was far too hard-headed for his own good.

"Nothing can come of this, you realize. She be the Shoring Water Maiden, and her parents already have a mate chosen."

Luik shook his head. "She shall fight for me. She did thus already before everyone in the throne room. She said she would not mate with him, and surely she must love me greatly to defy her parents in so public a fashion."

Sea-ena sighed and closed her eyes. "Luik, you be not a child. See reason. She has not spoken with you since you both were very small, so how—"

"And yet I have not ceased to think of her. We would be together even now if not for her heartless mother."

Sea-ena glanced around them nervously and moved closer to him to whisper. "Take a care. You should not be saying such things in the palace.

Do you so wish to lose your life?"

"A life without her be misery." His face fell. "You must help me see her."

Sea-ena shook her head. "I cannot, and you must swear to leave no more of these messages."

"But…"

"Swear it."

Luik hung his head in defeat. "It be so sworn, Aunt."

She nodded in relief. Finally, she could relax. She patted his cheek. "There we be, me boy. Find a nice, young mermaid of your station. That be not at all difficult for such a handsome young man as you. Forget this. It be for the best, for nothing could ever come of your affection."

She swam off for her bed, Luik's eyes following her.

"Nothing now, perhaps," he said softly to her disappearing back. "But the revolution be coming."

Boran was resting for the evening, relaxing back in bed and staring through the glass ceiling as sea creatures swam back and forth. Leading a revolution was hard work, and he rarely had time to do this anymore.

"Status report."

Boran jerked up in bed, scowling at the unwanted interruption.

"Oh, be it that time already?" he asked with a chuckle, but then he grew uncomfortable as the silence lengthened.

He should have known better than to try using levity. He cleared his throat.

"Yes, right. There be sixty-seven merfolk stationed in and around the palace with nine to eleven more expected to be positioned within the next week."

"And what areas are covered?"

"We have people in the storerooms and kitchens, servants that roam all around the palace, people in charge of weaponry and the heroshi stables…"

"Heroshi, Boran? What are these?"

Boran paused, but he knew better than to imply in any way

that everyone should know what a heroshi was. One lashing by the mastermind, whose true name was unknown, was more than enough punishment.

"The heroshi be the creatures that pull our chariots."

"The large ones with dragon-like heads, front flippers, back paws, and a tail with five long and thick, colorful flaps that spin at an impossible speed when they swim?"

Boran hadn't the vaguest notion what a dragon was, but the rest sounded perfectly accurate. "Yes."

"Good. Continue."

"Well...uh, as I said, we have people in the heroshi stables, and we have also positioned people in the sub stations and the airdomes."

"Airdomes? These are the circular, air-filled transports on rails that enable travel to and from land?"

"And that allow merfolk to switch between forms more quickly, yes."

"So we have people covering food, weaponry, transport, and there are those that can easily block entrance and exit from the palace...very good. I think we will have enough after next week. Stand by for initiation."

Just as quickly as he had come, he left. Boran sighed with relief. He always felt so conspicuous when talking with this strange leader. To anyone watching him, it would appear he was talking to himself...and perhaps he was. It seemed unlikely that his mind had conjured this person since common things like heroshis and airdomes had to be explained, but he had never seen the mastermind, only felt him and heard him, following his missives and telling no one that the words and ideas were not his own.

Diahyas woke the next morning in a very cheery mood. Of course, having a fantastic secret was bound to make her feel a bit giddy, and she was ready to go visit that secret right now. Quickly, she grabbed her favorite seaweed dress, one that had been dyed a deep purple with some lighter purple swirls twisting throughout, and swam into her new acquisitions' alternating chamber.

The water slowly descended, and Diahyas waited rather impatiently for the chamber to empty. Then with a twist of her finger she whisked away all moisture from her tail—a drying process that took anywhere between fifteen minutes to half an hour for mermaids without her particular gift—so that she could step through to the room beyond on her lovely two legs.

The moment she stepped inside, two gazes slammed into her. Fil was lounging on the floor, lying on his back as he most likely stared at the soaring ceiling, which was made of glass to allow guests the pleasure of seeing the ocean's creatures pass by. Eorian, on the other hand, appeared to have been pacing in frustration, and his expression was anything but welcoming.

"Why, Fil, look who deigned to visit our humble accommodations," he said with a mocking bow. "To what do we owe this pleasure?"

Diahyas frowned, her gaze sharp and assessing. "I understand not why you speak to me thus. Such insolence be certain to bring on me wrath, the consequence of which be a sharp shock from your band."

Eorian gave her a daring smile. "Go ahead."

The girl's eyebrows angled down severely, and she shook her head slightly as she studied him. "Such an unusual creature you be. There must be much courage in you to taunt me so."

Eorian's grin widened. "I'm just waiting until you get so tired of us that you'll let us go."

Diahyas laughed gaily at that. "You be far too interesting for me to release you."

"So you'll keep us caged in here for you to visit on a whim?" Eorian asked.

"No, I be training you now as me loyal servants. Soon you shall not wish to leave. Only bringing about me pleasure shall occupy your thoughts."

Fil snorted from his place on the floor. "Good luck with that."

"You have doubts?" Diahyas asked.

"No, I have no doubts at all," Fil replied as he slowly sat up and turned to face her. "Eorian definitely won't ever live to bring you pleasure."

"We shall see," Diahyas said with a shrug. "Now, come along. We shall find suitable servant attire, and then we shall go touring Haird... you shall carry me purchases as I shop."

Eorian and Fil shared a glance.

"You're taking us shopping?" Eorian asked in disbelief.

Diahyas nodded as she opened the door.

"Do not forget your oxys and vibrords," she tossed over her shoulder. "I shall be waiting just outside."

The door whisked shut behind her. Eorian stood completely still as he stared at the door in silence. Fil glanced from his cousin to the door and back again in confusion before pushing to his feet and grabbing for the interesting underwater gadgets necessary for human life under the sea.

"Here you go, E," he said as he held them out to his cousin.

Eorian didn't move.

"E?"

Fil examined his silent, unmoving cousin. Eorian's jaw was clenched tight; his eyes were fierce.

Fil reached up and snapped his fingers before Eorian's eyes. "Come on, E. She'll only wait so long."

Slowly, Eorian turned to look at him, a thoughtful expression finally replacing the stark fury present before. "Yes, we wouldn't want to keep the little princess waiting."

Fil watched worriedly as Eorian strode purposefully into the transitioning chamber before stepping in after him.

"What are you up to, E?" he asked.

"I'm not up to anything," Eorian answered casually, although the determined gleam in his eye stated the opposite.

Fil's alarm rose a notch, and his mind raced as he tried to think of a good way to change his cousin's mind before the chamber completely filled up.

"Look, cuz, I know she gets under your skin, but think long and hard about what you're planning before you do it. She's got some serious authority here, and you're just some oddity that popped out of nowhere."

Eorian glared at him. "I know what I'm doing, Fil."

Just as Fil opened his mouth to argue some more, the outer door opened to reveal the impatient mermaid. She grinned and motioned for them to follow her. "Come, the proper attire be this way."

"How exactly do you have 'proper' attire for humans if you've never had any on this planet before?" Eorian asked a bit snippily.

Diahyas took no notice of his tone.

"You be sharing the form of our mermen when they be on land. You shall wear the attire required for male servants at such times."

"Oh, goody."

Fil drew closer and gave a soft warning. "Seriously, cuz, reduce the sarcasm." What was with his cousin? Eorian was acting strangely even for him.

"In here," Diahyas pronounced as she swam through a doorway. Fil and Eorian followed, all of them stopping in the middle of what looked like a community closet with clothing of all sizes, styles, and colors. Diahyas swam over to one section and began rifling through the items. "Now, which to choose?"

She sent a glance toward them, her eyes narrowed in contemplation, before whipping back around to peruse the selections again. Not a minute later, she began tossing her choices toward them...although, due to the water, the pieces merely floated gently in their direction. After they each had four outfits, she turned toward them with a nod.

"Let us see which looks best." She pointed imperiously behind them. "There be an alcove for changing just there. Model for me."

She glided to a large cushion and relaxed into it with a smile. Fil and Eorian shared an uncomfortable look and didn't move.

"Go on," Diahyas urged. "I have not all day."

Eorian stared at her in disbelief before finally managing to speak. "Are you intentionally trying to demean us, or does it just come naturally?"

Diahyas's brows drew together in consternation.

"Why be you arguing with me when I try only to ensure that you and your cousin do not stand out any more than you already do? Stop trying me patience." She lifted her left wrist and poised the fingers of her right hand over the controls of her band. "Or must I give you encouragement?"

Fil sighed as he recognized the impasse between the two. He shoved into Eorian to shepherd him into the alcove.

"Come on, E, let's just get this over with," he muttered as he tried to silently break through Eorian's anger.

It took a few moments, but finally, Eorian relented. He turned abruptly and disappeared. Fil quickly followed to find his cousin roughly pulling his shirt over his head.

"The minute I find out where she's hiding my diamond dust, we're out of here," he said in soft ferocity. "I might even steal her little tiara while I'm at it."

Fil watched his vicious motions in silent wariness as he continued.

"Just wait until we're all on land. Then she'll find out who she's messing with. I don't have time for all these stupid, little games of hers. Who does she...where's the top to this thing?"

He started rifling through all the clothing for a shirt, only to come up empty. He closed his eyes and dropped his head as he slowly took in deep, calming breaths.

"Well, this is just awkward," Fil said as he finally got into one of his outfits. "Not only did she give us no shirts, but these bottoms are skirts. She does realize we're men, right?"

"I imagine we would have received shirts if she thought otherwise. I'm wearing mine."

Eorian pulled the soft cotton back on. Fil eyed his cousin's ensemble with a frown. The cream, long-sleeved top most decidedly looked like an undershirt from their world, and it fell loosely to mid-thigh. Beneath that, he could see the bottom of the knee-length skirt that was mottled with reds, pinks, oranges, and browns. Then, of course, to tie it all together, he still wore his black, scuffed boots that reached his calves.

"That's attractive," Fil said with a grimace.

Eorian scowled. "I'm not trying to attract anyone."

"What be taking so very long?" Diahyas shouted impatiently from the other room.

"Maybe if you tucked in the shirt?" Fil suggested, but Eorian ignored him as he stomped out to model for the princess.

Fil smothered a smile as he hurriedly followed. There was no way he wanted to miss her reaction.

Her eyebrows rose sharply, her eyes widened, and then she laughed happily...and continued laughing. Eorian stood with hands on hips as he waited for the mockery to stop. It took longer than expected.

"You're the one that picked it," he accused finally. "And you failed to give us shirts."

Diahyas rolled her eyes. "Mermen wear no shirts on land. And you be looking much less ridiculous without that one and those...what exactly be those on your feet?"

"You can't tell me you have no shoes on this planet."

"Why need we shoes?" She looked at him like he was an ignorant child. "We swim beneath the water, and those on land be required to make the ground tolerable. Now, come, be off with these unnecessary things."

"You may be able to swim through the water, but we're going to be walking. My shoes are staying right where they are," Eorian argued.

Diahyas glared at him while she debated, and then nodded slowly.

"You may keep them." A smirk began to creep across his features, but it froze at her next words. "The shirt, however, must go. It shall make you far too conspicuous in Haird. I told you that mermen wear no shirts on land."

"I'm keeping my shirt," he said hotly just before sucking in a quick breath and locking his jaw. As his eyes glared into hers, he slowly and angrily released the word clamped behind his teeth. "Ouch."

"Hey, hey, hey," Fil broke in with a huge smile. "Life is all about compromise, isn't it? How about we *not* shock my cousin here, and, E, really...she just let you keep your boots. Can't you meet her halfway here?"

"I am not going to be her half-naked bagboy as she drags me all over some city for everyone to gawk at."

"There be more gawking if you be wearing that ridiculous nonsense." Diahyas scrunched her nose at him in distaste.

"Come on, E." Fil gave him a coaxing smile. "Staying on her good side is in your best interest."

"Fine. Have it your way."

Again, he roughly yanked the shirt over his head and attempted to toss it aside, crossing his arms in annoyance when it merely glided downward. However, despite all the frustration coursing through him and the anger directed at the still lounging mermaid, he could not help but notice the spark of interest and appreciation now present in his tormentor.

"That be much better."

Was that a hint of gratitude he heard in her voice? Surely not. He must be imagining it.

He gave her a slightly mocking bow. "I am so glad you are pleased, your highness."

She completely missed the sarcasm. "Good. Now, you be not needing to call me your highness. I be referred to as Shoring in public, and you may call me Diahyas in private." She paused and bit her lip before looking at them a bit sheepishly. "What be your names again?"

Fil popped up a hand. "Filootego, here. Fil for short."

"Fil," she repeated as if working hard to commit it to memory. Then she turned to Eorian. "And..?"

"Eorian."

She grimaced. "That be too long, so many syllables to shout when I need your aide quickly."

"I call him E," Fil offered, which earned him a glare from his cousin.

"Your name has the same amount of syllables," Eorian pointed out to the pensive Diahyas.

She shook her head. "Me name be spoken in reverence. Yours need be shortened for brevity. I dislike Eorian, and I dislike E. What shall I name you?"

Eorian gaped at her in disbelief. "You've already taken my diamond dust, my shirt, and most of my dignity. You can't honestly be trying to take away my name now too."

"It be necessary," she said flippantly with a careless wave of her hand. "And you be rather impertinent. I think perhaps I should name you something to remind you of your place. It needs to be something that underlines my elevated status to your servitude, of my glorious being to your lowly self. I am like a great and mighty wave to your mere ripple, a vast and lofty mountain to your mound of dirt, a powerful whirlwind to your little wisp of air...that be it!"

Eorian's temper was very visibly rising with each self-important word she uttered. He was strung so tightly it would take next to nothing for him to snap. Poor Fil wasn't entirely certain how to handle the situation. His gaze kept volleying between the two of them, and he felt his stomach clench at her last pronouncement. Somehow, he knew she was about to make everything much, much worse.

Her proud and satisfied gaze found Eorian's, and she smiled. "You be Wisp. Perfect for an air breather, and a good reminder of the honor I have placed upon you."

Fil literally bit his tongue. So much irony, and he couldn't say one thing about it. His cousin would bite his head off...although, right now, all of his focus seemed to be on how best to kill the princess. His hands were clenching and unclenching, and his jaw must be hurting from the amount of pressure applied by his teeth. At least Diahyas finally seemed to be taking notice of his ire, even if it was a little late.

"Be you…angry?" she asked in confusion.

"Understatement," Eorian bit out.

"I be not understanding this."

"Clearly."

She crossed her arms. "Explain."

Eorian gave her a mirthless smile. "I don't even know where to begin."

Before she could respond, Sea-ena quickly swam into the room.

"Diahyas," she said urgently. "Come. Now."

"I be busy, Sea-ena. See you not this?"

"The Prime wishes you to join her for brunch…right now. There be a…*special* guest."

Diahyas' eyes widened. "Not…"

Sea-ena nodded.

"Get them back to the airie," Diahyas ordered. "And then immediately come to me room. Lands above! I have not thought yet how to handle this."

She looked close to tears. A mixture of fright, worry, and fear clouded her features just before she swam from the room. Eorian frowned, curious and a bit sympathetic despite himself.

"What was that?" he asked Sea-ena.

The woman shook her head sadly as she stared out the doorway. "She be facing a monster with no friend in sight. Her life hangs in the balance."

With those few cryptic words, she motioned them to follow her as she moved just a few doors down to their airie. Then she quickly left them to help her charge.

CHAPTER 5

She was late, although how that could be even remotely possible when her mother had summoned her just twenty minutes earlier was a mystery. Nevertheless, the Prime was angry at being made to wait, in front of a guest, no less!

Diahyas found it impossible to drum up any contrition. She didn't want to be here, and her mother knew that. She swam slowly to her place at the table. Because it was an intimate, informal luncheon, they were using the twenty-foot table with the Prime in the large, throne-like chair at the head, the Prime-Mate opposite her in a smaller chair, Diahyas on her left in a humble chair, and the guest of honor to her right in a chair matching the one across from it in the middle of the long, driftwood expanse.

Diahyas had refused to look at anyone or anything as she entered and took her seat, but after taking a slow breath to calm her nerves, she decided she should see what her betrothed looked like. Her mind instantly jumped to Wisp, and she found herself hoping that the man across from her was like Wisp. Perhaps the mating would not be quite so disastrous then...but, no, she would not give into her mother.

In fierce determination, she lifted her head in a smooth, swift movement only to find her view impeded by a large sponge, coral, and seaweed arrangement. She scowled and glanced at her mother, who smirked. The Prime knew her daughter well, and this was quite a nice, if subtle vengeance.

Had Diahyas not been so caught up in her inner turmoil, she may have realized the strangeness in the utter silence around her. As it was, she quietly weighed her desire to see this creature across from her against her repugnance of showing her mother that she cared even the slightest bit. Curiosity won out. She swept the large vase aside by moving the water around it with just a flick of two fingers, effectively breaking the silence with its scraping slide, and looked up to see…red. She blinked. Surely her eyes were playing tricks. But, no, the same image greeted her: skin so very pale, hair black as night, gaunt features, sharp chin, and those blood red eyes that studied her without warmth.

She shrank back slightly, converting the unconscious movement into a slow, graceful relaxation against the chair. Then she snorted and sneered at him. "You think you be worthy of a Shoring Water Maiden?" She turned to her mother. "What joke be this? You cannot mean it, surely."

A hint of doubt clouded the Prime's eyes before it was smothered, but that instant was long enough to make Diahyas' heart stop.

"Diahyas, this be Dehga of Randor."

The girl's gaze snapped to the frightening man in suspicion. This man looked nothing like her pets. "Randor?"

Dehga gave a curt nod, then he eased out emotionless words. "I am king there, just as the Prime is here."

"Then why do you not find a bride amongst your own kind?"

"This arrangement is mutually beneficial."

Diahyas waited for him to elaborate, but he did not seem inclined to do so. He must be lying, she decided, for there was no reason her beloved Faencina could benefit from a man like him. She turned to her mother.

"I be decidedly against this," she announced.

"You be having no choice."

Diahyas looked to her father for some source of hope. "You agree?"

His lips tightened in frustration at the situation, but he nodded.

Diahyas' eyes narrowed, but she calmly turned to face Dehga.

"As you can see, me parents be often in accord, which I find important when ruling one's people. Tell me, Dehga of Randor, how could *we* possibly achieve this when we be so very different?" She studied the man as he pondered her question. Her parents were a lost cause, but she may still be able to change his mind.

"Differences can strengthen a union as well, especially when dealing with such a variety of subjects. Being from two different worlds of thought may give us an edge that no other royal couple could claim."

Diahyas pursed her lips and drummed her fingers on the table. "You be knowing me none at all, and I be seeing you for the very first time this day. Surely you cannot determine if this eternal union be wise without first knowing to whom you be chaining yourself?"

The right corner of his lips edged upward, but the expression was not pleasant. He turned to the Prime. "I have been told that you have a summer estate, somewhere with less hustle and bustle. This seems to me to be a very good place for the two of us to get to know one another," he turned to Diahyas, "since it seems she feels the need to do so."

Diahyas's eyes widened in alarm. "We can get to know one another here just as easily. There be no need to travel so far."

The Prime, as usual, ignored her and nodded her head. "That be a splendid idea! I had been thinking it would be good to get away. We shall leave tomorrow at noon."

"But..." Diahyas began before she was drowned out.

"I think two weeks shall suffice," the Prime continued. "What say you, Dehga? Can you woo me headstrong daughter in so short a time?"

He bowed his head slightly and cut his eyes her way in triumph. "I believe so."

"Then it be decided." The Prime grinned at her great fortune. "Let us finish our brunch and then begin preparations for our journey."

Diahyas scowled down at the table where her plate of scallops, muscles, and kelp lay undisturbed. Perhaps it was for the best that she was leaving for a few weeks. Wisp and Fil would be unable to distract her at the summer estate, and she would be able to focus all of her energy on canceling this disastrous match. With that decided, she lifted her fork. There were some wars that one could not afford to lose.

A hurried meeting had been called for all the district leaders and a select few of the palace infiltrators, who would spread the news heard tonight to all the others. They were shuffling around in barely concealed anticipation. It seemed the wait would be over soon.

"Me brothers and sisters, I thank you for joining me on such short notice. I would not have summoned you if this be not of the greatest importance."

Boran looked around the room with a teasing smile on his face and an excited spark in his eyes.

"The time be set."

He waited as the crowd began murmuring, turning to neighbors with grins and pats on the back. Finally, he raised a hand for silence.

"We have twelve days to prepare, and then we strike."

Diahyas stared grumpily out at the coral reefs and watched some dolphins playing and heroshi munching on ribbon grass. It barely registered. Her mind was back at the palace, where she actually wanted to be instead of in this fast-moving chariot taking her to the summer estate. Ordinarily, she might look forward to the trip; however, this "vacation" was going to be anything but.

She sighed deeply. She didn't even have anyone to talk with on this journey. Sea-ena had always come with her before, but someone had to stay behind and take care of her Wisp and his cousin. Now she was going to have to adjust to someone else helping her ready herself in the morning and evening. What a chore. They never did it quite right, so it took twice as long.

Sea-ena had not wanted Diahyas to leave without her. She had said she could find someone else to take care of the humans, but it would be too dangerous to let anyone else in on the secret. Servants had a way of talking, and her humans would be quite a delicious snippet of gossip.

Diahyas smiled and allowed herself to daydream about how wonderful life would be when Wisp finally did her bidding without complaint. He would be so very attentive, speaking kind words and complimenting her. He may tease her a bit, which would make her laugh and smile, and then she would give him a hug…no, a kiss on the cheek, in gratitude of his service. And he would live for those small favors.

Yes, her life was going to be perfect, assuming she was able to avoid marrying that frightening man. Just the thought of Dehga, with his cold eyes and emotionless face, wiped the smile from her lips. How was it possible that he and Wisp were of the same race? The King of Randor vying for her hand certainly bore little resemblance to her Randorian pirate.

Instantly, Diahyas shot forward in her seat. Why had she not thought of it sooner? They were both from the same planet, one of them a well-known king…or so he claimed. Eorian must have heard of Dehga, and if he had not, then the imposter would be caught.

Slowly, Diahyas sank back against the seat again as yet another idea formed.

Even if all that Dehga said was untrue, the Prime and Prime-Mate had never been to Randor, nor were they ever likely to visit. She could not prove it without revealing her hidden humans. Diahyas sighed. She had no choice. If she could not convince Dehga to drop his suit for her hand within the next two weeks, then she would use her one last weapon: one Randorian's word against another.

She would bargain with Eorian: his freedom for his testimony against Dehga. If she brought Eorian before her parents and he spoke out against Dehga, they would have to call off this betrothal. They could not know which human to believe and must err on the side of caution. This last would be the only way to free herself from the wretched bonds her parents threatened to use. If all else failed, she would have to do this… even if she had to release Eorian in the bargain.

Ten days. They had been trapped in this room for ten days. Eorian was going crazy from the inactivity.

"Want to play cards again?" Fil asked half-heartedly. Even his chipper mood had waned after the first week.

Eorian turned from the desk where he had been scribbling on some kind of parchment to glare down at the cards lying on the floor by Fil.

"I am never playing cards again."

"Why? You won a few times." Fil smirked.

Eorian transferred his glare from the cards to his cousin. Then they heard the alternating chamber whirring and knew Sea-ena was about to bring them dinner, even if it was a little early for the evening meal.

Sea-ena walked into the airie carrying that sealed server that kept their food safe from water as it traveled from the land-creature's kitchen to them.

"Here you be, boys," she said with a smile. They had all warmed up to each other over the past several days, and it made her visits quite enjoyable. "It be clam chowder, and I even managed to grab you some bread. Be you needing anything else?"

"Fresh air?" Eorian begged half-heartedly.

Sea-ena chuckled and wagged a finger. "You be knowing I cannot let you out, and this air be plenty fresh. It be cycled in and out through the vents that lead to the surface."

"I am *dying* in here." Eorian sighed and hung his head. "When is she coming back?"

"I cannot be saying for certain, as the royals change their minds on a whim, but I be thinking she shall return in three or four days' time." She sent him a cheeky grin. "Think you shall make it?"

Eorian pushed up from the chair in front of the desk to walk over to the small dining table. "If you promise to try to convince her to let us leave, I will try to survive another few days of inactivity."

"It be so sworn. Though you should not be surprised..."

She broke off as a voice sounded through the room.

"Aunt Sea-Sea, can you come out? I really need to speak with you."

Sea-ena's mouth dropped open in surprise. Eorian glanced around the room, searching for the source of the voice and finding nothing. Fil's eyes were darting about the room too, but it looked more like he was searching for an invisible mermaid.

"They have ghosts here," he whispered as he moved closer to Eorian. Eorian merely rolled his eyes.

Sea-ena swam over to a small box on the wall by the door, and she held a button down.

"Luik...how did you know I be in here? And what be you needing that be so very urgent?"

Eorian stepped up behind her to examine the box. "How is this possible?"

Luik spoke at the same time he did. "Can you just come out here, please?"

Sea-ena sighed. "Oh, just a moment."

"What's going on? That's your nephew? How was he talking to you? That is incredible."

Eorian was grinning ear to ear as he studied the strange box.

"That be a speaker that projects the voice on the other side of the door. When I press this button, the microphone comes on to catch me voice and send it through to the other side. It be the quickest way for communication between the water and airies. Now, please excuse me, me nephew be needing me assistance."

She seemed incredibly worried, which puzzled Eorian a bit, not that he was going to complain. With a grin, he watched her leave without locking the inner door.

"Fil, grab our oxys."

"What? Why?"

Eorian didn't answer him, just moved to the door to listen more closely. Just as he suspected, there was no click when Sea-ena left the alternating chamber either. He hadn't remembered there being a lock on that door. His grin widened. Unfortunately, it would be a few minutes before the alternating chamber could be used again.

He turned quickly and grabbed a bag, throwing items into it. Fil merely watched him in confusion, not asking a single question during the two minutes that Eorian packed the few items they had brought with them and waited for the alternating chamber to be ready for another cycle. Then he grabbed Fil's arm and pulled him inside. Finally, Fil could stand it no longer.

"Uh, E, not that I don't enjoy the fun of being in the water whirlpool, but could you tell me why exactly we're doing this when we can't actually leave?"

"Sea-ena didn't lock it."

Fil's brows drew together. "Sea-ena didn't..."

"Lock the door," Eorian finished. "Now's our chance. I'm getting my diamond dust back."

"Okay, but you realize that Sea-ena will probably still be just outside talking to her nephew, right?"

Eorian paused. "True...but I'm guessing she doesn't want her conversation with her nephew overheard. Did you see the way she was acting? She won't be in sight of the hallway, so we can sneak past."

Fil looked like he wanted to argue the point, but he kept his mouth shut. Eorian's plan was simple and straightforward, and they did need to get home. There wasn't a better way.

The water finally filled the chamber, and Eorian slowly pushed open the outer door. He peeked out and scanned the hallway, sighing in relief to find that his hunch had been right.

"Let's go," he said with a grin, and they walked swiftly down the hall to Diahyas's chamber. Eorian glanced at his cousin with his hands ready to fling open the doors.

"Ready?" he asked, his eyes dancing at the mischief to ensue.

"Ready."

He turned the handles and threw the doors inward, a little worried that he might hear a startled yelp from Sea-ena. Diahyas's room would have been a good place for a quiet conversation with her nephew, after all. None came. His eyes examined the empty room from his place in the doorway just to be sure.

"Perfect."

"Not sure how this is perfect," Fil grumbled. "She could have hidden your dust anywhere."

Eorian frowned. "That will be a bit trickier. Oh, well. Come on. You take the right side; I'll check the left."

Eorian strode straight toward the bed while Fil started rummaging around some shelving on the wall holding assorted boxes and trinkets.

"This girl's a collector," he announced as he started on the second shelf.

"Of what?" Eorian asked absently while throwing around all the cushions from the giant shell that was her bed and then looking under and behind it.

"Everything."

Eorian tossed his cousin a bemused look, but Fil's back was to him.

"I mean, it's organized," Fil continued. "Probably Sea-ena's doing, but there's all sorts of items here…conchs, stones, figurines, a lot of boxes holding what-nots. Then she's got all these mermaid, doll things lined up. The dolls are actually creeping me out a bit."

Eorian paused to consider the shelving and what Fil had said, scanning the room fully himself to try and get a sense of the princess. What he noticed was that everything was grouped in twos or threes. There was not a single item in the room, other than the large pieces of furniture, that stood alone. Why would someone pair things up like that? It wasn't like inanimate objects could get lonely...

In a flash of insight, Eorian started to see Diahyas a bit differently. She was a collector, and surrounding herself with these items was an attempt to fill her empty life. It was like she was searching for something, but throughout the quest, she wanted to make sure that she did not leave her victims as utterly alone as she herself felt.

Eorian shook his head. What made him think that he knew anything about her? She was simply a pampered princess, used to life handing her whatever she wished, and she had imprisoned him and his cousin without a second thought, caging them for almost two weeks with nothing to do. Right now, instead of reading too much into his surroundings, he should be looking for his diamond dust so he could get back to his sister, his crew, his world.

He spun on his heel and started sliding open the drawers in the dresser. There was a lot of female paraphernalia, still in pairs—he wondered if she even realized she was doing that—which he ignored. Finally, he reached the last drawer and yanked it open. It had to be in here; by now they had looked everywhere in this room, and he highly doubted she would store it in that massive closet of hers. This drawer held still more pretty shells, but these had been crafted into combs that women used to adorn their hair. Eorian groaned in frustration.

"Please tell me you've had some luck over there," he called to Fil.

"Sorry, cuz. Found lots of stuff, but not your diamond dust."

Fil walked over to stand beside him and looked down at the dresser too.

"It *has* to be in here," Eorian said.

Fil glanced around at the now slightly rumpled room. "Where? We've checked it all."

Eorian drummed his fingers on the dresser top as he too surveyed the room again.

"If I were a princess, where would I hide it?"

"Getting in touch with your feminine side, E?" Fil asked with a smirk.

Eorian ignored him and walked to the center of the room. "I have unlimited resources, I have access to the most brilliant craftsmen, and I definitely have costly jewels that need to be hidden...speaking of which,

Fil, did you come across any expensive jewelry?"

Fil paused to think a moment before shaking his head. "Actually, I didn't. I think you may be onto something. Keep being a girl."

This time Eorian did scowl slightly.

"Check behind these wall decorations. There may be a safe of some sort."

Quickly they started removing the colorful, beautifully crafted coral artwork. There were also some mosaics of underwater scenes created with small pieces of shell. Unfortunately, behind each there was only blank wall.

"So much for that," Fil lamented. "What else you got?"

Eorian thought a moment. "Okay, so I would hide my jewels in a place that I could get to without a lot of trouble, but that I felt was still secure. I would want it to be near me."

Fil jumped in with more theories. "Personally, I would want it in arm's reach while I primped in front of the mirror so I didn't have to constantly get up and down from the chair. Girls never can make up their minds...can you imagine how many times she'd have to stand up and sit back down if she didn't..."

"Fil, that's brilliant."

Eorian immediately plopped down on the stool in front of the mirror, his hands poised over the dresser as his eyes skimmed it for something unusual.

"Let's see...it wouldn't be on top. The sides would still be too difficult to reach, so the front, where the drawers are."

He leaned down to scrutinize the line of drawers on either side of him. When he straightened, he had a satisfied grin on his face.

"Got it. Now I just have to figure out how to open it. Let's try..."

He pushed into the driftwood with two fingers, feeling the give of the secret compartment and hearing a slight click. When he pulled his hand away, the drawer followed, and he edged it out completely to reveal a plethora of extremely valuable baubles and an empty space...just the right size for his pouch of diamond dust. Somehow, he knew that was where she had kept it.

He closed his eyes and dropped his head. "She took it with her."

"What?" Fil exclaimed as he reached in to push around the jewelry. After several minutes, he plopped down on the floor and sighed. "Now how are we supposed to get home?"

Eorian's mind immediately jumped to his prophesy. With a sigh, he dropped his head into his hands. "All I know is that if we can't leave today, we'll be stuck here for quite a while."

CHAPTER 6

Diahyas had woken that morning with a stone of dread lodged firmly in her stomach. Nothing had gone the way she had planned over the last eight days. The first week had been frustrating because she could never seem to get Dehga alone to speak with him. She still wasn't certain how the man had avoided her for so long without even trying to, but she had finally found him yesterday evening. She hadn't even planned it.

After yet another horrific dinner with her parents and *him*, she had escaped to the garden. It was so lovely there. Colorful coral that had been carefully groomed, sea anemones and sponges of every shade and shape, and lovely sea urchins lined the pathways that were created with fluorescent plant life. There were also frilly slugs and bristle worms that crawled everywhere, lighting up the many wonders with their soft pink and green glows.

This was peace, in the softly swaying sea. She could breathe freely here, relax, and simply enjoy the nature around her. She swam along slowly as she admired each bright-yellow sunflower anemone or dark-blue spiky urchin. She wasn't sure how long she idled there, but after a time, she became aware of another's presence. She glanced up in surprise to find Dehga walking along a pathway, hands behind his back, but unlike her, he did not seem to be enjoying his surroundings.

She pulled in a deep breath before calling out to him. "Be you enjoying our gardens, Dehga?"

He stopped with his back to her for a moment before slowly turning her way, his face an emotionless mask.

"Shoring Diahyas," he greeted with a very slight bow of his head. Even that small gesture seemed a bit mocking somehow, but Diahyas could not be certain enough to call him out on it. "Although they appear lovely…" He paused to glance briefly at the happily swaying vegetation and animal life. "I must admit that I hardly noticed them."

At least he was honest.

"You must have much on your mind to be oblivious to such beautiful sights as these."

"Perhaps."

His intense gaze studied her, finally fastening on her tiara and somehow growing even more sharply assessing. "You have a regal air about you. The tiara merely enhances it. An heirloom?"

Diahyas raised a hand to touch it reverently with the tip of her finger. "This be passed down generations through me family. It be destined for me to further enable me to fulfill me role."

"As Shoring Water Maiden?" he asked. Something in his tone made her think he knew her answer already, but that wasn't possible, right?

"As the prophesied one."

They both waited in silence for the other to speak further. Diahyas had initially thought her answer would spur some questions from him, but he merely appeared arrogantly pleased about something he had no desire to share. Since he did not seem particularly inclined to continue the conversation, Diahyas decided it would be the perfect time to begin her campaign.

"May I ask a question?" she asked.

"You just have."

Diahyas' brows rose in surprise, but she tossed that snide comment aside and focused back on the issue at hand. "I would like to know why you wish for this union."

"As I said previously, it is beneficial for both your kingdom and mine."

Diahyas nodded, but she let her annoyance show. "Perhaps, but something like this…surely there be others that could provide benefit, others more similar to yourself. You know nothing of me, do not seem particularly interested in me, and we certainly are nothing alike."

Dehga frowned. "That is unnecessary."

"Un…unnecessary?" Diahyas repeated in disbelief. "This be a mating. It shall last throughout our lives."

A disturbing smile crept across his lips briefly. "Unless one of us dies."

The way he said it sent a chill down her spine. Surely he did not mean for it to sound threatening...

"That be true, I suppose, but would it not be better to avoid the misery altogether? Matings be difficult enough as it be."

"Mine will not be."

Diahyas shook her head. "How? How could it not be?"

His gaze met hers. "I will not allow it."

Diahyas was about to argue with him, explain that "not allowing it" wasn't an option for a Shoring Water Maiden, but he continued in that cold, detached way of his.

"This union is a necessary step forward in my plans. It does not matter to me who you are in particular. It is merely your position that I require. Emotion, interest, and similarities are not factors in this decision. You will see little of me, and I will see you only when it suits me."

At first, Diahyas could not believe her ears. She searched his face for some sign that this was all a horrific joke, but this man did not appear to be capable of levity. When it finally hit her that he was indeed serious and saw her merely as an object to obtain and then discard, she got angry, which, for the moment, overwhelmed her fear. Her blue eyes flashed as she swam a bit closer.

"How dare you think to treat me thus!" she exclaimed. "I be Shoring Water Maiden, soon to rule all in Faencina. I be not some toy that can be played with when it *suits*."

He did not respond at all to her outburst. There was no emotion, no small sign of nervousness. Just that dark, intense red stare.

Diahyas considered him for several moments, not understanding, and then her eyes narrowed. "Have you had your heart broken? Be this why you be so very cold and distant?"

Degha's gaze turned angry as it drilled into her. Fury had lit a fire within their red depths, but his voice was even and low as he replied. "To have your heart broken, you must first give it away. Then, after a time of ignorant bliss, it must be returned to you, used, scarred, bruised, and beaten. If you never trust another with your heart, they have no control over you, and you cannot be hurt." He paused. "Do I seem so foolhardy as to take such a risk?"

Diahyas took several deep breaths before nodding, dread beginning to fill her. "If you never trust another with your heart, it be true that they cannot break it, but neither would you ever reach your full potential together, as a unit, relying upon one another, trusting one another, completing one another. I believe this be a risk worth taking."

With that said, Diahyas abruptly turned and swam away, back through the lovely gardens that she did not see and into a lavish bedchamber that she feared might be her last. She did not slept though, not until the wee hours of the morning did she finally fall into a land of nightmares.

And now as she woke, everything came back to her, and she felt helpless. She would try her parents one last time. Perhaps they would see reason.

She did not get a chance to speak with them alone before she was summoned for dinner. For some reason, her parents had insisted upon them all eating together for that important meal every day during this vacation. Due to this, she had seen her parents more often in the past nine days than she usually did over the course of five or six months. She wasn't liking them any better.

Although she knew it would be less than ideal, she simply could not wait any longer to try to convince her parents that this mating was wrong. With that in mind, she quietly swam into the dining hall and eased into her seat. Dehga and her parents had already arrived, and once she joined them the servants began serving the food.

No words were spoken for several moments. Then her father broke the silence.

"I saw you enter the garden yesterday evening, Diahyas. Did you enjoy yourself?"

She swallowed a bite of redfish and nodded. "Everything be quite lovely there as usual. It be quite"—she glanced over to Dehga, who was watching her with a raised brow—"peaceful."

"I thought so meself when I swam through upon our arrival." Her father gave her a warm smile.

So maybe she was liking her father a tiny bit better. He certainly seemed to be trying to get to know her a little. Perhaps he would be more open to her suggestions now.

"I have been thinking about this betrothal," she began.

"Diahyas," her mother broke in, a warning in her tone.

Diahyas ignored her, her gaze never leaving her father. He had laid down his fork, and his eyebrows had drawn together tightly.

"Father, surely you must see that we be ill suited."

Without conscious thought, her eyes darted to Dehga again, watching him lean back casually in his chair and seeming to find amusement from the conversation. She pushed on quickly.

"We know nothing of one another..."

"You can learn," her father interrupted with a hopeful smile.

"He have quite a few years over me."

"His experience shall be helpful when the time comes for you to rule."

"He be human, and I be mermaid."

She heard her mother's utensils clatter to her plate.

"I see no reason for you to continue this conversation," she said crossly. "The decision be made, and our minds shall not be changed."

Diahyas scrambled for another argument. "Do you even know anything of him? Have you spoken to any from his world? What if all this be merely a con?"

"You tread a dangerous path, me girl."

"How?" Diahyas questioned her mother hotly. "This be a logical question."

"Do you think me a fool? How can you believe that your Prime has not already thought of this possibility?" Her mother's expression was full of ire, and she appeared to be moments from shooting from her chair and issuing orders to have her own daughter arrested.

Diahyas lifted her head petulantly. "Well, have you?"

Her mother sputtered angrily, and with this brief reprieve, Diahyas turned back to her father anxiously.

"Please, Father, surely you can see that this shall not do. You be dooming your only daughter to a life of pure misery. Can you not see this man clearly? He emanates anger and arrogance; he be cold and without pleasant emotion. You and mother match—do you not wish such a mating for me?"

He sighed and closed his eyes, his lips tightening in distress, but he shook his head. Diahyas's stomach dropped as the dread of the morning turned into fear and despair. She whisked through her options—not many. When she turned back to the Prime, she saw that her mother had calmed herself somewhat. Apparently, Diahyas's desperate plea to her father had struck a chord in her mother as well.

"You do not see this now, me child, but this be for the best. For me primage and for you."

Diahyas chuckled mirthlessly. "How could this possibly be best for me?"

"You must place trust in your Prime."

"You have given me no reason, and I shan't go through with this." She raised her chin. "You shall break this off, or I be forced to run away."

The Prime scoffed. "To where? You be known in every corner of me primage. You think I could not find you?"

"There be places beyond Faencina," Diahyas threatened without thought.

Her mother's eyes widened in shock before she nodded to her husband and responded in barely controlled anger. "You cannot think to leave this world, daughter. You know nothing of life outside the safety of me wealth and power. Do you have friends to aid you? No, for you have no idea how to mingle among common folk. Do you know how to barter with merchants, cook for yourself? Could you carry luggage for miles? How do you think to survive hunger, exposure, thirst? I do this to protect you."

Diahyas' eyes narrowed. "Do what?"

Her mother gave another nod, and Diahyas instantly became aware of her father floating just behind her. Before she could react, her tiara was snatched from her head.

"No!" she cried in alarm. "You cannot!"

She reached out for her precious treasure, the one thing that made her feel special and safe. It was more than a symbol of her position as Shoring Water Maiden, more than simply her means of travel when in need of escape. Her tiara had been with her since she was four. She had worn it daily, slept with it each night. She felt lost without it.

"Please," she begged as tears rushed forward, ready in a moment to fall. "Please."

The Prime shook her imperious head. "You cannot be trusted."

Empty. Empty and cold. Her entire being felt empty, cold, and alone.

She saw the Prime turn toward Dehga. "You be correct, Dehga. I thank you for warning me."

Deep within, Diahyas felt a strike of anger begin to burn, and she fed it desperately until it burst into flame. Nevertheless, her words were even and calm as she addressed her mother and Dehga.

"Do not think you have won. I vow that I shall never mate this monster, and if you try to force me, I vow that I shall renounce me throne, renounce this world, and neither of you shall get the chance to use me as you so wish to do."

A hard glare at each of them served to underline her stubborn intent before she swept from the room, leaving silence to again fall upon the occupants.

The Prime and Prime-Mate stared at the door in quiet surprise and would have continued thus for some time had their guest not coaxed their gazes to his smirking face.

"I see this arrangement working out quite nicely."

Throughout the long journey to her room, Diahyas somehow managed to keep angry tears at bay. Once there, though, she didn't stand a chance. With blurry sight, she swam around the room in a flurry, leaving trails of small, oily orbs in her wake. She gathered the items she would need and threw them into a small bag. She had to leave. She could stay here no longer.

With everything packed and thrown over her shoulder, she finally retrieved the pouch of diamond dust, which had been sealed within an air-tight, clear case, from her secret hiding place. She stared down at it in contemplation. If she used it now to get back to the palace, which was around two hundred miles away, she wouldn't be able to use it again for around two and a half hours. Surely that would be too short a time for her parents to locate and imprison her. They knew nothing about this diamond dust, so they would search for her nearby instead of the palace.

Diahyas worried her lip. She needed Sea-ena to help her pack essentials, and she needed to retrieve Wisp and Fil. They could help her survive on Randor until she could find another planet that was not within Dehga's domain on which they could live peacefully. There really wasn't a better way, not after this. Her parents would not listen to Wisp over Dehga; she had been a fool to ever think that a possibility.

No, she would have to disappear, and then after time passed, she could contact Sea-ena and see if her parents had relented. Eventually, she would return. Her parents needed an heir, and they would realize the error of their ways once she was gone.

With that plan made, Diahyas decided to leave early the next morning. A good night's rest was important, especially since she intended to travel to a whole new world. Yet despite this decision, she did not sleep well that night. She woke early, quickly gathered her things, and pictured the palace, building her very room within her mind. Every homey detail was delicately placed, and she felt a smile on her lips when it was completed. Not a moment later, she felt that familiar and exhilarating pull, and when she opened her eyes, all of her beautiful things surrounded her. This was where she was happiest...unless she was far away exploring somewhere. She would miss this.

Diahyas took in a deep breath and finally focused in on her room. Instantly, her eyes widened, and she gasped in surprise. Someone had been here, riffling through her things and leaving a trail of disarray in their wake.

"Sea-ena?" she called, though it came out quite softly.

There was no response. Her maid was not here. Who had done this? Had she been robbed? She quickly swam over to her dresser and depressed the panel that hid her jewels. In surprise, she reared back because her nicely organized drawer had been ransacked...but, wait...it was all still here. She sorted through the items again to be certain. Yes, everything that should be there was present. Why would someone leave them? What else could they possibly want?

She shook her head in confusion and then remembered how time-sensitive this trip was. Whoever had done this was not important at the moment. Besides, the true thieves were her parents. She felt her anger build again. How dare they take her tiara!

"I shall take back what belongs to me," she muttered viciously. "And it shall never leave me sight again."

Then she swam off in search of Sea-ena. They had very little time to pack and plan.

The door shut behind her with a soft thud, and just after, the door to her closet swung open. Eorian's tousled head poked out.

"She does have the pouch," he said with a grin. "We'll take it tonight while she sleeps."

"And are we hiding in her closet all day?" Fil grumbled with a yawn. "Not that spending the night in a girl's closet was terrible, but really…I'm ready to leave."

Eorian thought a moment. "Sea-ena will come in here at some point today since Diahyas is back. We can try the room across the hall. That way we can keep an eye out. What do you think?"

"Honestly, E, I think we're missing something here," Fil said softly. "Don't you find it a bit odd that she came popping back here several days early using your diamond dust?"

Eorian scoffed. "I wouldn't care if she had come back with three heads and a monkey on her shoulder. All I want is my diamond dust so that we can go home and save my sister, my crew, and my world."

Fil was quiet for a bit. "She could help us with that, you know."

Eorian gritted his teeth and shook his head obstinately as he pushed his way out of the closet and stalked across the room to the door.

"She is merely an obstacle." He tossed over his shoulder. "One that is soon to be overcome."

"Luik, this be madness," Sea-ena lamented as she wrung her hands. She had been in a wretched state ever since Luik revealed everything to her the other evening, which was why she had sought him out so early in the morning. "You cannot go through with this plan."

Luik growled under his breath. "This be why I did not tell you earlier, but I could not find her."

"You should have told me immediately! Then we could have stopped all this from happening. As it be, I highly doubt we could get a message to the summer estate in time…oh, Luik, whyever would you think a revolution to be a good idea?"

"As I said before, this be not me revolution. I heard of its coming, and it shall not be stopped. I be merely trying to keep Diahyas safe. But you let her go to the summer estate! I cannot be helping her there."

"I *let* her go?" Sea-ena stuttered. "You think me capable of convincing that girl of anything? Besides, that be her parents' decision. She had no choice."

Sea-ena looked away and mumbled. "Quite frankly, I see this as a good thing. Now you cannot commit treason by kidnapping the Shoring Water Maiden."

"I be *saving* her, not kidnapping her," Luik stressed. "I shall tell her all, and since we love each other, she shall be content to remain with me until everything settles down."

Sea-ena made a sound of great frustration. "She be not in love with you, Luik! If she even knows you, I would be surprised."

Luik moved away in shock. "What? But...no, she must. You be lying. I left many notes, and she has given me signs..."

"She never received the notes, me boy," Sea-ena said sadly. "I could not risk your life over a crush."

"You..." Luik gaped at her, anger beginning to creep across his features. "You kept me notes from her?"

Sea-ena rolled her lips inward as she nodded. "It be for your own good, for your safety."

He was building up to a loud burst of anger when a different sound caught both of their attention.

"Sea-ena! There you be." Diahyas swam over quickly, urgency and worry etched across her face. "I have been looking for you. I have great need of your aid. You must come now."

Sea-ena's face paled. "Dia-Diahyas? What be you doing back? Be your parents with you?"

Diahyas shook her head. "No, it be just me. I haven't much time, but I can explain while we pack."

Sea-ena glanced back at Luik in confusion and slight trepidation. "They began early?"

Diahyas finally noticed Luik then, who was staring at her with rapt attention and delight.

"Oh, I believe I have seen you before, yes?"

"I be Luik, and yes, we have met."

"He be me nephew," Sea-ena broke in. "But what has happened, Diahyas?"

Luik spoke up. "She has said, Aunt Sea-Sea, that things be urgent, and you need to pack. You should pack plenty of things she would need for a trip, and I shall be by to finish this."

Sea-ena's eyes widened. "No, Luik, you—"

"I be needing to leave now," Diahyas interrupted, not knowing or caring about whatever problems they were discussing. "It be not safe for me here, and I must find a place..."

"I can help." Luik jumped in. "I have just the place."

Diahyas paused. "I shall consider, although I had planned to be quite a bit farther than wherever you have in mind. Come, Sea-ena. Quickly."

Diahyas swam off toward her room, but as Sea-ena started to follow, Luik grabbed her arm.

"If you want her to stay safe, Aunt Sea-Sea, she has to come with me. A war be about to begin, something we cannot stop. Convince her to go with me."

Sea-ena shook her head. "I think it be unlikely that she will go with you, and where do you plan to take her?"

"I cannot tell," Luik said firmly. "But she shall be safe with me."

Sea-ena tightened her lips in indecision.

"Please," Luik pleaded.

Sea-ena slid her arm from his grasp. "I must go." She heard him call out to her as she finally followed her charge.

"I shall be coming by her room in an hour to speak with her again. Please, convince her to leave with me."

Diahyas had just finished reactivating the shock band on her wrist when Sea-ena swam through the door. She turned to face her.

"Good, now we must hurry," she said. "I shall need many, many outfits, but make them simple enough that I can dress meself. I shall need money and whatever other items you think necessary for a distant trip of indeterminate duration."

Sea-ena's brow creased in worry, and she questioned the girl while beginning to pack for this incredibly vague trip. "Whatever be happening, Diahyas? Why did you come back alone?"

"Me parents failed to listen to me complaints about this betrothal, and I spoke with Dehga. He be a heartless, cold monster who will discard me quickly enough if he does not simply kill me. I must go away."

Sea-ena shook her head. "So...there be no war..."

"War? Why would you think there be a war?" Diahyas asked with a frown before shaking her head and resuming her explanation. "Once I be gone for a while, me parents shall call off the betrothal. I shall be in touch with you to find out when it be safe for me to return."

"From where?"

"I had thought to go to Randor."

Sea-ena's eyes widened. "The humans' planet?"

"Why not?" Diahyas said with a shrug. "Wisp and Fil shall aid me."

"You overestimate the generosity of Eorian," Sea-ena responded with a shaking head. "He has been imprisoned here for almost two weeks now. It be much more likely that he shall leave you to your own devices once you arrive at his home."

Diahyas frowned. "I had not thought of that...but, no, of course he shall help. I be the Shoring Water Maiden. It be a pleasure to all to serve me, and besides, he still wears his band. He could not get far."

Tentatively, Sea-ena tried to give the oblivious girl some advice. "Diahyas...this man be one accustomed to being in control. If you continue to refuse him his freedom and treat him like your servant, he shall find a way to escape from your bonds, and you shall never see him again."

Diahyas chewed her bottom lip.

"If he be free..." she broke off. "He would not stay if he be free."

"You need to give him that choice," Sea-ena said, pausing in her packing to share a firm but understanding look with her charge.

For just a moment more, Diahyas wavered in indecision, and then her face hardened and she shook her head. "No, it be unlikely that he shall escape from his band, and soon he shall come to worship me as others do. This be the best way, I be certain, and besides, I shall need him. What alternative have I if he chooses to leave after I free him?"

Sea-ena had no response for that.

"No," Diahyas said. "I cannot do as you say. What else be I needing?"

Sea-ena looked down at the two bags she had packed. Not knowing anything about where the girl was going or for how long was posing a problem.

"I should pack some food, just in case you land where there be none to buy. You shall need plenty of water too. Give me some time to gather that from the kitchen. You should pack some of your jewels and money... hmmm...they would have different currency on another planet. Take the gold and silver coins, but none of the other. I shall return shortly."

Diahyas nodded and did just as she said, which didn't take long. Then she sat at her dresser and gazed into the mirror. She looked so different without her tiara. She could almost pass as a commoner. Diahyas sighed deeply. She would give anything to have that back, but it would be a very long time before she would see it again, she was sure.

As she pondered her misfortune, there was a knock on her door. Her brow creased as she called out for the visitor to come in.

"I hope I be not bothering you," Luik began as he slowly pushed the door open. "I thought I would stop by to offer me assistance with your escape."

Diahyas turned back to the mirror. "I be decided upon me destination already. Sea-ena be gathering the last few items I be needing, and then I shall leave."

"Oh." Luik frowned. "Where might that be?"

Diahyas's eyes flared as she whipped around to face the servant. "That be none of your concern."

"No, no, of course not." Luik put up his hands. "Many pardons."

Diahyas nodded her forgiveness.

Slowly, Luik swam a bit forward and pulled a small bottle from his pocket. "In that case, may I present a gift to you?"

"A gift?" Diahyas asked eagerly. "What be it?"

Moving toward her, he held it out and began to unscrew the top. "This be quite valuable. If necessary, you could sell it while away, but I truly give it to you because its flavor be as magnificent as your countenance."

Diahyas gave him a small smile, flashing her gaze up to him momentarily before her eyes again attached themselves to the bottle that was coming closer and closer to her.

"Here," Luik said as he finally got close enough to open the bottle and tip it toward her mouth. "Have a taste."

Some of the liquid within floated out into the sea surrounding her, and she flicked out her tongue to guide it into her mouth. Her brows drew together, and she frowned. It tasted incredibly strange...and not altogether that pleasant.

"I do not understand..." she began, but the words scrambled in her mind. "What...?"

She shook her head viciously and tried to get up from her seat but found the room crazily spinning around her.

"Whoa, now," Luik soothed as he twined his arm about her waist to steady her.

"Do not touch me!" she ordered loudly as she tried to swim from his grasp, but she began falling instead, the water getting dark as she grew tired and heavy.

She settled to the floor, her eyes finally fluttering shut. Perhaps everything would make sense after a short nap.

CHAPTER 7

Fil sighed loudly from his seat on an overturned bucket and rolled his eyes toward Eorian, who was propped up against the door to the small storage room.

"If we were going to wait somewhere, couldn't we have stayed in our nice, cozy air room?" he asked.

"This isn't so bad, Fil."

"At least we had cards in there to pass the time…and comfy cushions."

Eorian scowled. "We were also locked in."

"But she forgot to lock it back, remember?" Fil pointed out.

"And who's to say she hasn't already realized it and locked the room now? Besides, we need to keep an ear out so we know when she falls asleep."

Fil propped his elbows against his thighs as he stared at his cousin. "So we couldn't just wait until midnight or something and sneak in? Pretty sure she'd be asleep by then."

Eorian glared at his cousin without a word, and Fil gave him a cocky grin.

Just then, they heard a startled yelp coming from Diahyas's room that was quickly muffled. Their confused gazes met briefly before Eorian turned back to the door and inched it open. He peered across the hall and saw that Diahyas's door was only halfway shut. There were some packed bags on the floor, but he couldn't see anyone…except for a light blue arm and hand wearing a silver band that was lying motionless on the floor.

His eyes widened, and he felt his heart stop momentarily. Had she been killed?

He was just about to rush to her side when he felt Fil's restraining hand on his arm. He glanced up at his cousin, who merely shook his head and nodded toward the room to get Eorian to listen in. It was difficult to do through his slight panic…why was he panicked exactly? That girl had done nothing but torment him since he met her. He should be relieved, pleased even, but all he felt was a stone lodged in his gut as he stared at her small hand.

He needed to get over there, help her if he could. She might be arrogant and think she was the best creature on the face of the planet, but in reality, she was a defenseless young woman that knew very little of the world beyond her comfortable palace. She needed him.

"I have to get over there," he whispered to Fil as he began trying to push his way out of the storage room.

Fil applied more force to keep Eorian still. "Haven't you been listening? Just wait."

"She needs help," Eorian argued. "Let me go."

Fil looked at his cousin in confusion. "I really don't get you, you know that? You hate her, remember? Besides, she's just been knocked out with some drug. I told you to listen, so stay put and start listening."

With a frustrated growl, Eorian finally tuned into Sea-ena's conversation with the princess's attacker.

"I still don't understand why you would do such a thing, Luik," Sea-ena said pathetically. "Do you realize how much trouble you shall be in?"

"I be saving her from this revolution," Luik argued.

"She already had a plan. She would have been safe. This be unnecessary."

"She has to be with me. Only I can keep her safe. I love her."

Eorian frowned. He loved Diahyas?

"Help me gather all this to the chariot," Luik said, and it sounded like he tossed a bag onto his back.

Sea-ena spoke hesitantly. "How exactly do you plan to get Diahyas to a chariot without being caught? She be unconscious. Someone shall notice."

"I shall wrap her in this rug and throw her over me shoulder." Luik sounded incredibly proud of his plan, which was quite ridiculous in Eorian's opinion. "They will only think I be doing me usual cleaning. You shall follow with these other bags a few minutes after me. I have a chariot waiting just outside the door to the west wing."

"Luik, please," Sea-ena tried again. "Don't do this."

In the small sliver of room that Eorian could see, he watched Luik roll Diahyas up in the rug. Sea-ena was just barely visible, and she was wringing her hands worriedly.

"You shall follow with the bags?" Luik asked, looking up at Sea-ena from where he was tying a rope around the ends of the rug to keep it from unrolling.

Luik grunted as he hefted Diahyas over his shoulder. "See? Diahyas be not visible, and I shall not be caught. The bags?"

Sea-ena shook her head as she clamped her lips tightly together. "I cannot be a part of this."

Luik frowned. "Fine. Then those bags stay. Be there anything she absolutely needs? If so, slip it in the bag I carry."

Sea-ena bit her lip. "No, Luik. I cannot let you do this. I shall alert the guards if you take her."

"You would see me killed?" Luik asked in astonishment.

Sea-ena and Luik began a staring match that lasted a while. Then Sea-ena broke and shook her head with a grimace.

"Fine, but wait a moment. There be one thing more she needs." Sea-ena swam out of view but returned with a small container that she carefully wedged into the rug with Diahyas.

"What be it?" he asked.

Sea-ena looked down guiltily, though Luik could not see her. "Just some medication. She shall need it in a few hours. I want her to be able to get to it quickly."

"All right," Luik agreed. Then he turned to face her. "I swear to keep her safe. This be the only way to protect her from the revolution that will soon sweep through the castle. You know this. She cannot be here."

Sea-ena nodded and watched him swim out of the room with her charge. Then she turned from the door and sagged to the floor, crying helplessly. Eorian wanted to rush after Luik and take Diahyas from his arms, but he was worried about all this talk of revolution. He was missing something, and it would be best to gather all the facts before causing more trouble by acting recklessly.

He walked across the hall and pushed Diahyas' door completely open. Hearing the creak, Sea-ena yelped in surprise and clapped a hand to her heart as she spun around. Then she realized who was standing in the doorway, and she sagged in relief.

"Thank goodness," she sighed. "I worried you be the guards. Diahyas…"

"I know," he said angrily.

"You…how did you get here?" Sea-ena asked in confusion.

"That doesn't matter. Who was that, and where is he taking Diahyas?"

Sea-ena clamped her lips together, which just made Eorian angrier. They didn't have time for this.

"Is she in trouble?" he asked. "What is this about a revolution?"

"I packed the diamond dust with her so she can return here when the drug wears off," she replied without looking at him.

"You sent my diamond dust off with that fish?" Eorian yelled angrily.

Sea-ena's eyes flashed angrily. "That be me nephew, and he shall take care of her."

"If you think that, then why send away my diamond dust with them and why try to stop him?" Eorian asked.

Sea-ena began wringing her hands again. Eorian sucked in a deep breath to try to calm his impatient nerves. That's when he noticed a tugging on his wrist.

"What, Fil?"

He turned to his cousin but found only an empty space.

"What do you mean what?" Fil asked from his other side.

"I…" Eorian broke off when his arm started rising and the tugging increased. "What in the…?"

"Oh, no," Sea-ena whispered.

Eorian whipped around to face her and found her eyes wide and full of anxiety. "What do you mean, 'Oh, no'? What's going on?"

Before she could answer, he was yanked toward the door, just barely managing to keep himself from falling. Then the force ceased, and his arm fell to his side.

"What was that?" Fil exclaimed.

"Hurry, this way," Sea-ena urged as she began swimming quickly down the corridor.

Eorian and Fil followed, but Eorian did not do so quietly. "Tell me what's happening," he said.

"She must have activated her band," Sea-ena muttered and then turned back to Eorian. "I be so sorry. Had I known, I would have deactivated it."

"Wait…that was because of the band?" Eorian asked in disbelief.

Sea-ena nodded. "You cannot be beyond five hundred meters from her…assuming she set it at the farthest range."

"He's on a leash!" Fil couldn't completely keep the laughter from his voice.

"Turn it off," Eorian ordered.

"I cannot," Sea-ena said. "I would if possible, but only her band can control yours. I have to get you in a chariot quickly before they leave the city."

"Why? What will happen then?" Eorian asked, just barely able to keep the panic from his voice. He was beginning to get the unpleasant feeling that his life may be in the balance.

"The heroshi will go full speed once outside the city, and you shall be dragged behind by your band…by the shortest distance."

"Meaning…" Fil began and broke off to swallow. "Like through buildings?"

Sea-ena nodded. "Assuming his body can withstand the strain, which it likely cannot. Our chariots be specially designed to cushion us from the effects of heroshi speeds."

By this time, she had reached her destination and pushed open the castle doors.

"They shall have many stops while within the city, but at any time now…"

"Ahhh," Eorian yelled as he was pulled several feet away, trying and failing to run through the water just to keep on his feet.

"Fil, hurry, this way," Sea-ena urged him in the opposite direction toward the stables.

Eorian finally gave up on running and starting kicking furiously, but he didn't have a prayer of swimming fast enough. His arm felt like it was going to be ripped from his body. He could hardly catch his breath, and quite frankly, he was scared out of his mind. He could handle armies, he could handle heights, he could even handle drowning, but he hadn't planned on something like this. He was utterly helpless here, and this had to stop soon. His shoulder couldn't take much more.

Then he felt the tugging lessen before stopping entirely. He drifted to the ground, his lungs and arm on fire. Behind him, he heard something approaching quickly, and then his cousin shouted his name.

"E, are you all right?"

Eorian merely looked up at him, still breathing too hard to speak.

Sea-ena climbed from the chariot and motioned for Fil to help her get Eorian in the strange-looking contraption attached to the oddest animal Eorian had ever seen. Eorian supposed it was similar to the horse and buggie back on Randor, though the buggy part was definitely sturdier. It was made of metal, except for the windows – one small window on each side, and a large one covering the upper half of the front – and it was circular with four, short posts protruding from the bottom as support when the chariot wasn't moving.

"They shan't be stopped long," Sea-ena said breathlessly as she made a strange swiping motion with two fingers on Eorian's band. It began to glow for a bit before a bright red arrow appeared, pointing straight forward. "Follow the directions the band gives. It shall show you how to get back to Diahyas."

Eorian nodded.

"Thanks...but how do I direct..." he indicated the heroshi with his head. "that thing the way I need to go?"

That thing *has a name, you realize?*

Eorian's eyes widened in surprise. "You're like Relim!"

Sea-ena glanced from Eorian to the heroshi in confusion, then growing suspicion. "Be you speaking with the heroshi?"

"Uh...I..." Eorian instantly realized what admitting to that could reveal and shook his head with a smile. "Of course not."

Of course not. The heroshi mimicked in his mind. *You should be honored, Essence of Air. The things I must put up with.*

Eorian turned to Sea-ena. "I'll figure this out. Don't worry."

She nodded with a half-smile, as if she knew his secret...but she couldn't, right? Then he was distracted by the tug on his band. They were moving again.

With a bit more forcefulness than was necessary, he shouted within his mind for the heroshi to take off.

Sure, order the pack animal around, why don't we? They don't need respect.

"E, how do we drive this thing?" Fil asked in a slightly panicked voice as the chariot began racing through the streets.

"I can talk with him," Eorian said tightly as he tried to calm his own nerves. He had never traveled this quickly before.

Fil merely nodded. "I think I might be sick."

Where exactly be I going? Or must I be omniscient too?

Uhhh, Eorian thought. *Right! Go right.*

He felt the heroshi sigh. *Lovely. It be such a treat to travel using turn-by-turn directions.*

As Diahyas had collapsed to the floor, her thoughts had jumped to Eorian. He would rescue her, just like all the knights in the stories they told. She was the shoring, so she had to have a knight, right? Of course, there were also magical beings in those stories too, great wizards with long, gray beards. Eorian didn't have a beard. Did humans even grow beards?

Diahyas was most certain they could. Why? Her foggy mind jumped from place to place trying to puzzle this out. She had seen a beard before. It was almost as if there was some memory that was just beyond her reach, like a dream that becomes hazy after one awakens in the morning.

She felt herself moved and thrown uncomfortably face down across something that dug into her abdomen. There were words spoken that were incredibly garbled, and her mind was having trouble understanding, but that had happened before with words very similar.

Diahyas again began to search her mind as best she could. Finally, just before she lost consciousness, something floated softly to the front of her mind. It was a voice, a rough voice speaking in a language she could not understand. He was calling her...Si Dienoss.

Thump. She groaned at the impact that had partially brought her out of unconsciousness. She didn't wake much though. She was aware of being wrapped tightly, of something being tossed down right beside her head and something else being wedged by her neck, and then a bit later movement like a carriage.

She had thought something before...Diahyas wasn't certain exactly why it mattered, but it did. There were words, meaningless, *oh yes!* Her mind clung to those two strange words as she felt herself pulled deeply back down into that drugged stupor. That's when she began to dream. It had been a long time since she had dreamed in such a way, but the feel of it was familiar and exciting. When the world around her stilled, she found herself crouching just behind a screen in the corner of an airie... odd.

Then she heard a voice and quietly peeked around the screen to get a better look.

"Stop pushing yourself."

The order was terse and quite firm, certainly not something a wise person would challenge, so clearly the invalid had lost his senses when he had been wounded—and yes, he had been wounded, and wounded badly if those bandages were any indication. However, he had no qualms about arguing with his nurse.

Diahyas watched as he slowly swung his legs over the side of a beautiful and expensive four-poster bed, wincing at the pain in his side as he did so. Neither he nor his nurse noticed her, but even had they turned to see her step from behind the screen, they probably still would not know she was there. It was a dream after all, a strange one, granted, but being a mere observer wasn't unusual in a dream.

She supposed that it also wasn't strange that she was dreaming of humans, although the female human, who had yet to show Diahyas something other than the gorgeous brown hair that flowed sleekly down her back, was definitely new. The woman was speaking again, her voice full of frustration and worry as she tried to gently push the man back down.

"Please, lie back. You'll re-open the wound."

The man sighed, wrapping his arms around her waist. "I've been lying in bed for days and days. I need to move. Besides, I'm almost completely healed, just stiff and sore."

The nurse's hands cupped the man's cheeks lovingly. Diahyas tilted her head, a small smile gracing her lips. How very sweet and romantic! This was a couple, not a mere patient and nurse, and they cared deeply for one another. How Diahyas longed for a relationship like that...to feel wanted and cherished and adored.

"You almost died. I think a little more rest is in order, don't you?" the woman said softly.

They contemplated one another for a long moment, and then the man smirked.

"Make it worth my while?"

The woman threw back her head and laughed, the sound full of joy and satisfaction.

"Of course I will!" she replied happily.

Then she helped him lay back on the bed and pressed a gentle kiss to his lips.

"I'll bring you a visitor; how's that?" she asked.

Diahyas began to grow impatient. She really wanted to see what the female looked like. How had her mind conjured the face of a creature she had yet to meet? Unfortunately, her wish was not to come true. The woman slipped from the room without giving Diahyas a single glimpse of anything beyond her back and that long, swaying hair.

The man still wasn't looking her way either. His eyes followed the woman and remained on the doorway even after she disappeared. However, that very action is what finally brought Diahyas's attention to an oddity about this human. She had messed up...or rather her unconscious mind had erred. Were she consciously forming a human, she certainly would not have made such a mistake, minor though it be. That was incredibly curious though. Why had she...

All thoughts flew from the discrepancy when she heard a gasp from the doorway. Her gaze whirled to the source of the sound only to find that the long-haired woman had returned with the promised visitor. All eyes were now on her, surprise quite evident on every face and wariness on all but the visitor's.

"Who are you? What are you doing here?" the long-haired woman demanded as she advanced into the room. It seemed like she was speaking directly to Diahyas, but she couldn't possibly be.

The woman was very beautiful, a rival even to Diahyas's perfectly formed features, but again, Diahyas had messed up on that one thing.

Diahyas ignored the woman's impertinent questions. This was her dream; she had more right to be here than that woman did. Instead, she focused on the visitor, who was the only human in the room that she had imagined correctly...probably because she had seen him before, in another dream long ago. He looked older now, with more gray in his beard, and he was excited. It was almost like he had been waiting to again greet her, like she was a long-lost friend.

With a huge grin, he again whispered those strange words, *Si Dienoss*. It was still just as rough and guttural as she remembered. If only she could understand him.

The female whirled to face the newcomer in confusion, her hair swinging around with her and emphasizing again Diahyas's failure in the ear department. Why ever had she made them pointy?

With a scowl, she decided that she had been here long enough; it was time to change the dream. She felt herself whirled away, back to the uncomfortable carriage that was moving quite swiftly now. The drug was powerful though, and she felt herself slipping away again. She hoped she would dream something normal this time, something non-human... although it had been nice to see that old sailor again.

CHAPTER 8

"You still have not found her?" Dehga asked in concern as he entered the throne room. They had discovered Diahyas' absence when she failed to come down for breakfast. A search had commenced immediately, but they still had not located her after several hours. "Surely she must be nearby. How far could a young, naïve princess swim without being seen?"

The Prime's eyes flashed. "Me daughter be much more resourceful than you credit her."

Dehga just barely reigned in his anger. He still needed these creatures to like him. "She does not have her tiara...unless she managed to somehow retrieve it?"

Intense anger suffused the Prime's face, and she opened her mouth to retort when Leeyan laid a calming hand upon her shoulder.

"Bailena, Dehga be merely checking every avenue. We cannot fault him in this."

His voice was a soothing balm to her nerves, and Dehga found his own ire subsiding slightly. His eyes narrowed on the Prime-Mate.

Nothing about the merman really stood out; even his coloring worked to camouflage him. He was varying shades of pale sea-green, his tail a little darker than his skin, and his hair just a bit darker than both. He was of average height, average build, average attractiveness. Everything about him screamed ordinary until one glanced up to a kindly face that held mesmerizing eyes. One glimpse into those deep gray, calm waters was enough to silence any raging storm within the viewer. They demanded attention where his soft voice merely suggested, they commanded one's gaze where his physique requested but a passing interest, and they overpowered even the most dominating spirit. Dehga wrenched his own red eyes from him suddenly. There was more to this merman than most would recognize…more than even Dehga had guessed.

This lapse in judgment had him turning to scrutinize the Prime intently. Had he missed anything else? Where Leeyan could easily fade into the background, Bailena hadn't a chance. Her tail was shimmering silver with a few swirls of light pink, her skin was a deeper shade of that rosy hue—though it could darken to near red when she was angry—and her long and flowing hair was burgundy with streaks of gleaming silver mixed throughout. With an obstinate chin and stubborn, silver eyes, she truly was only what she appeared to be: a vibrant, strong-willed personality.

"You are still in possession of her tiara, correct?" Dehga persisted, continuing to look at the Prime in lieu of being pulled again into the Prime-Mate's calming current.

Although the Prime's eyes again flashed angrily, the Prime-Mate was the one who responded. "We still hold the tiara, yes."

"Then where could she be? Does she have any favorite places from childhood where she could be hiding? Does she know any country folk who may have taken pity on her? What about friends she could have called to her aid?"

"She has never been allowed to disgrace herself by associating with those beneath her, and she be never allowed outside the grounds of our summer home," the Prime replied haughtily.

Dehga took a deep breath to keep his anger in check. "Could she be hiding here? Perhaps some place was overlooked."

"Me servants have searched everywhere three times. There be nowhere left to look."

Dehga's lips tightened, and there was a long moment of silence in the room before another thought came to him. He pondered the possibility and then twisted his features into those of worry.

"Then we must accept the possibility that Diahyas has been kidnapped."

Surprised alarm skittered across both royal faces, and Leeyan shook his head as he absently patted Bailena's back.

"We should not assume the worst. Diahyas be very strong willed and capable of all sorts of mischief," he said.

Dehga bowed his head. "I am quite certain you are right." He paused briefly. "Perhaps...but no, what could I possibly do but get in the way?"

He glanced at the royals from beneath his lashes and heaved a great sigh.

Leeyan pulled himself up straighter. "Well, this inactivity certainly takes a toll, doesn't it, me dear? We should stay here, but Dehga, if you wish to join in the search, it would make me heart glad."

"I shall leave at once," Dehga replied hurriedly, tipping his head toward them slightly before striding from the room.

Immediately, his fist tightened. How dare that inconsequential, little fish run away from him! When he found her, she would realize her mistake, and terror would keep her chained by his side. Quickly, he entered the alternating chamber and waited in increasing impatience as the water slowly swirled through the vent in the bottom to allow him into his airie.

Ignoring the deep blue curtains that shrouded both windows and the rich, mahogany canopy bed, ignoring the costly pictures on the walls, the coral statue in a corner, and the other myriad indulgences that adorned his spacious room, he strode straight to a cream-colored chair and sank into it, closing his eyes immediately.

"Diahyas," he murmured beneath his breath.

A familiar feeling began to wash over him, the same feeling that had once filled him with dread but now gave him a sense of great power.

"Diahyas."

Because he made this journey alone, there was no need to drain his energy by projecting an image. Instead, he too would rest while he stepped into the mind of his fleeing captive.

There was a sudden jolt...had she just fallen? Dehga took stock of the girl's body. No pain, but she was wrapped up in something. Odd. Another jolt caused her to bounce, and then Dehga realized that she was moving, rather rapidly. Quickly, he delved deeper, searching out her subconscious so they could have a little chat.

Not a moment after deciding this, he was slammed by color—bright, swirling colors that were constantly changing. This was new. Usually when visiting with someone, he was shown into a room or walked through a door, and it was almost always pure white.

While he was not particularly drawn to the sterile environment, it was much better than this catastrophe.

Dehga also realized that he was not substance here. He could not walk; he could not talk. In fact, he had very little control over the situation. This was a space of thought only, and there was quite a lot of jabbering going on. Dehga tried to focus in, which was proving quite difficult, but he finally found one strand of consciousness that he could follow... more or less.

"Skip, skip, right we go!" She was mapping the course of her transportation, Dehga realized.

"Oooo, I shall win." Pause. "Sparkly, mine, no don't! Where? WHERE? Where be it?"

A giggle rang out.

"Nobody be knowing. SHHHHHHH! Secrets, secrets...what? Why pointy? No sense...no sense. No SENSE, he he, but...NO! It be not so good tasting. Away, AWAY, AWAY!"

Dehga pulled back a bit. Her shouts were painful, ringing and echoing all around him. They were fearful and angry and confused. What was wrong with her?

Instantly, everything changed once again. She seemed to calm, and all the bright colors dimmed to soft shades of blue and gray.

"I be sleepy." He felt her eyelids flutter, glimpsed a colorful pattern of whatever was wrapped about her, and then she sank back down again with a yawn. "But he shall save me."

"Who?" The word escaped before he had time to consider.

Noise began, loud and jarring. Bells and whistles, sirens and screams, all assaulted him while the gentle blues burst into flaming reds, oranges, and yellows.

"He be here! That monster...no drugs...no, OUT, OUT, OOOOOUUUUUTTT!"

Dehga slammed back into himself, surprise evident on his face. She *had* been drugged and kidnapped, but how? How could someone have spirited her away without any servants noticing? More to the point, how was he supposed to find her when she was drugged? Using his portal was out of the question. It was his only way off this water-logged planet, at least until he discovered the natural portal, which was "somewhere in the sea."

His well-laid plans were falling apart. The entire royal family was supposed to be imprisoned here in this house in two days. Everything, everyone was already in place. He wasn't going to call it off now.

Dehga forced himself to take several breaths, feeling his ever-present anger slowly recede. No, everything would be fine. Things would still go according to plan. The Prime and Prime-Mate would be trapped here, and he could look for the little fish at his leisure afterward. How much trouble could one little mermaid cause? After all, she was kidnapped, had no portal, and there were no friends coming to her rescue.

"Oh, thank Kiem above! We've stopped," Fil muttered from where he sprawled on the seat of the carriage. "That was one of the most terrifying things I have ever had to do."

Eorian ignored him as he opened the carriage door, looking up at a huge, metal dome. Rails shot out in all directions that had glass bubbles moving along them going in and out of the main structure.

"What exactly am I looking at?" he asked the heroshi.

Halfway through the ride, the heroshi had taken some pity on the poor, ignorant human and changed his frustrated sarcasm into more constructive lessons.

That would be the main substation for all travel above and below the water, called an airdome. It houses the largest alternating chamber for the mermaids, and the bulbs be the second fastest transport, falling just short of heroshi speeds of 65 knots. However, for land creatures visiting the capital, the bulbs be the only way to go. Most would be incapable of affording those nice oxys you be wearing. Once in the capital, they be provided a complimentary set of oxys and vibrords, but these must be returned before the trip home.

"Why?" Eorian asked. "Seems to me it would be better for all involved if everyone had them."

The heroshi, whose name was Bigs (apparently, a very wealthy merman had purchased Bigs as a gift for his son, who was the mastermind behind the name, and promptly sold the creature to the palace after the child decided he disliked the boring, white coloring of the animal), paused a moment before replying. When he did respond, it was stilted.

What you should realize, Essence of Air, be that you be on a planet of water. Mermaids be the supreme beings here. Land be...I be not sure quite how to explain. It must certainly not be like to your home. I suspect land be all encompassing there, with advanced creatures and beautiful cities. Here, land be backward. The culture be...well, it be more primitive, the peoples of lesser intelligence. Because of this, the mermaids prefer a separation. It be quite fine for the landlings to visit, but handing out oxys and vibrords be far too close to an invitation to remain. You understand?

Eorian nodded, still looking up at the huge structure as he moved to step from the carriage. Unfortunately, the carriage was a bit higher from the ground than expected, and he stumbled as he hit, propelling his arms through the water to keep himself upright. He heard Bigs snort behind him but chose to ignore it.

"So why did you bring us here?" Eorian asked before turning back toward the carriage to address Fil. "Are you coming out or not?"

"Just..." he waved his hand from where he still sat pressed tightly against the seat. "Just let me acclimate. I apparently have a fear of speeding through water uncontrollably."

"It wasn't that bad, Fil." Eorian sighed. "So, why here?"

You need to go on land. I can assure you this be the way they came. Diahyas and her captor would have need of the alternating chamber.

"Do you think they're still in there?" Eorian asked.

Perhaps...depends on how quickly they each can change. That differs from mermaid to mermaid.

"I think Fil and I should swim straight up here. Avoid the crowds and confusion, maybe even catch them as they leave."

You can swim? Bigs asked dubiously, clearly remembering his inglorious exit from the carriage.

"Yes, we can swim." Eorian ducked his head into the carriage. "Fil, you are capable of swimming, right, or is this case of swooning going to take you a little longer to overcome?"

Fil glared at him as he began to slowly remove himself from inside. "Look, I can't talk to the horse-fish, and I don't have a glowing band giving me directions. All that I saw were several near misses with other carriages, buildings, and that giant whale, not to mention the wild swinging to and fro. It's already weird enough to be breathing underwater, but flying through it in that reckless way…just be glad the contents of my stomach stayed right where they were."

"Honestly, Fil, you used to be a lot more adventurous."

"I used to be a lot of things, but then again, I was on another planet."

"Let's just get going. Thanks, Bigs, for the ride and information. It was a huge help. If I ever come back to the castle, I'll look for you."

Bigs nodded his head in farewell. *Safe journeys, Essence of Air.*

Then they swam off in opposite directions.

Luik had realized, almost too late, that taking the usual route to land simply wouldn't do. All creatures on Faencina knew of Diahyas; they may even have realized by now that she had been kidnapped, and carrying an unconscious mermaid into the busy airdome would have him caught instantly. Still, land was exactly where they needed to be. That would be the last place a search party would go, and the land communities were funny about helping out mers — to use their term. This was precisely why Luik found himself taking an excruciatingly long time to lose his tail in an isolated part of the beach just out of sight of the alternating chamber.

He could see the very top of the large dome from their hidden position and picture the nice rooms with warm blowers to speed the process along. It had been twenty, agonizingly slow minutes, and he was still only half changed. What made things worse was that Diahyas was fully altered beside him. For the first five minutes, absolutely nothing had happened with her, and he had started to get worried, but then she seemed to wake up a bit, groggily opened an eye, and then fell deeply back into sleep. Not five seconds later, she made a strange, circular motion with her finger, and instantly her tail vanished into legs.

It had been amazing, and if he was honest with himself, a bit scary, but now he was just annoyed. If she had been awake, she could probably do the exact same thing to him or show him how to do it himself… assuming he could. Why was she able to do that when seemingly no one else had the ability? Was that some trait passed down the royal line?

Maybe that's what had gotten them the position in the first place.

Luik frowned and shook his head. It didn't matter. He would dry out in just a bit, and then he would get himself and Diahyas to the safe house he had arranged. After five more minutes, Luik glanced down to his legs and smiled.

"Finally," he sighed and slowly stood to take some experimental steps.

He had only made this change three times in his twenty years, four if he counted this one, so his walking was unsteady at best. He stared down at Diahyas in contemplation. He was going to have to carry her, but how could he possibly do that while walking? Her weight would throw off his balance, which was more tenuous than he had anticipated. Could he compensate?

Luik shifted from foot to foot experimentally, leaned forward and back, jumped up and down, strolled up and down the beach a bit, and then finally squatted down beside Diahyas and slid an arm beneath her knees and shoulders. Three deep breaths later, he jerked upward, teetered on his feet, managed to avoid returning her ungracefully to the sand, and laughed in triumph.

"See? That be not so bad," he said to Diahyas with a small smile. "It be a good start, do you not think?"

He looked straight ahead. "Now to walk. I can do this. Don't you think I can do this? I can do this."

He lifted his left foot and felt everything shift. His eyes widened.

"Oh, no...no, no, no," he muttered as he stumbled backward, fighting to regain his equilibrium.

Finally, all control vanished, and he landed hard on his backside with a grunt, still holding tightly to the unconscious Diahyas. Luik sighed and hung his head.

"So what do I do now? The Yuens certainly won't help me, but I can't keep us here on the beach." He glared at the Shoring. "Why did you have to be so difficult? We wouldn't be in this trouble if you had come willingly. I be doing this all for your own good."

He waited for a response that he knew wouldn't come and then shoved her to the ground in aggravation, breathing a sigh of relief when her head landed on the bag Sea-ena had packed instead of slamming into the sand. That reminded him briefly of the medication that he had stashed in the top of the bag after removing her from the rug. Hopefully, she would wake up in time to take it. Everything was starting to go wrong!

"Fine," he said tightly. "We shall wait here until you decide to wake. Then we shall both walk to the safe house, and you'd better not make any more trouble. I can't deal with anything else today."

She was being gently rocked, back and forth, forward and back. It was soothing and familiar. Slowly, with a smile on her face, Diahyas opened her eyes. Water. Her smile widened as she took in a deep breath, but instantly blew it back out again with a frown. What was that smell? Fresh water did not have that hint of...what exactly?

Diahyas stared at the water, finally feeling the consistency of it all around her. This wasn't right. Very tentatively, she tasted the liquid. Her brows rose in surprise. Salt? What was this large expanse of water doing with salt in it? Only tiny, contained land waters were saturated with it. Where was she?

Swimming to the surface, she turned a slow circle. There was little to be seen, although the wall of fog before her certainly didn't help matters at all. Perhaps she actually was in some lake on Land, and that fog obscured it. She began swimming in that direction, certain now that she was right, and she continuously popped up to the surface to keep her bearings

Above her, she heard a bird cry out, but she paid it little attention. She needed to get on Land, figure out how to return to Wisp and Fil, and finally leave the oppressive hold her mother had placed on her.

Essence of Water?

Diahyas gasped in water and choked. How bizarre it felt! This must be how land creatures felt when drowning. She coughed a bit more before realizing the idiocy that had befallen her and quickly whisked the water from her lungs with the flick of a finger.

"How dare you!" She chastised the bird circling above her. "Know you not that it be rude to startle someone?"

I did cry out, if you bother to recall.

"I happen to be quite busy at the moment. I must reach Land and haven't the time to converse with you."

Then let us hope that you do *have enough time to listen when I say that you*

are swimming in the wrong direction.

The bird gave out another loud cry.

"Point me in the correct direction, then," Diahyas ordered.

She felt the bird's glare pierce into her. *I am a bird of quite some stature with friends just as powerful as you. A little respect would not go amiss, Essence of Water.*

Diahyas frowned angrily and looked away. How dare that bird defy her?

"You know who I be," she said roughly.

Yes, and you know that I hold the information you seek. The difference here is that you have nothing I need; I could simply fly off and leave you swimming in the wrong direction. Another loud cry ensued.

Diahyas flinched. "Why do you keep doing that?"

I must.

"Well, stop. It hurts me ears."

I cannot.

"Why ever not?" Diahyas sighed in frustration.

I made a promise that I intend to keep.

"To burst the eardrums of every innocent mermaid you pass?"

There are no mermaids here, Essence of Water.

Diahyas shook her head. "Of course there be. I be here."

No, Essence of Water. You are not fully here.

"You be making no sense."

Perhaps.

"Now, tell me how to get to Land."

The bird was quiet for a long moment, silently staring down at her from high in the sky. It was a bit unnerving. He flapped his wings quickly a few times, sketched a giant circle, gave another shrill cry, and finally, responded.

You could follow me. I fly in the direction of the nearest land, which is still a day's journey off...however, I believe that your quickest course would be to close your eyes.

Diahyas's eyebrows drew together. "Close me eyes? Whatever do you mean by that?"

Sleep, Essence of Water. If you sleep, you will return home.

"What? How could you know that? How be that even possible?"

She felt his chuckle. *I suppose I can't know for certain, but I do know that you are not truly here, which means you must be elsewhere. In dreams only can a person be in two places at once. So if you dream there and are awake here, then sleep should take you back.*

"Why do you keep saying I be not truly here? I feel this strange water, I am speaking with you, and..."

I can see through you. You are nearly solid but not completely.

In alarm, Diahyas quickly examined her hand. Her brow furrowed.

"This be some strange shifting of light, surely," she muttered as she slowly twisted and turned her hand. "Solid...not...solid...how be this possible, bird? What has been done to me?"

Once again, that same alarming, ear-splitting call rent the sky. Diahyas gritted her teeth in annoyance.

What makes you think anything has been done?

"I do not make it a habit to make meself transparent."

Seems a rather convenient thing to do on occasion, though. Does it not?

Diahyas's mouth slackened. "What be...? Why would...? That be not...ooooh, you frustrating bird! I merely be wanting to get to Land, yet each time I ask, you answer an unrelated question."

I answered you, Essence of Water. Land is in the direction I fly. I even gave you an estimated time frame.

"It cannot be."

Why?

"There be no lakes so very large that several days' swim be required to cross. If you be false with this, then why should I trust that swimming that direction will get me to Land faster?"

If this is a lake, why does it matter?

Diahyas scoffed. "*If* this be a lake? Of course this be a lake, silly bird. A mermaid knows salt water from fresh, and only lakes be having salt in them."

I believe you said that backward.

"Be you mocking me? I did no such thing. All know that on Faencina lakes be salty and oceans be fresh."

Perhaps...but that is not the case on Randor.

Diahyas' mind began whirling. Randor? The world her Wisp had left behind? She blinked and shook her head, feeling groggy and having so much trouble focusing on her surroundings.

I hope you visit again, Essence of Water.

The words were so faint. She must have heard incorrectly. She could not be on Randor in the first place, yet if she was, she certainly had no chance of returning to her own world so soon after arriving.

That thought was instantly replaced by a different concern. With an involuntary cry, she gripped her head tightly in her hands as pain speared deeply into it. What was wrong with her? Why was her head throbbing so? Why couldn't she see? Her breathing became choppy, and her heart matched that pace. Something was very, very wrong.

"You be okay."

Diahyas gasped and jerked. The voice was vaguely familiar, but she could not place it, and she could not open her eyes.

"Shhhh…it be all right. The drug be wearing off. Be slow and careful."

Hands gripped her face, stopping her movements, and then they began brushing back her hair. Her breathing slowed. Not a threat, then. She began focusing more on forcing her eyelids to open. It was a lot more difficult than she would have guessed possible, but finally, oh so slowly, she managed it.

The bright afternoon sun burst upon her, and her eyes instantly shut again. Fortunately, opening them a second time was not as much of a challenge.

Everything around her was blurry, but as her eyes roamed, edges began appearing, and a face solidified just above her.

"You!" she cried, yanking her face from his grasp and trying unsuccessfully to move back.

Luik held up his hands in a surrendering pose. "It be okay. I promise. I be keeping you safe."

"Safe from whom, exactly? I see no pending threat…present company excluded."

Luik shook his head. "I be no threat to you. I be here only to save you."

"Save me from what?" Diahyas asked.

"The revolution."

"What revolution? There be no revolution. You be mad." Diahyas stared at him warily.

"No, it be true. It just hasn't happened yet."

Diahyas chuckled. "Right. And when be this revolution occurring?"

Luik was silent a moment, his lips pulled tightly together.

"Come on then. Or do you not know?" Diahyas taunted. "When be it occurring?"

Luik took a deep breath. "In two days."

CHAPTER 9

"I feel so very helpless," Bailena pronounced to break the oppressive hush in the large room.

Neither she nor Leeyan had left the throne room throughout the day. There wasn't necessarily a reason for that either. It was not the most beautiful room in the summer home with its muted beige walls and light-blue banners. Although the intricate murals that graced the floor and ceiling were certainly eye-catching, one had to swim back from them to get the full effect, as each picture was quite large, so it was always amusing to welcome newcomers to this room and watch as they swam from floor to ceiling and back again to admire the artistry.

The problem with these murals, however, was that it was difficult to actually figure out what was happening. It was as if history had exploded on the floor with the different bits intermingled and bleeding into one another incorrectly. For example, in the most coherent section, one would see human men and mermen fighting one another, which had to represent when the sailors arrived on Faencina, and yet within the same battle, a heroshi pulling a chariot had been created even though that invention would occur hundreds of years later.

The more debatable mural, however, was on the ceiling. The images there could be perfectly figured out…they just made no sense. In the center was a crown with a large sapphire, and waves rippled from it, spiraling outward until they got closer to each of the four corners. In the corners, there were pictures that had imagery radiating toward the mural's center so that the ripples collided. The bottom left held a yellow beetle with lightning slashing outward, and wherever the flashes hit the ripples, the water either burned or melded with the electricity to spread it farther. In the bottom right, there was a white pile of sand, although some believed it was ash since smoke billowed from it. Some water seemed to be twisted and contorted oddly at the smoke's touch while the rest grew serene as glass.

The top right had a snake-like creature with red eyes. Its tongue was depicted as lashing out again and again to cause the water to dry up in some places. However, in others, the water twined around the lashing tongue, appearing to quench the snake's thirst to the point that steam rose from the parched flesh. Lastly, in the top left was a mirror with green glass instead of silver, and dark tendrils reached outward to block the water's progress and trap it or to absorb the water.

Although the Prime and Prime-Mate had spent much time in the throne room, and not just on this one, tumultuous day, the murals never seemed to make any more sense. As worry grew with the shadows of approaching evening, the Prime found herself frustrated at the confusion of the murals, at her inability to understand them...inevitably bringing her mind back to her failure in finding her daughter.

"You be not helpless, me dear," Leeyan responded softly after a moment. "We be doing much to find her."

Bailena shook her head. "No, our servants and soldiers be doing much to find her. They be out searching while we wait here; they be questioning all around as to her whereabouts while we swim round and round in silence; they...*they* be *helping* to locate our daughter, and I be doing nothing. She could be hurt, lost...kidnapped."

"No, Bailena, she be not..."

"You cannot know that. We have ourselves enemies, as well you know, and they be not so kind as to leave an innocent mermaid out of our affairs. She could easily be used as leverage," Bailena argued. Then she paused and hung her head. "We should never have listened to Dehga. We should not have taken her tiara. She would not have left had we refrained from taking it from her."

"You can't be knowing that. She be highly strong-willed and quite opposed to this mating," Leeyan said.

"All right," Bailena agreed with a shrug. "Then say she did still leave. If she were lost, hurt, or kidnapped, she could use her tiara to return home. Now what has she?"

Leeyan paused for one beat before swimming close and placing his hands on his wife's shoulders. "She has your courage, our intelligence, me persuasiveness. She be more resourceful than you credit her…which I believe you said yourself earlier today, did you not?"

Leeyan gave Bailena a small smile, urging one to creep across her lips as well. The smile he received was halfhearted at best.

"Come now," he continued. "You be not usually this despondent. Diahyas has given us many troubles before now. Why be this so very different?"

He saw guilt flash across Bailena's face just briefly before she masked it.

"Bailena?"

She sighed. "You be knowing that the unrest on Faencina has grown. It be more dangerous for her now."

"Perhaps. I cannot think that it be that much more troublesome than before, though."

"The stakes be higher now," Bailena said softly.

Leeyan backed away and dropped his hands to his sides. "I do not understand. Her life being at risk now should not cause stakes to be higher than her life being at risk earlier…" The Prime-Mate's eyes grew wide. "You cannot be thinking of the risk to this strange mating, can you? Be you honestly worried about *that* while our daughter be missing?"

The Prime turned her back to him as she replied. "Of course not! How could you say such a thing?"

"I know you, Bailena, or…I thought I did. Now…"

"It be not what you think," she said softly.

"I need you to explain," Leeyan ordered. His voice was hard and firm for once in his life. "I find it very difficult to understand how anything could be more important to you than your own daughter's life at this moment."

"We do not know she be in danger," Bailena protested weakly.

Leeyan took a deep breath. "You seem fairly certain of it, though, and that be why I wonder what could possibly be more important to you than our daughter."

"You don't understand," Bailena cried out, and it was the despondency in her voice that finally caught Leeyan's attention enough to snap him out of his righteous anger.

"Bailena?" He questioned as he slowly turned her around to face him.

"What do I not understand? Tell me."

"I cannot."

"Yes, Bailena, and you must," Leeyan urged. "This be what you would not tell me before, when first we presented the mating to Diahyas. I let you off then, but you must tell me now. You cannot keep this bottled inside."

Bailena closed her eyes. "You will wish you did not know."

"I will accept responsibility for the knowledge, but if it truly be so terrible, you should not shoulder it alone. I will not let you."

Bailena let out a slow breath and opened her eyes. "All right…but let us sit first."

Leeyan nodded and led them to some small chairs in the far left of the room. It seemed more intimate and secretive than the opulent thrones elevated in the center of the back wall. They took their seats, and Leeyan wrapped her hands in his.

"Now tell me what be troubling you," he said softly.

It took her a few moments to speak, which built his anxiety and worry to a near breaking point.

"There be rumors, Leeyan, about a curse in these waters."

Leeyan drew back in surprise and chuckled his disbelief.

"Since when have you listened to words such as these?" he asked.

"Since their truth be found out," she answered softly.

Leeyan stared at his wife for several seconds, searching her face in vain for something to help him make sense of her words. "Truth? In a curse? What be you saying?"

"Well, it be not a curse in actuality. Not as the rumor implies anyway."

"I still fail to understand."

She sighed in frustration. "That be because I cannot seem to find a good way to tell you."

"Be blunt."

Just one moment of silence followed the statement, and then she blurted out the awful truth. "We mermaids be dying out."

"Wh-what?"

"Many, many merfolk can no longer change to go on land. Thus, they cannot reproduce. Already our numbers be decreased by half over the past ten years, and each day I receive reports of more merfolk unable to switch. We cannot replenish our numbers, and yet we have the same rate of death. Then, to further muddy the waters, of all the children born thus far this year, none show signs of being able to alter. An entire generation unable to procreate."

"Why have you not told me?" Leeyan asked, finally understanding the multiple, unusual edicts that his wife had made of late.

"I be failing me people." The words were so soft, the tears in her eyes so genuine, Leeyan felt some of her pain himself.

"No," he shook his head. "You have no control over this."

She shook her head. "But I do. I be the one to keep this world isolated, to keep everyone confident in our own superiority. I have been told recently that humans be necessary for the survival of our race."

"You must explain."

"I be consulting with historians and scientists. In this case, the two needed to work together. Originally, we mermaids needed no land, could not go on land, in fact."

"This I know," Leeyan agreed. "But we adapted as all creatures do."

Bailena nodded. "We did, but it be because of the humans. According to the historians, when the fleet of ships full of humans sailed through to our world hundreds of years ago, they did not just leave. We did not immediately fight them. They stayed for a short time before the war was waged to send them back to their world…but a vast number of children were born of this visit. These children be the first to go on land, and it be so for their children and their children for generation after generation until all merfolk have this ability after years of adaptation. Now, though, according to the scientists, it be too long since human genes met with those of the merfolk. The new generations be having only mermaid genes, thus they be not able to go on land, but unlike the merfolk of ages past, they be unable to reproduce in any other way."

"This be why you agreed with the strange man on the betrothal?"

"He be human," Bailena stated with a helpless shrug. "Diahyas be me heir, and who knows how long she be able to switch? This man be the ruler of a great many humans, humans that can provide the means for our race to survive. This mating comes at just the right moment…but if something happens to Diahyas, Dehga will not stay; he will not help us. We would lose more than just our daughter. We would lose all our people."

"You be certain? Absolutely certain?" Leeyan asked.

Bailena nodded. "There be no other way."

"You must tell her," Leeyan said. "When we find her, you must tell Diahyas."

Bailena shook her head and looked away. "It makes no difference should she know. No need to air me failure."

"She shall be more willing if she knows."

"We shall not tell her," Bailena pronounced. "In fact, I think we must move the mating up. Waiting longer could be disastrous. We cannot put this off and risk losing our chance to save our people. Dehga shall be willing, I know, and Diahyas...well, in time, she shall accept it. Yes, when Diahyas returns, she and Dehga shall mate."

Eorian rolled his eyes as Fil heaved yet another huge sigh. Masking his annoyance, he turned back toward his cousin. "I'm sure it'll just be a bit longer. I think you can handle another five minutes or so, don't you?"

Although he had really tried, Eorian feared that a bit of condescension had still managed to slip out. Fil either hadn't noticed or chose to ignore it. Eorian couldn't really blame him for his impatience, though. They had been waiting outside the airdome by the main front doors for around fifteen minutes with no sign of Diahyas and her captor.

"We don't even know they're still in there," Fil pointed out.

"Bigs said that all merfolk have to go through this chamber before they walk around on land. We've been watching the entrance, and they haven't come out."

"Maybe there's another exit," Fil theorized. "Or maybe they left before we got here."

Eorian held up the band around his wrist, which had a slowly pulsing arrow pointing toward the building. Fil frowned and was quiet just long enough for Eorian to turn back toward the airdome's entrance.

"Okay, so let's say they left and kept walking in the direction of the arrow. It's not like that thing is very specific. It's not a map with a giant X marking Diahyas's location."

"If they were moving away, I'd feel it. There's a slight tug even when

I'm in the allowed radius if she moves away." Eorian's eyes narrowed as he saw his cousin fighting back a smile. "Will you please stop finding such amusement in this? I could have been killed because of it."

"And I swear, I would have been properly distraught had you died," Fil said with a chuckle. "But a girl has you tied to her with a collar that can shock you if you're disobedient. You *have* to admit that it's funny."

Eorian clenched his teeth. "How about you sneak around to the other side of the building and walk a ways down the beach, just in case we happened to miss them?"

Fil's brows drew together. "You just said…"

"I changed my mind."

Fil stared at him a moment and then started laughing. "All right, captain, anything you say, but this story is definitely being shared with our crew the first chance I get."

He jogged off before Eorian had a chance to retort. However, Eorian didn't have a good response in the first place, and simply ordering Fil to keep his mouth shut was the best way to ensure that everyone on the planet—*his* planet anyway—knew how very foolish he had been. He was never going to live this one down. He was really hoping that once he managed to save Diahyas from the maniac that had kidnapped her she would be willing to remove this band. She had to, right? She couldn't keep him trapped with her forever…but ten years wouldn't be out of the question. She could possibly hold him that long.

Eorian shook his head. No, she wouldn't. Then again, she had no friends and did not seem to get along well with her family…she would be all alone again once he and Fil left. Eorian's mind drifted back to her room with all the little treasures she had collected in pairs. Nothing was by itself in there, except her. She was alone. He looked down at the band. She wasn't alone while they both wore this. She had him, a captive that she tried to play dress up with and go shopping with and spend time with. She was trying to create a friendship; she just wasn't aware of exactly how friendships worked.

Eorian suddenly realized how very sad that was. He had always been surrounded by friends and family that he could rely on, laugh with, and just enjoy. He couldn't imagine always being apart from those around him, seeing them have fun while he could merely collect things. That must have been incredibly difficult. No wonder she didn't want to let him go. He just needed to show her that he would stick around without the band...

"Whoa," Eorian whispered to himself. Where had that come from? He would stick around? Of course he wouldn't *stick around*. He was on a foreign planet with a crew, sister, father, and a host of other people relying on him to return to his own planet to save them. He didn't have the option of sticking around, even if he wanted to. "But I *don't* want to."

"Don't want to what?" Fil asked from behind him.

Eorian jumped. "What are doing behind me?"

"Well, up until I scared you just now, I had thought you heard me coming." Fil smirked.

"Don't get cocky," Eorian grumbled. "And you left in the other direction. Why was I supposed to think you'd come up behind me?"

Fil shrugged. "Be aware of your surroundings at all times...sounds like some pirate thing you may or may not have said to me on one occasion or ten."

"Just tell me what you found."

"Well, I didn't find *her* per se, but I did find a lot of posters with her face on them."

Eorian sighed and rubbed a hand across his brow. "How is that supposed to help us?"

"Really?" Fil grinned. "I've just outsmarted my cousin?"

"Outsmarted me how?"

Fil held up a hand. "No, just let me have this moment."

"Fil," Eorian growled after a second had passed.

"Fine," Fil said. "It's this. After seeing the posters, it got me thinking that Diahyas is pretty high profile. Everyone would know and recognize her, right?"

Eorian's eyes widened. "So he couldn't possibly bring her into this hive of activity without alerting someone. Oh, I'm such a fool! Come on!"

Fil frowned as Eorian began hurrying off. "You could have at least let me finish explaining it," he called out as he followed. "Do you even know where you're going?"

Eorian gave his cousin a smile. "Just where you said: the other side of the building, where I suspect they are drying out on the beach."

Fil jogged to get even with his cousin. "So we just walk up and say, 'Hey, give us the princess back'?"

Eorian cut his eyes over to Fil with a raised brow and kept walking.

"I'm right?" Fil pushed.

"You're half right."

"Which half?"

Again, Eorian didn't respond.

Fil huffed. "All right, so we have no plan. We're just going to walk along the beach until we happen across two mermaids."

"That sounds like a plan to me."

"But what do we do once we find them? I mean, she can control water."

Eorian stopped and stared at his cousin. "You do realize that she's on our side, right?"

"Eh." Fil weighed his hands like a balance. "She has been sending electrical shocks to keep you in line, she kept us locked in a room for almost two weeks, and even though we are trying to help her right now, I'm not convinced she'd side with us instead of that merman that's in love with her."

"He's not in love with her," Eorian said a bit too loudly. He cleared his throat and brought his volume back down as he continued. "And anyway, I don't see why it would matter to Diahyas either way. She'll be on our side."

"Well, I'm glad you're sure that she'll pick you over him."

Eorian scowled but didn't rise to the bait. Instead, he looked down at his band.

"She's still ahead of us, but...I think she's moving this way."

"Well, that's courteous of her," Fil said with a grin. "How 'bout we just sit down right here on these large, smooth rocks and wait? Now *that* sounds like a good plan to me."

Eorian surveyed their surroundings. It was a rather narrow strip of beach that was at an incline as it moved inland. The incline had been growing steeper and steeper the farther they moved from the large alternating chamber. Currently, it was high tide, and the waves were rather loud as they crashed upon the sand. Just ahead, there was a bend to the right. Diahyas would be just beyond that, but because of the height of the incline at that point, she would have to come along this way to gain access to the town. With large boulders scattered around the beach, this would be the perfect place to reclaim her. He and Fil would catch that merman by surprise, quick and simple.

"It is a good plan," he replied.

"I know, right?" Fil agreed. "But why do *you* think it is, exactly?"

"I'll explain, but we need to get behind that boulder you're sitting on."

"Why? There's a really nice view from here."

Eorian rolled his eyes. "I am so very glad you're enjoying yourself, but there are more important things at the moment than your view."

"Such as...?"

Eorian grinned. "A surprise."

Diahyas's mind was swimming as she stared at Luik. Two days? How could a revolution occur in two days? Shouldn't she have had some inkling of what was to happen?

"You...you be lying," she said.

Luik shook his head. "You don't believe that. You know I would tell you only the truth."

Diahyas chuckled. "How be I knowing any such thing? You drugged me and kidnapped me; these do not seem to be acts of the truthful."

"I be merely trying to help you," Luik said yet again, his frustration overshadowing all attempt at convincing her now. "If you would but think back and remember, you would know you could trust me."

Diahyas's eyes narrowed. "Remember what?"

Luik scowled. "It shall not help if I tell you. You must remember on your own."

"I do not have time for this," Diahyas said as she pushed to her feet. "I order you to return me to me palace."

Luik slowly got to his feet as well, wobbling quite noticeably. "I cannot. You must not be captured when the revolution begins."

"You be saying that merely to keep me here."

"I swear I be not," Luik exclaimed as he took a step forward and nearly collapsed to the sand.

Diahyas eyed him scornfully. "Have you never before been on land?"

Luik blushed. "Just a few times, and I've never walked on sand before...at least, not any this loose and unsettling."

"That shall make me escape all the easier," Diahyas said with a smile as she whipped around and began to march off.

"Wait, wait, wait!" Luik called. "Don't leave. I be trying to keep you safe. We made a pact, Kessa, remember?"

Diahyas froze mid-step but didn't turn to look at him. "What did you say?" she asked softly.

Luik grinned his relief. "We made a pact, Kessa."

"Niev?" she whispered as she turned to face him, shock evident on her face. Her eyes roamed his face, searching for the familiar boy in the face of the grown man before her. There was excitement and hope in her eyes as she remembered their adventures and how he made her laugh, and she smiled when she finally recognized him. "Truly it be you?"

Luik nodded.

"But...how did you know it be me?" Diahyas asked.

Luik chuckled. "I knew the day we met. You be the Shoring, after all. Changing your name to Kessa did not stop me from recognizing your face even though we both be children."

Diahyas frowned and placed her hands on her hips. "Well, what be your excuse? Why change your name if you had nothing to hide?"

"Why give you me real name when you would not give your own?" Luik shrugged. "By the time I decided it be silly, you had already been ordered away and had no chance to find me...but I did not forget."

Diahyas looked down at the bright sand. "I tried not to remember."

Luik frowned. "Why? We had a lot of fun together."

Diahyas was quiet for a bit, then she cleared her throat and lifted her head haughtily. "A Shoring cannot fraternize with those beneath her. We could not have had fun; we merely broke the rules."

"Which be half the fun," Luik said with a lopsided grin.

"No." Diahyas's gaze hardened. "Whatever you remember you must forget...as I did."

"But you didn't forget. Not really. You remember playing hide and seek, scaring the kitchen maids, swimming after sting rays, catching seahorses...you said that..."

"It doesn't matter what I said!" Diahyas yelled. "I be young then, naïve, unaware of the trouble I could cause. I cannot have a friend now, and I should not have had a friend then."

"You said..."

"No!" Diahyas interrupted, throwing her hand out defensively.

Luik grabbed her wrist. "You said that you wanted us to be friends forever. That no matter what those around us did, no matter if we saw one another each day, we would be true. We made a pact."

"We be children and did not know what we be doing."

"*I* did. I swore it, I remembered it, and now I kept it. Why think you that I work at the palace? I want to stay near you, and I have been there watching out for you for many years."

Diahyas shook her head in disbelief. True, her subjects should live to do her will, should want to please her, but this seemed a bit obsessive. She had not asked him to do a thing for her, and in her experience, servants did not tend to do things if not directly told. "We have not even spoken since the last day we played together. Why would you devote your life to this?"

"Because I love you."

Diahyas blinked. Could that be possible? She was lovely, wealthy, powerful, and gifted with Kiem's essence of water. It would be very difficult not to love such a mermaid. Yes, his claim seemed perfectly reasonable, which meant that he truly was doing all of this to protect her.

She opened her mouth to answer, but he continued.

"And you love me."

Diahyas reared back and snatched her hand from his grasp.

"I fear you be mistaken," she said with great affront. "The Shoring Water Maiden would never degrade herself so far as to love a peasant."

Luik's face hardened. "Why be you refusing to admit it?"

"Because it be untrue." Diahyas turned and began walking away

"No! Wait!" Luik called out in alarm. "You must stay with me and go to the place I prepared to protect you."

"I must do no such thing," she said over her shoulder as she continued forward.

Luik began to stumble after her. "It be too dangerous; you don't understand."

"I be the Shoring. I understand everything. These revolutionaries you speak of would not dare to hurt me."

Luik growled in his throat, both at her naïve remark and at the pain that shot up his knee as he hit the sand yet again.

"Do you even understand what a revolution be?" he asked crossly.

"Out with the old, in with the new. These merfolk do not know you, only what you represent. They care not if you be hurt, left destitute, killed… they believe you deserve it. You be merely a figurehead not an actual mermaid, definitely not someone to whom they can relate."

Diahyas spun on her heel to face him, her fists propped on her hips.

"Yet you can relate to me? You believe this? You believe you know me, understand me?" She scoffed. "You know nothing of me. You may know the child I once be, but she has changed. I be very different from the image you hold."

Luik nodded. "You be hard and cross…but I still love you."

Diahyas sighed and closed her eyes, feeling a foreign sense of compassion toward the unhinged merman struggling through the sand. They had been childhood friends for a very brief month. He had made her laugh, push the rules, have fun. Now, in his own twisted way, he was trying to keep her safe.

"Come," she said as she moved toward him and threw his arm around her shoulders. "I shall help you to the airdome."

"That be not where I be heading," Luik argued.

"Yet that be where you shall end up. You need not be on land, as you well know, and I should do something about this revolution."

"What?" Luik glanced at her in alarm. "You cannot. You shall be captured. You must stay away."

Diahyas shook her head. "I do wish to be far from here, but there be responsibilities that I cannot overlook. Faencina be me home, and I do not see a warm welcome for me if me parents be overthrown and a new ruler set in charge. You understand?"

Luik was silent, but he finally nodded.

"You be heavier than you look," Diahyas grumbled as Luik began to fall again.

She glanced up at the large cliff to her left. The alternating chamber was out of sight at the moment, but once she rounded that bend, she would be better able to gauge just how far she would have to support Luik.

"Come now," she said. "Let's move a bit faster."

"I be not sure…"

"I shall keep you from falling."

She pulled him along more quickly, though he complained with each step, and smirked with satisfaction when they made the turn and saw the large airdome before them, gleaming in the sunlight. Unfortunately, that's when Luik began to collapse.

"Oh, no! Don't!" Diahyas gasped in dismay.

They landed in a heap on the sand.

Diahyas huffed and pushed against him. "Get off me!"

"I would do as the lady says, if I were you," came a familiar voice behind her.

She felt a smile split her face as she turned to face him. Standing there, tall and strong, he was the picture of a hero, even with the sardonic look on his face. The bright sunshine was hitting him full on, making his hair shimmer almost like he himself was radiating the light, and his eyes were dancing. Diahyas drank in the sight of him for longer than she should have before shaking her head and pushing to her feet.

"Where have you been?" she asked.

Those eyes drilled into her, making her feel as if the question was wrong somehow.

"Oh, I'm sorry," he replied. "I didn't realize there was a set time for me to rescue you."

"Rescue?" Luik piped in. "She be not needing a rescue. I be saving her."

"I'm going to need you to define what 'saving' means on this planet, because where I'm from, knocking a girl out, wrapping her in a rug, and sneaking her out of her home is not classified as 'saving.'"

Luik glared at him from his seat in the sand. "Who be you anyway? You look most unusual for a merman. You be not one of those strange Yuens, be you?"

"What? No," Eorian said just as Diahyas jumped in with, "Yes, of course he be."

They glanced at each other. At least he wasn't angry this time, just confused.

Luik's attention turned to her. "What be you doing with a Yuen?"

"I…I have found that he be a very good servant," she said.

A shout of laughter issued from behind a boulder, drawing all eyes to Fil as he stepped into view.

"You must have some lousy servants," he said with a grin.

Diahyas's eyes narrowed on him, but before she could respond, Eorian broke in.

"Fil, I told you to let me handle this."

"Yeah, well, I find the conversation mildly interesting, and there clearly isn't going to be any fighting what with fishboy unable to stand over there."

"Fishboy!" Luik exclaimed.

Diahyas swiped her involuntary smile away with a hand and watched Eorian roll his eyes in aggravation.

"He's sorry," Eorian said to Luik.

"No, he's not," Fil countered. "Have we already forgotten that he kidnapped the princess here?"

"Shoring Water Maiden," Diahyas enunciated. It did not seem that Wisp's cousin would ever learn the difference.

"I be *saving* her," Luik emphasized.

"Saving her from what?" Eorian asked in exasperation.

Fil crossed his arms. "You have an odd way of saving someone."

"I be bored with this now," Diahyas tried to break in. "I wish to return home."

No one seemed to pay her any attention.

"There be a revolution. It will occur in two days, and the current rulers shall be overthrown," Luik explained to Eorian.

"That seems a bit fast," Fil said.

"Why is it happening?" Eorian asked.

Diahyas walked to the center of the group. "It does not matter. It must simply be stopped. I need to return to me parents to warn them."

"What you need is information," Eorian argued. "There is no reason for them to believe you, or even for us to believe him without some explanation. You didn't have even the faintest inkling that this was going to happen, so how can we know that it actually is?"

"I have no reason to lie to her," Luik said in affront. "I never would. I love her and have sworn to protect her."

Fil snorted, and Eorian examined him skeptically without a word. However, Diahyas paused and glanced toward Luik briefly. What Eorian said was true. She had seen no proof of his claims or even heard a compelling argument. She bit her lip. Luik had been so earnest, though. He did not seem to be lying.

"We be childhood friends once," she said half-heartedly.

"People change," Eorian stated flatly.

Diahyas drew herself up as she came to a decision. "Perhaps, but we cannot be certain of anything while here. Me parents, on the other hand, have countless resources to uncover the truth. They shall decide after we deliver the warning."

"We?" Eorian repeated as he crossed his arms. "I came to find you so you could get this thing off my wrist and I could go home."

"That be where we be headed," Diahyas said in miscomprehension.

Eorian shook his head. "Not your home, my home. I want to go to *my* home."

"You would leave me alone with only me kidnapper to help me save me parents and me throne?" Diahyas asked with a frown.

Eorian opened his mouth and shut it again.

Fil spoke for him. "That's the plan. Great as our room was, it got a little old after the first week of captivity."

Diahyas ignored him and kept her focus on Wisp. He was struggling with himself. She could tell that he desperately wished to leave this place...to leave her, but he was a fair and just man. She did not believe him capable of abandoning her in her time of need.

"We don't need his help," Luik said angrily. "I can protect you on me own."

Eorian's jaw hardened as he shot a disdainful glance toward the merman. Then his gaze rested back on Diahyas.

"I will stay on one condition," he said.

"What?!" Fil exclaimed. "E, you can't be serious."

Diahyas's heart skipped a beat as she answered him. "Ask it."

"Take off this band and let me help of my own free will."

"Come on, E. Don't do this. Have you already forgotten the days and days confined in a room? She renamed you and shocked you and..."

"Fil, she needs help."

"We don't know that. It could all be a lie."

"Lucky for you, then. We'll get home sooner."

"Do you promise not to leave without saying goodbye first?" Diahyas whispered softly, drawing Eorian's attention back to her. She had not meant to sound so forlorn and desperate, but she couldn't fix it now.

"I swear you will know before I leave," Eorian said.

Diahyas nodded, pausing only briefly before entering the necessary sequence into her band. "Then I release you."

The click as the band opened made her heart sink. Once he had helped her, she was going to be all alone again…well, if she was lucky. She suppressed a shudder as her mind summoned Dehga's cruel face. If her parents would not call off the marriage after she saved their kingdom, then she would be forced to tag along with Wisp whether he wanted her or not.

Eorian was rubbing his wrist and celebrating with Fil when Diahyas finally pulled away from her thoughts. She held out her hand for the band.

"May I have the band?" she asked.

Eorian turned to her with a quirked brow and half-smile.

"You know, I think I'm going to hold onto it, if you don't mind," he said as he slipped it into his bag. "I'd rather not have you fasten it back on when I'm not looking."

Diahyas's eyes widened as she recoiled from his words. "How dare you! You believe me to be untrustworthy?"

Eorian shrugged. "Let's just say that I err on the side of caution."

Fury overwhelmed her, and she was just about to pelt the aggravation with water when he winked at her, throwing her completely off guard.

"I wouldn't," he said softly as if he guessed what she had been planning. "You do still want my help after all, and I think we should be going, don't you?"

She contemplated him a moment. He certainly seemed a lot more cheerful now that he was his own master again. She much preferred him this way, and he made a good point. She nodded.

"Let us use this diamond dust of yours. We shall arrive much more quickly," she said as she rummaged in her bag to pull it out.

"Diamond dust?" Luik repeated in confusion. "What has diamond dust to do with our travel?"

Diahyas gave him a devilish smile as she reached for him. "Take me hand, and you shall find out."

Eorian and Fil both touched her other arm as Luik looked at them all strangely and hesitantly grabbed her hand. She chuckled just a bit at the thought of his reaction before picturing her summer home and welcoming the sensation of instantaneous, distant travel.

A slow grin spread across Dehga's face as the messenger delivered her great news from the Prime and Prime-Mate. However, his grin did not mirror that of the young woman who practically spun circles as she swam from the room to continue spreading the joy. No, his grin was calculating and self-satisfied; it was a grin that made the viewer step back instinctively and search for escape.

Now, he closed his eyes briefly, picturing a face, and then was thrown into that very individual's mind.

"It is time."

Dehga did not bother to stay long enough for confirmation of his message, even though he was a few days early. Instead, he adjusted his ring and strode from the room in the direction of the returned Shoring. He had only managed five steps when the fantastic messaging system that this world possessed began relaying his command to every hibernating soldier throughout Faencina. The golden merman's voice was the one heard now, his face would be the recognizable target, but by no means was he in control.

"We rise," Boran announced.

Dehga continued along the hall to the stairway and began to descend.

"It be time for the tyranny to end."

Several servants were staring in confusion and worry at the small transmitters installed in each room. They paid no heed to Dehga as he crossed to the throne room and stood before the doors.

"There be troubling things occurring in these waters, terrible things that our rulers ignore or cause. It must be stopped!"

Dehga threw open the doors and marched inside, where the Prime, Prime-Mate, Shoring, and some fellow Dehga had not seen before all shared glances of great alarm.

"What is happening?" Dehga asked of them.

They hadn't time to respond before the voice boomed out again. "The time has come for our plans to be realized. To all me friends and fellow soldiers, AWAKEN!"

Dehga suppressed his look of triumph at the sound of the signal and the resulting lock of the throne room doors all around them. The royals in one place, safe and sound…it was working out far better than he had hoped, especially with Diahyas fleeing so inconsiderately. Now to play the rest of his hand, and if things continued just this smoothly, he should be mated, crowned, and widowed before a month had passed.

CHAPTER 10

Surprise came first, then relief, quickly followed by joy, but right on the heels of that was anger. All these signs of a parent's love flowed through Bailena and Leeyan, yet to Diahyas only the last emotion stood out, which made her quite cross.

"Where have you been, Diahyas?" Bailena nearly shouted.

"We be worried sick," Leeyan explained with more than a hint of frustration.

Diahyas crossed her arms, "Surprised, be you, that I be able to make me own way?"

She heard Luik clear his throat behind her and murmur something that she couldn't quite make out.

"This be not the time for childish games, Diahyas," her mother chided. "There be much going on in me primage of which you be unaware."

Diahyas smirked. "There also be much of which *you* be unaware."

Her mother reared back with brows raised.

"Diahyas, what mean you by this?" Leeyan asked.

"You want me information?"

Her mother's lips tightened. "It be not in your best interest to play more games with us."

"This be no game!" Diahyas snapped as her hands flew down to her sides and formed fists. "This be a trade. You want something from me, and I want something from you. Be you willing to negotiate?"

"Diahyas," Luik whispered behind her, which unfortunately drew her mother's gaze.

"And who be this?" she said coldly. "Be he the reason for a negotiation?

You wish to mate him instead of Dehga?"

"What?" Diahyas exclaimed, momentarily thrown off track. "No...why would...no. However, Dehga be exactly what I wish to negotiate."

Bailena shook her head. "That be not up for negotiation. In fact, your sudden disappearance has accelerated our plans. You, girl."

She pointed an imperious finger toward a young mermaid that was cleaning on the far side of the room. She startled and froze for a moment, but then slowly swam forward eagerly.

"Yes, me Prime?" she said with a bow.

"Spread the news that me daughter has returned safely. Go to Dehga first."

"Yes, me Prime." Another bow, and then she swept off.

"I do not wish to mate him," Diahyas said anxiously as the door shut behind the girl. "Please, you must not."

"I must not? I may do whatever I wish," the Prime declared.

Diahyas bowed her head and took a deep breath. "You be correct...I misspoke. You *should* not. We know nothing of him, and at the moment, you have far greater things to worry about. I can tell you precisely what be coming, but you must swear that you will not force me to mate Dehga."

"What do you know, Diahyas?" Leeyan finally spoke up. "If it be so important, you should not secret it away until your own purposes be met."

Diahyas looked down guiltily. "You leave me no choice."

"You, boy," her mother called to Luik. "You be knowing of this as well. Tell me, and I shall give you many riches and a high rank."

Luik swallowed. "I...I do not..."

"You do not know?" the Prime interrupted. "I find that unlikely. Why else would me daughter bring you?"

Diahyas broke in. "Release me from this betrothal, and I shall tell you."

"You shall not be released!"

"Then you be doomed."

The Prime laughed. "How do I know this be not a ploy to trick a swear from me? You must first tell me what shall doom me, and then I will consider releasing you."

"No." Diahyas shook her head. "I must have the swear first."

"You shall not have it until I know."

"Then you shall never know."

The two were locked in a stubborn duel of glares until an announcement came over the loudspeaker.

"We rise!"

Diahyas gasped and turned to Luik. "You said it would not begin for two days."

"What has begun?" Leeyan asked.

"...to end. There be troubling things occurring...," the man on the loudspeaker continued.

Diahyas gave in. "A revolution. There be an attack coming, and I be coming to warn you...but it came too soon."

The doors burst open, and Dehga walked in.

"What is happening?" he asked, though Diahyas did not believe him to be truly concerned.

Diahyas was just about to respond when the disembodied voice from the loudspeaker rang out again.

"The time has come for our plans to be realized. To all me friends and fellow soldiers, AWAKEN!"

Her head swiveled at the sound of one set of doors locking, followed almost instantly by another and another.

"Oh, no," she whispered, her mind jumping instantly to Wisp and Fil hidden away in her room.

"What be this?!" the Prime shrieked. "How dare they rise against me! I be doing everything in me power to help them. Know they not how tenuous our existence be? I be the only one to bring about change."

"What?" Luik asked, though he was ignored by everyone.

Dehga, on the other hand, received the Prime's attention. "I ask again, what exactly is happening right now?"

The Prime's tail swished back and forth forcefully. "I be informed, both by me belated daughter and by the traitorous coward behind the intercom, that what be happening be a revolution."

"Then we must leave. Get you all somewhere safe," Dehga said simply.

"Did you not hear the doors locking?" Diahyas asked snippily.

Perhaps Wisp would come to free her. She had told him she would return in an hour, so if several went by without her presence, surely he would come looking. If only he still wore his band! She could have sent him a message. How else...wait! He still retained his band in his bag.

Perhaps she could still reach him after all.

"I'm starting to detect an unfortunate pattern here," Fil said in disgust.

"Which is?" Eorian asked on a sigh as he rolled his head toward his cousin.

"Nearly every time we interact with the princess, we end up in a closet, and every single time, we have found ourselves imprisoned."

"We are here voluntarily this time."

Fil snorted. "You are, maybe."

Eorian opened his mouth to argue, but Fil pushed on. "Regardless, we can't really leave, can we? We're supposed to stay out of sight, you still don't have your diamond dust, and we don't have a clue where we are even if we decided to set out on foot."

"She'll give us the diamond dust once we've helped her. Besides, it can't be used for a few more hours anyway."

"Once we help her," Fil repeated. "How is this helping her? We are sitting in a closet while she and fishboy are down on the ground floor trying to…"

"We rise!"

"Shhh, Fil. Did you hear that?" Eorian asked as he moved to the door and put his ear against it.

"Hear what?"

"It be time for the tyranny to end."

"Okay, I heard that," Fil said with a frown.

"They started early," Eorian said with rising alarm.

"We need to find Diahyas and warn her." Fil grabbed the door handle.

Eorian shook his head. "No, we need to lay low. She and her parents are the targets. If we are anywhere near them, we'll be spotted and stopped. We'll stay here, scope everything out, and find a way to communicate with her."

"I'm not liking this," Fil said. "She's the only one that can help us get home. Shouldn't we try to find her first, before these revolutionaries do? We have our own war to fight. If we get caught up fighting hers, it'll be twice as long for us to get back, and…look, I need to know Lishea is safe. The last time I saw her, she was in a tiny rowboat disappearing into the fog covering a very large ocean."

Eorian ran a hand across his forehead. "I know… I know, but Fil…do you remember my prophecy?"

"I remember there being a prophecy, yes," Fil said in confusion. "I don't remember the details. What does that have to do with our situation now? Did it give us a clue?"

"Not specifically about what we need to do right now, no…although…"

"A lot of help those elders are, aren't they?"

"Well, they are…," he said slowly. "*From lands afar, her help she must send, To rid trouble, his hand he must lend.* They were talking about Diahyas…not Genevia. She'll help us if I help her."

"Maybe not," Fil said desperately. "Maybe that has nothing to do with this. It can't. We have to go home soon…sooner than helping her would allow."

"The prophecy said I'd be gone a total of ten." Eorian paused and gave Fil a meaningful look. Fil blinked at him, and he sighed in aggravation. "We're past ten days already."

"We're past…" Fil began then moaned. "Ten *weeks*? Really?"

He hit his head against the door and left it resting there. "Why did I ever join up with you?"

"You'd be bored out of your mind if you hadn't, and you know it," Eorian said.

"But two wars? *Two*? We don't even know who we're fighting in this one."

Eorian put a hand on Fil's shoulder. "We will get back home, Fil. Trust me."

Fil turned to look at him. "I'm going crazy with worrying about her. What if…"

"She's fine," Eorian said. "Relim is watching out for all of them, and my crew will protect her with their lives. She's my sister, too, remember? I made sure she was in good hands before letting her go."

Fil nodded and looked to the ground. Then his head shot up, his brow furrowed. "Do you hear buzzing?"

"Buzzing?"

It was very faint, but there was a definite hum. Eorian turned around, moving slowly to detect the source.

"Your bag," Fil said and pointed.

Eorian snatched it up and looked inside. There was a faint glow emanating from within, and he reached for it. When he pulled it out, he chuckled. "Why am I not surprised?"

"Is there anything that band can't do?" Fil asked.

Eorian turned it and shook it, poked and prodded, but he couldn't find a way to make the thing stop vibrating, much less use it to answer.

"I don't know what to do."

"Try that swiping motion thing that Sea-ena did," Fil suggested while miming the maneuver.

Eorian tried and failed, growing more agitated by the moment. He shook it again.

"Throw it against the wall."

"What?" Eorian glanced Fil's way to see if he was actually serious. He was. "No. I don't want to break the thing."

"Really? I seem to remember a few choice words of yours that contained the opposite desire."

"Well...I need it now."

Fil was quiet for a beat. "Then put it on."

Eorian stared down at the simple band with a grimace. Then he held it out to Fil. "How about you wear it this time?"

Fil took a step back and put his hands up defensively. "No way. She'd probably shock me to death for being impertinent enough to wear your band without her permission."

"She wouldn't..." Eorian stopped with a frown. Then he sighed. "Yeah, I suppose you have a point."

He stood indecisively with the vibrating and glowing band around his wrist but still unclasped.

"You really want me to do it, E?" Fil offered hesitantly.

"No." Eorian blew out the breath he hadn't realized he'd been holding. "Here we go again."

He snapped the band closed, and the vibrating instantly stopped. Eorian and Fil stood quietly, staring down at the silver circle of metal, but nothing happened.

"Maybe you weren't supposed to put it on?"

Eorian shook his head. "I don't think so. I mean, it did stop vibrating.

Maybe I'm supposed to..."

"Wisp?" came Diahyas's hushed voice from the band.

His eyes flew to it in surprise. "Diahyas? How're you doing that? And it's Eorian, not Wisp."

"Shhh," she whispered. "Do not say anything, or they'll hear you."

"Who?"

"Quiet, Wisp," she ordered again. Then there were some muffled words coming from someone else that he could not quite make out. "I be doing nothing, just like all of you."

"Be you talking to that human?" Luik asked softly.

"Yes," Diahyas responded. "Stay here by me so it looks like I talk with you. Wisp? You be listening?"

"It's Eorian, and yes, I'm still listening."

"Shhh, I told you not to speak."

"You asked me a question!"

Before Diahyas could respond, a different voice came through the band. "You are speaking with someone outside this room, aren't you?"

Diahyas laughed mockingly. "That be wishful thinking, Dehga. I be speaking with Luik."

Eorian clapped a hand around his band and leaned toward Fil to whisper, "Did that voice sound familiar to you?"

Fil shook his head. "No, why? Did it to you?"

Eorian nodded as he tuned back into the other conversation.

"...in touch with someone that can help us out of this room, you need to share it with us. Access to the outside world is mandatory if we wish to stop this revolution."

"You think I be not knowing this, Dehga? You think I have no wits?"

"I think you are a spoiled, stubborn little girl who likes to keep secrets."

Diahyas gasped. Fil chuckled and gave a muted shout of agreement. Then came a new voice that sounded a bit miffed.

"You be speaking with the Shoring Water Maiden, daughter to the Prime Water Maiden, ruler of all in Faencina. Respect be demanded."

Although he was quite some distance from the throne room, Eorian could feel the tension. There were far too many dominant personalities in that small space for this to end well.

"I have been under the impression that you needed me. Has this changed? Should I leave Faencina to its own devices?"

"Yes, you should," Diahyas said just as the new, feminine voice began to backpedal.

"No, of course not. There be no reason for you to leave."

"Mother!" Diahyas exclaimed.

"What is keeping me here?" Dehga challenged. "You're daughter does not seem to be submissive to our arrangement—running away, fighting against me at every turn, even now telling me to leave. I feel as if I am wasting my time here since you cannot find a way to rein her in."

"E, what is happening right now?" Fil asked softly in confusion.

Bewildered himself, Eorian shook his head.

"I believe we should each retire to different areas of the room," said a calm, rational voice. "There shall be words spoken soon that cannot be unspoken and cause irreparable damage to the relationships we share."

"I do not wish to have a relationship with him," Diahyas said.

There was a deep silence in which Eorian imagined that calm man staring the girl down. She sighed and must have moved away because everything said by the others at that point became muffled and indistinguishable again.

After a moment, Diahyas spoke to him. "Wisp? You can respond quietly to me now."

"It's Eorian. What was that? Who was that man?"

"Me father."

"Sounds like you have a difficult relationship," Eorian said as he thought back to the angry, harsh words that had been spoken.

"I cannot seem to persuade him to me side, and I have done all I can think to do!"

Eorian searched for the best way to respond. "Well, he does seem a bit...opinionated."

There was a pause.

"Me father?" Diahyas asked in confusion. "He be not opinionated at all. He do only what me mother wishes."

Eorian frowned. "He didn't sound like the submissive sort to me, what with all the yelling and derogatory remarks."

"Wha...? Oooohhh. No, that be not me father. That be Dehga."

The way she said his name sounded like a curse.

"Dehga, yes, you did call him that. Who is he? Your brother, uncle?"

"Me betrothed."

Eorian felt like he'd been slapped, which was ridiculous. He shook his head to clear it. "I'm sorry? Did you just say *betrothed*?"

"Yes. I need you to unlock one of the doors to the throne room—I will guide you there. I shall then try all the doors and miraculously find that one unlocked so we can escape."

"Who is Dehga? Have we met him before, because he sounds…"

"No," Diahyas interrupted. "Nor shall you. He be frightening and strange. The door? You shall unlock one?"

"Sure, yeah, I'm on my way."

"Good. Follow the hall to the left and swim down to the ground floor."

There was a click, then silence.

Eorian waited a moment for more instructions, and then sighed in frustration.

"I think they match," Fil said with a smirk.

Eorian frowned at his cousin as he opened the closet door. "How could you possibly think that?"

Fil fell into step beside him as he answered. "Because neither one of them is tolerable. They are both stubborn, opinionated, and feel superior to those around them."

"Diahyas isn't that bad…"

"Really?" Fil said doubtfully as he stared at his cousin. "You don't think she's 'that bad'?"

"No. She just takes a little getting used to."

He felt Fil's eyes drilling into him for several more seconds before finally Fil looked away. However, the chuckle that followed made Eorian uneasy.

"What?" he asked.

"Oh, it's nothing, really," Fil said with a smirk. "I just think someone has developed a little crush."

Dehga slowly scanned the room. They had each separated to different areas as requested. The Prime and Prime-Mate occupied the thrones, speaking softly with one another — most likely making futile plans. The merman that had arrived with Diahyas was hanging a short ways back from her, almost like a besotted puppy, and he followed her as she swam slowly around the room…once, twice. Dehga's eyes narrowed. She was up to something. She seemed agitated, impatient, and she kept turning toward the wall and lifting the wrist with the silver bracelet close to her face. What was she doing?

He walked toward the wall to intercept her on the beginning of her third circuit.

"Dehga." She glared at him. "You be blocking me path. Step aside."

He leaned against the wall and studied her. "I was just admiring that bracelet you're wearing."

He pointedly studied the jewelry before returning his gaze to a face that had grown a bit uncomfortable and wary.

"I thank you for the unexpected compliment. These be quite common."

"Common?" Dehga questioned. "I would think not. Surely, someone as grand as you would not wear a trinket so humble."

"You do not know me quite as well as you think. If you will excuse me…"

She made to swim around him, but he stepped to the side to block her once again.

"May I hold it?" he asked as he held out a hand.

Her lips drew tight. "Why would you wish to?"

"Humor me?"

"It holds sentimental value," she argued as she shook her head. "I would not dare to remove it. May I?"

She indicated that she would like to continue moving past him, and with a mocking bow, Dehga did step aside for her to pass, but he fell into step beside her as she swam along.

"What be you doing?" she asked.

"Can I not walk with my fiancé?" he asked simply.

"Not without good reason."

Dehga stayed silent but continued to move with her.

"I see you wish to keep your own council," Diahyas said.

Dehga glanced at her from the corner of his eye but still remained quiet.

Diahyas sighed. "That being the case, I do not wish to swim with you. Go away."

"Those are rather harsh and disagreeable words."

"You be a harsh and disagreeable man."

"I am a man accustomed to getting his way."

Diahyas stopped and stared at him. "And I be accustomed to getting mine. Seeing as we be on me world, in me summer home, me way be the one that prevails. I do not wish to be near you, so inasmuch as this room shall allow, you shall remain far from me."

Dehga gave her a slow smirk, and she swam away haughtily. The little fish could feel superior now, but it would not last. Besides, she was hatching a plan, one she desperately did not wish him to know, so allowing her a false victory was the best move.

Dehga watched as the wrist with the bracelet again moved to her face. She paused just a moment before whirling to face the room and making an announcement.

"Perhaps all the doors be not locked after all. I be trying them."

Red eyes followed her as she did just that. The first two she tried were locked, but the third responded to her touch. While the others in the room were excitedly praising her, each in their unique way, Dehga studied her once again.

So Diahyas was not completely friendless. There was someone here willing to help her, someone she was communicating with through that bracelet. That someone was going to die.

CHAPTER 11

Diahyas swam through the throne room door quickly, relieved that Wisp had actually done as asked and hidden himself away. Moving to the side, she allowed Luik, her parents, and her nemesis to exit as well.

"Now what?" Dehga asked drily, his red eyes looking around lazily.

"Now, we be leaving," the Prime announced and turned to quickly lead the way.

Dehga's response stopped her. "How exactly do you propose to do that?"

"We shall order a carriage, of course," the Prime narrowed her eyes as she stated the obvious.

Dehga nodded slowly and pursed his lips. "Yes, that does seem to be the thing to do, does it not?"

The Prime waited in aggravated silence for him to finally get to his point.

"However, at the moment, I believe that you are unaware of who can be trusted. Perhaps your carriage driver is in league with the rebels and will simply deliver you to his leaders. Then again...perhaps he truly is a loyal servant, willing to die to save you from imprisonment, but where will he take you? Do you have a secret bunker somewhere? Even then, the servants and soldiers that I am sure are paid to provide your comforts and protection could very easily be paid off or blackmailed. I'm sure they each have families, vices, money issues..."

"Your point has been made quite well, Dehga," the Prime said angrily. "And what do you propose we do?"

Dehga thought only briefly before replying. "Stay here. Find a place out of the way to hide out. I will go around the castle and weed out the loyal servants from the rebels, and once we have that small base to fight with us, I'm quite certain we can find a suitable place to hide. The rebels, for their part, will assume you have fled, so I will have a few hours at least to scout things out before they decide to look around here."

"Stay here." The Prime-Mate cocked his head in thought. "To remain within the claws of the beast, even though he thinks to have dropped you, be merely asking to be caught the more easily and swiftly once the realization be made."

"That is why we need to be sure to leave before they make the realization."

Dehga gave him a frightening, wolfish grin that seemed to only make Diahyas's father more pensive. "Where do you propose we stay?"

"The hay loft in the stables. We will be able to leave quickly once we know where to go."

The Prime-Mate nodded agreement, and both he, the Prime, and Dehga turned toward the stables. Diahyas stayed very silent as they moved away, hoping none would notice that she did not follow. Unfortunately, Dehga did and stopped abruptly before turning back.

"Diahyas. Come."

Those two terse words encouraged her parents' attention as well.

"There be no time for your stubbornness, daughter," the Prime urged. "Do as Dehga says."

Diahyas shook her head. "I shall not. You three may go, but I have other plans."

"To be captured?" Dehga snorted. "Because I can assure you that is all that will transpire if you do not come with us...and quickly."

Diahyas moved closer angrily. "And how do we know you be not in on this conspiracy? These troubles and your arrival do coincide, after all."

"No, they did not, Diahyas," the Prime interjected. "Now, come."

"Yes, they did, Mother," Diahyas argued before her attention returned to Dehga. "I shall not follow you anywhere. I do not trust you, and I do not think you mean to protect us. I believe you have plans all your own. I think you wish to rule Faencina in addition to your own world, so if me parent and I be out of the way, that would be exactly what you want. Why should you not help these rebels? In fact..." Diahyas's eyes widened. "In fact, why should you not be leading them? You do not strike me as a follower. I think you be leading this revolution to get me parents killed, and once Faencina be fully in your hands, you mean to kill me as well."

Instantly, Diahyas felt a strong presence in her mind, stealing her ability to speak. She heard Dehga faintly, as if from a far distance, speaking aloud to her.

"This is fear speaking, Diahyas. You do not truly believe me to be such a monster, do you?"

Well done, girl. Dehga's voice said within her mind, setting off all sorts of alarms and causing a pounding to begin deep within her skull. *Now say,* "Of course not, Dehga."

Never. Her mind was screaming against it, and yet, somehow, she heard those very words come from her mouth.

Good girl. Now say, "Please lead us to safety. I'm sorry."

No, no, no, no, no! She tried to revolt and managed to fight a few moments longer than before, but still the words escaped her.

That's when she became aware of some shift in the atmosphere. Something was happening outside of herself, but with this overwhelming presence in her mind, she couldn't make herself focus. How was Dehga in her mind? What strange power was this? He couldn't be here. He might discover...her eyelids fluttered closed, and she built wall after wall after wall, feeling the presence fading into the distance. Once it was a mere pinprick on the periphery of her mind, she opened her eyes to stare Dehga down and force him out.

But he was not looking at her any longer. His focus had shifted to the man who stepped in front of her. There was shock written on Dehga's features.

"YOU!" he shouted.

"So nice to know I've been missed," Eorian quipped. "Unfortunately, we're leaving now."

With one quick movement, he slammed his foot full force into Dehga's stomach and latched onto Diahyas's hand.

"Hurry, Fil!" he yelled over his shoulder as he began swimming toward the upper story. His cousin followed the order with Luik on his heels.

Diahyas looked desperately toward her parents. "Me tiara!"

Her father understood and made a quick decision. "Safe. 51615."

She gave him a grateful smile and took the lead. Rushing to her parents' jewels room, sliding away the secret panel, and punching in the code, she finally had her precious treasure back in her possession.

"We need to get away from Raef," Eorian said worriedly. "He's powerful, and we just made him really angry. I need air."

"It be fine," Diahyas said. "The oxys help regulate landling breathing so they cannot hyperventilate here."

"That's not..." Eorian shook his head. "Get the tiara to take us far from here. Take us to Randor."

Diahyas shook her head. "He rules there."

"He's not there now, and I need to be on land. Send us to Randor," Eorian said.

Instantly, she felt the presence in her mind again, and judging by the way Eorian clasped a hand to his temple, she was not the only one.

"Get us out, now!" he practically snarled.

Her eyes widened in surprise, but she grasped him and Fil tightly, seeing Luik grab Fil's shoulder as well. She pictured her pretty river on Land, such a peaceful place, and certainly better than this *Randor*. As the wonderful feeling of travel grew stronger, Dehga's presence grew weaker, and by the time they all landed, he was gone from her mind completely.

That had been too close. What was Raef doing here on Faencina? How had he known where to find him?

Eorian snagged the oxy from his nose and the vibrord from his neck, shaking his head to remove the moisture from his hair and running a hand across his eyes. He was soaked. Fil was frowning at his damp clothing, looking every bit like a bedraggled puppy. Luik was still half fish and looked all around at the trees above without actually seeing anything. Eorian could relate to that feeling; he would never get used to traveling this way.

Then his gaze fell to Diahyas, who was glaring down at him angrily, hands on hips, dry as a bone, not even remotely dazed from the trip, and gorgeous as ever. How was that even possible?

"You shall explain yourself this very instant!" she yelled.

Eorian closed his eyes briefly with a sigh before again looking up at her. "I didn't realize he was here, I swear."

Her brow furrowed, and she tossed some hair behind her back impatiently. "What be you speaking of? I refer to the harsh tone used just moments ago. How dare you think to order the Shoring Water Maiden to do anything!"

Momentarily taken aback, Eorian merely stared at her, and then he laughed. The princess just grew more miffed as the moments passed, and Eorian pushed to his feet as his laughter subsided.

He shook his head. "You can be one of the most hard-headed individuals imaginable, you know that? We are in a serious crisis, and you think you should scold me for my tone?"

Diahyas' eyes grew stormy. "You should not..."

"Yes, I should," Eorian interrupted. His gaze hardened instantly. "You do not know that man or the things of which he is capable. I do. It was paramount that we get far from him, and since you were determined to argue with me, my *tone* was necessary. Randor is the safest place for us, so while I do not apologize for ordering you around, I do thank you for doing as I asked."

"I did not."

The words were quiet, and it took a moment for them to register.

"I'm sorry?" Eorian said.

"We be not on this..." Diahyas waved a hand in the air, "...Ran-dor of yours."

Eorian took several deep breaths. "Are you telling me that we are still on Faencina?"

Diahyas nodded. "We be near the river on Land."

He wanted to shout, break something, shake her...she was so frustrating with her haughtily tilted chin, flashing eyes, and defiant stance. However, yelling at her would get them nowhere—it would make him feel so much better though...until he began regretting it a day later. Space. That's what he needed right now.

Without another word, Eorian began walking. There was no destination in mind, he simply needed to get away.

"Where...where be you going?" Diahyas yelled after him.

"I'll be back," he replied shortly as he continued walking.

Moments later he heard heavy footsteps running after him.

"Finally get your bearings, Fil?" he asked without turning around.

"Set you off again, didn't she?"

"As you have also decided to do, apparently."

"Silence it is then." Fil winked. "For my part, I'm content to be melancholy for a bit. Got my hopes up about being back in Randor...if only ten months could be so short."

Hands on hips, Diahyas watched Eorian stalk off. Why must he always test her?

"I'll just make sure he doesn't get himself into trouble, shall I?" Fil said with a grin before running after him.

Diahyas huffed, half inclined to follow as well...but no. He did not deserve her presence. She bit her lip. Why had he scolded her so? Not a soul had ever thought to treat her so poorly...excluding her mother, that is. She glared at the ground.

"We be better off without them," Luik said beside her. "Why should we wish to go to...wherever they be from? It be much better here."

Diahyas paid him no mind.

"Say, might you be willing to help me dry faster as well?" he asked hesitantly.

With a grimace, Diahyas twirled her finger his direction and instantly dried off his scales.

Luik chuckled in awe as he hesitantly stood. "That be fascinating. How be you able to do this?"

"That be none of your business," Diahyas snapped, and she turned her back on him to walk in the opposite direction of Wisp.

"Wh-where be you going?" Luik asked as he stumbled after her.

"I wish to walk and explore. If you be intent on following, do not speak, and do not expect me to wait for you."

"But..." Luik began.

Diahyas whipped around and narrowed her gaze. "Be you arguing with me?"

Luik opened his mouth, but the fierce look on her face had him closing it again without a sound. He shook his head.

With that, Diahyas spun on her heel and continued moving forward. It was so beautiful in these woods. Her eyes fell on the strong trees around her. She did not know their true names, but she had christened them herself years ago. Those strong, thick trees with such long, outreaching branches were guardia because they were the oldest and most protective of all the trees. They also provided many homes for the forest creatures. Next were the needra. Tall and straight, and occasionally sticky, their dangerous leaves would occasionally poke her bare feet as she passed. She had quickly learned to skirt around those. Then there were the small, gentle purerine. They were perhaps shoulder height with puffy, soft tops of various earthy tones. Their trunks were smooth and soft as well.

Diahyas found herself smiling as she looked all around her. This truly was a grand place. Wisp would realize this and apologize when he returned to her side.

"I told you we'd figure it out."

Diahyas paused as she heard the voice coming from just ahead. She quickly motioned for Luik to stop and crept forward until she was crouched behind a bush right at the edge of a clearing. Her eyes widened in surprise. She knew the owner of that voice...well, she had certainly seen her before anyway. What was interesting, however, was the shimmering orb behind her.

"We didn't figure anything out," her companion argued as stepped from the swirling opening. "Asben did."

Diahyas caught her breath as she saw him. It was the strange human man from her dreams. Both of them, here?

The female waved her hand absently at her companion's argument. "Details. We're here, aren't we? And, look, it's..."

"Devoid of all life?" the male interjected dryly as he looked around him. "Deserted? Vacant? Dead?"

"No," the female chuckled and rolled her eyes. "There's life all around us. Just look at the trees and grass and..." she spread her hands before her as if welcoming a friend into her arms, "...flowers."

Diahyas barely concealed a gasp as she saw beautiful flowers of all types and colors spread out before the human female. How had she done such a thing?

"Show off." The male shook his head, but his mouth and eyes smiled.

Diahyas could almost feel his love and adoration for the female. Why couldn't Wisp look at her like that?

She was pulled from her thoughts by Luik, who had crawled up beside her and was staring at the couple before them.

"Let us go to meet them!" Diahyas said to Luik, never taking her eyes from the strangers.

Luik frowned. Those creatures were human like all the others that were causing so much trouble...and that female one had some weird control over flowers.

"I do not think we should," he cautioned.

"You be questioning me?"

That testy look was in her eyes again. Luik shook his head. "I shall stay here just in case."

She nodded and rose, stepping forward into the clearing with a bright smile.

At her presence, both of her dream humans whirled to face her, and the male instantly pulled the female behind him in a protective gesture. Diahyas liked that, but when he pulled his knife out and pointed it at her, looking ready in a moment to pounce, she stepped back in surprise. She didn't like that.

"Sheesh, Frelati, there's no need to threaten her," the female said with rolling eyes. "She's alone and has no weapons."

The male, Frelati apparently, straightened a bit and relaxed minutely at her words, but immediately went on the defensive again when Luik stumbled from the bushes behind Diahyas.

"Harm her and you die, human," he threatened.

Diahyas sighed. What did Luik think he could possibly do? He could hardly walk.

However, her dream humans did not know this, and apparently, the female was alarmed. Before Diahyas had a chance to say a word, they were both wrapped in deep green vines and lifted high off the ground. Diahyas screamed in fear at the sudden, unexpected elevation.

"Let me down this instant!" she shouted at them as she strained against the thick vegetation restraining her. "I be Shoring Water Maiden, and this treatment be treason. I be having you thrown in prison, flogged, starved..."

"Stop with the threats," Frelati interrupted, thoroughly unmoved by her outburst. "I've been there and experienced that from a man much worse than you so don't waste your breath."

That did stop her. She stared down at him in shock.

"Who are you anyway?" the female asked in suspicion. "You were in our room just a few hours ago as a hazy apparition, which is precisely why we came. Why were you there?"

"I be no apparition!" Diahyas argued in affront. "You be dream beings intent upon bursting into me reality. Return to me imagination, strange humans."

"Dream beings?" Frelati repeated. "You think you were dreaming when you visited us?"

"Of course I be dreaming. Now let me down!"

"Genevia, I think…"

"Diahyas!"

Her head spun to where Wisp burst through the trees just a short ways to her left, Fil just behind him. "Diahyas, where…?"

His head tilted in confusion as he stared up at her vine covered form. "How…?"

"Eorian?!" Genevia exclaimed excitedly.

Eorian chuckled and shook his head with a huge grin. "I should have known it was you."

Genevia rushed over to give him a hug. "I am soooo sorry we left the way we did. I didn't know what I was doing, and Frelati was hurt so badly."

She pulled back in alarm.

"Everyone's okay, aren't they?" she turned to Fil with a sigh. "Well, you are, Fil, and if the two of you are here, then Lishea must be…"

"We don't know," Eorian said shortly.

Diahyas was growing more and more furious the longer she was left out of the conversation. "I wish to be released immediately!" she shouted. "And I order everyone to explain the meaning of things!"

Eorian's brows drew together as he looked up at her. "Perhaps if you asked nicely, my friends would do what you wanted. Would you like to try, princess?"

"Let me down!" Diahyas said angrily as she struggled once more.

Genevia bit her lip and started to do just that, but Eorian stopped her with a shake of his head.

"That is not nicely. Try again," he said calmly to Diahyas.

"Wisp, you be testing me patience. If you do not follow me orders like a good servant, I shall shock you. Now, release me."

"Servant?" Genevia asked him in confusion.

"Say please."

Diahyas poised her fingers over her band. "I shall shock you."

"Do that, and I promise you won't get down anytime soon."

Diahyas paused before crossing her arms and glaring down at him. Neither spoke for a few minutes.

Finally, Frelati sighed and walked forward. "Not that this stand-off isn't entertaining, but there are far too many unanswered questions at the moment for it to continue. Genevia, go ahead and let the two of them down, and we will all find a nice place to sit and figure all of this out. Sound like a plan?"

Eorian crossed his arms. "If you give into her now, she'll never learn."

"It doesn't look to me like she's learning now," Frelati pointed out.

"I still be up in this infernal vegetation and wish to be rid of it!" Diahyas yelled down.

Genevia looked between Frelati and Eorian. "Shall I?"

With a sigh, Eorian signaled with a hand for her to go ahead. A few seconds later, Diahyas was bearing down on him. Her eyes were blazing.

"How dare you be thinking to defy me orders?!" she scolded. "I be the Shoring Water Maiden, I be the commander of armies, and I be the essence of water gifted by Kiem!"

Eorian straightened. "I don't live on this planet, you are *not* my ruler, and have you already forgotten? Your armies have betrayed you. You are in the middle of a massive rebellion and would still be trapped and helpless if not for Fil and me. Lastly, you aren't the only essence on this planet, little princess, so I would be careful whom I ordered around if I were you."

How dare he! How dare he speak to her so roughly! Diahyas opened her mouth, ready to shout and scream, but she saw him sweep his hand, and her mouth and throat filled with air so as to take away her ability to speak.

Her eyes widened. What had he just done? This was…her mind raced back to his last sentence. Was he implying that he had Kiem's essence as well? This human she had kept prisoner, that she had shocked repeatedly, that she had renamed and ordered around and re-clothed, he was just as powerful as she was…just not when surrounded by water. The tables were turned. He was in control here on Land, and she had made him very angry.

"Nod if you're done scolding me, and I'll stop blocking your windpipes."

She gave a quick nod and instantly the pressure of the air went away.

She bit her lip. "Wisp…?"

He grimaced. "It's Eorian. There will be no more of this Wisp nonsense. Are we clear?"

She nodded. Eorian studied her curiously a moment, clearly surprised that she had acquiesced.

"By the way," Genevia jumped in, offering her hand to Diahyas, "I'm Genevia, and this is my husband, Frelati. Sorry for attacking you."

Diahyas eyed the outstretched hand for a moment before slowly taking it. "Diahyas. How be it that you know me human?"

Genevia's eyebrows rose. "I'm sorry?"

"Let's just find a place to settle in for a moment, somewhere a bit less…open," Eorian said as he looked around before meeting Frelati's gaze. "Raef is here."

"Raef as in…"

"Fezam is *here*?" Genevia exclaimed worriedly. "What is he doing here? We were trying to arrive before he did."

Eorian nodded. "Raef, Fezam, Dehga, as he's known here, regardless of what name you wish to use, he's still just as dangerous and causing a lot of trouble."

"Dehga has multiple names?" Diahyas asked at the same time Genevia said, "What kind of trouble?"

"Questions later," Frelati said with a nod to Eorian. "You're right. Let's find cover, then we'll go over the basics and come up with a plan."

CHAPTER 12

This was infuriating. Those two elves were monopolizing her two humans and paying little mind to the confusion of the two mermaids—most importantly, her—who had questions of their own that needed answering. Instead, the four buddies were chatting away about boats, some girl named Lishea, whispers of some sort, and other inconsequential nonsense that had no bearing on the present moment.

The only reason she was being this patient was because she quite enjoyed their surroundings. They had found a rather large tree with great outstretched limbs that held leafy vines draping to the ground. It provided a decent shelter while still allowing in some sunshine. Diahyas had been mesmerized by the ever-shifting shadows dappling the ground, and the sound of happy little birds and the river some short ways off had calmed her most efficiently. Now she was beginning to awaken from her daydream.

"I be wanting answers now," she demanded while crossing her arms, completely cutting Eorian off mid-sentence.

His brow furrowed slightly before he pasted on an insincere smile. "So sorry, princess. How inconsiderate of us. I'm sure your questions are just as important as discovering the fate of people's lives and trying to stop a war."

Diahyas's eyes narrowed. "You be showing me little respect. I be the essence of water *and* the Shoring Water Maiden! Do not think that any of you be me equal just because you have an essence of your own."

"So you don't want our help then?" Eorian asked with a mocking smile.

"I be needing no help," Diahyas answered stubbornly. "Faencina's royal armies be plenty strong enough to overcome a few rebels."

"You don't understand who you're dealing with," Genevia argued, her eyes full of worry for the Shoring. "Fezam is ruthless, and he now has an army here, an army from Randor, and an army from his own planet. He can get inside your mind, Diahyas. You *do* need us, and…well, we need you. Eorian has a war to fight on Randor, and my planet, Tiweln, won't be safe for long if Fezam takes both Randor and Faencina."

"Why be me people responsible for fighting in the wars of other planets?" Diahyas asked. "We have been separate for centuries."

"You aren't separate any longer," Frelati pointed out. "The parasite of the universe has already stirred up trouble right here on your planet."

Diahyas stood. "Me people shall not fight and possibly die for strangers."

Angrily, Eorian stood as well. "Then I think we're done here. Genevia, Frelati, I assume you now have a good grasp on how to do this inter-world travel. Care to give my diamond dust a whirl so Fil and I can go home?"

"No!" Diahyas exclaimed in alarm. Leave? He was going to leave her? "You cannot."

"If you aren't going to help me, I most certainly can leave," Eorian argued.

Diahyas thought furiously as Eorian turned back toward Genevia and Frelati, asking them once again how to open the portal. What could she do to keep him here? He clearly had no respect for her title or for her power…but if she could get him near water, she would have a distinct advantage. The river! It was just a short walk away, but how to get him close enough…

She saw Eorian pop his hands on his hips with a triumphant grin. "You ready to go home, Fil?"

Fil jumped to his feet. "You don't have to ask me twice."

"Genevia," Eorian offered a hand to pull her to her feet, and that's when Diahyas noticed his band.

She very quickly entered the command on her own band to decrease the distance that was allowed between them and pushed through the excited crowd to move closer to the water.

"Where are you going?" Genevia asked.

"Wait for me!" Luik called as he scrambled to his feet. Diahyas had completely forgotten about him.

She heard Eorian sigh. "Just let the little princess go."

Then he called out to her a bit sarcastically, "It was nice meeting you," before his voice changed to one of surprise, "what..." and finally to angry realization as he was pulled forward, "You little..."

"What's happening?" Frelati asked.

Eorian was tugging at the band ineffectually and muttering all sorts of things under his breath as he was pulled forward. Fil took it upon himself to answer as he followed the trio moving toward the river. Frelati and Genevia fell into step with him.

"Do you see that bracelet E's got on his wrist?" He waited for Genevia's nod. "Well, there is a matching one that Diahyas has on, and it functions as a training tool, in her words. She can communicate through it, set a perimeter past which Eorian physically cannot go, and she can also punish him."

"I'm sorry, *punish* him?" Frelati repeated.

"That sounds a little...odd," Genevia said as diplomatically as she could.

"Diahyas, get this thing off of me right this instant," Eorian ordered. She didn't even turn her head.

Fil nodded. "Yeah, so if E does anything she doesn't like..."

At that moment, Eorian realized that pulling against the band was utterly useless, and instead he charged toward Diahyas, throwing her to the ground and trying to pin down the arm with the band on it.

"Get off of me!" she yelled as she twisted her wrist from his grasp.

Fil chuckled. "Like that, for instance, then she can..."

Diahyas pushed a button on her band, causing Eorian to jerk back with a shout.

"Shock him," Fil finished as he pointed toward the scene.

Eorian growled in aggravation as he started grabbing for her wrist again. Diahyas was doing fairly well slipping out of his grasp every time he got a hold on her, but she was fairly certain she wouldn't be able to keep it up for much longer. Eorian was getting more and more frustrated with each passing second.

"A little help here, Fil?" he growled.

"No, no," Fil held up his hands as if in surrender. "I believe this is your fight."

"Why do you always have to be so very difficult?" Eorian mumbled as he yet again captured and lost her wrist, making him lose his balance.

Diahyas took that chance to roll out from under him, push to her feet, and begin running toward the water.

Eorian sucked in a deep breath as he quickly pursued, only to come to a screeching halt at the sight of her standing right by the river.

"Don't," he commanded.

"Be you leaving?" she asked as she took a step closer to the water.

Eorian's eyes narrowed. "Are you going to help us?"

Diahyas shook her head and lifted her chin imperiously.

"Then I'm leaving."

"No, you be coming with me."

Frelati spoke up. "You can't just take him. He's not your prisoner, and he needs to get back Randor."

Diahyas glared at Frelati. "He be not leaving me."

"How do you not understand?" Genevia said. "This is bigger than you and your wishes. We can't succeed without him, and we can't succeed without you. It says so in the prophecy. 'World to world they must defend/ earth, sea, fire, light, and wind.'"

Diahyas pushed her hair back with a quick, angry motion. "I be not caring for your poetry. He be me human, and you cannot take him."

"*Your* human?" Frelati questioned with a smirk at the same time as Eorian said, "I'm no one's human. We have been over this."

At that point, Genevia lost her cool. "I have tried to be nice about all this, but you really need to deflate your ego. You don't own any of us, and you aren't better than any of us. So you can throw around a little water; why does that give you any right to control Eorian, who, by the way, was actually willing to help you and your planet out of the goodness of his heart when he has a colossal mess waiting for him back home. So take that shock-y band thing off of him and try to come back down to reality."

Diahyas opened her mouth in shock. "Insolence!"

Genevia sent her a challenging smirk. "Yes, and what are you going to do about it?"

"Genevia," Frelati said softly. "Cool it."

"I will not cool it," she declared. "She is being difficult."

"ME!" Diahyas drew herself up to her full height, anger radiating from every pore of her being. "Difficult? I be showing you difficult!"

With that, she started throwing water at Genevia. Her hands moved and shaped the liquid into small balls that she pelted at the elf mercilessly. However, her attack was soon halted when Genevia lifted a mound of dirt beneath Diahyas, creating a column towering high above them. Diahyas screamed and fell to her knees as the dirt continually raised higher.

"Let her down, Genevia," Frelati said.

"No, she got me wet," Genevia retorted angrily. "She deserves it. She's spoiled and arrogant and…and…"

Eorian stared up at Diahyas. "I have to say that I'm on Genevia's side. Leave her up there."

"Genevia," Frelati said firmly. "Let her down."

Genevia was breathing deeply, but her anger was beginning to subside. Slowly, she lowered the column.

"Wisp!" Diahyas called. "Get me down. She be going to kill me!"

Something snapped within Eorian at her words. He motioned for Genevia to stop moving the column, and he flew up to get eye to eye with his tormentor.

"What in the last few minutes makes you think that I would have any inclination to help you?" he asked.

Diahyas refused to meet his gaze.

Eorian shook his head with a mirthless chuckle. "See, you *know* that how you're acting is ridiculous, which is why I am having so much trouble understanding. I offer to help you, and you rebuff me, yet when I try to leave, you go to ridiculous lengths to keep me here. What exactly do you want? Do you even know?"

Diahyas sat quiet and motionless for a moment before nodding.

"Will you clue me in?" Eorian asked with a touch of impatience in his voice.

Diahyas peeked over the edge at the four people below, all staring intently upward and probably hearing every word. She didn't want them all to know her greatest fear. That was a powerful weapon for someone to have. She looked back toward Eorian.

"Get me down?" she asked softly.

He leaned in and spoke equally softly. "That's not why you're causing all these theatrics. What is the problem?"

Her fingers dug into the dirt, and she stared hard at her hands. "I don't..." She took a deep breath. "I don't want to be alone anymore."

Eorian nodded, not appearing in the least surprised, and he seemed to understand...a bit. "You aren't alone, Diahyas. You are surrounded by people in your palace. You have your parents, Sea-ena, Luik...probably some other people I'm unaware of."

Diahyas nodded her head with a shrug. He didn't understand, no one did. She was merely a convenience for her parents, summoned at their whim, and necessary to keep the kingdom running. Sea-ena was just doing her job, and Luik...well, she didn't know him. In fact, he scared her a little bit with his over-the-top declarations of love.

Eorian sighed. "All right, I get that it's not the same as having close friends, but look..."

He ran a hand through his hair with a sigh. "I was trying. *You* were the one that decided you didn't need my help."

Diahyas's eyes shot up to meet his. "You be going back to Randor after you helped me."

"That has always been the plan," Eorian said with a nod.

"You shall abandon me when you be with your people, and I be alone again. And *they*"—she glared back down at the group below that had turned their attention to things other than the distant conversation—"be with us, taking away your attention."

"I'm not a toy, Diahyas. I'm a real, live person capable of making my own decisions. That means you do not get a monopoly on my time and attention. You have to share. Just because I start talking to someone else or go somewhere away from you does not mean that I have abandoned you. Although, if you keep acting the way you have been, I definitely will walk away and never come back. Do you understand that?"

Diahyas wrinkled her nose in distaste. "I do not like this."

"Yeah, I've heard that most women don't, which is why I'm still single." Eorian gave her a cheeky grin. "I suppose you've been good enough to be let down, but I would like you to remove this band first."

Diahyas's eyes widened, and she shook her head. "I shall be unable to find you if you leave me, and...and if we get separated again, like in me summer home, we shall be unable to communicate."

Eorian shook his head. "No. There is no way I am letting you keep control over me with this. You have abused that power enough. While it might be nice for all of us to keep tabs on each other and communicate easily, I don't think I can trust you with it anymore."

"Then…" Diahyas paused momentarily before forging on, "then I shall switch the controls to your band."

Eorian blinked. "Really?"

In answer, Diahyas started pushing buttons on her band. After a few seconds, she gave Eorian a smile. "Done."

Eorian lifted his wrist to see the band more closely. "How do I…?"

Diahyas reached over to instruct him. "Swipe your finger along the side here and then hold your finger there until the lights come on. Then you simply press the controls you want. This one at the top allows you to set the distance. The second down allows for communication between the bands. This third one gives you directions to reach me band if we be separated. This bottom one be the main controls…this be where I transferred our bands, and there be a few other options."

Eorian nodded. "And this button one up from the bottom that you skipped over…based on the picture, I'm guessing that's the shock button?"

Diahyas sat back from him and nodded. "You tap once and then hold it down for two seconds for anything to show up, and then you can choose the intensity. It be the best way to avoid accidentally shocking someone. I suppose…I suppose you be wishing to get me back now, yes?"

Eorian grinned.

"Most definitely, but I'm too much of a gentleman to give in to my wishes." He winked. "Come on; let's get you down now."

She wrapped her arms tightly around his neck, and he scooped an arm beneath her knees before gliding back down to the ground.

"That took long enough," Fil grumbled. "And you still have the band, I see."

"We've come to an arrangement," Eorian said as he set Diahyas on her feet.

"Thank goodness!" Genevia said. "Diahyas, I am so sorry about what I did. I don't usually get so…"

"Emotional?" Frelati suggested.

Genevia gave a sheepish smile. "Yes. So I wanted to apologize, Diahyas."

Diahyas nodded once. "Although it be terrible insolence to treat me, someone of royal birth, in such a way, I concede that I *may* have slightly provoked a bit of your anger."

"Thank you?" Genevia said. "Although, since you mention royal birth, I feel the need to clarify something. You do realize that there is royalty on other planets as well?"

"Of course," Diahyas agreed immediately.

"And you would agree that those royals on other planets are your equals?"

For a moment, she pondered the question before nodding. "I suppose this be so."

"Then that makes me your equal. I am the princess of the elves on my planet." Genevia paused to let that sink in, watching Diahyas closely all the while. "Although, my station should not come into play at all. I agree that respect should be given, but that goes both ways. You are only deserving of the respect that you give to others, whether they be lowly or highborn."

Diahyas started in surprise. She was no longer quite so special. There was another royal essence.

"Oh."

"My cousin isn't beneath you either, since we're on the topic," Fil said.

"Fil," Eorian warned in a near growl.

Fil ignored him. "He's just as much your equal as Genevia is, and due to the way you've treated him of late, I think you should apologize. Imagine how you would react if you, a ruler on your world, came to our planet, were forced to live on land instead of in the water you're used to, had your name changed, and were being given shock therapy so that you would learn to be an obedient servant. I'm not sure your ego could withstand it."

Diahyas glared at him. "Shoring Water Maidens do not apologize. That admits fault, and we be faultless."

Eorian snorted. "Look, I'm not asking for an apology—it would be nice, but I don't see it coming. All I want is your final decision: are you with us, or are you going it alone?"

"I be with you...Eorian," she said softly.

He grinned. "That makes this a whole lot easier. Now, let's come up with a plan to save both our planets."

It was a shame how very terribly soldiers followed orders. It was not necessarily that they ignored them or even that they executed the mission poorly, but rather their timeliness left much to be desired. The first few near-misses could easily be chalked up to sheer luck, but after the fourth failed attempt of the revolutionaries to capture the royals, Dehga was beginning to lose faith that it would ever happen.

He was giving these merfolk point by point directions as to where their targets were headed—first to the barn, which they left just before the soldiers arrived, then as they left the gate that closed far too slowly, next as they left the city where half of a barricade hadn't a chance of holding them up, and this last time at an outcropping of large boulders perfect for an ambush…that never came. Unfortunately, Dehga just did not know these waters well enough to stage a believable capture and allow time for everyone to get together to carry it out. He *had* to stop them from reaching Geola, and now he could not return to the summer home since Eorian was here. They must be secreted away elsewhere, some place Diahyas would never think to look, a location that was remote and held few friends for the Prime and Prime-Mate.

In an instant, his mind stilled as the perfect hideaway came to mind.

"I have been thinking," he said aloud into the heavy, fear-filled silence.

Two pairs of eyes connected with his.

"You say that reaching the capital is the only way to stop this coup, but have you considered the possibility that Geola is already overrun with these traitors? You could very easily be riding into a trap, and what are you to do from a prison cell to put down this revolution? Your people need you to be free and able to direct your armies if they are to overcome this threat. I feel that our current destination could be a mistake. Perhaps you could stop elsewhere, somewhere they would not imagine you to go, and send out inquiries as to the state of Geola before you completed your journey there. Just as a precaution."

The Prime was nodding her head in agreement, but the Prime-Mate appeared to be less convinced by the argument.

"Geola be quite a large city, and surely not all there be on the side of the revolutionaries. We be certain to find friends there." He studied Dehga closely. "Where would you have us go if not to Geola? It be far more likely that the smaller towns house many who be now against us."

Dehga took in a deep breath to calm his frustration. Perhaps he would also orchestrate a fatal accident for the Prime-Mate as part of the capture.

"You do bring up a valid point, Leeyan. I agree that the small towns could be dangerous for you. Let me think." He brought a hand up to his chin. "We are presently going around the Olis Chasm, yes?"

"That be correct," the Prime-Mate said.

"Then if we are to avoid the smaller towns, that really only leaves one option open, doesn't it?"

Leeyan shook his head. "I be afraid I do not follow."

"Land," Dehga said matter-of-factly, taking in the royals' startled faces.

"The land folks merely tolerate our presence because they be far lesser in number than we, but if only the two of us go on Land and try to hide among them, they would instantly use that advantage and either kill us themselves or find some of this rogue group chasing us and deliver us to them," Leeyan argued.

"I am quite certain there are ways that you could convince them to help you. Greater access to the capital, money, provide them with some of your scientific cunning to make their way of life a bit less primitive, perhaps? I could be the ambassador between you. They will easily see that I am not a mermaid but a land creature as they are, so they should be content to negotiate with me." Dehga saw the stubborn glint still in Leeyan's eye and decided to change tactics. "As you said, Leeyan, the Land folk are known for their hostility toward the mermaids, so why would anyone think to look for you on Land? You will not be there long anyway, assuming you are correct in thinking that the capital still holds many of your friends. And although you believe the Land folk capable of delivering you over to your enemies, do you truly think they would *help* mermaids by either giving you over to them or killing you themselves as opposed to merely tolerating your presence and ignoring you?"

"I believe his argument to be sound, Leeyan," the Prime said. "We should do as he suggests."

There was still doubt in the Prime-Mate's eyes. "You truly think this,

Bailena?"

Dehga grit his teeth. The Prime-Mate was using that uncanny power of his to lessen Bailena's conviction.

"He does not know the Land folk as we do," Leeyan continued.

It was time for him to take matters into his own hands, Dehga decided. Very carefully, he probed the Prime's mind, whispering a few words to keep her firmly on his side. *Caution be good, but when time be against us, action be necessary.* He truly despised the way these people spoke, but when convincing one of her own thoughts, it had to sound like her.

"We must act now, Leeyan; there be not enough time for discussion, and Dehga has made a sound argument." She rapped on the carriage three times, and a small window connecting to the driver's section opened. "Change course to Land."

"Land?" the driver repeated in surprise.

A single nod from Bailena, and the window closed. Dehga barely suppressed a grin as the carriage turned northward.

"If you will permit me, I would like to close my eyes for a bit," he said humbly.

Bailena waved a hand. "Whatever you wish."

Dehga settled down more firmly in his seat and then began the process of contacting Boran to stage this fifth and final capture.

CHAPTER 13

In general, the Yuens were a peaceful people. They didn't squabble among themselves, and they didn't pick fights with the mermaids who treated them so poorly. They were a small group of like-minded—if not similar looking—creatures. It was a bit amazing that this was the case, given their origins.

Every time Gorn thought of it, he grew angry. In fact, most of the leaders of the small communities of Yuens held a deep-seated hatred over their history, though the populace seemed to have grown used to the idea—assuming they knew the full truth, which Gorn suspected they did not.

The Yuens were a hodge-podge of things. No two Yuens, even in the same family, looked alike…except on those very rare occasions. Some looked more feline, some looked reptilian, some canine, some of indeterminate species. There were those with spikes, tails, claws, fur, and there were several that looked slightly more mer in appearance. All were primarily humanoid, however. They were all capable of speech and forethought; they just looked a little different.

The Yuens had been around for perhaps 150 years or so. It was around that time that the more forward-thinking, scientific mers discovered the high probability of their species going extinct due to complications of reproduction. In an effort to plan ahead, two older scientists, Himlin and Folku, put together a team of highly inventive, brilliant young minds and gave them only one guideline with their experimentations: discover a way to alter mer genes that would enable them to more easily go on land. Himlin and Folku called this experimental group Youths Undertaking

Evolutionary New Science, YUENS for short.

There was a lot of gene-splicing, test-tubing, animal-altering, and generally unacceptable practices that went on in those laboratories, and it continued for twenty years before anyone caught on. There was a huge outcry once the experimentation was accidentally spilled to the public, and the royals shut the project down. However, they faced the ethical issue of what to do with the intelligent, living beings that had been created.

After months of discussions, during which time the poor Yuens were held in terrible prison conditions, it was decided that since the creatures were primarily land-based, they would be exiled to Land. So the Yuens were abandoned on Land with no provisions, no explanations, and no instruction as to how to care for themselves. The mers did not believe them capable of reproducing or surviving for long, so these unfortunate, scientific mistakes would be wiped out after another twenty or so years, by their most conservative estimation.

They were wrong.

The fifty Yuens that had been created found a way to survive, and they did have children, and those children had children. After sixty years, the mers finally realized that this culture was there to stay, so they began to finally make some allowances for them: travel to the underwater capital, mechanisms to help them breath and speak while there, and their leaders were recognized for negotiation purposes. It was far from what they deserved, but it was a great deal more than the mers had wanted.

To the mers, the Yuens were mistakes that just wouldn't go away; they were hideous monstrosities that spoiled the beauty of Faencina.

To the Yuens, the mers were cruel and heartless, having little value for life and striving to keep those on Land under their thumb.

Gorn often wished there was a way to leave Faencina, start somewhere new with peoples that would accept them. He realized it was most likely a fantasy, but his people deserved so much more. They were beautiful, brilliant, and so full of compassion and acceptance...all of which would soon be lost if the mers persisted in their persecution.

"Lord Gorn," a messenger with bright green, vertically slit eyes said as he stepped through the doorway of the log structure that served as the community council house. "There be a visitor asking to see you."

Gorn's brow creased. "A visitor? You mean from one of the other tribes?"

"No, sir." Villis, one of the more reptilian of the Yuens, stepped fully inside and shut the door, lowering his voice slightly as he glanced behind him. "I do not recognize where he be from, but…he says he be advocating for the mer royals."

"Advocating for the royals?" Gorn repeated in confusion. "What could they possibly need advocating for? They demand; they do not negotiate."

Villis shrugged. "I cannot say what the man means, but there be something about him. He be not a mer, but he be not one of us either."

Gorn's small cat nose twitched a bit, and his pointy ears flattened slightly before the brilliant orange eyes fixed back upon Villis. "Do you trust this man?"

Villis's tongue flicked out quickly, and he shook his head. "I taste deceit around him, but I do not feel that it be directed toward us."

Gorn stood gracefully. He was fully covered in tawny fur, but there was a black patch of hair that traced around the right side of his face. He wore a flowing white shirt with long sleeves and tan britches to his knees. As the mers did, the Yuens went barefoot unless they were traveling in untamed places. His fingers and toes had sharp claws and were covered in the same tawny fur, but they were formed like those of the mers when they walked on land.

"Let us go meet this stranger, Villis. Signal two guards to keep watch out of sight."

Villis nodded, and they both left the council house. The stranger was a short ways from shore and was just as Villis had described him. He surveyed Gorn as they approached, and Gorn studied him just as intently for several moments before saying a word.

"Greetings, stranger," he said without a smile as he offered a hand. "Where be you from?"

"Randor," he replied simply as they shook, not bothering to elaborate on his answer even after Gorn silently requested further information.

Gorn took a step back from him and crossed his arms. "You be here for a reason. State it or leave."

"Are you aware of the revolution raging beneath the water?"

Gorn looked toward Villis, who shook his head in bewilderment, tasted the air, and gave a shrug to say it flavored as truth.

"News of this has not reached us yet."

The stranger waved a hand. "Not surprising; it has just begun. However, the goal of the revolutionaries is to capture the Prime and Prime-Mate."

Gorn's lips curled in distaste. "Let them take the royals."

The stranger shared a malicious grin. "I intend to. However, I need your help."

"We do not fight the wars of the mers."

"I am not asking you to. What I ask is a place for the royals to stay here on land that could be easily compromised by the revolutionaries."

"I do not understand."

"Just below the water are the Prime and Prime-Mate. They are waiting while I negotiate with you for temporary protection from the revolutionaries so that they can send out a missive to the capital inquiring about its safety."

"As I stated before, we do not fight the mers' wars."

"And as I said, I am not asking you to. I am merely requesting that you provide them a place to stay that is a bit away from your village and make a show of protecting them. Tonight, I will have the revolutionaries sneak in and take them captive. None of your people will be harmed, and the Prime and Prime-Mate will not think that you betrayed them. They will believe that you were overpowered by the forces of the revolutionaries. Meanwhile, the revolutionaries will see you as allies, so you will be handsomely rewarded once they are victorious. It is truly a win-win situation for you."

"You do not appear to be a trustworthy man. It seems unwise to do as you say."

The stranger gave a vicious smile. "It is a shame how often casualties of war are mere bystanders, don't you think? The protection given by the revolutionaries could assure your continued existence throughout the remainder of this war."

"I be beginning to believe that the revolutionaries be the greater of two evils."

"Not toward allies," the stranger paused before slowly extending a hand. "Are we in agreement?"

Gorn studied him for several seconds. "I did not get your name. It seems poor taste to come to terms with a nameless man."

"Dehga." The hand extended just a bit more forward.

"It seems you leave me little choice, Dehga." Gorn clasped his hand, feeling his gut twist just a bit as if it also knew he was making a mistake. "I be Gorn. Bring the royals. I have just the place for them."

Eorian and Frelati looked back over the rough map of Faencina that they had created in the dirt with the help of Diahyas. Diahyas had relished relaying her knowledge of her magnificent world, but now she had another task to accomplish. While Eorian and Frelati poured over weaknesses, strengths, strategic points, potential traps, and the best way to gather allies to win this war and the one on Randor, Genevia and Fil were in a quiet location with one task: getting Diahyas to take a nap.

Eorian had initially thought that sending Fil with the girls would be a terrible idea, but since Diahyas was being hunted by the revolutionaries and Dehga could easily put both her and Genevia into a deep sleep, it seemed wise to have a third person to watch over the girls and send back reports if necessary. There was a purpose behind the nap beyond just getting a little peace and quiet from the haughtiness of the princess. After they had all sat down and discussed her strange dream and the vague apparition of her that had simultaneously appeared before Genevia and Frelati on Tiweln, they had discovered that she had a way of projecting herself using her portal without physically traveling and using up all its juice. They were still unsure of the details, but she had done it several times in the past apparently.

They discovered this when Genevia had mentioned a talk with a sailor friend of hers that said he had seen Diahyas as a child playing out in the middle of the sea. He had thought she was a Sea Goddess. Diahyas had remembered the old man. Then Diahyas mentioned speaking with a rather sarcastic bird that kept crying out very loudly, and that's when Eorian realized that they had a way of contacting his sister and his crew. He could run both wars from here, keeping the portals as a last resort.

The final piece of their plan for the moment involved Luik. They had sent him back into the water, which really was for the best since he was so terrible at walking. His task was to collect information and to retrieve more bands so that everyone could communicate. He was to find out where the natural portal was located and to find potential allies that would help them in their fight both here and on Randor. At the moment, they still weren't certain how much trouble the revolutionary threat posed. That was another key piece of information.

One thing that Diahyas had been strictly opposed to was trying to convince the Yuens to fight on their side. She felt this was completely useless and that their time should not be wasted. However, Eorian saw the potential for an influx of fighters and believed it was worth a shot to speak with their leaders. Just as soon as Diahyas was asleep, he and Frelati were going to walk to the nearest Yuen village and request a meeting.

"The bulk of the fighting here will be in the water, if Luik's skill on land is any indication," Frelati said. "Diahyas will be able to aid them, but I'm not positive if any of the rest of us will be any good. I am hoping that most of the royal army she keeps talking about is still on their side. If not, I have a feeling this world may be lost to us. At that point, we will need to get all of our allies to Randor, where we should have a good chance of beating Fezam...assuming you haven't lost any of your allies in your absence."

Eorian shook his head. "No, we have to succeed here as well. If not, then Raef will have at least half of the mermaids on his side that he can bring to Randor. We'll have the same fight between mermaids there as we did here, and we will be just as evenly matched on land as we were before."

"That's assuming Fezam can convince the mermaids to fight a war on another world. Diahyas certainly didn't seem enthused about it, and it sounds like they want to preserve their isolation."

Eorian looked Frelati in the eyes. "Raef managed to convince an entire army of creatures from another planet to revolt against their long-time rulers. He will find a way to do the same to get them to Randor."

Frelati nodded. "That does seem likely, unfortunately. All right, then let's postpone our what-ifs until we get the numbers. Do you think we're free to leave yet?"

Eorian shook his head and stood. "I'm quite tired of catering to the princess, and we've waiting a good thirty minutes already for her to fall asleep. I say we go and deal with any consequences later."

"It be extremely difficult to fall asleep when there be two creatures staring at you and it be so very bright. Could this not wait until closer to night?"

Genevia gave Diahyas a strained smile. "Look at this from Eorian's perspective. He left a lot behind when he arrived here so unexpectedly, and he's quite worried. Besides, this will help your planet as well. This will better help us to strategize."

"Be his people coming here?" Diahyas asked as she sat up to better question Genevia.

Genevia settled a light hand on her shoulder and gently pressed her back downward. "That is a bit unlikely as his people are already engaged in battle on Randor."

As Diahyas again began to sit up to argue with her, Genevia pressed a bit more firmly on her shoulder and continued. "That being said, I am quite certain that they would be little help to you. Your battle is underwater, and although you do have several apparatuses to help land folks survive underwater, you do not have nearly enough to equip an army. Also, I imagine that our people would be just as terrible in water as Luik is on land. Do you disagree?"

"I suppose I cannot," Diahyas replied grumpily.

Genevia gave a harried look toward Fil, who was leaning against a tree a few feet away.

"Fil, can you think of any way to help her fall asleep?" she asked.

He winked and rubbed a fist. "I can think of one, but I don't think either of you will like it."

"Fil." Genevia rolled her eyes. "You can't pull off fierce and threatening; stick with your classic sarcasm and jokes. How about a song, Diahyas? If you close your eyes and focus only on the music, perhaps that will lull you to sleep."

Diahyas gave a great, heaving sigh in response and closed her eyes.

Genevia smiled at Fil in triumph.

One of Diahyas's eyes popped open. "This shall not work, you realize?"

Genevia frowned. "Only if you go into it with that negative attitude. Close your eyes."

She waited until Diahyas acquiesced.

"Now, Fil taught me this one while Frelati and I were on Randor. It is quite lovely and soothing." She motioned for Fil to move closer. "Fil will sing with me. He has a charming voice. Just clear your mind of everything but the song."

"I'd rather not sing, if it's all the same…"

Genevia cut Fil off with a fierce look.

"Sure, yeah, right-o. And which song exactly are you wanting to sing?"

"*Autumn.*"

"That one, really?" Fil complained.

"Well, we can't do any of the upbeat ones you taught me. She's trying to fall asleep."

"Which be less and less likely as the two of you continue bickering."

Fil brightened. "*Luna.* It's perfect, you've got to admit."

"Oh, yeah! I forgot about that one…and I may not remember all the words." Genevia bit her lip.

"I'll start, and you pitch in when you remember something."

Fil plopped down beside Genevia and began the soft ballad.

> *As the sun fades on the horizon*
> *And the darkness starts to fall*
> *The earth grows still at twilight.*
> *And the moon shines over all.*
>
> *Luna, oh, luna*
> *Light the sky each night*
> *Luna, oh, luna*
> *I am awed at the beautiful sight.*

Genevia nodded to Fil that she remember the second verse, and he bowed out for her to take the lead.

> *There is calmness and peace,*
> *There is hope and rest and dreams,*
> *There's a tranquil feel at midnight,*
> *As the world sleeps in your beams.*

Together Fil and Genevia harmonized the chorus.

> *Luna, oh, luna*
> *Light the sky each night*
> *Luna, oh, luna*
> *I am awed at the beautiful sight.*
>
> *Alkina, Artemis, Celina, Cyra*
> *Diana, Iantha, Kynthia, Miah*
> *So many names for the beautiful moon,*
> *Though none quite as fitting as Luna.*
>
> *Luna, oh, luna*
> *Light the sky each night*
> *Luna, oh, luna*
> *I am awed at the beautiful sight.*

When the song had begun, Diahyas had thought that Luna was a beautiful name for the moon. She had never heard it called that before. Her mind began to picture the lovely celestial being before realizing that doing so could redirect her to an unintended location.

Genevia had been correct in saying that Fil had a charming voice. It surprised Diahyas. From what she could gather, he was in love with Eorian's sister, the girl Diahyas was to go see. That was what she should focus on, not the moon. Luna…a lovely name…perhaps that was Eorian's sister's name. It had been mentioned before, she was certain, but she could not recall what it was. She was pretty certain it began with an L. If she imagined the girl's name to be Luna, then she could better focus her mind and listen to the soft, sweet song all at the same time.

Diahyas felt herself begin to relax; her breathing became deeper and more even. Was it actually working? As they sang the chorus, Diahyas tried to imagine what Luna looked like…a female version of Wisp, perhaps? Luna…pale blonde hair, light blue eyes, milky white skin…the moon in human form. Eorian's sister was simply a paler, more luminescent form of him. She had to be with a name like Luna.

Yet once Diahyas fell fully asleep and found herself transporting, she came to face to face with almost the complete opposite of her vision for Eorian's sister. Dark brown hair, dark blue eyes, and tanned skin as if she'd been out in the sun for a while. Maybe this wasn't Eorian's sister?

She was sleeping on dirt, and all around her were sleeping men, except for the one on guard facing away from her that was settled against a depressingly shriveled tree. Diahyas could be in the wrong place, but Eorian had mentioned something about his sister being with his crew. She walked over to the girl and knelt down.

"Wake up," she said, but there was no response.

Diahyas frowned and stretched out a hand to shake the girl awake only to discover that she was not solid enough to do much more than slightly tickle the girl. In frustration, she growled.

"Wake up," she said more loudly, which was no more helpful than the first time around.

However, it had been loud enough to capture the attention of the lone man against the tree. He stood in confusion and started walking toward her.

"Who are you? You ain't one of our crew…" he finally drew close enough to see her in the moonlight, and his eyes widened. "G-g-g-ghost!"

"I be *not* a ghost," Diahyas scoffed, standing and placing her hands on her hips.

It did no good. The large man was well and truly frightened.

"Ghost!" he yelled as he pointed at her.

The men around her began to stir and awaken. Diahyas turned around to face Eorian's sister, who was still fast asleep. Great, she was going to wake the whole camp except the one person to whom she needed to speak.

"Ghost! Ghost! Ghost!"

"Shush," she yelled. "I told you before; I be not a ghost."

"Barro, shut up, man!" one of the men yelled.

"There's a ghost! It's come to eat our souls!" he yelled before dropping to his knees. "Please don't rip out my soul and eat it!"

Finally, a man sat up, put some spectacles on his nose, and walked over to Barro.

"What is all this fuss, Barro?" he asked with a yawn.

"Ghost. Right there, Gallutam," he said as he pointed, grabbing the bespectacled man's arm with his free hand.

Gallutam sighed but looked toward Diahyas, noticeably starting awake as his eyes found her. He pushed his glasses farther up his nose.

"This is impossible. There cannot be a ghost standing before me." He took a step forward with an outstretched hand.

Diahyas watched him cautiously. "You be correct, sir. I be no ghost."

Gallutam snatched his hand back, and his eyebrows rose in astonishment. "Who are you? What are you? Why are you here?"

Diahyas ignored the first two questions. "I be needing to speak with Eorian's sister, and yet I cannot wake her because of this infuriating lack of substance."

Gallutam shook his head. "You know Eorian? What do you need with Lishea?"

"Lishea! That be the name he used," Diahyas muttered to herself before looking back at Gallutam. "Awaken her."

Gallutam shook his head, and Barro started pulling on his arm urgently, eyes wide.

"You shouldn't argue with the spirits," he whined.

"She's not a spirit, Barro."

"No, I be no spirit; however, me time here be limited, and I must deliver Eorian's message. Where be the strange bird I met last I be here?"

"Relim?" Gallutam shrugged. "Out hunting. He'll be back in the morning."

"Lishea?" Diahyas nodded toward the sleeping girl. "You will waken her?"

Finally, Gallutam nodded with a sigh. "Fine, but you do not leave camp, and I hear every word. You may not be a spirit, but we have too many enemies now for me to trust you. Besides, you are a little too close to being a wisper for my liking, and half of them would like to see Eorian dead. Are we agreed?"

Diahyas pursed her lips momentarily before giving a curt nod. She really did have limited time, and there was a lot of information to deliver and gather. "We be agreed."

CHAPTER 14

"So what do these things looks like, the Yuens?" Frelati asked.

Eorian shrugged. "I've never seen any, but they must not look anything like we do."

"Why do you say that?"

"You should have seen Diahyas's reaction when she saw me for the first time," Eorian chuckled. "She was feeling my skin and my hair and had no idea what I was."

Frelati frowned. "That's not particularly comforting. Do we even know if these creatures talk, think critically? Would they be capable of making a treaty or fighting our wars? Perhaps Diahyas was right to scoff at our suggestion of seeking their aid."

"Well, they have their own villages. That's something."

Frelati paused a moment beside the river they were following to find the nearest village, and Eorian stopped as well and turned to face him.

"What?" he asked.

"I'm thinking that maybe we should scout them out, maybe talk to the lower level people first, just to feel them out a bit before speaking with their leader. That way we have a better idea of what we're dealing with. It would be bad to form a treaty with them only to realize that they are more harmful than helpful."

"All right," Eorian agreed. "That makes a lot of sense. Best to be prepared. While we're stopped, though, I'm going to get some water. I'm parched."

Eorian knelt down by the river and scooped up a handful of water, already relishing the blessed refreshment of the cool liquid on his throat.

However, once he took a sip, he realized his error, and he spit it all out and wiped his mouth.

"What's the matter with it?" Frelati asked in alarm.

"It's salty," Eorian responded with a moue of disgust. "This world's water is all backward. The seas are fresh, and the rivers are salty."

"Really? That's bizarre. Although it does explain why the trees and grasses aren't growing up against the river like they usually do."

"Okay, I say that we find this village pretty soon and ask for a nice place to eat, where I can get a large mug of water."

Frelati nodded with a grin. "Seems to me that would be the best place to learn about the people anyway. Lead the way."

It took another fifteen minutes of walking before they saw the village. It was a bit crudely built, but everything looked sturdy, and the wood and stone buildings were all in straight lines. Along the outskirts of the town were small wooden huts with gardens. There were also quite a lot of small felines and canines roaming freely.

"Are those miniature bobcats?" Frelati asked.

Eorian cocked his head. "Looks like it, and over there is a small tiger and coyote."

"It's like their growth was stunted because they are all living on the sole, small land mass. At these sizes, they could all feast on rats and mice as opposed to antelope and deer."

"Huh. That's interesting." Eorian surveyed the area a bit more before pointing out another odd creature. "Look at that one! It almost looks like a puppy, and it's walking on two legs."

In that moment, the small creature turned to look at them, and the intelligence in the eyes was unmistakable.

"I think it heard you," Frelati muttered.

Then the creature startled them by crying out in a loud, frightened voice. "Mama! Mama, mama, mama!"

"It can talk?" Eorian said in surprise.

Then they saw a more mature creature race from within the house toward the child. The woman had the sharp features of a coyote up top but as Eorian moved his gaze down her body, she became more and more reptilian. She wore a pretty, yellow sundress with a well-used apron draped around her neck and tied around the waist.

"What be the matter, Equinus?" she asked as she stroked the boy's floppy ears.

The boy frowned and pointed toward Frelati and Eorian. The woman quickly turned to find them, gasping and pulling the boy behind her as she took them in.

Eorian gave a small wave and a tentative smile.

"Who be you? What be you?" she asked cautiously. Then, a little more gently. "Be you Yuens as well...from another village?"

"Uh...no," Eorian replied. "We're not really from around here. We were wondering if there might be a good place to eat and get some water."

The woman's brow furrowed. "You do not look exactly like a mer, but...they be not experimenting again, be they?"

She seemed quite worried by the prospect.

"No...well, not that we know of," Eorian hurried to reassure her. "And we are not...mers? Is that what you call them?"

The woman nodded, and then a period of awkward silence ensued.

"You don't happen to have any water to spare, do you?" Eorian finally asked. "I'm parched, and trying to drink from the river just made it worse."

The little boy laughed. "He drank river water, Mama!"

She gave the boy a small smile and nudged him toward the house. "Go grab these men some water, Equinus."

The boy nodded and rushed inside.

"I'm Eorian, by the way, and this is Frelati."

"Mia," she greeted with a small bow. "I hope you do not think me childish to ask this..."

They waited a moment for her to continue, but before she could finish, Equinus was running back out with two clay containers of water, half of which was sloshing out in his excitement.

"Equinus," his mother scolded. "Slowly."

He very barely checked his speed before handing the cups to Eorian and Frelati.

"Thank you," Frelati said with a grin.

"His ears be pointy like yours, Mama," the boy said to his mother as he pointed them out.

"It be rude to point, Equinus," she chastised gently.

Equinus turned to Eorian next. "Be you a hoo-men like those stories?"

"I'm sorry?" Eorian asked, looking toward Mia for some clarification.

She brushed the fur back on her cheek in a nervous gesture and gave a small smile. "That be me question as well. He be asking if you be the mythical creature described in some of our stories. Our forebears heard the scientists speaking of creatures called humans who lived on land and walked on two legs. They came in large ships on the sea, and they gave the mermaids the ability to go on land as well, but not to easily dwell there. These humans be the reason we Yuens be created. They wished to form more mythical creatures that could help them continue to walk on land. I had not thought it more than a story, but..."

She shrugged and gestured toward the two men. "I have no other way to explain you."

"I'm not human," Frelati said. "I'm an elf. Though we are closely related. Eorian's a human, though."

"An elf," Mia repeated.

"What be an elf?" the boy asked in wide-eyed wonder. "You look the same to me."

Frelati shrugged. "We live longer, we have varied gifts, and we have pointed ears."

"Gifts?" Mia questioned.

Frelati grinned. "My wife can make flowers grow."

"Really?" the boy exclaimed. "Where be she? I want to see!"

"I'm sure that can be arranged." Frelati winked.

"So...about food. Is there a pub or tavern around here?" Eorian asked.

Mia shook her head. "I be not knowing of these pubs and taverns, but there be Cooks just a short way from here. Firnan be the best cook in the village, and he prepares meals for anyone who wants or needs food. We bring him spices, vegetables, or items of our trade, and if we have none to trade, we clean the dishes after everyone eats. We do not use currency here as the mers do."

Eorian chuckled. "I am quite glad that's the case, because we don't have any local currency anyway. Thank you for the water. I think we're going to wander around a bit, stop in at Cooks to eat something, and then head back out to meet our small traveling group."

Mia's eyes grew suspicious again. "Small traveling group...how small?"

"Just five of us. My cousin, Frelati's wife, and a friend of ours. We're exploring." Eorian sent her a charming grin, and she noticeably relaxed again.

"You can bring them here to stay the night. Rosie keeps a small inn for Yuens from other villages. I can send Equinus to tell her to prepare."

"That's very kind, but I'm afraid we don't have anything to barter with. We have no way to pay her."

Mia grinned. "Stories. After dinner, stay downstairs and tell tales of your homes; it be certain to bring a crowd, and they will bring many things to her. Shall I send her word?"

"Frelati?" Eorian asked with a raised brow.

"Seems like a great way to meet everyone."

"We're in."

Gorn swept out an arm to present the small, stone cottage chosen to house the royal mermaids. It was sheltered by many trees and bushes, and although the village could still be seen through the windows, it was far enough away that most of his people could be kept in the dark about their guests.

"I realize it be not quite as grand as you be accustomed to, but I hope it shall suffice. You will not be disturbed, and we shall do our best, with the few skilled men we have, to keep an eye out. Although, I must advise that you get your own protection. We be few in number, and it sounds as if your enemies be great."

Without being too obvious, Gorn was trying his best to warn the royals, although why he was bothering after all they had done was a mystery. It just seemed so underhanded. He felt Dehga's eyes spear into him, silently warning him to keep his mouth shut. He really disliked that man.

"We appreciate your kindness," the Prime-Mate said with a smile of gratitude. "I realize this decision be not a popular one among your people, so I hope we did not cause too much dissent."

Gorn studied the mer closely in confusion. He seemed different from the others; more reasonable, thoughtful, and kind-hearted. He gave a nod in acknowledgement of the Prime-Mate's words.

"If you need anything, ring the bell here by the door. Me second, Villis, will be by to assist you."

The Prime-Mate walked over and offered a hand to each of them in turn, giving a firm handshake of acceptance.

"We shall take up no more of your time."

Gorn and Villis turned to leave, sparing not even a glance for the silent Dehga or the haughty, disapproving Prime. They listened intently for the door to close and then waited until they were still more steps away before speaking.

"What think you, Villis?" Gorn asked.

Villis's tongue struck out once, then twice before he responded. "The Prime-Mate be sincere. The Prime be...just as expected. I fear we be better treated under these two than whoever be fighting against them. We may have made a grave error."

Gorn sighed. "I feel the same. But we were given little choice."

Villis nodded. "I would not have made a different decision be I in your place."

"As always, Villis, I thank you for your counsel."

Then Villis stopped and tasted the air. A small smile graced his lips. "Excitement be coming."

Gorn tilted his head. "Excitement? Whatever do you..."

"Chief Gorn, Chief Gorn! Guess what, guess what?!"

A familiar, small form came bounding around the corner of a house, bouncing around and tripping over his feet in his hurry. Gorn chuckled.

"Yes, Master Equinus. What have you to tell me?" he asked as he crouched to be on the child's level.

"There be these two strangers, and they came up. I be scared at first because they be so funny looking. They be not mers. And Mama, she be talking to them, and then they wanted water, so she sent me inside. But then they asked where to eat, and she sent me to Rosie's to tell her to get all her rooms ready."

Gorn nodded, although he had barely followed the excited chatter. "Could you tell me a bit more about the two strangers?"

The boy nodded and jumped from foot to foot. "They be sooo tall, and one had pointy ears. He said that be what makes an elf different from a hoo-men."

Gorn startled back. "A human? Equinus, be you saying that a human came by to speak with your mother?"

Equinus nodded. "A human and an elf. They be really nice, and they be eating at Cooks now, but Mama told me to run tell you…after talking to Papa, since he be the peacekeeper."

The boy swelled up with pride as he spoke of his father. The great bulldog-like man was large, bulky, and had quite a fierce look to him, though he was as sweet as they came. He doted on his little boy and treated his wife like the greatest princess in the land – partly because she was the princess of a neighboring village and partly because that was his nature.

Gorn straightened. "Run ahead and tell your mother I be coming to speak with her."

"Okay," the boy cried out, and he shot off like a bullet.

"You be thinking they be two of Dehga's allies?" Villis asked.

Gorn nodded, deep in thought. "Perhaps. It seems strange, though. We could very easily have run into them as we took the royals to the cottage. It be sloppy for Dehga to send spies at the same time they arrive, and I do think him to be sloppy man."

He stood pondering a moment before coming to a decision.

"You go to Cooks. Watch them, inquire of Firnan, and if you feel it safe, speak with them. I will talk with Mia and meet you there."

Villis nodded, and they parted ways. Gorn was slightly worried and also a bit hopeful. If the two men were not allied with Dehga, he may be able to convince them to bring more of their people here to fight against the rebels that were to attack. They hadn't a lot of time though, so he would have to work quickly.

All the men were gathered around Lishea and Gallutam, eager to here news of the midnight visitor. Barro had been causing quite a ruckus about it all morning, and they were ready to hear some reliable information.

Gallutam cleared his throat. "As I'm sure you are all aware, we had a semitransparent guest last night. By her own testimony, she was from another planet, and she knew Eorian."

Lishea's excitement overcame her in that moment, so she blurted out the good news. "He is alive, and he is not captured by Raef!"

All the men roared their happiness, and many made smug comments about how their captain could never be captured by that no-account tyrant.

"Settle down, please," Gallutam said, not nearly loudly enough. He adjusted his glasses, took in a deep breath, and tried again in a slightly louder tone. "Everyone, please, quiet down! There is more!"

Gradually, he got everyone's attention. "Thank you. Now, our visitor followed that up with some rather distressing news. Apparently, Eorian and Fil are not the only ones from Randor on her planet. Raef is there as well."

"What?" Lius shouted. "What's he doing there?"

Gallutam ignored the outburst. "And he's started a revolution. He has gathered quite an army, and it is likely that this new batch of warriors will be sent here once they finish their mission on this other world."

The group was deadly silent.

Finally, Burk spoke up. "We were barely going to have a fighting chance when it was only Randor's people involved. If Raef brings over a whole new batch of troops…"

Gallutam held up a hand. "Now, now, I know it sounds a bit grim, but Eorian is over there now helping in the fight against Raef. He has aligned himself with the rulers there, and if they are successful, he will have an army to bring over as well…maybe. Our visitor did not seem particularly enthused about her people making the trip."

"If Eorian is helping them, they can't refuse to help him!" Lefta shouted in anger.

"Hopefully, they won't, my boy, but it is a possibility we must be prepared for. We do have two other pieces of good news, however." He paused momentarily to ensure everyone was listening. "The elves are there with Eorian. Both are well, although I believe Frelati is still recovering from his wound. He is mostly healed. Lastly, the visitor that came to us is the ruler on her world, and she happens to have control over water. For those of you that may not be privy to the most intimate information we possess, that means we have the essences of air, earth, and water on our side against the one essence of darkness. That definitely puts the odds in our favor. I know many of you will have more questions, and we can go into more detail later, but for now, we have a job to do. We can no longer sit around waiting for answers and hoping that Eorian will show up. We must go to the leaders we've identified as potential allies and convince them to fight with us. The more people we have allied and ready to fight once Eorian comes back with the foreign fighters, the better chance we'll have of taking Randor back. We will win this!"

Again the whole camp roared its approval, and then they began to plan.

Luik was surprised by how far the revolutionaries had come in so short a period of time. The outlying cities and towns were almost fully in agreement with them. Geola was still holding out, however. There were signs everywhere in the city preaching the revolutionary propaganda, but for the most part, people seemed to be going about their daily lives, seeing the revolutionaries more as nuisances than as an actual threat.

There was still quite a thick blanket of tension around the city, though. It felt like a bomb that was definitely going to go off, but no one was certain what time had been set. Yet another difference was the lack of royal patrols. Usually, they would swim along leisurely, just watching and keeping the peace, but there were none in sight. Luik's best guess was that they were all surrounding the palace, trying to give the appearance that the royals were in attendance there. That would be his first stop.

As Luik walked up, one of the guards greeted him with a smile and nod. Luik relaxed a little, finally beginning to hope that this might be easier than he initially imagined. However, once he passed through the outer guards and was trying to pass through the inner doors, another guard stopped him, and this one was definitely more suspicious.

"It be Luik, right?" he asked.

Luik nodded. "That be right, Ubenius."

His eyes narrowed. "I haven't seen you around for the last two days. Where have you been?"

Luik shrugged. "I be asked to go to the summer house before all this mess started, and then not long after I got there, that message goes out.

Creepy, right? So I be trying to stay out of sight for a little while because the summer house be crawling with revolutionaries. Oddly enough, the Shoring finds me while she's trying to get away, so we…"

"The Shoring?" He had the man's full attention now. "Be she all right?"

Luik gave another shrug. "As far as I know. She ordered me back here to scout things out."

"Where be she?" he asked intently as he leaned in far too closely.

Luik reared back. "Slow down, now. There be traitors everywhere here. You think I be telling you if I knew? I be not *that* ignorant. Besides, she moved after I left her, so I be having no way of knowing exactly."

The man frowned. "Then how shall you tell her your findings?"

"That be for me to know. For now, I be needing to speak with the commander."

Ubenius chuckled. "You think you be important enough to take him from all of this mess right now?"

"Did you forget our conversation just now? I be thinking the Shoring be the highest importance…well, just short of the Prime and Prime-Mate, that is. Have you found them yet?"

The man's face said it all.

Luik nodded. "That be what I thought. The commander?"

"This way."

"This be just a suggestion, but you may want to work on your impassivity. I would think keeping the masses in the dark about their apparent lack of royals be of utmost importance."

Ubenius glared at him without response, and they continued in silence throughout the short walk to the commander.

The guard led him inside, down the familiar back passageway for servants, up through a narrow hatch to the great hall on the second story, and over to a small door at the far end of the room. He rapped twice.

"State your name," came the call from within.

"Ubenius, with a visitor to whom you shall want to speak."

"One moment."

The two waited in silence until the door opened.

A very young, light-gray merman swept his arm inside importantly. "He shall see you now."

It was at that moment that Luik began to feel nervous. He hadn't really thought about it until now, but the commander was a top leader of the world, just below the royal family. Diahyas was no problem to talk with; she was young, kind-hearted, maybe a bit haughty and demanding, but they had grown up together, and deep down, he knew she loved him. This man was huge, with a commanding presence. His eyes screamed that he would abide no nonsense, and there was a hint of danger around him that was underlined by his blood-red coloring and intense, brown eyes. When the door snapped shut behind him, Luik jerked and became even more keenly aware of his humble existence before this mighty man. At least the assistant was still in here.

"You have information for me?" the commander asked Luik in a soft voice. Despite his overpowering and almost threatening appearance, his voice was welcoming.

Luik nodded a bit self-consciously and took a deep breath. "I be sent here by Diahyas."

The commander instantly swam up from his seated position and moved around the large desk to get closer to Luik.

"This be not a topic to joke about, boy," he warned. "You swear Diahyas sent you?"

Luik nodded. "It be so sworn."

The commander studied him one moment longer before nodding.

"Jenns, leave us, but stay just outside the door in case I call."

The small, gray merman quickly and silently left the room. The commander waited for the door to click closed before the interrogation began.

"Be the Prime and Prime-Mate with her?"

"No. We escaped the summer home separately from them. Diahyas had to retrieve something of great importance."

"Do you know where the Prime and Prime-Mate be now?"

"No."

"But you do know the whereabouts of Diahyas?"

"Well..." Luik began.

"Do you, or don't you?"

"I *will* know," Luik explained hurriedly. "I just have to retrieve a band first. She has one, and once I put it to her frequency, she shall tell me where they be. It be safer that way in case I be captured on me way here."

The commander leaned back and studied Luik some more. "Wise precautions. Your idea?"

"No."

"A member of this 'they' you mentioned?"

Luik nodded.

"And who be this 'they'?"

"I be not certain you will believe me."

"Try me. This can be tested when we contact Diahyas."

"She be with two humans from Randor and two elves from another planet…I cannot remember the name. They say they be the essences of air and earth and that they need Diahyas, as the essence of water, to help them fight a war on Randor that be caused by the same human that be causing the revolution here."

The commander frowned. "A human did not cause this revolution. A merman did, and we believe we know who."

Luik shook his head. "The human be essence of darkness and can get inside of the minds of others…at least, that be what the other two essences be saying. It sounds unlikely, but I witnessed him get into Diahyas's mind and the Essence of Air's mind. The Essence of Air—Eorian be his name—helped us to escape, but the Prime and Prime-Mate did not understand and be still with Dehga…he be the essence of…"

"Dehga?" the commander's voice grew disbelieving. "You believe him to be behind all this? That be nonsense. He could not."

Luik shrugged. "That be what the others say."

"You should take a care with those words. Dehga be the Shoring's betrothed. Do not speak against him."

Luik nodded nervously.

The commander continued. "Why be you here instead of with them?"

"Eorian wanted me to find allies here in the capital, and we needed four more bands so we could all communicate. Eorian and Diahyas already have bands. They be planning a way to put down the revolution, and they also be wishing to get our aid in fighting on Randor."

"Who be this Eorian? He sounds as if he has experience leading men and strategizing wars."

Luik shrugged. "He be the essence of air, and he said he be leading the fight on Randor. Frelati…that be the elf from the other planet…he be helping Eorian plan. They both worked together on Randor as well."

"And this Frelati is the essence of earth?" the commander questioned.

"No," Luik shook his head. "That be his wife, Genevia. She be a ruler on her planet, and she says that the elves will help in the fight on Randor."

"This be a lot to take in. There be so many new variables," the commander muttered. "First things first, we get you a band, and you put me in touch with Diahyas and Eorian. We will strategize from two fronts. Tell no one else that Diahyas be alive, and especially do not give anyone her whereabouts. Understood?"

Luik nodded.

"I still have not determined who all be working with the revolutionaries. There be traitors all around us."

"I may be able to help," Luik said very softly.

The commander frowned. "Explain."

"Before the revolution began, I went to a meeting and spoke directly to Boran. That be the man in charge, by the way...well, sort of. As I said before, Dehga..."

The commander's eyes narrowed. "It be best for you not to continue that sentence. It be treason that I cannot overlook much longer."

Luik swallowed and nodded.

"Good. I knew of Boran, but why be it that you attended such a meeting?"

"Whispers among the poor and middle class caught me attention. Especially when the children who could not go on land be brought up. Me brother be one, you see. I got curious, went to a few local meetings, and then I heard that they planned to overthrow the primage and take down the royal family. I work here in the palace, and I grew up with Diahyas. I did not wish to see any of that happen, so I contrived to get into the meeting for all the village heads. It took a while, but I finally heard the location of one. I went, I listened, and afterward, I managed to speak with Boran. He be *very* intrigued that I worked at the castle. Ever since then, I got missives from the revolutionaries. I have not checked the last few days, but I imagine there be notes for me, and I can find other revolutionaries they have been installed around the palace and the city."

"A double agent. That be notoriously risky for all involved. Can I trust you be not a triple agent, or perhaps even just their agent tricking me?"

"Me allegiance be to Diahyas and Diahyas alone. You can test me if you wish, and you will find no fault in me."

"Then let this be the first test." The commander swam to the door and opened it. "I will grant you access to the bands, and you will grant me access to Diahyas. Know this, though, boy: if you be lying, these will be your last living moments on Faencina."

CHAPTER 15

"Okay, so explain to me how exactly you are traveling without actually traveling while you are asleep," Genevia asked. "This would be incredibly helpful…if I could do it."

Diahyas shrugged. "I do not know. I had not realized me dreams be more than that until I met you. Perhaps because me tiara has always been in me possession since I be a mere child and because I knew of its abilities even then? I have been consciously visiting places using me portal since I be six years of age."

Genevia's eyes widened in shock. "You were traveling like this when you were six? It's terrifying, especially for a child! At least, until you get used to it."

Diahyas gave a small smile. "I have always found it comforting, like a hug from time and space."

"I guess…" Genevia still stared at the girl in shock. "But your parents actually let you go?"

"They had no idea. Me servant, Sea-ena, certainly tried to stop me, but she be a mere servant and cannot tell me what to do."

Fil leaned over toward Genevia and softly muttered, "I'm starting to see why she's so…*her*."

"Oksy, so you've had the portal and been using it so long that it's second nature to you. That part makes sense, I suppose. I haven't been using mine often enough to get comfortable with it yet, and I always thought you had to say words up until Lishea mentioned the possibility of not needing them."

Diahyas rolled her eyes. "Words, ha. No, focus be all you need."

Genevia nodded.

"Well, I suppose we have a slightly better idea of how all this works. I always take my necklace off before I go to sleep." Her expression grew wistful. "I used to move around a lot at night when I was little, and my father worried that somehow my necklace would get so twisted that I would choke. He would always take the necklace off and lay it on the bedside table so that I could be safe and still see it. After...well, I've done that ever since then. It's almost like remembering him each night."

Fil awkwardly patted her on the back, and Diahyas examined her with great curiosity and sympathy. Genevia shook her head to remove the gloom and gave them both a big smile.

"Anyway, my point is that I have never worn that necklace while I was asleep. It was never physically touching me, but from what Diahyas is saying, it sounds like it *does* have to be on me or close enough for me to touch to use it the way she does. I'm going to try wearing my necklace tonight and see what happens. Maybe I'll be able to focus correctly."

"You must be careful, though," Diahyas warned softly. "I feel as if you do not quite understand how to focus yet, and you could accidentally physically transport yourself. As I said, I be not certain exactly how I be doing this. It be different from me usual focus to travel. Just...try not to do this focusing while you be still conscious."

Genevia's brow furrowed. "Perhaps I shouldn't try this yet. I was just hoping that maybe I could pop over to Tiweln and speak with my parents and Asben. They would help us strategize, and I need to let them know what is happening over here. They are gearing up to go to Randor, and they don't need to do that until we have this mess settled first."

"Hey, I believe in you," Fil said with a huge grin.

She gave him a small smile. "Frelati won't want me to try. He can be a bit of pessimist."

"Then let's give it shot before he gets back," Fil said with a wink.

"Gets back? Where has he gone?" Diahyas questioned. "He be with Eorian, yes?"

"Yeah, he's with E," Fil said with a chuckle.

Diahyas's eyes narrowed. "They be just a short ways from here, yes? I can go speak with them about me conversation with Lishea?"

Fil leaned forward. "Did she ask about me?"

"We be discussing important matters about wars, and you ask if she stopped to ask after you?" Diahyas asked.

"Of course," Fil said, giving her a look as if he thought she was crazy.

"I be going to the clearing now," Diahyas said as she stood.

Fil and Genevia exchanged a look. Fil shot to his feet and rushed to block her.

"You didn't answer me. What did she say?" Fil asked.

Diahyas sighed. "She asked if you be well, and she asked after her brother. She wished me to say, 'I love you both, be safe.'"

Fil puffed up noticeably. "She loves us both, hear that? She loves me."

Genevia laughed and shook her head. She had remained sitting comfortably on the ground and leaning against a tree.

"So, Diahyas, I really need you to do me a favor," she said, waving the girl over.

Diahyas appeared intrigued and settled on the ground near her. Fil gave Genevia a thumbs up behind the mermaid's back.

Genevia cleared her throat and fiddled with the grass on the ground, occasionally making a small, colorful wildflower pop up here and there.

"I need to try to get in touch with my people on Tiweln, and I know that Frelati would think it too risky and would tell me not to do it. If you wouldn't mind, could you postpone going to tell Fil and Eorian anything until I try? They won't be expecting us back yet, so I have time. Just give me one hour...maybe two. Then we can go talk to them. Could you do that for me?" she asked.

Diahyas pondered the request a moment before nodding and grinning like a child in on a very important secret.

"We females must stick together, no?" she said with a wink.

"I would like to point out that I am not a female," Fil said as he too sat back down.

Genevia settled more deeply against the tree before sitting back up quickly with a frown.

"Darn. I forgot that my necklace is all out of juice from our trip." She frowned at her beloved trinket. "I suppose I can't do it after all."

"Well..." Diahyas said before breaking off.

Genevia looked up at her. "Well, what?"

Diahyas took a deep breath before reaching up and removing the tiara from her head. "You can use mine."

"Oh, no," Genevia said, shaking her head vigorously. "That's yours.

If I do end up traveling physically, I don't need to take that from you."

Diahyas bit her lip before straightening and giving a nonchalant shrug. "We still have Eorian's diamond dust, and there be a very good chance that nothing at all will happen. Besides, if I see you leaving, I shall jump in with you."

"You're sure?" Genevia asked as she reluctantly reached out her hand to take it.

Diahyas nodded.

Fil spoke up. "Okay, you close your eyes, I'll hum, and Diahyas, can you go gather some soft moss, leaves, something like that to put behind her head?"

Diahyas jumped to her feet eagerly and nodded.

"But…" Genevia began before Fil quieted her with a look.

As soon as Diahyas was out of earshot, Fil spoke. "Look, I'm all for you trying this thing, and I admit it's a great way to keep Diahyas occupied for another few hours until they get back, but…if something does go wrong and you're not here when Frelati gets back, I'm going to have a maniac on my hands. He'll never forgive me. I didn't actually think you'd go through with it without talking with him first. I was joking before."

"You were right, though," Genevia said. "I love him to death, but he can be a bit overly protective sometimes. After everything we've just learned, I need to talk to Asben and my parents. If they go to Randor early, it could be a massacre, and we'd lose the advantage of surprise. There's too much risk here."

Fil bowed his head a moment. "So what do I tell Frelati if something does go wrong?"

"Tell him…"

"I just had a great idea," Diahyas exclaimed as she rushed over with her arms full of moss. She tossed the vegetation at Fil and glided to the ground. "Now, this be only if you end up actually traveling, mind you, but you can record a message on me band! I can play it for Frelati afterward."

Genevia's brows rose in surprise. "Your band can do that?"

"Short messages only. Ten seconds."

Genevia planned out her short message, recorded it, and set the band on the ground nearby. Then she settled back with the moss cradling her head and closed her eyes.

"Are you going to sing me a lullaby, Fil?" she asked teasingly.

"One a day; that's my limit."

"Spoilsport," Genevia muttered before yawning. "It's a good thing I tend to get a little tired around this time of day."

"Stop talking," Fil ordered. "Listen to the birds or something."

It was amazing how lively the forest sounded when all was utterly still and calm. The wind swept through the trees and rustled the leaves. Small insects wandered over and under the fallen foliage. The claws of squirrels climbing up and down tip-tapped all around the area, and quarreling birds tittered in the treetops. It was quite nice, soothing and relaxing. Fil was convinced that Genevia was close to dream world, and he listened to her breathing to verify.

"She's out," he whispered to Diahyas. "Cross your fingers."

"Why would I cross me fingers?" she asked in confusion.

"It's just an expression for wishing someone luck. It's like saying 'cast a long shadow' if you're advising someone to influence people or 'slay your dragon' if you want someone to overcome an obstacle. You don't actually *do* those things, just what they represent. Get it?"

Diahyas nodded. "It be like our saying, 'fight fire with fire', yes?"

"Exactly," Fil grinned.

"And what be the origins?"

Fil sighed. "Don't overthink it, princess. Just say it and move on."

"I do not wish to move," Diahyas said as she crossed her arms.

"Oh, Kiem," Fil muttered and smacked a hand to his head. "Must I endure this; take me from here!"

In that instant, both were startled by a bright blue light coming from Genevia.

"No!" Diahyas exclaimed in dismay, eyes wide.

Fil looked between them as the light continued to brighten. "That's not good, is it? Stop it...stop her...DO something!"

Diahyas was shaking her head. "I can do nothing!"

Fil moved forward. "Maybe if we shake her awake?"

Diahyas lunged forward and dragged him back. "Do not touch her! If you do, you will go too."

"Go where?!" he asked.

"I hope somewhere nice!" Diahyas yelled as she reached out a hand to grab Genevia.

And then it all stopped. The bright light disappeared, the wind died down, and the girls were gone.

Fil's entire body sagged as he continued staring at the empty space where only moments earlier two women had been. Two women that had two protective men looking out for them.

"I am in so much trouble."

Genevia awoke to the feel of a powerful tugging sensation, and instantly she was alert. This was not good. After just a few more moments, the world around her stopped spinning, and she came to a halt. There was not a tree in sight.

"Frelati is going to kill me," she whined as she looked around, surprised to find Diahyas brushing some dirt from her skirt. "What? You actually came with me?"

Diahyas looked surprised. "I swore that I would. Me tiara, please."

"Yeah, right," Genevia passed it over, still feeling some mild shock. "Why did you come? You had no idea where we would end up."

"It be better if two be together than one alone…even if she does happen to be essence of earth," she explained. "Besides, I enjoy adventures, and you had me tiara."

Genevia sent her a smile and, on an impulse, gave her a quick hug. "Thank you so much!"

"Sure," Diahyas said with a very pleased smile. "It be not *that* meaningful."

"It really is, though," Genevia said. "And I appreciate it more than you can know. I would be a bit frightened here on my own."

"You be welcome," Diahyas said, and she held out a hand. "Friends. They stick together."

Genevia grinned as she shook hands. "Friends. They stick together."

Diahyas took in a deep breath. "So, where be we?"

"I have no idea," Genevia said as she turned a circle to better survey their surroundings.

"Well, what be you thinking when you began traveling?" Diahyas asked.

"I'm not sure...I remember hearing words. I think it was you and Fil talking, actually. Let's see; something about shadows and dragons... maybe fire?"

"We be discussing phrases that represent meanings. I do not see how that could transport you to another place."

Genevia shrugged and began making another slow circle to view the landscape. It was dark, ash-like ground. It almost appeared as if a fire had burned through here recently, destroying whatever life had been in its path. In the distance, there were some mountains, and far, far away in another direction, Genevia could just barely make out the tops of green trees. Then, as she moved to face south, she noticed something she had bypassed before. Instantly, she grabbed Diahyas's arm.

"Don't move or say anything," she hissed softly.

"What?" Diahyas asked in an equally soft voice. "What be wrong?"

Genevia slowly pulled them down to a crouch. "Do you see that darker shadow straight ahead? The one that has nothing to cast it?"

"I do not think...oh, there, yes! That be strange; what be it?"

That's when the shadow moved...not very far, but it was definitely moving toward them.

Diahyas squeaked a bit in fear. "What be it?!"

"I'm not *positive*, but based on the descriptions that Frelati has given me, I am fairly certain it's one of Fezam's wraiths."

"Fezam?"

"Dehga. Remember, he went by Fezam on my planet."

"Right. And a wraith is...?"

"Something we *really* don't want to encounter."

Diahyas was quiet a moment, and then the creature began moving toward them again. Her eyes widened, and both women began backing slowly away.

"It's huge," Diahyas said. "What can we do?"

Genevia shook her head. "Frelati said there was no way to kill them... or, at least, that he doesn't know how to yet. We were working on that."

"We need to know *now*."

The creature stopped again, and Genevia and Diahyas did likewise.

"Be they all that large?" Diahyas asked.

"I don't know. This is the first one I've seen in person. I certainly hope not."

Then the creature flew upward, and both women screamed in fright and surprise. Yet the wraith did not attack or come toward them. Instead, it hovered in the air, its wings beating at regular intervals, and studied them. Genevia straightened, her curiosity getting the better of her sense.

"It looks like a dragon," she said, and she began to walk closer. "It's still that same shadow-y, insubstantial substance that Frelati described... almost like our daughter, Dayze...but he never said they looked like dragons. That would be an odd thing to leave out."

Diahyas trailed a bit behind Genevia.

"I do not believe we should walk closer," she cautioned.

"It's not attacking, though," Genevia said. "And I don't think it's going to. Besides, if wraiths looked like dragons, Frelati would have described them that way, and he didn't."

"Would it not still be better to leave it alone?" Diahyas asked.

Genevia shook her head. "Maybe it can help us."

She cupped her hands around her mouth and called up to the creature. "Excuse me! If you can understand, would you please come down? We need some help."

This is no place for the essence of earth, and it is definitely not the place for the essence of water.

Genevia grinned in relief. "You're like Relim and the dolphins."

Diahyas walked up to stand beside Genevia.

"Yes, Relim, and also the heroshi on me planet," she agreed before calling up to the creature. "Why be it especially not the place for me?"

Mermaids need a lot of water. That is something we do not have an abundance of in this particular location. Although, this planet is not abounding in water anywhere, quite frankly. We are going through a widespread drought.

Diahyas reached to her side to feel the container of water she had been keeping with her while on land. Half full.

"Genevia, I cannot survive here for two weeks if there be little water, and I be certain that be how long it will take me tiara to recharge if we be on another planet."

Genevia's face hardened in determination. "We won't be here that long. We'll find another way."

The creature slowly settled before them, lowering her head to the ground to look them in the eyes.

The two of you are far from home. Why are you visiting this planet?

"Well, which planet is this exactly?" Genevia asked.

They felt the creature chuckle. *Small essences that know not where they are traveling. That is a dangerous game you are playing. You know there are other essences, some not particularly friendly.*

"We've met one," Genevia said.

You have, have you? And from which planet is this essence?

"Ashneer."

The dragon's countenance instantly clouded over, and a whole range of her emotions washed over Diahyas and Genevia, jumping from rage to guilt to sadness to determination. *We have someone in common then. I was exiled from Ashneer because of him.*

"You know Fezam?"

"He calls himself Dehga as well," Diahyas offered.

"Also, Raef when on Randor," finished Genevia.

None are his true name.

There was a moment of silence before Genevia got up the courage to ask an important question.

"So you are from Ashneer?"

Yes.

"Well, you look a lot like…well, I guess 'look like' is a bit much, but, um, your physical substance, I guess, is similar to…"

He is attacking you with wraiths, isn't he?

Genevia nodded.

We are two separate creatures with a common history. Mine is an older, mightier race…or, it was. We have all but been wiped out. I am the last, and I was exiled from my home. The wraiths are like parasites, as I imagine you have seen. My race began as typical dragons, and they traveled to Ashneer from their home planet…here, actually. The wraiths left us alone at first, but then they began attacking while we slept. Just as humans can be changed into a wraith, our physiology altered as well. However, we merely adapted to become a hybrid of dragon and shadow. We cannot change others into wraiths as they do, but we can easily hide in darkness.

"Where be *here?*" Diahyas asked.

Zilcemi. The essence of fire is here, though she has not been awakened yet.

"Since you seem to not get along with wraiths all that well, perhaps you might be able to give us some tips on defeating them?" Genevia asked.

Light. Fire will work as well though it takes more of it.

"We haven't found those essences yet, and we have wars on two planets going on!" Genevia exclaimed in dismay. "Is there nothing else?"

The creature grew pensive. *There is another thing you can try. Essence of Water, you could be very instrumental.*

"How?" Diahyas asked. "They be shadows…how can water defeat that?"

Have you watched a shadow on the water? It is not particularly good at retaining its shape. It is weak, jagged, a poor copy of itself. Trap the creatures in water, and you can defeat them with a small torch of fire…even a fiery arrow.

"Really?" Genevia asked. "That seems so…unlikely."

Take it from an insider. It will work. Besides, the essence of darkness had to find a way to control the creatures. He knew of their dislike of water, and he developed it. They now all have an intense fear of water. You will not see them out fighting in the rain, and they will not be on boats fighting in the ocean He must keep them frightened of water in order to rule them. There is a very good chance that many will simply die from fright if trapped in water and fire will not be necessary.

"You're positive?" Genevia asked.

I have given you no reason to distrust me.

"Thank you," Genevia said. "I have one last request, if you don't mind."

The shadow dragon nodded her head.

"Could you tell us where the nearest natural portal is on this planet?"

I can do you one better, Essence of Earth. I can take you there.

"Oh, Kiem, thank you!" Diahyas shouted in great relief. "How long will it take?"

Two hours by air. You have my permission to climb onto my back.

Hesitantly and very carefully, the two climbed up and settled in.

"What can we call you?" Genevia asked just before the shadow dragon took off.

My name is Cerinos.

And with that, she took to the air.

CHAPTER 16

Eorian and Frelati were pleasantly surprised by the tastiness of the food served at Cooks. It was quite different from the meals they had on their own planets, but it had its own charm.

"I should bring some of this back for Genevia," Frelati said. "She does tend to be a bit selective with her food, but I think she would like it. What was it called again?"

Eorian paused in his eating a moment to think. "Ummm…the special of the day?"

Frelati snorted. "I'll ask before we leave."

Because they were eating lunch so late in the day, they were the only customers in the fairly large building. Firnan had been quite wary of them at first, but he warmed up soon enough after they complimented his food. Firnan was quite an interesting Yuen. He almost resembled a squid, especially with the six arms that aided him quite handily in the kitchen, but there was some amphibian in him as well. Neither of the men could pinpoint which amphibian.

As they continued eating, another patron entered the building and went up to order. Frelati thought that the two may be related because the new chap looked quite lizard-like, or maybe snake-like. Perhaps Firnan was part lizard instead of amphibian? Regardless, the newcomer soon sat down at a table nearby and began eating the same thing they were.

It was quiet in the room except for the sound of rattling dishes in the back and wooden spoons scrapping up food from wooden bowls, so it was quite startling when the other man spoke out of the blue.

"Who be you here to see?" he asked.

Frelati and Eorian looked at one another a moment before Eorian replied.

"We aren't really here to see anyone. We just wanted to visit the village."

"You be not from around here."

"No."

There was a moment of silence.

"Where be you from?" he pushed.

"I'm from Randor, and he is from Tiweln. I'm sure you haven't heard of..."

"There be no such places on Faencina," the man said.

"We are not from Faencina," Frelati said.

"And why did you leave your own planets to come to this one? How did you even know of Faencina?"

Again, Frelati and Eorian shared a look.

"It was an accident," Eorian said with a shrug. "We'll be back in our rightful place soon enough. We just have to wait a bit."

The stranger stared at them both a moment before nodding and turning back to his food.

That odd conversation essentially ruined the atmosphere for the remainder of their meal, but Eorian and Frelati refused to be rushed from the building so they took their sweet time finishing up.

"Ready to wash?" Frelati finally asked.

Eorian nodded, and they both pushed away from the table and grabbed their bowls.

"It was nice meeting you," Eorian said as they walked toward the back.

The stranger gave no sign of hearing him.

There were a lot of dishes piled up when Frelati and Eorian entered the kitchen area. Firnan chuckled at the sight of their widened eyes.

"I suppose you wish now that you had another form of barter, yes?" he asked with a grin.

Frelati began rolling up his sleeves. "We can handle this."

As they began tackling the dishes, another man entered Cooks and joined the odd lizard man. Firnan instantly went out to take his order. Frelati and Eorian shared a look of unease.

"You think there's something odd about this too," Eorian said.

Frelati cocked his head to one side. "The first man was far too inquisitive. It was like a cross between interrogation and information gathering, and this new man meeting with him does not seem coincidental, more like a planned meeting. If there was anyone else in here, I probably wouldn't think a thing of it, but I'm fairly certain they are here only because we are."

Eorian nodded. "So how should we proceed?"

"Well, we're trying to get them to trust us so they will become our allies. I would think straight-forward might be best. They don't seem hostile."

That's when another huge man entered Cooks, his face fierce and hard like a bulldog.

"That one, on the other hand…"

"Gorn," the man called out. "I be informed there be strangers in the village. Do you need me assistance removing them?"

Gorn stood, walked over to the bulldog, laid a hand on his shoulder, and began propelling him toward the door. "Thank you so much, Flen, for stopping in to check with me. Villis and I have been discussing the newcomers. Would you wait just outside for us, please? Ensure that no one else comes in."

"Certainly, Gorn," the man replied with a huge grin, and he walked back outside.

"Do you think there's a back door?" Frelati asked softly.

Eorian glanced around. "Don't see one. Maybe we could go through that window?"

Frelati glanced over to the right. "That's a bit small, don't you think?"

"Gentlemen!" Firnan boomed, and they both whirled around to face him. "It looks like most of the dishes have been washed. I count your debt paid. Chief Gorn would like to see you now."

"Great!" Eorian said with equal, slightly faked enthusiasm as he dried off his hands.

Frelati did likewise and unrolled his sleeves as they walked out front to the table with Gorn and lizard man.

"Please, take a seat," the cat-like man said as he indicated the chairs across the table from him.

Frelati and Eorian sat.

"Me name be Gorn," the man said, "and this be me right-hand man,

Villis."

Eorian and Frelati introduced themselves.

"I spoke with Mia and her son, Equinus, just a few moments ago. She told me some very interesting things about the two of you." Gorn waited a moment before continuing. "I have a question for you."

"All right," Eorian said.

"Do you know a man named Dehga?" he asked while closely watching each man's reaction. Anger from both of them was paramount before they both tried to mask it.

"What do you know of Dehga?" Eorian asked.

"Not much," Gorn replied with a shake of his head. "I would like to know more."

"Do you know where he is?" Frelati asked.

Gorn nodded. "He be in me village."

"What?!" Frelati exclaimed as he stood. "Eorian, we have to get back now."

"Wait a minute, Frelati," Eorian said. "Gorn wants something; don't you?"

With great reluctance, Frelati sat back down. "If Dehga does anything to Genevia while we're sitting here talking, I am holding you responsible."

Eorian ignored him, his focus fully on Gorn, who was clearly impressed by Eorian's insight.

"From your companion's reaction, I believe I can assume the two of you do not work for or with Dehga."

"Not even a little bit," Frelati said scornfully. "The man is a monster, an incredibly dangerous and powerful monster."

Gorn frowned. "Powerful? As in, he has many soldiers at his disposal?"

"No, powerful as in..." Frelati began angrily before Eorian cut him off.

"Frelati, how about you let me explain this to him?" he said softly. "I'm a little more distanced than you are."

Frelati gave a wave for him to proceed and leaned back in his chair.

"First things first," Eorian said. "Are you working with Dehga?"

Gorn frowned. "In a manner of speaking."

"We should leave now," Frelati warned Eorian.

"Explain that...please," Eorian continued.

"Dehga approached me not long before you arrived asking for me village's assistance in housing the royal family. However, he does not wish for them to be safe; he plans an ambush tonight. He be working for the revolutionaries to overthrow the kingdom."

"And you're helping him to do that?" Eorian asked.

"I do not wish to," Gorn replied. "However, he has threatened me village, and we have no means to defeat him. I fear that under his rule, we Yuens be treated worse than we already be, so if you have a way to help us, I be willing to strike a bargain."

"Diahyas's parents are here? With Dehga?"

Gorn nodded.

"And you said they are planning on attacking tonight? Do you know where they plan to take the royals...or are they going to kill them?"

"He did not say," Gorn replied. "He merely stated that it be happening tonight, and I should look the other way, perhaps put up token resistance so the royals believe I be on their side."

"Interesting. And he's there with them now?" Eorian asked.

"He be pretending to be hunted as well. I be not certain why," Gorn replied with a frown.

"Because he's trying to keep their trust. He is betrothed to their daughter, so if this revolution of his doesn't put him on the throne, he has a back-up plan."

Gorn's eyes widened. "That man be betrothed to the Shoring Water Maiden? He will become Prime-Mate either way?"

Eorian thought a moment. "If I understand your culture, then it is the female that tends to be the high ruler and the male is merely a helpmate, yes?"

"That be correct."

Eorian sighed. "Then, no, Dehga will not become the Prime-Mate. He will make sure that he is the highest ruler, and I imagine the entire royal family will be killed to make that happen."

"This be quite troubling."

"It definitely isn't good," Eorian agreed. "All right, Frelati and I need to get back to the rest of our party and come up with a plan. I advise you, both of you, to stay away from Dehga. Very. Far. Away."

"He can get inside your minds," Frelati stated flatly.

Villis's tongue flicked out nervously. "Truly?"

Both men nodded.

"How many be in your party? Do you believe you can stop this on your own? Will you need me help? We could perhaps get the aid of some closer villages before nightfall."

Eorian nodded. "If you can do that without calling attention to your plans, then do. Just know that Dehga is very intelligent, so it will be difficult to surprise him. We don't have a lot of people with us, but those that we have are good fighters. We stand a good chance. However, it would be better for Dehga not to know that it is us helping you. He needs to continue believing we are no longer on this planet."

Gorn nodded. "Leave it to me."

"We will be back by sunset," Eorian said as he stood. "Oh, and Mia had made arrangements for us to stay with someone here in the village. Can you make sure she understands why we will not show up?"

"Yes; I will relay that message. We will be ready by sunset."

With that, Eorian and Frelati shook hands with the villagers and left. They both hurriedly walked straight for the woods, and once they were out of sight, Eorian fiddled with his band until he found the communication button.

"Diahyas?" he said.

They waited a moment, but no response came.

"Maybe she's still asleep?" Frelati said. "Try calling for Fil or Genevia."

"Fil, Genevia, are you there?" Eorian said.

Still nothing.

"I need someone to answer me now. Diahyas, Fil, Genevia, someone say something."

Not a word came over the band.

"Something's wrong," Eorian said.

They both began running.

"I don't like this," Frelati said. "Fezam may already have them."

Eorian shook his head. "I doubt he knows about the bands. He wouldn't think to take them off, so someone would have answered us. Maybe it's out of range."

"Even if he doesn't have them now," Frelati said, "if we attack tonight, we are putting out a giant signal for Fezam to follow. He'll get them then."

"This is the best way to get the Yuens' allegiance. If we help them, they help us. It's that simple."

"I'm not saying you're wrong, but Gorn admitted that they had very few fighting men. How much help could they possibly be? It may not be worth the risk."

"They are clearly hunters. If we put bows in their hands, they can hit a target. Hand-to-hand combat may not come naturally to them, but we can still use them."

By that point, they both decided arguing and running was not the best idea, so they continued to the campsite in silence. What they found was Fil sitting cross-legged in the middle of the camp, staring at the ground.

"Hi, Fil," Eorian said as he tried to catch his breath.

"E! So glad you're back," Fil said, though his voice sounded like he didn't mean it in the least.

"Where's Genevia?" Frelati asked. "I need to speak with her."

"Fil, you're acting weird. What's going on?" Eorian asked.

"That's a lot of questions you're both asking me at the same time," Fil said.

"Fil."

Fil held up his hands in surrender. "I need you both to promise to hear me out completely before you kill me."

"What did you do, Fil?" Eorian asked.

Frelati was increasingly looking more worried and angry. "Where's Genevia?"

"I'm not hearing that promise," Fil said with a nervous chuckle.

"I'll kill you right now if you don't tell me something," Frelati threatened. "Where's my wife?"

"And where's Diahyas?" Eorian said.

"Okay, so you remember how you told the three of us to get Diahyas to fall asleep so she could contact Lishea and the crew?"

"Cut to the chase, Fil," Eorian ordered.

"Hear me out," Fil said. "This backstory is necessary."

Both men sucked in a deep breath to tamp down their impatience.

"All right, so that went really well," Fil continued. "Diahyas woke up, she told us about her discussion with Lishea...who missed me, by the way..."

At Eorian's glare, Fil cleared his throat and pushed on. "Anyway, uh, Genevia started asking her questions about how she managed to travel without actually traveling. I thought it was bad idea."

"She didn't," Frelati moaned. "Tell me she didn't."

"Well, she left you a message on Diahyas's band just in case it went wrong."

"Wait, she couldn't travel. Her necklace was out of juice," Eorian pointed out.

Fil looked away guiltily. "They *may* have decided to use Diahyas's tiara."

"You're kidding me. So now we can't go get her. Wait...where is Diahyas? She actually let Genevia use her special tiara?"

"Where is the band with the message?" Frelati asked.

Fil looked between the two increasingly angry men. "I just want to explain that the two of them had this whole woman-bonding thing happening. It was really strange, and I was defenseless against it."

"Where's the band?" Frelati repeated.

Fil reached behind him and held it up. Frelati instantly snatched it from his hand and started fiddling with it to get it to play.

"Why didn't you answer when I called?" Eorian asked.

Fil shook his head. "That didn't seem like a good idea."

"You had us worried you were all captured by Raef," Eorian chastised. "You could have at least let us know that you and...wait, where is Diahyas?"

Fil was quiet a moment before responding. "She may have gone wherever Genevia went."

Fil got to his feet slowly, just in case he had to run.

"And where did they go?" Frelati pushed.

"I..." Fil sucked in a deep breath. "I have no idea."

Frelati ran a hand through his hair angrily. "You lost my wife?! She could be anywhere!"

"This is really bad timing, Fil," Eorian said angrily. "We have an ambush coming tonight, and we need both of them."

"I'm sorry!" Fil exclaimed. "I honestly tried to stop them, and I had no idea that Diahyas would lunge forward to go with Genevia. Listen to Genevia's message; that'll prove it."

"I don't think this could get any worse," Frelati said.

"Oh, no," Fil said. "Take it back. Never, *ever* say those words. Those are death words. They basically ensure that something else terrible is going to…"

"Shoring Water Maiden Diahyas, this be Commander Wynedor. I have been informed by your messenger Luik that you be awaiting me contact."

Every eye jumped to the band on Eorian's wrist.

"See?" Fil said as he pointed toward the silver transmitter. "Worse."

Luik was starting to get nervous. Diahyas should have answered immediately. Why wasn't she responding? She wouldn't intentionally ignore this call and risk his life, but what if she had been captured? He had always been unsure about trusting those strangers.

"Commander Wynedor?" came a male voice through the device. "This is Eorian."

"Eorian, put Diahyas on," Luik said into the band, earning a glare from the commander.

"Unfortunately, she can't come at the moment," Eorian said. "Sorry. We'll get her to call in as soon as we can."

"How do I know you be not her captors?" the commander asked.

"They be not," Luik said. "That one be a human."

"Ah, so you be the human," the commander said.

"Well, one of two. And who are you? Is that Luik I hear?"

"I be the commander of the royal army, and Luik be here with me. He tells me there be other foreign creatures with you. Please describe them."

"Well, at the moment, there's my cousin, Fil, and me. Both humans. And we have one elf, but his wife, also an elf, was here earlier. She's gone off with Diahyas."

"They will be back soon so I can speak with the Shoring?" the commander asked.

"I'll be honest; I have no idea how long it will take them. Women, you know," Eorian chuckled.

The commander sighed. He could not argue; he had a wife and knew exactly what the human meant. Apparently that was the same on every world.

"Listen, since you contacted us, I wonder if you might be able to help us," Eorian said.

"You have me attention."

"We just found out that the king and queen…"

"I think they call them Primes," another man muttered. Luik thought it sounded like Frelati.

"Oh, right, the Primes. They are currently in a Yuen village with Dehga, and there will be an ambush tonight by the revolutionaries to capture them, maybe kill them. We are going to help the Yuens fight the revolutionaries off, but it would be quite helpful if we could have a little more manpower."

"Yuen traitors," the commander muttered angrily.

"No," Eorian said quickly. "It isn't the Yuens' fault. They came to me for help. Dehga threatened them, and I'm sure you are aware that they have no soldiers to fight him. They had no choice in the matter, but they're trying to make it right."

"You be misplacing your trust. Those things be scientific creations that have no thought beyond survival. They be tricking you. Dehga, however, be the betrothed of our Shoring and has the complete trust of the Prime and Prime-Mate. You should not speak out against him."

Eorian clearly sounded angry. "I'm beginning to believe that you have never actually met any of the Yuens. If you had, you would realize immediately how imbecilic that statement is. From the little I've been able to gather, the mermaids have treated the Yuens like dirt, and yet here they are trying to protect your rulers. Show a little gratitude. We need their help, and you do not mistreat your allies. Lastly, it is *you* who have greatly misjudged Dehga, not me. He is a stranger on your planet, but I know him intimately."

The commander's eyes widened in surprise before he began chuckling. "You have spirit. Although, I feel the need to point out that your speaking out against Dehga, in whom we have put our trust, be misguided. If you request our help, you will not abuse his character again."

Eorian was silent on the other side for several moments. "You have no reason to believe me…yet. But you will, and I will not say another word against him until you do. The ambush is tonight. You can pinpoint my location through the band, so come to *me*, not the Yuen village. We have some planning to do."

Then he hung up, again surprising the commander.

"How dare he give me orders," the commander muttered with a hint of annoyance. "He be full of smoke with no fire, that one."

"Actually," Luik said quietly. "He be the one that be full of air."

CHAPTER 17

The commander had delivered. There were quite a lot of soldiers sitting around waiting for sunset. Eorian and Frelati had gone over the plan, and fortunately, the commander had no complaints with it. They were going to allow the ambushers into the village, and the soldiers would slip in behind them, hiding in the trees until just the right moment. Eorian's group would be waiting around the house to make sure that no one made contact with those inside. They were assigning the Yuens to watch over captured revolutionaries since they didn't seem too skilled in fighting. The ultimate hope was that Dehga would believe the ambush never took place. It had taken some convincing on the commander's part, but he finally agreed to leave them out of his explanation since they had been kind enough to help them locate the Primes. He would instead mention something about a tip from someone working with the revolutionaries.

Assuming Dehga took the bait, his focus would then be on trying to locate the traitor in his midst instead of paying attention to Eorian and his group.

"Where be Diahyas?" the commander asked after the strategy had been determined.

It was the question Frelati and Eorian had been trying to avoid. Eorian's brain was racing as he tried to figure out the best way to explain. How much was the royal family keeping secret?

Frelati started speaking. "Assume for now that we know everything about Diahyas, every secret big or small there is to know about her. Now we need to gauge how much *you* know before we start explaining things. Are you following me?"

The commander straightened and scrutinized each man suspiciously. "I shall not divulge any secrets of the royal family. This be trickery."

"No," Eorian said hurriedly. "It's not. We just aren't positive how much of the explanation you'll understand if you don't already know some things. How about this: is her tiara in any way *unique*, other than its history?"

The commander's eyes widened.

"Okay, good. Next question: does water ever do anything unexpected around her?"

This time, the commander nodded. "So we do seem to be on the same page."

Eorian grinned. "That will make this a lot easier. Diahyas and Genevia have gone traveling...accidentally. We aren't positive where they went, but they will be back eventually."

"You allowed her to travel during all this?" the commander asked angrily.

"She's a big girl," Eorian pointed out with a frown. "And she has enough resources to take care of herself. That being said, I wasn't here to stop her. Frelati and I were scouting around the Yuen village over that way."

"Hemlon," the commander supplied.

"So it does have a name. Good. Well, Frelati and I were scouting around Hemlon, and apparently the girls...Frelati's wife and Diahyas... decided to test a theory that backfired on them. We imagine they won't be back for...a while."

Not long after he said that, the air began whipping around ferociously.

"I take it you are not the cause of this?" Frelati asked Eorian, who shook his head. "Good. It seems I'll get to yell at my wife soon."

Just as expected, a portal opened and out came Diahyas and Genevia. Genevia instantly ran to give Frelati a big hug and kiss.

"I'm so sorry, Frelati! You must have been so worried. Can you ever forgive me? I know I should have talked to you first. I'm so sorry," she said.

All the anger and frustration Frelati had felt melted away into relief and content. She was safe.

"Yes, you should have talked to me," he said softly. "But I am so glad you're back."

"Me too, and you won't *believe* what we found out!" Genevia said excitedly, turning to look back at Diahyas. She had moved to stand near Eorian, but both were saying nothing despite all the things they had to say.

"Thank Kiem, you're back!" Fil exclaimed as he came rushing from the edge of the camp, where he had been keeping low and out of sight of the angry Frelati and Eorian. "What were you thinking, Diahyas? And Genevia, seriously, how could you leave me behind to face *him*?"

Fil pointed an accusing finger at Frelati, who shrugged and gave a slightly sheepish grin.

Genevia frowned at him. "Frelati, you didn't give Fil a hard time, did you?"

"It was justified," Frelati argued.

"Can we finish this squabble later?" Eorian broke in. "I seem to remember someone mentioning something about finding out some information. I am assuming it would be useful, and since we are about to start fighting, I would like to be educated."

"Oh, right!" Genevia said as she whirled to face him. "It's about the wraiths."

"Wraiths?" the commander asked.

"They're shadow beings," Frelati explained briefly, barely able to contain his anger over the commander's disbelief of Dehga's character. "We haven't encountered any on this planet yet, but..."

"And we probably won't," Genevia broke in.

"You can't know that," Frelati said.

"Yes, she can," Diahyas responded vehemently as she stepped more to the center of the group. "The planet we visited be home to a shadow dragon, and he knew of these shadow beings."

"More specifically," Genevia continued excitedly. "He knew how to defeat them!"

"How?" Frelati asked intently, his excitement beginning to rise as well.

"Light or fire, the essences of which we haven't located yet," Genevia began, and Frelati's face fell.

Diahyas finished. "And water."

"Water?" Eorian and Frelati chimed in together.

Diahyas nodded. "It destabilizes their shadow-like substance, so a torch or a fire arrow could kill them. That also be the way they be controlled, so they be terrified of it."

"And since this planet is mainly water, Fezam most likely will not bring them here. They would be more of a hindrance," Genevia explained.

Frelati was so glad she had referred to Dehga using that name.

"Who be Fezam?" the commander asked.

"He's..." Genevia began before seeing Frelati shake his head.

Frelati finished for her. "He is a man that caused some trouble on our planet and is now causing trouble on Randor."

The commander's eyes narrowed a bit, but he did not push the subject.

"Well, as fantastic as that news is," Eorian said to break the tension, "it won't really help us in the upcoming battle, but the two of you can. So listen up, we have to expand upon our plans a bit."

The village was quiet. There were three Yuens patrolling the streets and a few stray animals roaming about, but beyond that, everything was still. It was to be a simple job, that's why there were only twenty fighting men here. Although it seemed unlikely that the Prime and Prime-Mate were staying voluntarily, the revolutionaries had it on good authority that the targets were indeed waiting in this small village before continuing on to the capital.

Silently, the signal was given for six men to quickly subdue the patrolling Yuens. This was completed a little more slowly than usual because the men were still getting used to their land legs, but not a sound was heard as the three Yuens were incapacitated and moved into the shadows.

Another signal was given, this time for everyone to advance. One unit would come from the south, one from the west, and one from the north so nearly every angle of the cottage was covered. The east side was right up against the thick woods, so it would not be a wise point of egress.Everyone moved slowly and carefully. Barely a whisper was heard. The central unit that was coming from the west toward the front of the cottage halted and waited for the signal from the other two units.

It didn't come.

The group of seven mermen began looking at one another in confusion. They waited a bit longer, ears straining. Still nothing. Finally, the leader of the unit appointed one man to go around and find out what was happening. The entire unit faded into the shadows as the scout quickly and silently moved around the buildings and toward the northern unit.

He began to slow up as the cottage came into sight. Where was everyone? He checked the shadows of the closest building with no result. Then he faced the thick forest, and he nearly yelled from his surprise. The seven men were all entwined with vegetation, immobile and useless. Their eyes were scared and darting every which way, some of them trying to warn him to run away. However, what was so puzzling was that their mouths were free. Why were they not calling out? It wasn't *that* important for them to stay silent during this ambush.

The scout weighed his options. He could try to set the men free now, or he could go back for help. After examining the vegetation again, he decided getting help was the better option. He turned to leave, and instantly a vine shot out and wrapped around his ankle. As he was plummeting down, a shout formed, but the air caught in his throat, and he couldn't make a sound. His eyes widened, and he kept trying to scream with no result. Then he began to be pulled toward the forest. He grabbed at the dirt, trying to stop himself, but again, his actions were useless.

Soon he was dangled up with the rest of the revolutionaries, silent, still, and wondering what the western unit would think.

What they thought was that they should send another scout to the southern group. Clearly something was wrong with the northern unit, and back-up may be needed from the south.

That scout also carefully snuck around to where the southern unit was to be stationed. However, what he found was very different from the scene in the north. Unconscious mermen, with tails instead of legs, were strewn all over the ground. How was that even possible? It wasn't raining. They had made sure of that before attacking. The scout rushed over to the closest victim and checked his pulse. He was definitely still alive, but what had happened?

That's when he felt himself wrapped up in a cocoon of water. His legs morphed into a tail, and he knew that no matter how much he shouted, it would be too muffled for anyone to hear him. Then, just as he was beginning to wonder how the others had lost consciousness when they had gills to breath in the water, a man broke out of the forest and delivered a very powerful blow to his head. Blackness.

The five remaining men in the western unit were getting nervous. What had happened? They did not believe moving forward would benefit them, but retreat would not be looked on favorably by the other revolutionaries. However, if they did retreat, they could get more people and have a chance of winning. With that decided, they began slowly exiting the way they had entered. At the edge of the village, they realized their mistake.

Creating a barricade was a line of sword-wielding soldiers loyal to the royal family. There were at least thirty of them. All ten hands of the western unit went up in surrender.

After that, it was all pretty easy. The soldiers rounded up all twenty rebels and placed them in a roughly built containment area guarded by the Yuens. Ten of the royal soldiers were to stay and help guard the prisoners in the Yuen village until more men were sent to help with their relocation to the palace prison. The remaining twenty royal soldiers, including the commander, marched up to the cottage and retrieved the Prime, Prime-Mate, and Dehga.

Dehga had inquired about any resistance as the soldiers came to rescue them. With just a hint of unease at the lie, the commander had waved a dismissive hand and informed Dehga that he need not worry about the small, untrained group of revolutionaries that had tried to capture them and instead ended up retreating back to the water. The traitors were no match for his soldiers, and all three of them were perfectly safe.

The commander was profusely thanked, and they all left for the capital. It had gone smoothly, and as long as Dehga did not inquire too closely after the failed ambush, he should remain clueless as to the whereabouts of all of his rival essences.

The next month was filled with activity. There were a lot of pockets of revolutionaries to roust, there was an entire population to educate about the current reproduction crisis, and they had to figure out the best way to convince the Prime and Prime-Mate to call off the betrothal with Dehga. None of it was going very well. It seemed every attack was quickly countered, and no one seemed to believe the broadcasts about the reproductive issue. They needed to find Boran, who of late had been the primary focus of their efforts. He was proving to be incredibly illusive, however, and everyone in Eorian's group was fairly certain how he was managing it.

"We have been in these woods quite a long time, you realize?" Diahyas said as she walked up to Eorian one morning. He was staring down at a map peppered with X's but still having far too many hiding places that they hadn't checked.

"Yes, I am aware," he replied distractedly.

"We should not go back to me comfortable palace, where you will have easier access to the commander, and I can be much more persuasive with me parents in getting this betrothal called off?"

Eorian sighed, finally dragging his eyes and attention away from the map and onto Diahyas.

"I know you aren't comfortable with roughing it out here." Even as he said it, he realized it was a huge understatement. "But you know how dangerous Raef...Dehga...is. We can't let him know we are still on this planet, although I imagine it's just a matter of time now before he figures it out. Do you also remember telling me that your parents had tried to immediately marry you off the last time you showed up, just before the revolution started? I imagine they have not changed their mind on that score, and they still think he's helping them."

Diahyas pouted. "I do not believe it to be *that* bad if we stay at the castle. We could, perhaps, stay at the other end of the palace?"

Eorian sighed and turned back to the map.

"You could at least try to make it more pleasant out here. Have large tents with comfortable beds and tasty food and..."

"A big sign that says, 'Diahyas is here, everyone,'" Eorian said sarcastically.

Diahyas stalked off, probably to gripe to Genevia, who was her new best friend. Eorian sighed as he watched her go. She was doing a lot better, and Genevia was helping with that. He was just having trouble adjusting to their new dynamic. She wasn't lording herself over him or ordering him around—as much – and she couldn't shock him whenever she liked anymore. However, he still felt like disagreeing with her or making snappy remarks every time she was around. He would then instantly regret it after seeing that hurt look on her face. Why did he keep doing that? If he kept it up, she would stop talking to him altogether.

"So, E," Fil said, breaking through his thoughts quite effectively. "Care to explain to me why we are still here? We can leave anytime now. We've pointed the mermaids in the right direction, and we've gotten the Yuens to agree to help us. What exactly are we waiting for?"

Eorian grimaced and looked up at his cousin guiltily. "Would you believe me if I said that I felt obligated to help the merfolk now and that I didn't want to leave until they had everything settled?"

Fil shrugged. "I mean, that sort of sounds like you."

Eorian nodded. "It does, doesn't it? And it really is the best strategic move. We couldn't exactly ask the mermaids to send any of their forces over to Randor while they were still trying to clean up over here. It'll all move so much faster if we help them out."

"That makes sense too," Fil agreed. "However…"

"What?"

"I can't help but feel like there's a much bigger reason behind it all. *Maybe* if so much wasn't going on in Randor, I could see it, but your father's in jail, you're leaving your ragtag crew to gather allies, and the wispers are in disarray. Not to mention your witch friend, also in jail, who you promised to help. Care to share?"

"Not really." Eorian gave him an impish smile.

"All right, then why haven't you sent Frelati and Genevia back to Tiweln to get the allies together over there? She made a very good point when she said that she needed to give them some information before they rushed over to Randor…and it's been a month. Don't you think it's about time they were clued in on the developments?"

"Frelati and Genevia are free to leave whenever they want, Fil," Eorian said. "They don't need my permission."

Fil snorted and crossed his arms. "You know as well as I do that Genevia is not going to go anywhere without your approval. She's still completely wracked with guilt for leaving you in the heat of battle last time. Frelati…well, quite frankly, he's obsessed with doing anything in his power to thwart Raef's plans, and you are giving him all the toys he needs to do it."

"I haven't asked them to leave because I was planning on going with them once we got a few more things settled here. I just want to ensure that Raef doesn't get his claws back in after we leave."

Fil blinked. "You're going with them. To Tiweln. And was I supposed to go there with you because it would have been nice to know ahead of time."

"I was going to give you the choice, but I had thought it would be better if you met up with my sister and familiarized yourself with everything that's been going on in my absence."

"Is there a reason you're going to Tiweln?" Fil asked in confusion. "You don't have to convince them of anything. They've already seen what Raef can do, so they are all in."

"The elves are, yes…maybe even some humans, but I thought it might be worth a shot to try to convince some more people. They apparently have quite a lot of different creatures on that planet. They could come in handy."

"Why?" Fil asked.

"Because we need more soldiers," Eorian said slowly.

"Let me rephrase," Fil said. "Why can't Frelati and Genevia, the *natives* of that planet, do the convincing? Why don't you want to go back to Randor?"

"I *do* want to go back to Randor."

"It really doesn't sound like it."

"Fil, I *do*. Just not yet," Eorian said in frustration.

"Not yet?" Fil shook his head.

"The prophecy, Fil. What did my prophecy say; do you remember?" Eorian asked in a slightly louder tone. Fil blinked at him in silence. "'Gone he will be for a total of ten.' The prophecy was right about everything else. I'm worried that if I go back before that ten, which I'm guessing now is ten weeks, that it will make us lose."

"So you're waiting to go back because a prophecy told you to?" Fil asked for clarification.

Eorian nodded. "I know it sounds a little crazy, and I don't think I would have done anything like this even six months ago, but I heard what Genevia said about her prophecy coming true, and I've seen all the things in my life that have aligned with mine. We don't know what

Diahyas's is yet, and it could be that hers hinges on my decisions since mine relies on her. I really don't want to test it."

"Have you asked her?" Fil asked.

"Asked her what?" Eorian said. "You heard me ask her for her help right after Genevia and Frelati popped over. She was less than enthusiastic."

"No." Fil shook his head. "Have you asked her if she knows her prophecy?"

Eorian frowned. "I figured she wouldn't know. Neither Genevia nor I knew ours until the time was right. Someone else had to share it with us."

"Neither of you knew that you were essences until someone told you, but Diahyas grew up knowing she was one. Seems to me it is quite likely she knows her prophecy too."

Eorian was silent as that revelation hit.

"The two of you have been walking on pins and needles around each other for a while now," Fil said. "Why don't you go for walk, talk it out, and you can ask her what she knows about her prophecy? It can't hurt, can it?"

Eorian's stomach tightened. Fil smirked as if he could read his cousin's mind.

"Have fun," he said with a laugh and smacked him on the arm. Then he walked off with a wave.

As was their normal routine, everyone gathered around the fire in the middle of camp to eat dinner. They didn't usually have a lot to say, but small comments here and there would be passed, and occasionally someone would tell a humorous story. Fil generally tried to lighten the mood by telling a very tall tale or describing some ridiculous antic of one of Eorian's crew members. Tonight, Fil's focus was quite different, and he said very little to the group as a whole. His attention was on Eorian.

"Have you asked her yet?" he whispered between bites.

Eorian glared at him and said nothing.

"You scared of your first date in…" Fil paused. "Actually, have you ever dated a girl before?"

"Fil," Eorian said in his dangerously low, threatening pirate tone.

"You haven't, have you?" Fil said confidently. "I hadn't ever thought about it before. I guess I always figured you to be a top catch."

"Why would you think that?" Eorian asked before he could stop himself. He groaned. "Ignore that. I never asked."

Fil only ignored the last part. "Well, you've got that aloof, mysterious quality. You also come across a bit like a wounded warrior, so I bet a lot of girls would feel an urge to soothe your broken soul. And, as long as we don't compare you side-by-side with Frelati, you aren't exactly hard to look at, I guess."

"Well, thanks, Fil. That makes me feel marvelous," Eorian said drily.

"What are you two whispering about over there?" Genevia asked loudly with a mischievous grin.

Eorian caught Fil's look and issued yet another warning. "Keep quiet, Fil."

Fil grinned. "We were discussing what an eligible female might find attractive in Eorian's rather rough self."

"*He* was discussing," Eorian clarified. "I was an unwilling listener."

Genevia's face brightened. "Oh! This should be fun. Diahyas, what do you think?"

Diahyas's blue skin turned a bit purple. "I...um...I..."

Genevia chuckled. "I'll go first, then. See if you can outdo me."

She grew theatrically serious as she stared Eorian down.

"Confidence," she announced after a moment. "A girl wants someone that knows his mind and knows how to achieve what he wants...just, not if it's overdone. Your turn, Diahyas."

"His hair?" she said hesitantly.

Genevia shook her head. "You can do better than that. Think it over a bit more. Would you like to play, Frelati?"

Frelati shook his head with a laugh. "I think I'll bow out on this game, but you go ahead."

"Fil?" Genevia offered.

"Why not?" Fil said. "If my answers aren't right, you can correct me. I may not be that great at knowing what a girl wants."

"I'm sure you're not," Eorian said.

Fil ignored him. "I'll use one I mentioned to E. An air of mystery. You girls like that, right?"

"It does keep things interesting, just as long as he knows what needs to be revealed," Genevia agreed.

"Pretty sure he needs to work a bit on the sharing of his secrets, but he's getting there," Fil said as he grinned at his cousin.

"Can we end this game now?" Eorian said. "I think the torture has gone on long enough."

"No!" Genevia said. "Diahyas never really got a turn. What do you think, Diahyas? Did you come up with something?"

She nodded with a small smile. "I do still think his hair be quite marvelous. Very different from me own. However, I believe the quality best about him be his heart. He be very willing to help others…even if at first they may have done him wrong."

Fil and Genevia both beamed at her.

"I think she's the winner here. What do you think, Genevia?" Fil asked.

"I agree. What's her prize?" she asked.

"Why, a romantic walk through the enchanted forest with a prince charming, of course!"

Genevia clapped her hands with a laugh. "That's perfect!"

"Fil, really, you are…" Eorian began, but Diahyas cut him off.

"Would you truly go on a walk with me?" she asked, her face so very hopeful that he couldn't bear to say no.

He pushed to his feet and offered her a hand up. "It will be my pleasure."

As they disappeared from sight, Fil winked at Genevia.

"Let me guess," Frelati said. "This was all planned."

Genevia snuggled up against him. "I may have learned a thing or two from Jezzie."

Fil laid back on the grass. "I was just ready for E to get out of his foul mood."

"Then I will offer you both my conditional congratulations."

"Conditional?" Genevia asked.

Frelati nodded. "If the two of them come back to camp together without having had an argument that has made them hate one another, then I will fully extend my congratulations."

"You are so pessimistic, Frelati," Genevia said with a sigh.

Frelati looked off in the direction the two had walked. "I'm relying on history here, so think of me as more of a realist."

"A realist would have said we wouldn't get together," Genevia pointed out.

"Which makes it all the more likely that I'll be right this time."

CHAPTER 18

It was beautiful at this time of evening, just a bit after sunset. The air was crisp. Lightning bugs began to flash between the trees, and crickets hummed softly all around. There was still a bit of light to allow for better navigation, and the world felt magical.

"I have never walked in the forest with someone before," Diahyas said excitedly. "I always travel to Land on me own, and never at this time of day. It be very beautiful, do you not think?"

Eorian nodded. "It's quite nice out here."

They lapsed into silence as they continued walking beside one another, close but not touching. Diahyas cast around in her mind for something else to say to fill the void.

"Tell me something," she finally said.

Eorian glanced over at her. "Tell you what?"

Diahyas shrugged. "Anything. I know little about you."

"I prefer for people to know little about me," Eorian said. "Fil, unfortunately, knows too much because he grew up with me, and he has no qualms about sharing everything."

Diahyas bowed her head to stare at the ground, and they continued on in silence.

"My mother is the best cook anywhere," he said softly. "She always made my favorite dishes when I came home because she is a firm believer in showing love by supplying those around her with food. She is a baker's daughter."

Diahyas smiled at him. "She sounds marvelous! Will I get to meet her?"

Eorian's eyes grew very sad as he shook his head. "Raef killed her."

"What?" Diahyas exclaimed.

Eorian came a stop, taking deep breaths to keep his emotions in check. "I'm sorry. I shouldn't have said anything. That's not exactly what you wanted to hear."

Diahyas stepped closer and laid a hand on his arm. "How long ago did this occur?"

"Not long before I arrived here. Everything has started running together, so I'm not positive exactly how long ago it was."

"You have not spoken to anyone of this, have you?" Diahyas asked.

"They all know," Eorian said.

Diahyas shook her head. "Not of your feelings on the matter, though, yes? You keep that inside where no one can see, a deep ache that nearly rips you apart."

Eorian stared at her in surprise and confusion. "You are quite perceptive. I hadn't thought compassion and sympathy for another's plight would be in your repertoire."

Diahyas flinched and backed away. Her arms wrapped around her middle defensively.

"No, I didn't mean that in a bad way," Eorian rushed to assure her. "I just hadn't expected it, is all. You've only ever shown me an arrogant princess fully emersed in herself. How was I supposed to know..."

Diahyas' eyes flashed dangerously. "I should not have remained here with you. Everyone, even strangers from afar with looks so very different from ours, be the same."

"What did I say?" Eorian asked. "I was giving you a compliment."

"Wrapped in barbs, just as me mother does. Others be callous, domineering, and wish not to get close to anyone," Diahyas said angrily, getting close to tears.

"Sea-ena didn't seem that way to me," Eorian replied softly.

Diahyas paused and nodded. "She be kind to me, but she be me servant. She be required to please me. She can leave whenever she wishes to be with people she wants to be with. That be cruel as well, the superficial kindness."

Eorian shook his head. "She cares for you, Diahyas. Trust me. It is a job, and she does have to serve you, but doesn't she also look out for you, try to keep you safe? She was terrified when you brought us back because she worried that we would harm you. That goes beyond a mere servant arrangement. And what about Genevia? I've seen you grow close to her. She's kind to you, and there is no reason for her to choose to talk to you or laugh with you unless she genuinely enjoys your company. Do you deny that?"

Diahyas shook her head.

"Okay, now me," Eorian continued as he took a step closer. "I don't necessarily say things the right way, but I would not still be here if I didn't want to help you."

"You wish to have me help in return," Diahyas argued.

Eorian nodded. "That's true, but there is no guarantee even if I help you that you will send people to help me."

"There be a better chance."

"That's not the point I'm arguing here. Yes, I need your help, and yes, if I help you, you will be more inclined to help me. But why am I keeping you here instead of in the palace?"

"You wish me to suffer without me comforts here in these woods?" Diahyas asked with a slight smile.

Eorian chuckled. "Not really, no. You will be safer here with us than in the palace surrounded by all the soldiers. If I truly did not care or wished to be cruel or wanted to push you away, I would send you there."

"You also wish to keep me away from Dehga. That be a good reason to keep me here."

"You really don't want to believe me, do you?" Eorian said on a sigh.

"Perhaps I just really wish to keep meself safe…inside."

"Attachments are always risks. Some of them you can't choose… family members, for instance, and some you can, like friends and lovers. You can miss out on a lot if you don't give it a shot."

"You have a lover back home?" Diahyas asked.

"Not even close, actually," Eorian said. "I have lots of friends, though, and they would do anything for me. Just as I would do anything for them. If you would like to have someone to rely on, Diahyas, you can rely on me."

"And…and you will rely on me?" she asked hesitantly.

"If you'll let me," Eorian agreed with a nod.

Diahyas smiled widely. "Truly?"

Eorian laughed at her enthusiasm. "Truly."

"I wish to give you a hug the way Genevia did when she first saw you here. May I?" Diahyas asked.

"I guess so," Eorian said with a shrug and opened his arms.

She bounded inside with a giggle, squeezed him tightly, and then bounced back out again.

"Thank you," she said.

"No problem. Are you ready to head back?"

Diahyas nodded. "It be growing quite dark now."

Eorian offered her a hand, which she happily took.

"This has been a marvelous walk," she said.

"Except for that bit I messed up," Eorian replied with a frown.

"You fixed it, and that be what matters."

They walked along quietly, each in their own thoughts, and just a bit before they reached camp, Eorian remembered one of the reasons Fil had wanted him to go on this walk.

"Oh, Diahyas, I've been meaning to ask you something."

"Yes?" she asked curiously.

"You remember Genevia mentioning her prophecy, and I have one as well that I can share with you. I was wondering…do you happen to know what yours is?"

Diahyas bit her lip. "I be told that I should tell no one of it, just in case they use it against me."

Eorian nodded. "And I agree with that completely. We do not want Dehga to have any more information on you than he already has. If you wish to keep the prophecy to yourself, I will respect that. It is helpful, though, to know that you are aware of it and can follow it yourself. That is enough."

Surprisingly, he actually meant those words. On a whim, he leaned forward and kissed her on the forehead.

"Good night, Diahyas."

As he started to leave, she grabbed his arm.

"I will share with you only. Our secret?" she asked.

"You're sure?" Eorian asked. "You really don't have to; I trust you to follow it."

"It be not all that helpful. Perhaps it will mean more to you?"

Eorian chuckled. "I doubt I'll find any hidden meaning. I'm still trying to figure out parts of my own. We can give it shot, though."

Diahyas nodded, closed her eyes, and took a deep breath before reciting.

Born to wealth and title high,
Water flows at her beck and cry,
When evil comes, she shan't stand by,
A lasting alliance they all must try.

Unyielding pride that must bend,
Meeting up with foe and friend,
World to world they must defend,
Earth, sea, fire, light, and wind.

"Let's see here..." Gallutam looked down at the map of Randor intently. Lishea, Burk, and Lius were gathered around as well. "Acentia is a yes. Kenorin is a no. Dohsyc..."

"A resounding yes!" Lius yelled victoriously. "With their awesome new blasting invention and warships. No thanks required for my efforts."

"Yes, thank you, Lius," Gallutam said as he adjusted his glasses. "The islands off Sohsena are a no. Omwoe is a yes. Burk, how did it go with Fracen and Grionia?"

"They decided it was too risky to go against Sohsena. They rely on trade with them."

Gallutam sighed. "You told them that they may lose trade with several other countries if they do not side with us?"

Burk nodded. "Their response was that they could survive without trade with all other nations, but they would starve without Sohsena."

"Sounds a bit dramatic to me," Lius huffed.

"All right, so Fracen and Grionia are both nos. Lishea, how did Hius Yifwa respond?"

"They wanted to remain neutral at first, but after a lot of convincing on my part, they have decided to side with us," Lishea said with a small smile. "I had been getting really worried for a while. It seems they've had a lot of casualties during Raef's reign, and he had reduced a lot of trade with them."

"Not a wise move," Gallutam said as he made a mark on the map to show Hius Yifwa's support. "Another yes. And on to me. I went to speak with Surrea and Relis. Both are stubbornly refusing to fight on either side, but I did convince several of their scientists to provide us with specialized weaponry, more advanced communication, and, if necessary, some strategic advice. We will have to be extremely cautious, however, when we go to retrieve any of this. They have essentially locked down their cities from outsiders in the hopes it will keep them out of the war."

"This is a *global* war. What makes them think they are exempt?" Lius exclaimed.

"Relis believes they are exempt because they are men of intellect, above the petty games of regular men. Surrea...well..."

"They are simply following in the footsteps of their smarter neighbor because it appears easier," Burk finished. "I imagine before this is over, they will have joined our side."

"Let's hope," Lishea said. "Although, if we do get help from that other planet that Eorian is on, then we have a very good chance of getting Raef off of our planet for good."

"Yeah! We'll show him!" Lius said excitedly.

"Not necessarily," Gallutam said.

"What do you mean?" Lishea asked.

Burk answered for him. "He is referring to the resources available to Raef on his own planet. We have no way of knowing exactly how extensive those are at the moment."

Gallutam nodded. "Exactly. In addition, the ghostly visitor mentioned a revolution on her planet. That division of loyalties will not remedy overnight, and I imagine many will remain dedicated to Raef's cause. In which case..."

"I got it," Lishea said in defeat. "He's still outnumbering us."

"Weeellll..." Gallutam began.

"What else have I overlooked?" Lishea asked in exasperation.

"The elves."

Lius cheered. "That's right! The lovely lady will send her fighters to avenge us!"

"It still may not be enough," Gallutam shook his head. "There are too many unknown factors at present."

"So we wait?" Lishea said. "Is there nothing else we can do?"

Burk shook his head. "We need to retrieve the witch and Eorian's father, but Eorian set those plans in place before he left. We just need to finish what he started."

Clim, Grov, and Roas worked surprisingly well together. The wisper trio had grown up knowing each other, but until Eorian gave them this chance, they had not really cared to spend time with one another. Now they had a mission, a semi-dangerous one. They may come out all right, since most humans had no idea how to catch or punish a wisper, but their targets could easily be killed if even a small mistake was made. That was why they decided to enlist one more wisper.

Now, they all silently glided to the castle. To the humans, they were simply curious arrangements of nature floating through the air: clovers, maple leaves and pine straw, dandelion seeds and colorful wildflower petals, and differing shades of pollen. It was because of this last wisper's bizarre choice of substance that she had been chosen. Finley kept away from everyone. She was a little younger than the other three, and none of them knew too much about her. However, she seemed excited to be a part of this group and to have the chance to meet Eorian in person. Also, every wisper who knew of her spoke of her analytical mind and drive for success. That seemed to be a good combination for the current mission.

They had all done a few run-throughs, and they had brainstormed about potential issues and how to overcome them. Maps of the castle had been studied, and three different points of exit had been chosen. Perhaps they were ready.

As agreed, Clim, Grov, and Roas waited outside while Finley brushed along the floor toward the dungeon. She was the best choice for this job since she could easily look like dirt on the ground if anyone passed by.

Finley carefully moved downward, feeling the damp and gloom descend around her as she entered the lowest level of the building. When she reached the bottom and saw the long central hallway, her confidence fell. There were a lot of cells down here; it was going to take a while to determine which held the prisoners. Methodically, she started with the front cell and began working her way down the left side of the prison. There was a very small sliver of space beneath the doors that she could whisk under to check. That did make things a bit easier.

One by one, she moved along. There were some cells that held people, but none were female. The first priority was the witch, who could then describe Eorian's father and help them retrieve him. After half an hour, she had managed to go through all the cells on the left-hand hallway. Most of the cells were empty, but those that contained an occupant were so depressing that it made it difficult to leave them behind. Finley decided at that moment that while she would not jeopardize this current rescue, she would come back to save the poor souls rotting away down here…even if she had to do it alone.

She continued on to the right wing and started the search again. Once she was halfway down and still hadn't found Uratia, she started to get worried. What if she wasn't down here? Raef could have moved her. How would they find her then?

She took several deep breaths to calm herself. First, she had to determine that Uratia was not in any of the remaining eight cells, then she would deal with the outcome. She flew forward, ducked under a cell, and saw emptiness. One down. Crossing the hall to the left side, she peeked under that door. Again, nothing. Two down. Back to the right side, slide under the door, and Finley saw a person crouched in a corner. Was it her? She couldn't tell from the way the figure was curled up.

Excuse me, she called softly.

Instantly, the prisoner whirled around with wide, frightened eyes. "Who…who's there?"

Finley sighed. It was another man.

I will free you; I promise, she said.

"Rida?" came a slightly hopeful voice.

Finley. Is Rida in prison down here too?

The man sagged and turned away. "Rida is nowhere."

Finley hovered there a short while, staring at the forlorn man. Sympathy washed over her. There was something different about this prisoner. He seemed more lost and alone than the others. He would come with the other two escapees. She could not leave him here any longer.

I'll be back for you, she said as she withdrew from the cell.

She paused outside his door, feeling a deep pain inside herself on his behalf. She didn't wish to leave him now, but she could not help him if she did not. Slowly, Finley turned around to the cell across from him. She closed her eyes and prayed that this one would hold the prize. Then she swept under the door.

The image that met her was different from the others. This prisoner was in chains, sitting cross-legged in the center of the cell. It almost looked as if she was meditating.

Uratia? Finley called out hopefully.

The woman's eyes opened, but nothing else moved. She scanned the room for the source of the sound before landing on the whirling yellow and brown motes floating at the bottom of the door. She smiled.

"I had hoped today might be the day," she said. "And what is the name of my rescuer?"

I am Finley. Clim, Grov, and Roas are waiting above for my signal.

"And you have a plan," she stated, then cocked her head as if listening to something before nodding. "A good plan, I see."

You truly are a witch, Finley said in awe.

"Clearly not a good one, since I was captured."

Clim said that Eorian said that you did that on purpose.

Another small smile graced Uratia's lips. "Perhaps. Now, you wish to know how to locate Eorian's father, Jano."

Again, another tilt of her head, and her eyes fluttered closed briefly. "You have seen him already."

I saw many prisoners before I found you.

"Yes, but you remember this one most of all…I cannot pinpoint which cell you were checking, however." Uratia sagged. "I need to stop this if I expect to walk out of here. My body is drained enough."

Yes, rest while I go through the plan with you.

Uratia shook her head. "No need for that. Go tell Clim that all is ready. I will do my part. You have the item I requested?"

Finley pushed all the way into the room and flew over to Uratia, who opened up a palm. Finley deposited that heavy bit of metal she had been asked to carry into the witch's hand.

Can you really undo those locks with such a small piece of metal? she asked.

Uratia quickly bent the long, thin piece of silver into shape and began fiddling inside the lock. After a few minutes, there was a click, and the manacle fell from Uratia's chafed wrist.

"Much better," she said on a sigh. "Go now while I do the other."

Finley nodded and hurried to the other wispers waiting outside.

She is ready.

You all remember what to do? Clim asked.

Each wisper nodded.

Finley, did you see the guard on duty?

Top of the stairs.

Perfect. Let's go.

A scream rang out through the halls that instantly caught the prison guard's attention. He straightened from where he had been leaning against the wall and looked in the direction of the commotion. Another shout rang out, this one seeming to come from a man, though it was no less frightened than the female.

Footsteps ran up behind him.

"What's going on?" the soldier asked in confusion.

"I'm not sure," the prison guard said.

Then another cry rang out. *Stay away! Please don't curse me, witch!*

The prison guard's pulse began racing. "The witch escaped!"

"How? She's locked up tight," the soldier said, equally worried.

The prison guard removed the keys from his belt and tossed them to the soldier. "Check to see if she's still in there. I'll go investigate down that way."

The soldier nodded and raced down the stairs while the prison guard rushed to the rescue of the frightened castle workers. In a few moments, the soldier had reached the cell, and he flipped open the small window to look inside. His stomach twisted at the sight of the empty chains on the ground.

Check inside, came a shout that sounded like the prison guard.

He fumbled with the keys, taking several tries before finally getting the door unlocked. Quickly, he threw the door open and stepped inside.

That's when Uratia attacked him from behind, effectively knocking him unconscious and chaining him to the floor just where she had been. Quickly, she set an illusion charm over him so that any who looked inside would see her. That would hold for a few hours. Then she grabbed the keys and locked the cell.

Eorian's father be in this one, Finley said as she indicated the cell across the hall.

Uratia nodded, unlocked the cell, and both of them went inside.

"Leave me be," Jano said pathetically.

We are setting you free, Finley said as she swept over and laid a hand on his shoulder.

He didn't even turn to look at them. "I will never be free."

Uratia's face hardened. "Jano, don't you jeopardize this. Eorian worked far too hard to get you out for you to ruin it now."

"Eorian?" Jano repeated as he sat up. "Eorian is here?"

"Not here, no, but we will take you to him," Uratia said. "You must move quickly if you wish to see him."

Jano nodded and slowly got to his feet. Finley helped support him as best she could by providing an air barrier around him. He was quite weak. As they stepped from his cell, they heard the prison guard call down.

"Is she still down there?"

She's here. What was all the ruckus? Finley replied in the voice of the soldier.

"Not sure. Never saw anyone."

Let me check the other cells just to make certain.

"Good idea."

They moved to the base of the stairs and stopped.

"We can't go up," Jano said. "There's a guard."

Patience. We have a plan. Listen.

That was when another series of shouts rang out.

He's got a sword. Help! Help!

Please don't kill me. I'll do anything.

What do you want?

The prison guard shouted back down in alarm. "Stay down there and check all the cells. Someone is free. I'm going to check it out."

They heard his footsteps recede and quickly climbed the stairs.

This way, Finley said as she pulled them to the left. *We have one more flight of stairs, and the door to the outside is at the end of the hall to the left.*

They followed the corridor for several feet before coming across the stairs on the right.

Uratia, you can support Jano?

"I've got him," she said as she threw his arm around her shoulders.

Finley flew to the top of the stairs to survey the area. A bit down the hallway to her right was a cleaning maid. She would need to be forced to look the other way. Finley turned left and flew beneath the door to check outside. As planned, Clim was waiting, and it was a good thing, too, because there were several guards that had an easy view of their escape.

Clim, get their attention elsewhere. We're ready.

Instantly, he glided off to call the soldiers to another area of the castle while Finley returned inside. She flew back down to Uratia and Jano and told them to wait at the top of the stairs until they heard the signal, then they were to hurry down the hall to the left and out the door. Finley waited as they slowly made their way upward, and once they were in place, she flew toward the softly humming maid.

Reaching out a hand, she blew some pollen toward the woman. Her nose crinkled and wiggled, but that was all. Finley blew a bit more pollen her way, and this time the woman sneezed forcefully. She rubbed her nose and shook her head.

"Dust must be getting to me," she muttered as she began wiping down the small table again.

Finley sent more pollen her way, continuing to push it toward her nose relentlessly. Finally, the poor woman began to have a sneezing fit, and she turned to bury her face in her apron to muffle the sound.

That's when Uratia and Jano began hustling toward the door. Finley kept an eye on both parties, sending a bit more pollen toward the maid when she began to straighten a bit, and then the prisoners were free. Finley flew after them.

They were blinking furiously in the sunlight, which was not altogether that bright.

"Where's my son?" Jano asked.

You will need to follow me. We will get you to your son in time.

"Where are you taking us?" he asked tiredly.

Into the woods just a short way from here. There is a cave for you to rest a bit before we continue on.

"Continue on to where?"

To your son's crew.

With that, Finley left a sign on the ground by the door so that the other three wispers would know to rendezvous back at the cave, and then the three of them cautiously left the palace behind.

CHAPTER 19

They had finally found him. It had taken over a month and a lot of manpower, but he was now in their grasp. They could put down this revolution on Faencina for good. Commander Wynedor stepped through the door of the room they were using for interrogations. The golden man within looked quite frightened. This would be easy.

With a smile, Commander Wynedor pulled out a chair and sat down across from Boran.

"Be you comfortable?" he asked congenially.

Boran glanced around the sparse room that hadn't a single window. "Not particularly."

"Thirsty? Hungry? Cold?"

Boran shook his head. "They brought me food earlier."

"Good." The commander folded his hands together on the table and leaned slightly forward. "You understand why you be here, yes?"

"You believe me to be responsible for the trouble around here."

"And be you?" the commander asked.

"The people be acting on their beliefs. Me involvement be not necessary for their continued resistance," Boran responded diplomatically.

"So you admit to being involved?"

Boran said nothing.

The commander leaned back and looked at a point beyond Boran, as if he were speaking to the air instead of the prisoner. "We received intelligence placing you at the head of the revolution. Several people named you as instigator, riling up the country folk with talk of repression and manipulation of the genes of their children. However, I do not believe that. You do not seem to be a man capable of it. What do you think? Could you pull it off?"

The commander returned his intense gaze to Boran.

"Playing to me ego will not work," Boran said.

Commander Wynedor nodded. That had been one unusual outcome in their background on the man. It was quite curious, which made Commander Wynedor think there may be someone above him.

"True. You do not have much of one, do you? We spoke with childhood friends, old teachers, even your estranged brother. Quiet, reclusive, and passive. Those be the words used most often. And yet, here we sit. There be a reason for that. The most logical assumption be that you be a scapegoat. That be a rather terrible position, do you not think?"

Boran's lips tightened for a moment, and he swallowed.

"The scapegoat rarely comes out alive. Estrangement followed by death be the usual outcome. Be you prepared to die, Boran, for something you did not do?"

Boran's eyes darted to the door and then down to the table.

"Look," the commander leaned forward again as if imparting a secret. "I already told you that I don't think you be the mastermind behind this. Level with me. If you do, maybe you will be the scapegoat that beat the odds. What do you say?"

"I say I be dead either way," Boran said.

"What makes you say that?"

Boran closed his lips tightly.

"Be it because of the invisible hand instructing you?" the commander asked.

Boran's head jerked up, his eyes full of surprise as he stared at the commander. "How do you...?"

Clearly, the commander had hit on something, though he wasn't positive what exactly he had said to do that. Best to keep it going, in any case.

"It be me job to know things. However, there be a bit more that I wish to know about this; for instance, I want the name of the man directing you."

"I do not know it," Boran said earnestly.

The commander nodded and gave a comforting smile. "That does not surprise me. Be there anything distinct you could share?"

"He does not..." Boran began and then he stopped. His eyes grew very fearful again, and he visibly began to retreat within himself. "He will kill me."

"You be safe here. He cannot reach you," the commander explained.

Boran shook his head. "He does not have to reach me. He be *here*."

With that, he began beating against the side of his head.

"Whoa, now," the commander shouted in surprise as he leaned forward to grab the man's wrist. "Calm down."

"He always be here, issuing orders. At first, I thought him me friend, but then he made me do things, and he gets so angry. He always comes back. I think I be free, and then he returns. Me thoughts be scrambled; he turns me into someone else, puts words in me mouth."

"Be he in your mind now?" the commander asked worriedly.

"He be always here now. I cannot make him leave."

"Can I speak with him?"

"No, no, no!" the man shouted.

Before the commander's eyes, he began to spiral down into insanity.

"Boran, Boran!" the commander yelled, trying to get the man to look at him.

He grabbed Boran's head with both hands and brought him close so they were almost nose to nose.

"Boran. Think. Tell me what I need to know. What has he done to you?"

"He knew," Boran panted. "He knew when you advanced; he knew when you found; he knew when you captured. He warned not to speak of him. Dire consequences. Memories taken, knowledge lost. He set the trap that I then entered. Gone."

His eyes grew even wilder.

"'Listen, Boran, you must tell me all,'" Boran began again. "'What strange things be occurring? What bad things be the Prime doing? What be a heroshi? Politics, economy, society. So many questions! Listen, Boran; go, Boran; begin, Boran; quiet, Boran.'"

Then his mouth snapped shut, his eyes glazed over, and he began rocking back and forth.

"Boran?" the commander shook him slightly with no response. "Boran."

Slowly, the commander released the man and sat back with a sigh.

That had been so completely unexpected, and he had learned absolutely nothing. He had not gotten a name to verify their suspicion, and the revolutionaries would probably be even more incensed now that their leader was...what exactly? He was alive, but he could no longer function. They would all assume the royals were responsible.

"How did this go so very wrong?" the commander asked aloud.

Then he stood and rapped on the door. The guards outside opened it, and he left the room.

"Get him some help," the commander ordered.

"Sir?" one guard questioned.

The commander whirled around, his anger over the past few minutes overcoming him. "Medical attention be needed swiftly, and you take the time to question me? Look at the man in there and tell me he be all right. Do you know nothing, man?"

The guard straightened, saluted, and rushed off. The other guard simply tried not to draw attention to himself. However, the commander's mind had already jumped elsewhere as something clicked into place.

"So many questions..." the commander muttered. "About things all mermaids know. What be a heroshi?"

"Do you need me to answer that, sir?" the nervous guard asked haltingly.

"What?" the commander asked as he focused in on him. "No, no."

Then his face contorted to one of dread as he remembered Luik's mention of the essence of darkness who could get into a man's head. "They be right. It be him."

"Who?" the guard said in confusion.

"Dehga."

"I don't know what to do."

Fil's brows drew together in confusion. "Come again?"

"You heard me the first time, Fil."

"But...this is what you do! You are never out of ideas."

"I am now. Do any of you have a brilliant solution?"

Eorian looked at each face in turn. Frelati and Genevia began thinking through scenarios intently, Diahyas looked bewildered, and Fil was still focused on the fact that Eorian was asking for help.

"What do you expect us to come up with that you haven't already?" he asked.

"Fil." Eorian rubbed his brow. "You do realize that I am not the only one with ideas aboard my ship, right? Gallutam and Burk are greatly instrumental, and even Lius with his very different outlook on life has come up with some interesting suggestions. Each of you has experiences that could give us an idea that I would never think up, which is why I ask the question: do you have any solutions?"

Fil shrugged. "I don't."

"Thanks, Fil, that's very helpful."

"We don't know this culture very well, so it's difficult to anticipate how they will respond to things," Frelati said.

"Diahyas can help there," Eorian said as he sent a smile her way.

She nodded. "I can certainly help...if I can. I be not convinced that me subjects think in the same way that I do."

"Luik would, though," Genevia said thoughtfully. "By the way, where is he? That commander brought the bands to us, but Luik wasn't with him. I know he was supposed to be helping get information on the revolutionaries, but have you heard directly from him recently?"

Eorian nodded. "Yes, he contacts me periodically...mainly to check on Diahyas. He's playing a dangerous game right now, though, so he can't be in touch too often."

"When did you hear from him last?" Genevia asked.

"Maybe three days ago, and he actually had some decent news. It seems there are a few revolutionaries that are defecting...although, they may join back up if Boran is replaced."

There was silence after that, and Eorian hurried to break it. "So... ideas. What do you have?"

Fil looked to Diahyas, who looked to Frelati.

Frelati shrugged. "This isn't really my forte. I can plan out fights fairly well, but trying to convince people of things...I'm not a people person."

"Genevia?" Eorian asked in a voice that was close to pleading. "You're good with people."

Genevia bit her lip. "Individually, I suppose I am. When you get into group mentality, it starts to get convoluted."

"I just need something to start with. How can we convince the mermaids that this revolution was started by a foreigner? Someone who simply wishes to rule over them any way he can."

They all avoided his gaze.

"Come on," Eorian said.

Finally, Genevia gave in. "All right, I have an idea, but it may not help."

Eorian grinned. "I'll take anything right now."

"We need to talk to Asben."

Eorian blinked. "Who?"

Frelati smiled. "You're right, Genevia. I should have thought of it."

"Asben is a brilliant friend of ours on Tiweln. It's possible that he won't be able to help, but I'd be willing to bet he's read about situations like these and can come up with a good solution," Genevia explained.

"And you know that he'd love to get a look at this place," Frelati said with a chuckle.

Eorian was nodding slowly as he mulled it over.

"I know that going to Tiweln is not anything that you had in mind, but you wouldn't have to go. Frelati and I would be perfectly willing..."

"Actually," Eorian interrupted. "It works quite well into my plans. I had hoped you would allow me to travel with you to Tiweln so that we could perhaps try to convince more people to fight with us on Randor. Now we'll have two purposes."

"And if we're all going, then we won't have to stay as long because we'll have three of those portals to transport us," Fil pointed out. "No waiting on recharges."

"I believe I would enjoy seeing this planet Tiweln," Diahyas said. "New places be quite exciting."

"All right, it's settled then," said Eorian. "We'll let Luik and the commander know what's happening, and then we'll start our journey."

"Eorian. Respond."

Every startled eye stared at Eorian's band.

"Uh...this is Eorian."

"Commander Wynedor. I have important information for you."

Eorian chuckled a bit at the irony. "We were just about to call you. We have something..."

"Boran has gone insane," the commander interrupted him.

"As opposed to how incredibly sane he was when he started the revolution?" Eorian asked a bit sarcastically after a brief pause.

"No. You misunderstand," the commander said tersely. "He be literally insane. One minute, he be fine as I interrogated him, and the next…"

Eorian waited a moment for him to continue.

"It be very strange," the commander concluded. "Had I not witnessed it…but he said something during his rantings."

"Which was?"

"He spoke of some other man, someone in his head asking questions. I had not thought much of it, but he also said the man asked what a heroshi be…"

"Yeah, those are the horse-dragon things that pull your carriages, right? We met one named Bigs."

The commander seemed to pull in a deep breath. "Your response further verifies me beliefs. There be no beings on Faencina that know not of heroshi. Only someone not of this world would ask such a thing. When paired with the mental breakdown and his speaking of someone in his mind…I remember Luik saying that the essence of darkness could control one's mind. Be this true?"

"Unfortunately. That's what makes him so incredibly dangerous."

"And you believe this essence of darkness to be Dehga?"

"It *is* Dehga," Eorian stressed. "I knew the moment I saw him because I am fighting with him on my own planet."

"It be difficult for me, but I believe I made an error in not believing you initially. I intend to right this wrong. I be going to speak with the Prime and Prime-Mate about him, but I wished to tell you beforehand, just in case."

"I'm not sure talking to them is a good idea. They could very easily tell him your suspicions," Eorian cautioned.

"It be me duty to warn the Prime of all potential dangers," the commander argued.

"Sure, but doing it this way is too dangerous. You may want to wait—"

"No, the Prime must be told immediately," the commander interrupted stubbornly.

"All right…but whatever you do, don't talk to them with Dehga around," Eorian warned.

"Understood."

"We will be gone for a short while...by that I mean, we will be on another planet. We won't be able to help you; you're sure you don't want to wait?"

"No. Time be essential. Safe travels."

"Thanks, and good luck to you," Eorian said just before the commander clicked off. He faced the group. "Now to message Luik, and we'll be on our way."

Ancient and beautiful trees were scattered all around. Beneath them grew deep purple, red, and blue flowers with vibrant, yellow centers and thick, green leaves. Along the dirt path that lazily ambled through the forest were bright patches of sunlight where happy, little flower faces opened up to create mini-rainbows on the ground.

It was quite a serene and majestic picture. Then the animals started peeking out curiously. There were some tall, camouflaged creatures keeping behind the trees as they scrutinized the newcomers. Small, furry creatures with long snouts snuffled along the ground, pausing to look up at their visitors periodically before starting back on the search for food.

Finally, the music of the birds started up. It was a glorious sound to hear, and as the feathered musicians flew from tree to tree, their brilliant colors flashed in the sunlight, creating a mesmerizing display.

"It's this way," Genevia said as she pointed up the path.

Slowly, each of the foreigners to the planet tore their eyes from the spectacle around them and followed her. They walked along the path for a quarter of a mile before the forest opened up a bit to reveal a beautiful and interesting castle.

Unlike most regal structures, this large building did not overwhelm its surroundings or instantly grab one's attention because of its sheer contrast with the landscape. Instead, the palace seemed to be a part of the earth and trees and stones. The architects had quite cleverly used every aspect of the hill to its fullest when creating their masterpiece.

A swift river ran around its base, serving as a moat of sorts, and a bridge intricately carved out of one large stone arched from bank to bank. Once the bridge was crossed, a magnificent, wide-spread tree welcomed them at the base of the hill. This tree was unlike any other tree in the forest. Its trunk was so large that a human could not see all of it without turning the head both right and left, and its branches were wide enough that small houses could easily be built atop them…in fact, there were some structures built on a few of them.

Built into the foot of the large tree were tall double doors. A few sparkling gems had been encrusted in them, but it did not detract from the overall natural feel. In fact, the truck was decorated all around with vines yielding colorful flowers of all kinds.

"This is beautiful," Fil breathed. "You live in a tree; how elf-like is that?!"

"Well, the rooms are actually beneath the hill. The tree is reserved for the public places like the ballroom, dining hall, and library," Frelati explained. "They built an open courtyard between the tree and the hill to serve as the transition between the two; although there is also a tunnel below ground that can be used as well."

"It be so very grand," Diahyas said. "Me castle pales in comparison."

Genevia laughed. "I'm quite certain it doesn't."

"You're right, Genevia, it doesn't," Eorian agreed. "It's just *very* different from this. I have never seen anything remotely like it."

Genevia's cheeks turned slightly pink with her pleasure.

"Come," she said excitedly. "We'll show you around."

Eorian had been wondering how exactly she was going to open the gigantic doors that towered over her, but she did not walk toward the great doors. Instead, she moved to the left and pulled on a loose vine hanging down at her level. To his surprise, a small door folded inward in a move similar to a petal falling back as a flower opened. A faint, warm light glowed from within. Genevia walked inside, and Frelati motioned them forward.

"After you," he said with a smile.

Each of their guests ambled along after Genevia, who walked down a short hallway and then up some winding stairs. At the top, everything opened up into a grand welcoming hall, complete with a chandelier. This light source was unique as well and perfectly matched all around it. The base near the ceiling was a deep, luminescent green in the shape of leaves.

The rest of the chandelier formed petal after petal of an ever-changing colorful flower. The artistry of it almost convinced the eye that it was a living, glowing plant. It both slowly changed color, from vibrant red, to soft pink, to vivid orange, to pale yellow, and so on throughout the spectrum, and also changed shape from being a mere bud to a full-blown blossom.

"I can't decide if that's alive or not," Fil said. "Is it?"

Genevia chuckled. "I said the same thing when I first saw it! But no, it's not."

"Do we get a tour first?" Diahyas asked. "Or must we conduct business up front?"

"Frelati?" Genevia asked.

"Half a tour now, business, dinner, and then the rest of the tour before bed?" he offered.

"Suits me just fine," Eorian agreed.

"Really?" Fil asked incredulously.

Eorian chuckled self-mockingly. "I know usually I wouldn't agree to it, but what I've seen so far is absolutely amazing. I think we deserve a break to take it all in."

Genevia clapped her hands together happily. "Where should we start?"

Frelati raised a brow. "I believe we should start by calling the girls down. You know they won't forgive us for excluding them."

"Oh! Right!" Genevia said as she looked all around. "Now, where… ah!"

With a grin she raced over to a large horn-like contraption by the top of some fancy stairs that led up from the great doors. Eorian assumed that those must only be used for special occasions. Genevia grasped the large horn in both hands, sucked in a deep breath, and then blew two short blasts and a long one. All the guests instantly covered their ears, seeing Frelati's huge grin at their shock. He had covered his ears ahead of time without bothering to warn them.

Genevia bounded back over, and both she and Frelati stared at a hallway leading off to the right of the great hall. A few minutes passed without a sound.

"Is something supposed to be happening?" Fil finally asked.

"Give it a bit longer," Frelati said. "The castle is large, and knowing the girls, they had to run back to their room to grab something before coming to meet us."

"Who be these girls?" Diahyas asked.

That's when they heard the tapping of feet running down the hall. Even before the source of the sound could be seen, a great shout came ringing forward to greet them.

"Papa! Mama!"

Frelati knelt, just barely getting his arms open enough to allow a young girl to rush inside. Genevia was engulfed around the midsection by a shadow-like creature.

"You were gone so long!" the shadow accused. "You said it recharged in two weeks."

"I know, Dayze. I'm sorry. We hadn't expected to run into friends while there. They needed our help," Genevia explained as she brushed a bit of the girl's gray, wispy hair back.

"Look, Papa," the elf child said as she popped from his arms to display a sheaf of papers. "Dayze and I wrote a story. It has pictures and everything. Captain Traynord sewed the pages together for us, see? So you can flip through more easily, just like the books in the library!"

"That is absolutely beautiful," Frelati praised each of them. "How about we read through it tonight before bed?"

Both girls nodded excitedly.

"For now, we have guests," Frelati said as he straightened. "And they want a tour of our lovely home. I told them I knew the best two tour guides around. Lela, Dayze, do you think you could help me out?"

"Yes!" both girls exclaimed happily.

Lela bounded over to Eorian and Fil, grabbing their hands to pull them along with her up front. Dayze glided over to Diahyas.

"You are beautiful," she said.

"Yes, I..." Diahyas began before giving the girl a warm smile. "Thank you. I believe you be beautiful too."

Dayze grinned up at her and offered a hand. "Do you want to walk with me?"

Diahyas nodded and took her hand. "I be delighted to do so."

Genevia and Frelati shared a smile over the success of this introduction. If only everything else could be so easy.

CHAPTER 20

"Me Prime," Commander Wynedor said with a bow.

The Prime, who found herself rather bored this morning, waved the commander forward. Perhaps he could liven things up a bit.

"Be the Prime-Mate nearby?" the commander asked.

The Prime sighed. "He be with Dehga and the scientists discussing solutions for our reproduction problem. The humans can help future generations, but this current age of children will still have an issue that needs to be corrected…if possible."

"You did not wish to join them?"

"Science be tedious," the Prime replied with a wave of her hand. "What be you wanting?"

"It be…sensitive."

"As you see, we be alone," the Prime said as she opened her arms to encompass the room. "The servants be grating on me nerves so I sent them away."

The commander nodded in such a way that she felt he was merely appeasing her. That did not improve her mood any.

"Go on, then," she snapped.

The commander paused just a beat before speaking. "You know that we captured Boran yesterday morning, and I interrogated him that afternoon."

"Yes," Bailena said as she leaned forward in her seat. "And what information did he yield?"

"Unexpected information, me Prime."

"Helpful, I hope."

The commander's gesture was quite noncommittal. The Prime sighed. "Let's hear it."

"I request that you please allow me to describe everything to the end before you begin asking questions," he said slowly.

"You think me so rude as to interrupt you?" the Prime asked, completely affronted by the insult.

"Trust me, me Prime, you will understand me request as you listen. I mean no offense."

Something about his manner as he said that calmed her entirely and further intrigued her. Perhaps the morning would end on a better note than it had started.

She listened as he described the interrogation. It was quite odd that the man would suddenly lose his sanity. She began to have questions, just to verify some things, and realized then that the commander's request had indeed been necessary. However, he continued by going back to a meeting that had occurred over a month prior, back when she and the Prime-Mate had been staying in that pathetic, little cottage in the primitive Yuen village. Apparently, he had learned of their location through a young man who was employed at the palace. She would have to ask his name to reward him.

At the time, the man had said that he had met Boran at a meeting. The Prime also wished to ask why the boy had attended such a meeting. This young man had since been quite helpful in sharing information about the revolutionaries and instrumental in the capture of Boran. Although the Prime was still intrigued, she began to wonder where all of this was leading.

That's when the commander finally began to connect the dots. It was at that first meeting, he informed her, that the young man had said something meaningful, something that the commander had disregarded at the time as misinformation. The Prime, who had been relaxed back in her chair, moved to the very edge of the seat and leaned forward.

"We know that Diahyas be Kiem's essence of water."

"Yes," the Prime agreed in confusion. So many jumps the man was making.

"This young man told me that the essence of darkness was causing the revolution."

"You be saying the essence of darkness resides on this planet as well?"

the Prime asked, completely forgetting his request.

He sent her a look of weak chastisement, and she instantly realized her mistake. She huffed and sat back in her throne.

"He did not say that the essence of darkness resides here. He merely said that he be the cause of the revolution," the commander explained. "According to this young man, the essence of darkness has the unique ability to get inside your head...speak to you, convince you of things, or...break you."

The Prime's eyes widened. "He be the cause of Boran's mental state!"

The commander nodded. "That be the conclusion I came to as well. However, since the young man appeared to be right on that point, I now have to assume he be correct on the other point, which I absolutely refused to hear that day."

The commander pulled in a deep breath. "Please think on me next statement a moment before you react."

Now the Prime was nervous. She had a feeling deep in her gut that what she was about to hear would change everything. She gave the commander a nod.

"This young man gave me the name of the essence of darkness. We know who he be and where he be."

"He must be imprisoned then. I will not have a traitor in me midst," the Prime stated angrily, already running through all of the individuals of her court to determine who might be the culprit. "What be his name?"

Again, the commander took a deep breath. "Dehga."

The Prime blinked. She opened her mouth to ask...she closed her mouth again as she realized she had no idea which question should come first. That action was repeated twice more before she finally got something out.

"Dehga?"

The commander nodded.

"How...?" The Prime paused, knowing she needed to better phrase her question. "How could the boy know this? What proof has he?"

"*He* has no proof. He be relaying the information," the commander said carefully.

Now the questions were coming quickly. "Relaying the information from whom?"

"You remember me saying that we had found Diahyas and that we be keeping her in a secret location far from here just in case somehow the revolutionaries capture the capital?"

"Do not tell me this be a lie," the Prime said angrily.

"No! No, it be no lie," the commander said hurriedly. "However, there be some additional information that may have been withheld."

"Explain," the Prime said angrily.

"You remember telling me of the two other humans that took Diahyas away?"

"They have her?"

"Well, yes and no. She be *with* them, and with two other creatures not of our world. I met them and strategized with them to help retrieve you from the Yuen camp. The yellow-haired human you saw be the essence of air, and one of the other creatures, she be essence of earth. They be more good to Diahyas than me army."

"We now have three additional essences on our planet? How do we know these other two be not conspiring with the essence of darkness and merely be placing the blame on Dehga?"

"I suppose that could be the case," the commander allowed. "But I did think of it, and I find it unlikely. They recognized him when they grabbed Diahyas. He be causing a war on one of their planets, and they be needing reinforcements. That partially be why they be helping us to defeat the revolutionaries. You must admit, Dehga be strange, and he does not look quite as the other two humans did. According to Eorian, the human with power over air, Dehga be not from his planet but yet another planet, and he has tried to cause this trouble on one other planet besides—the one that the essence of earth inhabits."

"I find this all suspect. If Diahyas be with these creatures, she has told them of her betrothal. This be her attempt to halt the mating," the Prime argued stubbornly.

The commander's face fell. "Me Prime, I do not believe..."

"Enough! I must have proof of this. Dehga states he be the ruler on Randor. This other human states that Dehga be a mere usurper causing wars and strife on other planets. For all we know, it be the other way around."

"Perhaps if you met them..." the commander began.

"I shall, in due time, but I require me proof first. I shall not confront Dehga with such flimsy accusations. He be the salvation of this planet;

we *need* his good will. Only with irrefutable proof shall I break off this betrothal...although, it seems to me, either way Faencina be doomed."

It had been quite marvelous to sleep on a proper bed again. Diahyas felt better than she had for over a month now. She stretched as she stood and walked over to the curtained window. As she pulled the fabric back, bright sunlight hit her full force. She blinked.

"I must have slept quite a long time," she observed softly as she focused out at the scenery beyond.

The view that met her was lovely. Her room was up close to the top of the hill, on the backside, and she could see, far below, the stream amble along. There was a garden directly beneath her at the castle's base, and then trees began again. Perhaps she could walk through the garden before they left.

She turned away and grabbed for the jug of water that she had requested be left in her room. She was beyond parched. Once half of the large jug was empty, she moved to the door and opened it. A smile spread across her face when she saw a picture had been attached to the outside of it. Dayze's signature graced the bottom, left-hand corner of the paper that held quite a good picture of Diahyas and Dayze together before the gigantic tree that formed half of the castle. Carefully, Diahyas rolled it up and stashed it in her small bag before heading downstairs.

On their tour the night before, Genevia and Frelati had pointed out the breakfast room, and they made certain that everyone knew how to get there the following morning. Diahyas's stomach rumbled at the thought of food. Hopefully, they still had some breakfast out...and if she was really lucky, it would be something she would eat. Diahyas paused mid-stride. Dinner last night had been quite interesting. Everything had been so different from meals she was used to at home. Some of them had been quite enjoyable, especially the dessert of chocolate, but there had also been some questionable items that she did not care for, mainly those of the vegetable variety.

It would be an adventure, she decided as she continued on. Today, they were going to see Traynord, the old sailor she had met in her youth. According to Genevia, he always told the best stories; although, Diahyas doubted they would get to hear any. They were going there on business. Traynord lived in a human town, when he wasn't out on his boat, anyway, and they were planning to speak with him about gathering possible volunteers for the war on Randor. His was the closest location they were traveling to, a place called Wilksom Olem, so it was the first stop.

After the first half of the tour the prior afternoon, they had gone to see the king and queen of the elves. The two had been quite nice, which surprised Diahyas immensely. Her parents were nothing like this, giving hugs, sharing smiles, and genuinely listening when their daughter spoke with them. It was so very foreign that Diahyas had been enthralled just watching them. She actually didn't remember much of what had transpired when they visited with the elf rulers, but she did remember the conversation they had after dinner in the room full of books and maps.

Frelati had pulled out a very impressive specimen from the latter collection and spread it out on the table. Its edges were held down by great tomes, and all five of them crowded around to examine the world of Tiweln. Frelati had described each place they would need to visit, and they had drawn up a step-by-step plan for their travels, the first stop of which she was quite excited about. She and the sailor would be unable to speak the same language, but with Genevia translating, it should be quite a pleasant visit.

Diahyas grinned as she walked down the final hallway to the breakfast room. She heard laughter from within and eagerly pushed through the doors. All of her party was there with plates half empty.

"Look who finally decided to join us," Eorian said with a smirk.

"Did you sleep well?" Genevia asked in concern. "I know it must be different from what you are used to."

Diahyas nodded. "It be very different, yes, but it be marvelous to relax into soft bedding. I slept quite well, thank you."

Frelati swept out an arm toward the sideboard. "The food is all ready. Grab a plate, select what you like, and eat up."

Diahyas followed his instructions; however, once it came time to select the food, she found herself at a complete loss. Funny looking yellow lumps, tan rounded things with dark blobs splotching them, strips of brown-ish red that looked like some type of meat. She grabbed the last one, feeling it to be safer than the rest, and continued down the line, growing more and more overwhelmed at the sight of each new and unusual food.

She heard a chair scrape back, and Eorian walked over to the sideboard. He started dipping up some yellow lumps.

"This food is fantastic, Genevia," he said. "It's been a while since I've had food this good; hope you don't mind me getting seconds."

Genevia laughed. "I'm sure Frelati will be joining you over there in just a minute."

Eorian glanced at Diahyas's plate. "What? No eggs?"

Diahyas was quite certain her confusion showed on her face, along with a tinge of embarrassment.

Eorian's eyes widened in understanding. "I am so sorry! I hadn't realized. This is all foreign to you. That's why you didn't eat much last night. Here, I'll put some of my favorites on your plate, you try them, and we'll go from there. Sound good?"

With relief, Diahyas nodded, and Eorian quickly loaded her plate with what he said was eggs, a blueberry muffin, grits, and toast with jelly. He also generously grabbed multiples of each for himself before they headed back to the table. Just before she sat down, he pointed to the beverages behind her.

"Are you familiar with milk, orange juice, tea, coffee?" he asked.

"Babies drink mother's milk, but adults drink only water...although, on very special occasions, there be a liquid created from one specific type of urchin that be quite delightful. It be difficult to make correctly, so not many supply it."

"I'll have to try it sometime," Eorian said. "However, today, you get to try a lot of different types of liquid."

He walked over to the beverage table and filled four different cups with a little of each drink and then placed them before Diahyas.

"These two are cold, and these two are hot. The hot drinks can be very bitter, so if you don't like the taste initially, we will try them with some cream and sugar."

Diahyas nodded, feeling a bit overwhelmed by it all. They had so very many choices here. However, as she tried everything, she began to understand Eorian's excitement about it all. The food truly was fantastic. The dinners served at her home in the palace were not terrible by any means, and they did have some variety, but the different types of fish did tend to taste somewhat the same, and there was only so much one could do with seaweed. Eel was disgusting, though there were many that enjoyed it. All in all, it was the variety that they seemed to be lacking... and perhaps the seasonings.

They soon finished breakfast and headed to their rooms to pack. Frelati and Genevia said their goodbyes to two tearful, young girls and the king and queen. Then they used Genevia's necklace to pop over to Wilksom Olem.

Diahyas had been expecting another place similar to the elves' home, but this was a lot more similar to a Yuen village...just a bit less primitive. Traynord's home was quite small and near the water. He answered the door quickly and gave Genevia and Frelati a huge grin when he saw them. As expected, Diahyas did not understand most of what was said, but he seemed to agree to ask around Wilksom Olem for volunteers. Genevia told her that Traynord knew some roughnecks who were always looking for a fight, so he was sure he could find a few allies.

He was informed of the rendezvous point on Wefleca, near the natural portal, and then the conversation moved on to more pleasant things. They stayed the night with him, hearing fantastic tales — all of which were translated by Genevia — and the next morning, they moved on. The next stop was Rom, the home of Jezzie and Asben. They had rebuilt after a fire burned down their original dwelling. Asben, the genius who was to end the war on Faencina, greeted them warmly and took a particular interest in Diahyas. He ushered them into his library, which he informed them was much larger and grander than the original had been. Fortunately for the foreigners on Tiweln, Asben had picked up a lot of the Elven language, so they could actually speak with one another.

"Fascinating," Asben said after Eorian had complimented him on his library. "It is just as you said, Genevia. Other worlds do speak the same ancient language of the elves. There is a difference of accent, I see, but... fascinating!"

He turned to Diahyas. "Would you please be so kind as to say something as well?"

"Umm...thank you for welcoming us into your home. I also believe your library to be quite magnificent. I be Diahyas; it be a pleasure to meet you."

Asben's grin grew even wider, which Diahyas had not believed to be possible.

"Another accent! Fascinating! And, I'm sure you all heard it as well, she does not use the 'be' verbs as we do. Instead of is and are and were, she appears to be using only the word be. Interesting. Are there any other words that you've noticed have a variation?"

"My," Eorian said. "They all use the word me in place of it."

Asben's eyes turned to Diahyas again. "Could you please demonstrate?"

"This be me tiara?" she said hesitantly.

"Fascinating!" Asben said excitedly. "But you did not come here for me to gawk. What can I do for you?"

"Actually, I think this will be mutually beneficial," Frelati said.

"It does involve rather distant travel, though, so you may want to speak with Jezzie before you give us an answer. Where is she, by the way?" Genevia asked.

Asben grinned. "Where she always is, my dear. The bakery. However, I can summon her with this new invention of mine. Come, take a look."

He waved them over to the door, where a contraption with a handle protruding from it had been built into the wall.

"I...crank..." Asben said with a puff as he began to demonstrate. "This handle here. And...whew...a current is created through the... pipes...running along the...walls...and ceiling, see?"

He stopped cranking the machine and pointed to the bit of pipe that they could see. "The current hits a funnel that makes a whistling sound as the air is pushed through, and that whistle sounds through a vent in the bakery, so she knows to meet me here in the library."

He adjusted his glasses and turned to the foreign visitors. "The bakery adjoins our home, you see."

"That's quite handy," Eorian said thoughtfully as he studied the invention, and Asben swelled with pride.

"There are several adjustments I need to make. For instance, making it easier to crank, but for now, this rather crude design is quite effective." He paused to listen to the footsteps nearing the library. "Ah, here she comes now."

And in came a flour-covered, aproned, middle-aged woman. There were a few gray hairs amongst the brown that surrounded a surprisingly youthful face. Sadly, Diahyas was unable to understand her language, but her actions spoke so clearly it was almost unnecessary for the translation that Frelati and Genevia gave.

"Oh, my dears!" she greeted happily as she rushed to give Frelati and Genevia each a welcoming hug. "You've been gone far too long. And look how thin ya are! Don't you leave without some bread, ya hear? How long are ya stayin?"

"Of course," Frelati said dutifully. "And we'll be here until tomorrow afternoon, I imagine."

Then Jezzie turned to the other guests in her home. Genevia translated for Eorian and Fil, much to Jezzie's delight. "My! Look at these two strapping, young fellas! So handsome. I bet ya both turn the girls' heads, but the two of you need fattening up as well. You be sure to tell them that, Genevia."

The two shifted a bit in embarrassment as Genevia finished.

Jezzie turned to wag a finger at Frelati and Genevia. "You make sure they eat the bread I'm gonna give 'em."

Genevia smiled and nodded.

Finally, Jezzie focused on Diahyas and offered both of her hands. After a second's pause, Diahyas placed her own hands within the flour-covered, strong and slightly chubby ones. Again, Genevia quickly translated the woman's words.

"You are quite a lovely, young lady," she said. "Look at the color of your skin. What I would give for that! Blue is my favorite color, you know. Oh! And look there at those little sea creatures swimming about in your hair! Asben, have you ever seen the like?"

"No, dear," he said with great affection. "She is from another planet. All three are."

"Another planet! My, but you've traveled far," Jezzie exclaimed. "You must all be famished. Let me fix you up some goodies."

She was just about to bustle from the room when Asben stopped her.

"Dear, Genevia and Frelati have come to request my help with something, and I imagine it will involve travel away from Tiweln. I am correct in this, yes?" He turned to Frelati for verification, who nodded. "Yes, well, that will involve me being away from Tiweln for at least two weeks."

"That travel has always seemed dangerous to me, Asben," Jezzie said cautiously with a frown. Then she turned to Frelati and Genevia with a twinkle in her eyes. "However, I am quite certain they would not take you from my side if not for a very good reason, so if I would be permitted to spend two weeks with my goddaughters while you are away, I may give my approval."

Genevia laughed happily. "They would love to see you! But you had better not spoil them too much."

"I would never," Jezzie said with a wink. "All right, I'll leave all of you. I'm sure you've got some scheming to discuss, and I need to get back to the bakery. Asben, you be sure they get back by dinner time."

"Of course, dear," he agreed.

Then Jezzie hustled off. Diahyas was sorry to see her go even though she couldn't understand a word she said. She really liked the affectionate woman. After that, Frelati and Eorian explained a bit of what would be expected of Asben, and they asked him who they would need to speak to on Rom about recruiting fighters. Asben thought just a moment before sharing a name and taking them to meet the man.

Eorian, Fil, and Diahyas waited outside while the other three spoke with the leader of the city. They all decided it would be too confusing for everyone to be there with the language barrier. Genevia and Frelati summed up as they walked back to Asben's house. Apparently, the leader had agreed to send a few men, assuming they were willing, and he would speak with leaders of other cities on Rom. They all remembered the terrible treatment of Fezam and feared that he would return.

Just after lunch the following day, they gathered Asben, his books, and all of Jezzie's goodies and headed off to the dwarf undergrounds on Yima Olem. Pilloop, an old friend of Genevia and Frelati, welcomed them gruffly, but that had been the only good thing about the trip. The dwarf king was non-committal, as Frelati had expected, and Genevia was sorely disappointed.

"They were so happy about me being the essence of earth the last time we were here, and yet all they did to help was send Pilloop to guide us through the tunnels. We saved them from Fezam! They owe us *something*," Genevia lamented that evening.

Frelati sighed as he wrapped his arm about her shoulders. "They are a closed community. The fact that he offered any help at all is amazing. At least he allowed us to stay here a few nights while the necklace recharges."

That did not cheer Genevia, but as unhappy as she was with the dwarves, she was not particularly looking forward to leaving for their next destination.

Suta had been the location chosen, the land of the nomads. Diahyas and her five companions popped up right beside Quiz, the nomad leader, who nearly had a heart attack at their sudden appearance. He exchanged some choice words with Frelati before Asben stepped in to quiet them. The big, burly man listened intently and thought for a while before responding. Genevia explained to Eorian, Fil, and Diahyas after they had left that he said it would be difficult for him to send members of his family to a foreign war to fight a man that, although terrible, had never succeeded in harming any of the nomads. Asben had argued that Fezam had certainly tried to locate them, and had he succeeded, Quiz may no longer have anyone to call family. In the end, Quiz requested the location from which they would leave Tiweln to travel to Randor, and he said if he changed his mind, he would show himself at the appointed time. He then offered them two tents for the evening, which had been unexpected but quite nice.

After their time on Suta, they traveled to Lonyi. This place had many large trees in a very well-kept forest. There were two people in particular that Frelati and Genevia were trying to meet up with, twins named Sizzle and Slice. Although the words were foreign, the exchange between the two men and between them and the elves was quite amusing. They also kept changing into one thing or another. Sizzle even morphed into Diahyas and sidled over to stand beside her. He gave a bow, morphed back into himself, kissed her hand, and then re-joined the conversation with Frelati and his brother. Diahyas imagined he had left because of the rather fierce look Eorian had sent his way.

The twins were quite enthusiastic about another fight against evil. They agreed to round up whatever other shapeshifters they could, if any, and they would join in the fight. Then they showed the travelers to a small, cozy inn to stay the night.

That evening, Frelati and Genevia discussed trying other places. Pixies were mentioned, but neither of the elves thought that involving them would be good. The dragons were mere animals here, unreliable and untrustworthy. They had no contacts with any of the humans on other continents, and they were hoping that word of mouth would work to gather more people. The elves were already all signed on to help. With that decided, they traveled back to the beautiful castle on Meufa, where they had marvelous food and comfortable beds for another five nights before leaving to continue the fight on Faencina.

CHAPTER 21

It was always fun to be met with terrible news after a short vacation. It seemed that both the commander and Luik had been waiting for Eorian's band to become accessible again because Eorian had not been back on Faencina more than five minutes before they both tried to hail him.

"Eorian!" came Luik's frantic call. "Thank goodness you be back!"

"Eorian, we have a situation that must be discussed."

"Luik, do you mind waiting a moment while I speak with the commander?" Eorian asked.

"This be *important*," Luik stressed.

Eorian frowned. "Commander, do *you* mind waiting a moment while I speak with Luik?"

"You do not understand the gravity of the situation," he said.

"Great. Inform me in five minutes," Eorian said before switching over to Luik. "All right, Luik, go ahead."

"She be missing, me aunt, and I think the revolutionaries took her."

Eorian did not completely follow. "Do you think they found out you were helping the royals?"

"I don't know; I don't think so. They haven't tried to do anything to *me*. I think they be hoping she knows the whereabouts of Diahyas."

"Can you find out where she is?" he asked.

"I don't think so. Everyone I speak with does not seem to know."

"Luik, calm down," Eorian said evenly. "We will find her. You keep checking with your contacts, discretely. I'll talk with the commander and see if he knows anything. Are you positive that she didn't take a vacation somewhere or that she isn't taking care of a sick friend?"

"I…" Luik paused. "I suppose I do not know that. She never mentioned a vacation, not to a soul in the family, and she *always* does that because she wishes someone to take care of her precious cuttlefish. When I visited her home, the cuttlefish had not been fed for a while. That be not like Aunt Sea-Sea."

Eorian sighed. "All right, well, try to inquire a bit more amongst her friends, and as I said, check around with the revolutionaries. I'll get the commander to search for her as well. We'll be in touch."

He closed the channel with Luik and switched over to another. "Commander."

"Present."

"Have you heard about Luik's Aunt Sea-ena?"

"No. How be this relevant?"

"Later," Eorian said. "Tell me your news."

"The Prime refuses to do anything about Dehga without proof that he be the mastermind. She states that you could just as easily be the one plotting against us. You must discover a way to convince her."

"Oh, lovely."

Yet another challenge to overcome before possibly getting the mermaids aid.

"All right, well can you inquire after Sea-ena? Luik's aunt, who also happens to be Diahyas's ladies maid, is missing. Luik believes the revolutionaries may have kidnapped her to get information about Diahyas."

"This be disturbing news. I will do me best to locate the woman."

"I'll be in touch."

With that, Eorian shut off his band and walked off to the deliver the unfortunate news to the rest of the group. As expected, Diahyas took Sea-ena's absence terribly. She was shouting about sending armies to trample the revolutionary troops until they revealed Sea-ena's whereabouts. It took quite a few minutes to calm her down.

Asben shifted his glasses higher up on his nose. "It appears there are quite a few problems present on this planet. I am not certain that I am the right person to help you."

"We've run out of options, Asben," Frelati said. "You are our best bet. I'm sure there's something in all those books of yours that could be of use."

"Perhaps…" Asben began flipping rapidly through one entitled *Strategies of Wars Past.* "If I remember correctly, there was one war on Tiweln over three hundred years ago in which a woman was manipulating a human king. He had several advisors who tried to warn him of the destruction the woman was causing, but he beheaded each one for treason…at her request, of course. Finally, one man decided to trick the woman into telling the king of her evil machinations. I can't quite recall all of the details, but his plan did work, the king executed the woman, and the war was ended. From what you have told me thus far, we could employ something similar to reveal Dehga to both this Prime person and the revolutionaries. Unfortunately, I'm afraid it will not be much good for locating Sea-ena. My apologies, Diahyas."

She nodded sadly.

"Tell us what we need to do; we'll do whatever you think best," Eorian said.

Dehga was not particularly pleased with how the war was going. The revolutionaries were beginning to get discouraged without Boran to bolster their spirits. Dehga had not yet located a suitable replacement either since the commander and his patrols were greatly limiting his movements. Dehga had not decided whether or not the commander was suspicious of him; either way, it may be best to dispatch of the man soon. He was bound to cause more trouble.

Another unfortunate development was the security measures put in place for Diahyas. She had been secreted away according to the Prime and Prime-Mate, but Dehga knew that Eorian had taken her off the planet. Perhaps he should journey back to Randor and flush them out. Then again, if he was wrong and Diahyas was still here somewhere, they would definitely try to undermine him while he was away.

Dehga once again considered jumping into the princess's mind, but he still remembered the chaos he had encountered the first time, and then there was her strange ability to create walls to block his access. It was as if someone had taught her to fight him, and he began to worry that she could find a way into his mind. Once the door was opened, it could be entered from either side.

Dehga growled in frustration. He couldn't locate Diahyas, he had been unsuccessful in locating a suitable replacement for Boran, and his forces were losing members every day. He needed a plan. As Dehga pondered the situation, he realized that there was one really good way to solve all three problems…and a fourth one besides. He had to pick one special person's brain. With a grin, he settled back into a comfortable, high-backed chair and closed his eyes.

Good evening, he greeted as he felt around inside his victim's mind. *I believe you have been looking for me.*

"Who be this?" came the demand. Why did people always feel the need to speak aloud when he contacted them this way?

One moment. Let's get a bit more comfortable, shall we?

With that, Dehga pulled himself more fully into the man's mind. He felt the man drift asleep and collapse. Then, as expected, a white room appeared with a table and two chairs set across from one another. The man was sitting in one chair, looking around in confusion, and Dehga walked over to take the other chair.

"So it be you after all," he said.

"I had been wondering if you suspected me. However, you do not seem overly surprised by this power I am using. Why is that?"

"You used the same power on Boran…although, I be not positive that this be the same way he saw you."

"Correct. I was a mere voice in his head. Now, I need information from you. We can do this the easy way or the deadly way."

"So you be not planning to kill me regardless? I find that difficult to believe."

Dehga smiled cruelly. "I forget that you, too, are a man of war. As such, I suppose you will make me work for my information."

"We understand each other."

Dehga shrugged. "No one would know. If you willingly share, then I will kill you quickly and painlessly."

"No deal."

"Very well then."

Dehga stood and began to send electrical shocks into the man's mind. He screamed and gripped his head tightly.

"Let's see. Where to begin?" Dehga reached out and forcefully removed an old, deeply embedded memory. "Cute child. A little sister, perhaps?"

He tossed it aside and reached for another. "Oooo, she didn't last long, did she? This memory is a painful one for you; you won't miss it."

The man continued to scream his pain as Dehga ripped more memories out, glanced at them, tossed them aside, streaming painful shocks all the while.

"You realize that it is unnecessary for me to delve this far back. The answers I seek are much closer to the surface, but because you are making me go to the trouble of finding the information myself...you understand? Are you positive you do not wish to help?"

"Soon you be getting what you deserve. Every tyrant be overthrown eventually," the man said through gritted teeth.

Dehga shrugged. "There have been no tyrants like me. Ah, you have a family. Do you think they will miss you much?"

The man made no response.

"Look at this proud moment. You finally reached the ultimate title, *commander*."

Dehga riffled through several more memories before getting bored with that and moving on to the fresher batch that would hold the jackpot.

"Well, what do we have here? Quite a young boy, isn't he? Do you think he'll be proud of how his father handled himself in his last moments? Oh! That's right. No one will know. You will have died of unknown, natural causes. Too bad for you."

Yet another memory was tossed aside, although Dehga made sure that this one landed just beside the commander with an image of his little boy facing him.

"Hmmm...let's see here. What is this one?" Dehga mumbled. An image of a light-green young man floating in the commander's office presented itself. Something about it caught Dehga's attention just before he was going to toss it aside. "Who are you?"

He dug around the same area and found a history of the entire conversation.

"Ah! This boy knows much more than he should, doesn't he? And it seems you lied to me, commander, about your mission in the Yuen village. I do not appreciate being lied to. You have no idea what this means; it actually makes things much easier for me. What other jewels do you have hidden away in here?"

As he pricked and prodded around, he found information that Diahyas was on land with all of those troublemakers from both Randor and Tiweln. He would definitely have to do something about that. He also discovered that the boy, Luik, was the nephew of Diahyas's ladies' maid, which completely explained why he had been involved initially. Then he located the coup de grāce of information.

"Someone has been quite naughty. You could have easily destroyed my well-laid plans. As it is, I can still salvage this." Dehga turned to face the commander, who was on the ground, staring at his young son with tears in his eyes. "Because of this, I will have to do more than kill you. You must be completely discredited now. What a disappointment you will be to your son. He will swim the streets with his head hung in shame, hoping no one recognizes him as the son of the late Commander Wynedor."

Dehga squatted down to whisper. "You should have listened to Eorian. It truly was far too dangerous."

Dehga laid a hand against the top of the commander's head. If not for the emotionless glaze to the cruel red eyes, it may have been misconstrued as a compassionate gesture.

"Rest assured. The Prime will have her fears assuaged."

Then Dehga left, shooting one final, high-voltage shock to end all the pain.

They would not have known about the tragedy had a bulletin not gone out over the loud speakers at the same time that Fil had been gathering some supplies from Hemlon. He hastened back to their camp as quickly as he could.

"Raef...I mean...Dehga...killed him," Fil panted with hands on his knees.

"Killed who?" Eorian asked in alarm.

"The commander. That guy that helped us at Hemlon," Fil explained as he continued to gulp in breaths. "It was just announced...over those loud speakers. Natural causes, they said."

"That's unlikely," Frelati murmured.

"But...if Fezam was in the commander's head..." Genevia began.

Eorian was nodding. "Then he now knows where Diahyas is and where we are."

"You forget," Asben broke in hesitantly.

"Forget what?" Eorian asked.

"We never told the commander of our most recent plans. If we strike now before Fezam has a chance to make any moves, we may still win this."

"We must do something," Diahyas urged. "The commander said he spoke with me mother, told her about Dehga. He may try to kill her now too."

"Alright, so we move up the time table. How are we supposed to get everything in place now? The commander was going to handle part of the plan."

"Luik?" Genevia suggested.

"There isn't really another option, is there?" Frelati said.

"Do you think he'd be able to set it all up?" Eorian asked Diahyas.

She shrugged. "I do not know his capabilities. Although I do not believe that what you be asking be too much trouble for anyone."

"All right, then we'll contact Luik and hope he can get it done."

"This will be easy, Luik, she says," he mumbled. "Does she not realize that the loud speakers be guarded to prevent the revolutionaries from gaining access again?"

Luik had tried swimming up to the front and talking with the guards. That had failed. He had then talked to a friend, who knew a friend, who had a cousin, whose wife worked as the secretary of the man who ran the loudspeaker. The only thing he had gleaned from that was that the man would be out to lunch from noon to one and that the water circulators would be offline during that time...the vents of which were large enough to fit a small man.

"This be ridiculous," Luik griped. "Someone will catch me, and they'll take me to the new commander who does not know me, and I will be executed for treason."

He squeezed his way out of the vent and faced a huge array of buttons and levers. He gave a great sigh. How exactly was he supposed to work this thing?

"I be in the building, but there be so many controls, I cannot guess which to use," Luik explained through his band.

"Is there a manual anywhere?" Eorian asked.

"I have less than an hour before the controller returns. Do you think I have time to read through a manual?"

"Perhaps if he describes it to me, I could be of assistance?"

"Who be that?" Luik asked. "I do not recognize his voice."

"I am Asben. I'm not positive that I will be of any use, but it can't hurt to try, can it? Will you describe what you are seeing?"

"I can do one better."

Luik pressed a few buttons on his band and scanned the entire control panel.

"Eorian, get Diahyas to open the shared image."

"Fascinating!" Asben exclaimed. "How do you think they managed such a thing? I would love to tinker with one of these. Diahyas, do you think...?"

"Asben, we're on the clock," Frelati said.

"Oh, right, right. Let's see here. This button here, the red switch, appears to be the main power. That will need to be turned on after everything else. Hmmm...volume is there, frequency, and those appear to be adjusting the levels of different sounds. I would leave all of that alone...well, maybe turn up the volume. Ah! This entire left section, the labels are a bit hazy on my end, but it looks as if it could be locations. Each switch that is flipped up should receive the broadcast."

"Yeah! I see that now," Luik agreed excitedly. "And here be the palace. I can turn all of them off inside except the one in the throne room. That be the most likely place for the Prime and Prime-Mate to be, correct?"

"This be true," Diahyas said. "Although, how be we to get them there if they be not there already?"

"First, let's get Luik finished up in here," said Eorian.

Asben took over again. "All right, Luik, switch all the location switches as appropriate, set the volume a bit higher, just in case. Check the microphone to make sure it is on."

Luik searched the microphone and found a button on the back side that he pushed. A glowing light appeared.

"It be on now."

"Then set your band around it and flip the main power switch."

Luik followed the instructions. "Band on. You need to turn off your side, and then I will flip the switch."

"Luik," Eorian said hurriedly. "Make sure that you block the door with something so that no one can rush in to stop the broadcast."

"Got it."

"Good luck."

Luik heard the signal click off. Then he locked the door and wedged a chair beneath the handle before turning back to the control panel.

"Here we go."

He flipped the switch, and all the other controls instantly lit up. He tapped once lightly on the microphone and listened as it sounded outside the door. He grinned. Then he wiggled his way back out the ventilation system.

"I should be a spy," he said as he swam off.

How about something greater?

Luik paused. "Who...who said that?"

A friend, Luik.

"In me head?" he asked.

Do not be frightened, Luik.

"I know who you be! You cannot trick me the way you tricked Boran."

I have no intention of tricking you, Luik. This will be a business arrangement. There is something I need you to do for me, and in exchange, I can do something for you.

"What could you possibly do for me, Dehga?"

I can keep your aunt alive.

Luik's blood ran cold. "Where be she?"

Now, Luik, you know I won't tell you that.

"You wish me to betray Diahyas to save me aunt," Luik realized in horror.

Smart boy. Now, it is my understanding that you have been undermining my revolution. I do not appreciate that, but you can make it up to me by becoming the new leader. Your people need someone to follow, and you would be perfect for it. You just have to do exactly what I say, and you cannot tell your meddling friends any of this.

"Why me? How did you know I be involved?" Luik asked.

The commander's mind was full of useful information.

Luik frowned. The commander died after his aunt had been captured. That meant that Dehga had other plans for Sea-ena beyond controlling Luik. Although he had no idea what those other plans might be, it meant that his aunt would be safe even if Luik did not cooperate…hopefully. However, if he said no now, Dehga would go through his mind and discover Eorian's plan. Even if he said yes to Dehga now, it may end in the same result.

Luik looked around him at the bustling city. People were swimming all around him, some shopping, some getting food, and some trying to get a little exercise. What he wouldn't give to be one of them right now.

I need your answer, Luik.

Luik took several deep breaths as he looked all around for some way out of this situation.

Luik, I am not a patient man.

"You want me answer," Luik said with a slight tremor in his voice. "Well, here it be."

He closed his eyes, sucked in a deep breath, and swam right in front of a swiftly moving heroshi pulling a carriage. It slammed into him with terrific speed, and Luik felt his body roll under the creature's body and into the churning tail. There was quite a lot of pain, and he was fairly certain someone was screaming, but then blackness descended and with it came blessed silence.

CHAPTER 22

The Prime and Prime-Mate were enjoying lunch in the small dining room when Diahyas burst in upon them.

"You must come with me, quickly," she said.

"Diahyas? Why be you here?" her father asked in confusion.

"*Please* come with me. We have no time for questions."

"Do you not see that we be eating, Diahyas? This interruption be most unwelcome," the Prime said before taking another bite of food.

Something snapped inside Diahyas at that moment.

"You selfish woman. Your world be under attack, and your daughter, whom you have not seen for over a month now, be trying to help you save everything. Yet here you be, too focused on filling your stomach to listen." Diahyas looked at her mother in disgust. "I have met rulers from another planet, and they be both compassionate, loving parents and beloved rulers. Perhaps if you had tried their method, we would not be in the middle of this war."

The Prime gaped at her in sheer astonishment.

Her father frowned. "Diahyas, it be cruel of you to say such things when you know not your mother's motives."

"Then perhaps she should have shared them with me," Diahyas snapped. "Or *you* should have."

Her father bowed his head. "It be an error on me part, I agree. Though I did wish to confide in you. Would you listen to us now?"

Diahyas paused in surprise and curiosity. However, she instantly remembered the importance of time at the moment and shook her head.

"I will listen later. For now, you both must come with me."

"Where be you taking us, me wayward daughter? Have others filled your head with lies and now you wish to kill us?" the Prime said nastily.

"I be here now because, unfathomably, I do *not* wish you dead. We have little time, though, so you can either trust your only daughter and come with me now or you can regret the decision for the remainder of your short lives."

Her father looked at her intently, and she met his gaze with confidence. Then he turned to the Prime and nodded.

"We must go with her."

The Prime crossed her arms. "I refuse to leave without knowing our destination."

Diahyas glared at the woman. "We be going to the throne room. You can take your food if you like."

Leeyan snatched up both their plates and swam toward Diahyas.

"We be coming, daughter. Lead the way."

Diahyas nodded once, seeing Bailena finally get up from her chair as her daughter left the room. Diahyas was surprised that she was more anxious than angry at the moment, despite the recent provocation. This was their only shot. Dehga could not be tricked again.

They all entered the throne room. The Prime and Prime-Mate sat upon their thrones while Diahyas swam around to ensure all the doors were closed.

"Eorian, we be ready now," she said into her band.

"Frelati, Asben, Fil, you are near the loudspeaker building?" Eorian asked.

"We are," Frelati said. "No one seems to have noticed anything wrong yet, but we'll cause a diversion the second they do."

"Good. Genevia and I have found Dehga. He's in his room. I'm leaving my line open in ten seconds, so make sure you have all of yours turned off."

"Right." Frelati said.

"I love you, Frelati," Genevia called out hurriedly.

"Be safe, Genevia," Frelati responded a bit hoarsely.

He had been adamantly against Genevia going with Eorian to face off against Dehga, but according to everyone else, she knew how to goad the man quite effectively.

There was a click as he closed down his signal.

"Diahyas, make sure you stay safe too and keep your parents in that room," Eorian said.

"I will do me best," Diahyas said. "Please do not die."

With that, she broke her signal as well.

"How long must we wait here for something to happen?" her mother griped.

"People be risking their lives this very moment to help you," Diahyas responded angrily. "Have a little respect and sit quietly while you wait."

"I do not have to stay here and take your abuse," the Prime retorted, and she started to get up.

The Prime-Mate laid a gentle hand on her arm to restrain her. "Me dear, our daughter be anxious, can you not tell? She be not trying to goad you to anger, but her nerves be tight already, and you know the two of you have a strained relationship at best. Please be patient, me dear."

Diahyas breathed a sigh of relief as her mother relaxed back down into her chair. In that moment, Diahyas vowed that she would not say one more word, despite the provocation, until Dehga had shown his true nature to the entire world.

Eorian laid both hands on Genevia's shoulders and looked her in the eyes.

"Are you sure you are okay doing this?" he asked. "I promise I will not think badly of you if you back out. You have a family to think about."

Genevia gave him a small smile. "A family that will no longer be safe if we do not succeed. You will not face him alone."

Eorian nodded and turned to face the door. "Ready?"

Genevia nodded.

Eorian opened his channel to Luik's band and threw the doors to Dehga's bedchamber wide open. He caught Dehga's look of surprise and then smug satisfaction as he recognized the intruder. Genevia slipped in behind and shut the doors. When Dehga saw her, pure hatred filled his eyes.

"Why are you here, girl? Shouldn't you be frolicking in the woods somewhere?" he said maliciously.

She gave him a cheeky grin. "I heard there was another mission to stop you, and you know how I so love to thwart your plans. You would have missed me if I wasn't a part of this one, *Dehga*."

"Hardly. Although I see you have learned my new name. Brava." He eyes were hard and his expression infuriated. "You realize I will kill you both now?"

"And *you* realize we will not make that easy for you," Eorian said. "How about a pleasant conversation first?"

"Why?" Now Dehga's eyes were suspicious.

"That's what we want to know. Why did you kidnap Sea-ena...or, more accurately, why did you have the revolutionaries do it?" Genevia asked.

Dehga scoffed. "I will not answer that question."

"Fine, then answer this one. Where is she?" Eorian said.

"I will not answer that question either. You are wasting my time." Dehga sent Genevia a terrifying smile. "I believe I'll start with you."

"And what do you think will happen if the Prime and Prime-Mate discover a dead elf and a dead human in the room of their soon-to-be son-in-law? My guess is that they will call off the betrothal."

"I can convince any number of these slow-witted, fish people to dispose of you both."

"That's harsh," Eorian said. "You wouldn't keep your army of revolutionaries if they heard those words come out of your mouth. By the way, how *are* you managing to keep everything together since you effectively killed Boran? Have you found a new replacement yet?"

Dehga glared at him a moment before a look of malicious pleasure creased his features. "Actually, I had found just the right replacement. A young man that would have quite easily stirred up the passions of all the lower-class, uneducated fish. I even had the proper leverage to motivate the boy to do my bidding. However, the loyal idiot decided to kill himself this afternoon...let's see, what was his name? Ah, yes. Luik."

Genevia gasped and started to rush at Dehga, but Eorian quickly held her back.

"You murderer! How could you?!" she yelled.

"How could *I*?" Dehga asked with a soft chuckle. "My dear girl, I did not touch him."

"You don't have to. You simply reached into his mind and started playing games with his brain, you despicable…"

"There you are," Dehga said in triumph. "I knew there was a murderer in you somewhere. Everyone has a dark corner, even a happy little elf princess. So glad I got to see it before I kill you."

"You're a monster," she hissed.

"I'm a manipulator," Dehga corrected. "All of you have such weak minds. Humans are very susceptible, but then, these mermaids proved to be an easy conquest as well. Just a few short conversations with Boran led me to the stress point that would rile everyone up. Their *children*."

Dehga snorted his derision. "It appears that evolution selected this useless race to perish, but of course, it is so much easier to believe that someone caused the problem. If they believe that, then they can also believe that there is a cure. Who should they blame? Why, the royals, of course! Not a one of them questioned *how* the royals could possibly alter their children's ability to go on land or even *why* they would have such a motive. This was mere child's play, really, and it will continue to work once I dispose of my opposition."

"If this was working so well, why cater to the royals? Why are you here trying to ensure that they still want you to marry their daughter?" Eorian asked.

"Everyone needs a backup plan, even if they don't believe they need it," Dehga replied. "This is tedious. Any last words?"

"Yes," Eorian said with a grin as he held his band up close to his mouth. "Did you get all that?"

Dehga's eyes jumped to the contraption in miscomprehension.

"Everyone out here heard it loud and clear," Frelati said with a laugh.

"Me parents be properly mortified," Diahyas confirmed.

"What is this?" Dehga asked in fury as he advanced toward Eorian and jerked his wrist closer to investigate the strange contraption.

"Oh, that's right. You don't know about these, do you?" Eorian asked as he forced himself not to yank his arm free. "You can talk between them. For example, if you were to be speaking to me, my band could pick up your voice and send it to another band that was strategically placed on a microphone that was connected to the loudspeaker system broadcasting to every corner of Faencina…excluding a few well-chosen areas. I know you are familiar with their loudspeakers. You used it to announce the start of the revolution, correct?"

The usually pale face that was quite distinct about Dehga turned a ghastly shade of purplish gray, and he forcefully released Eorian. His livid red eyes pierced into Eorian as Dehga took three slow steps back.

"You may have thwarted me on this planet, for now," Dehga said as he glared at Eorian, "but your planet will soon be entirely within my control, and once I have all of the resources of Randor and my own planet..." —he turned to Genevia with a malevolent grin—"I will re-capture Tiweln. With all three of those worlds in my grasp, it will be no trouble to subdue this ghastly planet. Know this: I allow you to live now so that you will soon witness my triumph, and once that day dawns, you both will face slow and painful deaths."

Before either Eorian or Genevia could make a move, he had rubbed his onyx ring and was gone.

Everyone on Faencina remained in a state of shock. The Prime and Prime-Mate, in particular, had quite a lot of trouble coming to terms with the revelation, although they had much less time to dwell on it than the rest of the populace. They had decisions to make, and Eorian was not being incredibly patient.

There had been quite a lot of questions, and he answered every one of them. However, they were not answering his one and only question.

"Will you help us or not?" he asked for perhaps the third time.

"Young man, this be not an easy decision. If you be a ruler, you would understand," the Prime-Mate said.

"On the contrary, it is a very simple decision," he argued. "And I have quite a lot of experience leading others, so I most definitely understand the gravity of your responsibilities. It comes down to this: do you send your people to help us fight, or do you sit back and hope that somehow we'll win without you? If you send your people, we have a very good chance. If you bow out, there is a very high probability that we will lose, and you heard Dehga's plans. *He will come back.*"

"You be asking our people to fight and die for strangers," the Prime said.

Eorian realized then where Diahyas had gotten her ethnocentric beliefs. He sighed.

"I am asking your people to fight and die for both their own families and children and those throughout the universe. This is bigger than just your planet or mine, but if even one of us decides to sit back and do nothing, it could affect everyone."

Diahyas swam forward to speak to her parents. "I be going to help with or without your support, but it be much easier if you help me."

"You be the heir to me throne," the Prime said. "You will not fight in wars, much less those on other planets. Besides, an alliance through mating with a human be our race's only hope. Your fate be not the only one you throw away by going."

Diahyas glared at her mother. "Explain that. This be why you saddled me with Dehga, yes?"

"Yes," the Prime responded with an uplifted chin. "We must reintroduce humans into our populace so that they may share their genes. It be no solution for the children already born, but it will allow halflings to continue our existence. Perhaps our scientists will find a cure, even temporarily, for the current afflicted children, if we can take samples of human DNA."

Fil popped a hand up. "So if I were to volunteer a sample or two, would you help us then?"

The Prime scrutinized him. "A sample would be greatly appreciated and would allow our scientists to begin experimentation. However, we will need more than what you can give."

"Would any human work?" Eorian asked pensively. "For the arranged mating, I mean."

"We do not want a commoner," the Prime said. "They would have no clout to further our cause. We need someone who has the authority to demand or the ability to convince humans to come here."

Eorian nodded and looked to the floor, still deep in thought. Diahyas began arguing with her mother again about going to fight on Randor, trying to convince her mother that they needed her as the essence of water.

"What are you thinking?" Fil asked softly as he sidled over to his cousin.

Eorian lifted his head to respond but was caught in the eyes of the Prime-Mate before he had a chance. Those eyes were relaying a simple message: he knew what Eorian was thinking. The Prime-Mate leaned over to his wife and whispered something. She nodded absently and continued arguing with Diahyas. Then the Prime-Mate motioned for Eorian to follow him.

"I'll be right back, Fil," Eorian said. "Please keep the two of them from killing each other...or making things worse."

"No promises."

Eorian started to walk off when Fil stopped him.

"E...don't do anything rash, okay?"

Eorian shot his cousin an unconvincing smile. "When have I ever?"

With that, he followed the Prime-Mate through a small door and into a study.

"Please shut the door, Eorian," the Prime-Mate said. "And you may call me Leeyan. I have always abhorred the formality forced upon me position."

Eorian shut the door.

"Leeyan it is then," he said.

"I believed this should be a more quiet conversation, do you not agree?"

Eorian nodded.

"I see you be still unsure about it," Leeyan said with a comforting smile. "What we say here by no means shall be binding. This be exploratory only."

"In that case, what if I were to offer myself as the means of an alliance?"

"Then I would ask if you met our qualifications."

"I'm not positive," Eorian said. "I'm only half human."

Leeyan's brow furrowed. "I must admit, you have surprised me. Continue."

"We have creatures called wispers on my planet. They are insubstantial, air-like beings. One of them was my biological father. He also happened to be the ruler of the wispers, which is the only reason I am still alive. I am his only heir."

"So you come from royalty, but the ones you rule be not those that could help us."

"No, they couldn't, and I do not rule them. Nor do I plan to," Eorian said. "I will help them find another ruler."

"Admirable. However, it be beginning to look like you would not be an ideal candidate," Leeyan said gently.

Eorian nodded, debated with himself a bit more, and then pushed ahead rather reluctantly. "Except for the fact that I have a considerable amount of allies. I am the leader of the resistance on my world. There are multiple countries that will follow my decisions in this coming war. I have united them all, and they will grant me whatever I wish if we win."

"This be so," Leeyan said. "That does change things a bit, doesn't it?"

"I thought it might," Eorian agreed heavily.

"I will speak with Bailena. After you think on it a bit longer, if you come to decide you do indeed wish to pursue this, I can assure you that you will have our support. We have not many options in any case."

Eorian nodded and sucked in a deep breath.

"May I ask…" Leeyan began softly before stopping.

"Go ahead."

"Why be you doing all of this? You do not wish to rule, you do not appear to want power or riches…I understand you feel a duty as the essence of air to help your world, but…you seem to be sacrificing much when you have so little to gain."

Eorian shook his head and smiled. "I do not see saving the lives of millions of people as little gain. Besides, Dehga already took a lot from me, and I want to return the favor."

Leeyan was quiet for a short while as he studied Eorian. "I see you have made your decision then."

"I suppose I have."

"And there be no one back home that you be leaving broken-hearted?" Leeyan asked.

Eorian shrugged self-consciously and shook his head. "Never had the time. I suppose that's a good thing now."

"Allow me one evening to discuss this with Bailena privately. We will come to you in the morning with our decision."

Eorian held up a hand. "One other thing, Leeyan."

"Yes?"

"I will require Diahyas to come with us. That is part of the agreement. We get your troops, and we get her. You understand?"

Leeyan frowned. "Bailena will not be pleased with this."

"Diahyas is the essence of water. We need her with us, and I swear to you, I will do everything in my power to keep her safe," Eorian said.

"I believe you." Leeyan nodded. "It be agreed. Tomorrow morning then."

"You did what?!" Fil exclaimed.

Eorian shushed him. "I told you to keep it down. We haven't actually agreed to anything yet."

Eorian and Fil were sharing the same airie in which they had been prisoners. Frelati and Genevia were in the adjoining airie, and Eorian was not positive how thin the walls were around here.

"Did you not hear me when I said not to do anything rash?" Fil asked.

"This wasn't rash, Fil."

Fil shook his head. "Sounds pretty rash to me. What were you thinking?"

"I was thinking that it would ensure that they would send fighters and allow Diahyas to help us," Eorian said fiercely.

"You do realize that this marriage thing isn't temporary, right?"

Eorian scowled.

Fil continued. "I just wanted to check since apparently you haven't been on many dates. Maybe you didn't realize it. This will be for the rest of your life."

"I know that, Fil," Eorian said.

"Are you sure?" Fil asked.

"Do you intend to continue going around in circles like this all evening?" Eorian asked. "I *knew* I shouldn't have said anything until it was a done deal."

"You've already decided, so for you, it *is* a done deal," Fil said. "What do you want me to say? Congratulations?"

"No, but a little support would be nice."

Fil crossed his arms. "I'm not supporting something I think is stupid. You're making a terrible decision."

"No, I'm not," Eorian argued.

Fil stared at him. "I'll be right back."

He moved to the door and stepped into the alternating chamber.

"Where are you going, Fil?" Eorian asked.

"I need backup," Fil said with a smug grin as he shut the door and started the alternating process.

Eorian slammed a fist against the door. "Fil, I swear, if you bring Frelati and Genevia into this…"

"You'll listen to them," Fil said.

"Fil!" Eorian shouted. "Don't you dare!"

Eorian heard the outside door open and growled his frustration. However, there was no stopping him now, so he might as well get comfortable, because the upcoming confrontation certainly wouldn't be.

Fil had brought Frelati and Genevia into the room in a matter of minutes, and whatever he had said to them had thrown them both into a bit of a tizzy.

"You *don't* want to do this, Eorian," Genevia said earnestly, looking as if her entire world was about to fall apart.

Eorian's brows drew together in confusion. "It's not *that* bad."

"It's a fairly permanent decision," Frelati argued with great gravity. "You don't come back from it."

"Well, yeah, but how bad can Diahyas be?" Eorian asked. "And I have a fantastic reason, you have to admit."

The elves paused.

Frelati turned back to Fil. "You said he was killing himself. What is he talking about?"

Eorian chuckled. "That was a bit dramatic, Fil."

"It's an expression!" he said defensively.

"Someone explain," Frelati ordered.

"I am guaranteeing that the Prime and Prime-Mate send troops to Randor to fight and that they allow Diahyas to fight with us," Eorian said.

"That doesn't sound bad," Genevia said hesitantly.

"He's not done yet," said Fil. "Go on, tell them how."

"I'll form an alliance between the mermaids and the humans and ensure that some people from Randor come over here."

"By…" Fil pushed.

Eorian paused just a moment. "Marrying Diahyas."

"That's what you were speaking with the Prime-Mate about," Frelati said as realization dawned across his face.

Genevia was shaking her head. "I don't think this is a good idea."

"See?" Fil said happily. "I told you they wouldn't agree."

"I do."

Everyone turned to Frelati.

"You do not!" Genevia said.

"Actually, I do. Sorry, honey," Frelati said with a shrug. "It makes sense, and the needs of the many outweigh the needs of the one. Everyone throughout the universe needs this war to be won."

"But…he'll be miserable, and Diahyas will be miserable," Genevia argued. "Marriages only really work if you love each other."

"Marriages happen all the time on Randor for reasons worse than mine," Eorian pointed out. "Mostly, people get married for more money or better status."

"That's terrible," Genevia replied.

Fil frowned. "You were supposed to side with me, Frelati. Now it's two against two."

Genevia straightened. "Diahyas will be the tie breaker."

Eorian stood. "We're not bringing her into this too."

"Are you saying that women have no right to make decisions about their own lives?" Genevia challenged hotly.

A very uncomfortable silence fell on the room. Genevia glared at each of the men in turn.

"All three of you think that you have more of a right to influence Eorian's decision than Diahyas, and yet did any of you think of asking her opinion? This does not concern you, Fil, or you, my misguided husband, or even me. This is between Eorian and Diahyas." She turned to face each man in turn. "Frelati, you and I are going back to our room. Fil, you are staying here with your mouth shut, and Eorian, you march over to Diahyas and get this settled. I don't care what you decide, but you had better both be in agreement."

Frelati gave a small shrug to Fil and Eorian as if in slight apology and followed Genevia out of the room.

Eorian glared at Fil as he waited his turn for the alternating chamber.

"Do you see the trouble you've caused?" he asked.

Fil shook his head. "After *that* display, you still want to go through with this…with someone you have no feelings for at all? I mean, I suppose Genevia was right, but if I'm gonna have a woman explode at me, I had better at least get her loving side too."

"Just be glad you have that choice, Fil," Eorian said on a sigh, and he stepped into the chamber.

CHAPTER 23

Being back in her room among all her familiar items made Diahyas feel lonely once again. As much as she hated sleeping on the hard ground, there had been something peaceful about being around all of her new friends while they were on Land. She was also very acutely aware of Sea-ena's absence. Before, she had been upset, but it hadn't quite felt real. It was almost like her mind still thought Sea-ena was waiting here for her. But now Diahyas was here, and there was no Sea-ena. She hoped that the kind woman was not being mistreated.

That line of thought inevitably brought her back to the moment she had heard Dehga's cruel words. He was going to use Luik as a replacement for Boran, use Sea-ena as leverage to control Luik, so Luik had...Diahyas closed her eyes tightly. It was all so *real*. As marvelous as it felt to be around friends, this terrible sadness she felt now would never have occurred had she just remained alone. Was it truly worth it?

She felt her salty tears melt with the fresh ocean around her. She had never thought she would cry because she had friends. How strange to think of all the times she had cried because she had none.

A rap sounded on her door.

Who could possibly wish to interrupt her solitude now? She had not sent for anything, her parents certainly wouldn't come for a nice chat, and Sea-ena was...

"Who be there?" she called.

"It's Eorian. Can I come in?"

"Eorian?" Diahyas swam over to the door and opened it. "What be you needing?"

"Can I come in?" he repeated.

Diahyas nodded and moved aside to allow him entrance. The door closed, and silence descended.

Eorian looked over at her uncomfortably, then he frowned. "Have you been crying? Your eyes are red."

Diahyas's cheeks tinged purple. "Sea-ena."

"Oh, right." Eorian nodded. "I'm sorry we haven't found her yet."

"We will," Diahyas said fiercely. "And we shall not stop looking until we do."

Eorian sent her a smile. "Exactly."

Another silence fell.

"So, why be you here?" Diahyas asked.

"I have been informed by Genevia that I need to discuss something with you."

Diahyas frowned. "All right. This sounds quite serious. Do you wish to sit down?"

"Ummm, no, not really." Eorian ran a hand through his hair. "You can sit down if you want, though."

Diahyas took him up on that and settled on the stool before her dressing table.

"I be warning you that I be not up for more bad news tonight," she said softly.

Eorian thought that over. "This *may* not be too bad."

Diahyas sighed. "That means it be not good either."

She sucked in a steadying breath, closed her eyes a moment, and then looked up at him. "I be ready now. Tell me."

"What would you think if I made a deal with your parents to get them to send troops and allow you to come with us to Randor?"

"What deal?" Diahyas asked in curiosity.

"Well...you know what they want," Eorian said with a shrug.

He looked very uncomfortable talking with her. Diahyas felt a bit sorry for him, but she also felt sorry for herself right now.

"You be a much better alternative to Dehga," Diahyas said simply.

Eorian's face clearly showed his relief that she understood him. "I don't have to make the deal. I'll do whatever you want me to."

Diahyas shrugged. "Me parents care not for me thoughts on the matter. They will find me a mate one way or another whether I like him or not. At least I like you. Besides, it will help you."

Eorian frowned. "I wasn't expecting you to be happy about it, but you aren't really reacting...well, at all."

Diahyas looked up at him with heavy eyes. "I be sad, and I be weary, Eorian. I cannot find the strength within me to feel much of anything beyond that right now."

"But you must have some opinion on the matter," Eorian argued.

"Will you be kind to me?" she asked.

"Of course," Eorian readily replied.

"Will you listen to me opinions?"

"Yes."

"Will you try on occasion to make me happy?"

"Just on really special occasions," Eorian said with a wink, which drew a very slight smile from Diahyas.

"Will this mean we be no longer friends?" she asked softly as she looked down at her tightly clenched hands.

Eorian knelt down in front of her and tilted his head to look her in the eye. "I would think it would make us better friends...but I'm not going to promise that I won't get angry at you from time to time. We will probably have some of the most colossal fights."

"You be not encouraging me much," Diahyas chastised.

"I wasn't finished yet," Eorian said with a smile. "We'll also laugh a lot, and we'll make some wonderful memories. We're both going to have to work at this, but friendship is a great way to start; don't you think?"

Diahyas nodded.

"Then what do you say, Diahyas?" Eorian wrapped his hand around hers. "Will you marry me?"

Diahyas began to nod, but then she stopped and got a mischievous look in her eye. "One condition."

"Am I going to regret this?" Eorian asked warily.

"You must make me parents agree that we finish up this war before the ceremony. I do not wish to have all of this hanging over me head, and I want Sea-ena to be there."

"Will you settle for me saying that I'll try?" Eorian asked.

Diahyas sighed. "I suppose so."

"Good. I'm leaving now. Try to get a good night's sleep."

His hand slipped from hers, and he stood.

"Good night, Eorian. Thank you for speaking with me about this," Diahyas said without looking up at him.

He slipped a finger under her chin and raised her head up so her eyes met his.

"Thank Genevia," he said, and he bent down to press a gentle kiss against her lips before leaving the room.

The Prime seemed to be in much better spirits the following morning. Once Eorian gave his final decision and she heard that Diahyas was not going to fight them on it, she was over the moon...at least, for her. However, when Eorian mentioned postponing the ceremony, she grew quite suspicious.

"Diahyas wishes to find a way out of this arrangement," the Prime said angrily. "This be a trick."

"It's not a trick," Eorian explained. "She wants Sea-ena to be present, and as you can see, we have not located her yet."

The Prime sat back in her chair in surprise.

"She wishes to postpone this momentous occasion for a mere servant?"

Diahyas swam forward angrily. "She be much more than a servant. She be more mother to me than you have ever been. I shall not go through with this without her, so you had best put forth all manner of resources to locate her."

The Prime looked ready to explode again, but the Prime-Mate gently calmed her. Then he turned to his daughter. "We will do as you request. I believe it be time that we start considering the needs of the lesser folks, do you not agree, Bailena? This recent revolution has opened our eyes."

Reluctantly, Bailena nodded her head.

"Good." Leeyan smiled in relief. "We will need a few days to gather our soldiers. How do you propose to get them to Randor?"

Frelati stepped forward. "Asben is working with your scientists to locate the natural portal on your world. We will need to use that since there will be so many people. Also...there may be a slight issue that we had not originally considered. Asben, of course, did."

"Which be?" the Prime asked.

"Your oceans are fresh water; those on Randor are salt water. While your people can survive in salt water for a while, prolonged exposure could lead to severe dehydration, even death."

"This be quite troubling," the Prime said with a frown. "How be it that your waters be so very salty?"

Eorian shrugged. "They just are."

"You realize that with this news we cannot in good conscience send our people over there," the Prime-Mate said.

"Well, Asben may have a solution for that as well," Frelati said. "It would require Diahyas's agreement, though."

"Of course," Diahyas said.

"Asben believes that with your power over water, you could separate the water from the salt...at least, in the area around the mermaids."

"That sounds as if it would take a great amount of her power. How long would you expect her to keep that up?" Leeyan asked.

"Well, initially, quite a while," Eorian said. "Inland there is plenty of fresh water, and the ocean water around the river outlets would be quite tolerable for mermaids. Our plan is to send troops to different rivers around Randor, and some are closer than others. However, we will need to send the mermaids from the natural portal here through to the natural portal on Randor, which is in the middle of the ocean. The reason we are doing this is for two reasons. One, it will be easier to go both ways between worlds; it won't just be a one way trip for everyone. Two, it is in a location that everyone avoids because of the heavy fog and some superstitions, so no will accidentally happen upon us. As I said, initially, it will be quite draining for Diahyas, but once everyone is in position, she won't have to do a thing for them."

"Can you do this?" the Prime asked Diahyas.

"Of course," Diahyas said as she flipped some hair over her shoulder.

Frelati leaned over to Diahyas and spoke softly, "Asben was actually hoping to practice with you using some of the salt water rivers here."

Diahyas rolled her eyes. "I need no practice. Water does whatever I wish."

"A week's time, then," the Prime-Mate said. "Assuming we have found the portal. Within a week, we will have our supplies and troops ready."

"Perfect," Eorian said.

The natural portal was down in the Chasm of Olis, which was why many people did not know its location. It was also why Boran had been able to evade them for so long; he had been living right beside it. Exactly ten weeks from the day Eorian had arrived on Faencina, the mermaid troops began swimming into Randor. Diahyas had gone through the natural portal first and started to desalinate the water for the mermaids swimming through. It was proving to be a lot more difficult than she had thought it would be.

Finally, after quite a few minutes, she started to feel a change in the water, and she signaled to the first of the troops. They came through four at a time, and they did so slowly. It was taking time for Diahyas to freshen the water, and they wanted to make sure there was enough room for everyone in the ever-widening circle she was creating.

When all the mermaids were through the portal, they began the journey to the Riffa Canal, which was fed by a large river that greatly reduced the saline content. It was going to take several hours of constant swimming to reach it, and Diahyas was already getting tired. She started reaching out into the water a little bit farther, trying to find a way to make the process easier. She definitely should have practiced with Asben. Why had she been so very cocky?

After an hour, she was so weak that her mind grew fuzzy. She needed to find some source of strength; she needed to focus on something other than this difficult task. Her mind flittered back to Eorian. He had been so calm and sure of himself as he stood before the natural portal and spoke to everyone. He had even looked a little worried before she swam through the portal, but he believed she could do this.

Focus on Eorian just before you parted, Diahyas thought, and she clung to that image tightly. After a few minutes, she felt it begin to energize her. She felt less weak, and it seemed that her herculean task grew easier. She could make it the next hour and even the next, if it took that long. *Just keep your focus on Eorian as he stood before the portal.*

Eorian and Frelati had traveled through Faencina's natural portal after all the mermaid troops had gone, excluding the five left to monitor the portal; however, their destination was Tiweln's natural portal on Wefleca. They were both very pleased with the number of elves, humans, shapeshifters, and even several nomads that had gathered there. Frelati told them to wait three hours and then they should cross through by saying his name. That would put them right where they needed to be.

Then Eorian and Frelati traveled to Hemlon to tell the Yuens how to get to the portal and how to use it. The longest part of their trip was the travel back to the palace via heroshi to meet up with Genevia, Fil, and Asben. They would all be taking the trip to Randor together. It ended up taking the two men a little over an hour to get back, but they still had plenty of time. Unfortunately, when they got back to the palace, they were met with bad news. It was Asben who rushed up to meet them.

"Eorian, we've encountered a problem," he said with a great frown as his fingers fidgeted with each other.

"What problem? Dehga isn't back, is he?"

"No, but this could also potentially be world changing."

"Go on."

"It seems that Diahyas may have changed the way she is desalinating the water," Asben said.

"I'm not following."

"About ten minutes ago, the men you left at the portal sent us a message. They had to leave the site of the portal because the water had grown too salty for them to remain."

Eorian blinked. "The water *here* was too salty."

Asben nodded. "I believe that Diahyas may have inadvertently started pulling fresh water from here through the portal to help her remove the salt over on Randor. I'm not positive, but that's the only theory I can come up with. These two portals have been in existence since the dawn of time, and there has never been an issue of water crossing over and changing ecosystems. The only factor that is different here is her."

"So how bad is it, and can we fix it?" Eorian asked.

"Fixing it could be incredibly problematic, although we could lessen the overall negative affect. At the rate the salt is spreading, there will be at least one fifth of the planet that is uninhabitable for quite some time… generations possibly. The remainder of the planet will absorb some of the salt but will still be quite livable. Diahyas would have to help to reduce the spread initially until we could somehow cordon off the affected area. The issue now is that she is still pulling fresh water over to Randor and allowing more salt to come into Faencina. I'm quite positive she is unaware that this is happening, but someone needs to tell her to stop *now*. We are already evacuating the closest towns and cities."

"How did this happen?" Eorian said with a sigh. "All right, take me to the others."

Asben led him to where they were all waiting in a small sitting room. It looked like Genevia and Fil were playing some kind of game.

"I hope everyone is ready to leave," Eorian said.

"We were ready the moment Asben brought us the news," Frelati said as he stood. "What's the plan?"

"We use Genevia's necklace to take us to my boat on top of Mount Measine, and then we use my diamond dust to take all of us and, hopefully, my boat out on the ocean where Diahyas is."

"Got it," Genevia said. "Gather 'round, everyone."

They each grabbed their bags and huddled together.

"The name of the place again, Eorian?" Genevia asked.

"Mount Measine."

She smirked. "That is such a weird name. It's like someone saying 'give *me a sign*.'"

Eorian frowned as that registered, but he didn't have time to respond.

Genevia had closed her eyes while focusing quite intently upon those two words and Eorian's boat. They all felt the tug of travel, and when she again opened her eyes, she was quite pleased to find them all standing on familiar wooden planking.

"Well done, Genevia," Frelati praised and gave her a kiss on the brow.

Eorian nodded his thanks.

"Let's crowd on the side and each put our hands on the ship. Maybe if we're all holding onto it, it'll come with us," he said.

They followed his advice and made sure that they were also all touching one another.

"How does this work again, Genevia?" he asked.

"Focus only on Diahyas, nothing else. Reach out to her, and the diamond dust will make real your desire," Genevia described. "At least, that's what I do."

Eorian nodded, took a deep breath, and closed his eyes.

Focus only on Diahyas, he thought, and he began to picture her. He sketched her in his mind, trying to see her as she would be now, swimming through unfamiliar ocean and trying her hardest to keep the salty sea at bay. She would be mortified to learn of what had happened, but they had to tell her now before more damage was done. *Focus on Diahyas. Diamond dust, if we are somehow psychically linked, I need to see her now.*

CHAPTER 24

They were almost there. Another thirty minutes, and she could finally rest. They were swimming closer to the surface since it was easier for Diahyas to keep the water fresh there, so when a dark shadow passed over them, it caught everyone's attention. Diahyas looked up at the bottom of the large ship in confusion. Eorian had said that no one ever came into this part of the ocean. What was a boat doing here?

Just a moment later, someone dove into the water not far from her and began looking around.

"Eorian?" she called in surprise. "What be you doing here?"

He turned around to face her and pointed to the surface. She nodded, shouted for everyone with her to halt, and then swam up to meet him. Eorian sucked in a big breath and then began explaining.

"Diahyas, we have a problem."

Instant alarm shot through her. "What problem?"

"It seems that water from Randor has been trading places with water from Faencina," he said carefully.

"How be this possible?" she asked. "The portals do not regularly exchange water like this, correct?"

"No, they don't," Eorian said slowly, as if choosing his words very carefully. "Do you think it might be possible that you were inadvertently pulling fresh water over here as you worked on desalinating the water?"

"Of course I would do no such thing!" she exclaimed in affront. "That would be dangerous for all me people."

Eorian nodded. "Well, the facts are these. We opened a portal between Randor oceans and Faencina oceans. There was no exchange of salt and fresh water as people went through, nor was there an exchange for an hour afterward. Then, almost an hour after the portal had closed, the water around the portal began to grow increasingly saltier, and it started affecting nearby towns. They are being evacuated as we speak. How do you think it happened?"

"Well...," Diahyas began, her expression becoming a bit worried. "Perhaps...perhaps the portal never really closed? Maybe the exchange was slow at first and then...and..."

Her face fell, and she shook her head.

"That be the same time that I grew incredibly tired and thought that me power would break," she said softly. "I did not think that I had changed the way I be working me gift, but I suppose...how terribly did I hurt Faencina's waters?"

She looked so very fragile, and Eorian did not wish to make it worse. However, she had to know so she could fix it.

"According to Asben, about one fifth of the planet will be uninhabitable for some time, but if you go there now, you can use your power to decrease the damage temporarily while they come up with more permanent measures."

Diahyas nodded.

"You'll need to use the natural portal," Eorian said. "We still need you here, though, so work on it for an hour and half and then come back. We'll wait on my ship for you here and then travel through the portal to meet up with my crew."

Diahyas nodded, but she looked ready to cry. "What if I make it worse?"

"You won't," Eorian said confidently. "Your parents have already sent scientists to the affected area, and those from the closest towns and cities will have arrived by now. Talk to them, see what they suggest, and do your best. I believe in you."

"I'll try," Diahyas said, though she sounded as if she were going off to die.

Eorian gave her shoulder a quick squeeze and sent a smile her way before flying up out of the water. When he looked over the railing of the ship, he saw her slowly slip beneath the water and swim off.

"How'd she take it?" Genevia asked worriedly.

Eorian shook his head. "Not very well."

"She did believe you, though, right?" Fil asked.

Eorian scowled at him. "Yes, Fil, she believed me. Her confidence seems to be shaken, though."

"That's not necessarily a *bad* thing," Fil said.

"Fil," Eorian shouted crossly. "I realize you're not particularly fond of her, but she is incredibly upset at the moment, so when she gets back, keep your mouth shut. Also, if you had bothered to think this far ahead, you would realize that her confidence in her abilities is exactly what makes her useful to us when fighting the shadow beings that Frelati has told us about. If she starts second guessing every decision she makes now, it could cost lives."

"Whoa, you don't have to bite my head off, cuz," Fil said softly.

Eorian sighed and rubbed his brow. "Sorry," he said shortly. "Things are not going well."

"I imagine they will get worse before they get better," Frelati said pessimistically.

Genevia hit him on the arm and sent him a glare before giving Eorian a smile of encouragement. "But they *will* get better."

Your son is on his way, Jano, Finley said softly as she laid a hand on his shoulder.

"Eorian?" Jano said. "Where?"

He has just docked. Relim sent word. He'll be here in twenty minutes, maybe less.

Jano's eyes lit up for just a moment before grief settled over his features once more. "He won't want to see me. Rida is dead because of me."

That's not true, Jano, Finley said.

"It is," he argued as he swung around to face her. His eyes had grown wide and vibrant, and his jaw was set. "Raef was supposed to kill me, and I couldn't convince him to leave Rida out of it. Eorian's mother is gone because I failed; how can he stand to look at me? I should leave."

Jano made to stand, though he was still quite weak from lack of food and severe punishment while within Raef's care.

You will stay here, and you will greet your son. Finley said. *Promise me.*

"He doesn't want to see me, and I…I just can't face him."

He does, and I will be right beside you the whole time.

Jano sagged back to the ground wearily. "Why do you care for an old, broken man?"

I don't. I care for a man who has lost his way due to tragedy. My purpose is to help you find your path once again.

"But…why?" Jano asked again. His hands gripped his head, and he stared at the ground.

Perhaps you are helping me as well.

"I can't help anyone. Not anymore."

Sure you can. Finley blew some wind toward Jano, and it rustled his hair. *You know, I'm not really very popular back home. I don't have any friends. I could use at least one; don't you think? That seems to be a simple thing you can do for me. In fact, you've been doing it without trying for some time now.*

Jano glanced over at her, a hint of life finally showing in his eyes. "You sound like some head doctor. Step number one to overcome grief, give the person a sense of purpose."

Finley laughed. *It may sound trite, but if it works, you cannot find fault with it.*

"We'll see," Jano shrugged.

The two sat side by side in silence, simply listening to the wind as it swept through the tall, brown grass that covered the small hill upon which they watched the ever-present waves crash against the shoreline some distance from them. Time faded away in that moment; even their very beings were engulfed by the sheer constancy of the elements surrounding them. How could beings with such time constraints think their problems insurmountable in the face of these ancient, never-ending forces that witnessed every moment in history as they slowly beat away at the earth? This was peace to Jano, having a few precious moments of stasis in which all thought was whisked away, and he could sit mesmerized by both sight and sound.

"Eorian's here, Finley."

The burly voice broke through and shattered Jano's illusion.

Thank you, Barro, Finley said as she glided up. *You will help us to meet him, yes?*

"'Course," Barro said eagerly. "I sure know the cap'n will be wanting to see his pa."

Barro hustled over to Jano and helped him stand. "You're doing so much better now, for sure. I was worried when you first got here, but look at you now."

"Thank you, Barro," Jano said as he leaned slightly on his arm.

Barro had irritated him at first, but there was something about his childish and over-eager demeanor that was a bit charming. The large man also never looked at him pityingly, which was something everyone else around the camp had trouble with...even Lishea. She had stared so long when she saw him; it was as if she had been searching for the strong father she idolized and found only a broken beggar. Then she had started crying, and Jano had tried to walk over to reach her, to comfort his daughter, but his legs had been too weak, and he had collapsed to the ground just a few feet from her.

It was there as he knelt beneath her that he saw her pity. She had reached out, helped him to his feet, given him the quick, required hug, told someone to see to his wounds and get some food, and then she rushed off. Every day after that, she had stopped by for a few moments to ensure he was getting enough food, had enough blankets, or some other trifle, and then off she would go again. She hardly looked at him, but when she did, pity filled her eyes. Jano was terrified that he would see that same pitying look in his son as well.

They continued over a second hill, and then there was the camp below. Eorian was striding up confidently, and Lishea ran over to greet him, nearly jumping into his arms in excitement. Then she began greeting the others with Eorian as he shifted his focus to his men. Every one of them was pleased at his return. The two young boys were jumping up and down in their excitement. Lius broke into song. Eorian was smiling.

They were still a short ways away when Jano stopped them all again.

"No, I can't," he said. "He can't see me like this."

Finley turned to him. *Like what? What is there about you that is not worthy to see?*

Jano could not explain. He no longer wore the rags of prison, but he still felt them about him as heavy as chains. He would forever walk with a limp after the nasty break his left leg had suffered at his tormentor's hands. He was not the man he had been.

"Eorian wants to see you," Barro said. "You shouldn't keep the cap'n waiting, you know."

"He doesn't want to see me," Jano said with a shake of his head as he stared at the ground.

"Pa?" came the familiar voice.

He cringed and kept his head down, but his ears still picked up each step his son made toward him.

"You're safe," Eorian said happily, his voice full of relief and awe. He threw his arms around him and held him tight. "You're safe. They got you out."

Slowly, he pulled back to look his father in the eye. That's when Jano saw his shock, which quickly turned to anger.

"What did they…" He stopped, took a breath, and gave his father a forced smile. "Never mind that. Has everyone here treated you properly? Barro, I see you've been helping him, and you have my sincerest gratitude." He turned to look at Finley. "And I don't believe we've met."

She shook her head and looked to the ground in nervousness.

"Did you help my father escape?" Eorian asked.

Yes, she said softly.

"Then whatever you may want, I will do my best to grant it," Eorian said. "I don't have too much to give, but for now, I hope you will take my thanks. I'm Eorian, by the way, though I imagine you knew that already. What's your name?"

Finley. Pleased to meet you.

"You look tired, Pa," Eorian said. "We have a lot to talk about, so why don't you rest until dinner? We'll spend the rest of the evening catching up."

Jano gave him a very small smile and a nod. "I'm glad you're back, son."

"Me too."

Barro and Jano turned to go to Jano's tent. As they walked slowly, Jano heard Eorian speak to Finley.

"Come with me while I talk with my sister and Asben. I imagine you have many things you can tell me as well."

Eorian's voice was tight as he spoke to her, as if he was trying to repress excess emotion. He had seen the broken man Jano had become, which was just what Jano had feared. However, instead of pity, it was causing in Eorian fierce anger. Jano closed his eyes. Would either of his children ever look at him the same way again?

The small towns and villages along the coastlines of all the countries that had sided against Sohsena were the first victims. Many had been burned to the ground. Then Raef threatened to stop trade with his allies if they did not give him information and more soldiers and supplies. Sohsena had been overrun by shadow beings, and the natives were now scared to go out even in bright daylight. The seas were covered with Raef's ships, and they attacked maliciously, leaving only one survivor with each attack. Tales had to be spread after all.

Eorian closed his eyes. "And has there been any good news?"

They had more allies. The wispers had finally all decided to help since Raef had begun to turn his attention toward them as well. A powerful blasting weapon for their ships had been created and shared that Raef did not have, and there was bound to be more inventions coming with the Relians working hard on it. Lastly, Uratia and his father were out from under Raef's control...which seemed to be the main cause of the vicious attacks of late.

"Is Uratia all right?" Eorian asked. "Where is she?"

"She's —" Lishea began before she was interrupted.

"Right on time, as usual," Uratia said as she walked up. "As are you. Ten weeks exactly, just as the prophecy foretold."

"We ran into quite a lot of trouble on Faencina," Eorian said. "However, we were able to bring back a rather large troop of soldiers, so overall I think it was worth it."

"I don't," Lishea muttered crossly.

Eorian studied Uratia. "You seem to be in much better shape than my father. Do you know what was done to him?"

"I am in better shape because I am a witch," Uratia said softly.

"Can you not help him heal more quickly too?" Eorian asked.

Uratia smiled. "You misunderstand. I am doing all I can for your father at present. What I meant was that I was not as ill-treated as your father because I am a witch."

Eorian's eyes still held great confusion.

"It seems our enemy has a chink in his armor," Uratia said. "He is scared of witches."

"Really?" Frelati said in surprise. "Witches are frightening, but power from Kiem's essence is not? How does that work?"

Uratia shrugged. "I was unable to get an understanding of this strange fear beyond the fact that it was caused by some tragedy in his past."

"Well, you're definitely coming with us when we face him then," Fil said.

"But what happened to my father?" Eorian asked.

"I cannot tell you," Uratia said. "And I believe my use in this conversation is at an end, so I am returning to my tent to rest. I am still not quite healed. Welcome back, Eorian."

She walked off, and silence followed her absence.

I know a bit about what happened, Finley finally said hesitantly.

"I had hoped you might," Eorian replied as he turned to her.

He does not say much, but I know he received little food and water. He was given no blanket to shield him from the damp and cold of the dungeon. Soldiers beat him, which is the cause of the damage to his left leg. Finley paused.

"What did they do to his mind?" Eorian asked.

He will not speak of it, Finley answered, and she saw Eorian sag a bit at the news. *But he calls out at night because of the nightmares, and I was able to piece a bit together. I think that those nasty shadow creatures caused the damage. They replayed his worst fears over and over, but they intensified it. They made him relive Rida's last moments; they even made him watch her die…though, it is my understanding that she was taken away and Jano did not actually witness it.*

Eorian looked out to where his father's tent stood, sadness and fury warring with each other inside him. "How can we fix it?"

Surprisingly, the answer came from Frelati. "Time."

"What?" Lishea and Eorian asked in unison.

Frelati shrugged. "He just needs some time. Their poison is still in his system. It tends to stay a while, and the side effects are intense fear, depression, and paranoia. However, it would also help if both of you treated him like he was still normal, which neither of you are doing. He'll find his way back faster if he recognizes what he used to be."

"How could you know that?" Lishea asked.

"He experienced it," Eorian responded before turning back to Frelati. "I still vividly remember your description of it too. Do you think, maybe, you could talk to him? Maybe if he knows someone else has experienced it, that it *can* get better, it'll help him."

Frelati nodded. "Since I'm not needed here right now, I'll go ahead and get started."

Eorian gave a smile of thanks as Frelati walked off. Then he turned back to the people still gathered around him: Genevia, Fil, Lishea, Diahyas, Asben, Gallutam, Burk, Clim, Finley, and Lius.

"We need a plan," he said. "We have support underwater for areas around freshwater, and keep in mind that the mermaids are capable of coming on land as well. We also have a lot of ships that can cover the salt water areas. There are foot soldiers, cavalry, and archers that are from all over Randor, Tiweln, and some from Faencina. The wispers can help as well. The majority of the fight is going to be on Sohsena, most likely centered around Cekogel. We have hundreds of shadow beings that will need to be contained, and we have only one weapon against them: Diahyas. Gallutam, Asben, the two of you are the smartest men I know. You have the list of our resources, and you have the numbers of the enemy we're fighting. I need you to tell me the best scenario in which our forces are used in their greatest capacity. Just know that Genevia, Diahyas, and I are going to need to stay together at all times, because all three of us are going to need to face Raef if we're going to get him off our planet."

They had decided on six factions, not including the groups of mermaids that had been placed at every river entrance around Sohsena. The faction names had been decided as well to make communication easier: Hy, Der, Eyd, Soh, Cek East, and Cek West. Each faction leader had been given a band so that everyone, regardless of distance, could keep track of the war and send reinforcements if needed.

Hy was the group fighting on Hius Yifwa. As the second largest continent on Randor, Raef saw it as the biggest threat. Once he had determined that they were no longer neutral and were instead allied with the enemy, he had sent a rather large force to beat them into submission.

The Hy faction was mainly made up of the people from Hius Yifwa, but Eorian had also allotted some fighters from Omwoe, the Yuens, and the shapeshifters to their cause. The fighting there was vicious, although Raef had fortunately not dispatched any shadow beings there.

Raef had emptied Nohaf Dosam, Randor's prison, for the most violent of prisoners, and drafted the meanest of the bunch into his army. They had been given free reign; several had even been placed in positions of leadership. As such, targets consisted of anything that moved. Civilians, children, even stray animals were not exempt from the fighting that began in Soothsa, Hius Yifwa's capital. Fires burned and many fell in the streets, but slowly, Hy faction fought back. Their numbers grew as they fought through a ransacked town; the civilians picked up whatever they could get their hands on as weapons to help push the invaders back.

They did manage to send the enemy out of the city, and they posted guards along the city wall to bar re-entry, but they remained under siege. Eorian was notified the moment the town was taken back under Hy's control, and the Hy commander assured him that they could hold it for some time. However, he cautioned that provisions were already low since much had been lost in the fire. They would need either reinforcements to rid them of this menace or more provisions within three weeks, or they would be forced to surrender, which could easily turn the war to Raef's favor.

Der was made up of a large fleet of ships in the Deras Sea. These ships contained some archers from Acentia, and they were all armed with new cannons, courtesy of Omwoe. Several countries had been the suppliers of ships, men, and weapons for both this group and Eyd, which was the second sea-based faction. Many humans from Tiweln were also stationed on the ships. Eyd was in the Eydizum Ocean and was essentially a mirror image of Der. Both groups were having an intense naval battle with the King's Army. However, they were both having a much easier time of it than Hy.

Eorian received countless reports of Raef's ships sinking because of a well-placed blast from the cannons. At least on the sea they outmatched Raef, whose ships were not equipped with anything to fire at Der or Eyd ships from long distances. However, there were still several of the King's Army vessels that managed to get in close, and once the soldiers boarded, everyone was on even ground again. There had been several reports of that happening, but overall, their victory was assured on the seas.

If only the fighting on Sohsena, where the factions of Soh, Cek East, and Cek West were stationed, could go so well.

CHAPTER 25

Eorian, Diahyas, Frelati, and Genevia were traveling with Cek East toward Cekogel. This group was made up of half of Eorian's crew, half of the soldiers from Tiweln, and half of all the other soldiers that Randor's countries could supply. The plan was to meet up with Cek West, which had the same soldier ratio as Cek East plus Fil and Lishea, in the middle of the Cekogel, and then push all of Raef's troops north toward the river, where the mermaids and wispers would be waiting. The capture of the city was paramount. If they could take control of Sohsena's capital, they would win it all. This was why, although everyone was in position around Cekogel, they were waiting to make sure that there would be no surprises to compromise this.

Relim was doing a sweep overhead, checking for any troops that could come at them from behind or the side. Until he gave the all clear, no one would move.

"Why be we concentrating all of our forces here, Eorian?" Diahyas asked. "Be there not enemy troops elsewhere to fight?"

Eorian nodded. "There are, but not in any great numbers, fortunately. Raef pulled his troops back here the moment we began attacking on Hius Yifwa and at sea. The other countries that sided with him are all busy in one of those three locations, so they can't come in to help him here. He knows how important his hold on this city is; we're in for a fight."

Diahyas frowned. "Then why be not all of the mermaids at the river to the north? You left several still in the Riffa Canal."

"Yes," Eorian replied. "As I said, Raef still has troops elsewhere. The wispers are covering any enemies to the north, though I doubt he'd send any there. We have Cek West and Der covering the west side, and Eyd and Cek East are covering the east side. That leaves the south wide open, and Hius Yifwa is not in the best position to hold. We need your mermaid troops as a buffer in the Riffa Canal to both watch for any men coming from Hius Yifwa and to stop whatever troops Raef still has in the south."

"Gallutam and Asben did well thinking this through," Diahyas praised.

"They had far too much fun working together, but their results speak for themselves."

Eorian's band buzzed, and he heard a hushed voice speak through it.

"Eorian, there be trouble down here at the Riffa Canal."

"What do you mean?" Eorian asked.

"There be several of the shadow creatures you mentioned in addition to the soldiers. I believe they be planning to come your way, but we cannot stop them. One of me men…he be touched. Everyone else be quite shaken by it."

Eorian thought quickly before asking another question. "Where exactly are they located? North or south of the canal?"

"South. The town they be staying in be utterly deserted, on the east coast right up against the canal. They be trying to cross over. We be doing our best to halt their progress, but as I said, there be not much we can do."

"Can you estimate the numbers?"

"A couple hundred troops, maybe fifty shadow beings?"

Eorian cursed. They couldn't fight the shadow beings on two fronts. They needed all of them close to the river so Diahyas could douse them.

"Stay put; I'll be in touch," he said quickly before shouting for Asben. Then he spoke into his band again. "Cek West, get Gallutam."

In a few moments, Asben and Gallutam were both by the bands to discuss the issue.

"It would take too long to send troops down there to fight," Gallutam said.

Asben argued. "Troops wouldn't help. Diahyas would be needed to stop the shadow beings, which are the only things making this a threat."

"Look at this logically," Gallutam countered. "It'll take days before they get here. Weeks if they're on foot. I say we ignore them. We could have Cekogel taken before they get here."

"Or it could take us longer than planned to capture Cekogel. It's a walled city. We may have to put them under siege, which could take a month. At that point, we'd be running low on supplies, and then the troops and shadow beings would arrive for us to fight. We'd be far from the water, so it would be difficult to stop the shadow beings, if not impossible, and once we were distracted by them, Raef could then send out his troops from the city to surround us. The war is lost."

"That is the most likely scenario," Gallutam agreed. "In fact, if I were Raef, that is exactly what I would be planning. However, if we leave now, we lose the element of surprise, which may be the only way we can get into the city."

"What about me tiara?" Diahyas asked, startling everyone.

"Interesting," Asben said as his mind began to factor in that piece of information.

"Her tiara functions as a portal, yes?" Gallutam said.

"Yes," Eorian said.

"That being the case, you could send Cek East down in a matter of seconds. You fight them, which realistically will take several hours, at which time her portal should be recharged, right, Asben?"

"The distance being...let's see, best estimate...fifteen hundred to sixteen hundred miles. At most it should take about five hours for the tiara to be ready to use again."

"That's a reasonable time frame for us to postpone the attack to ensure that we do not get surprised later," Gallutam said.

"I concur. We may want to retreat a bit, though, to ensure that our cover is not blown."

"Agreed," Gallutam said.

"I also have my necklace," Genevia said. "If we have to leave sooner for some reason, we can travel back here with it."

"That's a good contingency," Gallutam said. "Are we all clear on the plan?"

"Wait," Eorian said. "Do I need to bring this whole faction, half, a handful?"

"The entire faction," Gallutam said. "It will both reduce our chance of being seen, which would of course eliminate the surprise factor of this attack, and also will increase your chance of success down south. There isn't a limit to the number that can travel using the personal portals, is there, Asben?"

"Not as far as I am aware, but then again, I have not tried to transport this many before. This is the best course of action. Make the mermaids to the north aware of the change. They should relay the information to the wispers. Once we arrive at the Riffa Canal, we will send word."

Gallutam closed the connection.

"Asben, do the mermaids at the canal need to be ready to do anything specific?" Eorian asked.

Asben shook his head. "The shadow beings are afraid of the water, which will greatly work in our favor. Have the mermaids focus on whatever it is the shadow beings were planning to use to cross the canal. If they keep water flowing across it, it will keep the shadow beings at least partially distracted."

Eorian nodded and relayed the information before getting the attention of everyone in Cek East. "Grab your bags and make sure that you are physically touching those closest to you. We're about to travel to the Riffa Canal to do a little practice fighting."

"King Raef is expecting an attack on the capital any day now. You've all heard the reports of how well the war is going everywhere else; do you want the battle at the capital to go the same way because we couldn't get there on time?" Malnor glared at the men around him. "Do you want to go back to Nohaf Dosam? And for those of you here who haven't been there yet, you've heard the stories; do you want to go there at all?"

All the men around him shuffled their feet and shook their heads. His troop was a ragtag bunch. There were some soldiers with a bit of experience, but the majority of the group around him was made up of hardened criminals, just like he was. They did not coordinate well together, and most of them fought with wild abandon, focusing only on preserving their own lives at the expense of the allies that they accidentally took down with their enemies. All in all, Malnor did not care overly much about any of them, but if his troop did well, Raef would reward him handsomely. He was not going to let these incompetent fools take that away from him.

"Get those hydrophobic shadows across the canal, now!"

One of the larger hotheads challenged the order.

"And how exactly are we supposed to do that?" he asked. "You can't shove a shadow onto a boat or across a bridge, and even if you could, who wants to touch those things? You've seen what they can do. I don't want to try to force one across, have it splashed by one of those mermaids in the water—which aren't supposed to be *real*, by the way—and then have the shadow turn against me."

Malnor walked up until he was nose to nose with the man. "You can either take your chances by helping them across, or I can tell them to turn you right now. What'll it be?"

The man glared at him a moment or two, but his fear of the shadows was quite intense. It didn't stop him from making another comment though.

"I didn't agree to fight mythological mermaids. Have you seen them? They could pull us all under and drown us. We can't win against them."

The other men started nodding their heads in agreement, and Malnor knew he had to put an instant stop to it.

"Look there!" he yelled as he pointed toward the one unfortunate mermaid writhing on the ground from the touch of a shadow being. "The mermaids can easily be hurt, but you had better stay on the shadows' good side if you want their help."

That seemed to motivate all of them. Finally. They couldn't handle any more delays. Raef had wanted them to arrive at the capital a week from now. As it was, they would be lucky to get there in two weeks. Raef would not be pleased with that, but at least they could warn him that there were mermaids. That could put Malnor back in his favor...unless they were delayed again.

That's when he heard a shout of surprise. He closed his eyes briefly before turning to face the next obstacle.

"What's the problem..." he began at a shout but it quickly fizzled. "...now..." He stared in shock at the sight before him.

"The problem," said the tall blond man standing before a large number of fighters, "is that you are threatening our well-laid plans. That's going to have to stop."

Malnor was beyond confused. "Where did you come from? Who are you?"

The man answered the second question first. "Eorian."

Then he looked around at the faces of all of Malnor's frightened men with a grin.

"And we came," he began to rise off the ground, "from the sky."

At that, two of Malnor's more superstitious men took off running. Malnor hated them for it...partially because that's exactly what he wanted to do, but he had to lead his men and defeat this odd group.

"Attack!" he yelled.

In that moment, both groups charged forward. Eorian's focus was on Malnor, and he met up with him swiftly. Malnor grinned and spun his sword as Eorian stopped before him.

"Ready to play, little bird?" he asked.

"I don't think you're in my league," Eorian replied calmly. "If you want to run now, I won't tell a soul."

Malnor gritted his teeth angrily. Somehow, this man knew about his momentary wish to flee, but he would pay for the comment.

Malnor swung his sword, and it clanged against Eorian's as he parried. Several more jabs, stabs, and wild swings later brought Malnor to the conclusion that he had no chance against this man. He was a master swordsman. However, sheer numbers could easily overcome him. He whistled loudly, the signal put in place with four of his strongest men so that they would know to come to his side.

Five men now encircled the smug, blond man.

"Think you can win now?" Malnor asked.

A half grin appeared on Eorian's face after he had taken a quick glance to his left. "You aren't the only one with friends, and unfortunately for you, your friends can't do this."

With that, he flew up and over Malnor, landing softly behind him and putting the point of his sword in Malnor's back. The four other men, however, were paying him no attention. Instead, they were fighting against rapidly growing vines that twined around their arms and legs. Malnor's eyes widened in fear.

"What magic is this?" he asked.

"Kiem's kind," Eorian said softly. "And unfortunately, you picked the wrong side of the war. Genevia! How about tying this one up too?"

She nodded, and instantly vines began creeping up and wrapping tightly around Malnor.

"That should hold you while we finish this up. Don't you think?" Eorian said before he moved on to fight another battle.

Frelati, Genevia, and Diahyas already had their jobs for the upcoming fight, so once the battle cry was made, there was no confusion about where they should focus. Diahyas was to drown the shadow beings in water. Frelati was to keep soldiers away from Diahyas and stab the shadow beings with a torch if need be. Genevia was to ensure that no one escaped, whether they be human or shadow being. She had almost lost the first two men that had tried to run, but she'd managed to snag them both around the ankles with vines and drag them back.

Diahyas easily got the shadow beings in thrall as she threw water around. She was steadily backing them into a corner that was surrounded on all sides by water, and the mermaids in the canal were ready to help once they were all in position. There were a few shadow beings that tried to escape, but Genevia had carefully forced them back to some mermaids, who then splashed them back into the fold.

Frelati was nearly back to back with Diahyas as he fought off soldiers. The moment they realized what Diahyas was doing, many had focused in on her as a high-priority target, so Frelati had his hands full.

"Ready to test our theory?" Diahyas asked Frelati.

He sliced the arm of a soldier who had come a little too close, and as the man backed away, Frelati lurched forward to snag a rather large stick on the ground between them.

"I need some more men over here," he shouted before turning and holding the stick high in the air. "Asben, find a way to light this."

Diahyas whipped some more water around as a few of the larger shadow beings started creeping forward.

"Come closer," she said. "I have a present for you."

She threw a few balls of water toward a batch of them, and they skittered and hopped in fright to avoid being hit. Behind her, she heard several men arrive to cover Frelati's position, and he moved over to

Asben, who quickly lit the stick.

"Now, Diahyas," Frelati shouted as he began pushing his way back toward her.

Diahyas focused on surrounding one of the larger shadow beings in water. He darted back and forth to avoid being covered, but soon she had him wrapped in a bubble of liquid and lifted a bit off the ground. Just as the shadow dragon had said, the creature lost its form. It began fading in and out of shape, though it still tried to struggle out of her hold.

Then Frelati ran forward and shoved his stick into her water orb. She allowed the fire to pass within without the water dousing it, and the moment it struck the heart of the creature, it vanished. Diahyas allowed the water to cascade to the ground.

"It worked!" she said excitedly.

Frelati nodded in utter bemusement. "It did work."

"Don't just stand there and gawk; get rid of the rest of them before one can slip past and reach us," Eorian said as he fought his way closer.

"Right," Frelati said. "Diahyas, surround some more of these things in water; I'll go grab the special torch from Asben now that we know this works."

Frelati jogged off again, stopping briefly to check on Genevia, who was yelling at a man that she was surrounding in vines.

"I told you to stay put," she said angrily. "Cutting through my plants and running is the opposite of that."

"Ouch!" the man shouted as he squirmed some more.

"Oh, is that too tight?" Genevia asked sarcastically.

"You doing all right over here, honey?" Frelati asked with a raised brow.

She gave him a smile. "I'm handling the borders, but if you distract me, I could miss someone."

"Just stopped to tell you we killed one," Frelati dropped a kiss on her forehead and then jogged off to Asben.

"You hear that?" Genevia taunted the vine-covered man. "Your little shadow beings have a weakness that we just exploited."

Then another man caught her attention a few yards away.

"Where do you think you're going?" she called, and he began to run faster. "I swear, I need a wall...ah, that's what I'll do."

Frelati reached Asben just as a rival did, and he barely managed to divert the blow from digging deeply into Asben's shoulder.

"You all right, Asben?" Frelati asked as he fought the guy off.

"Not particularly, no," Asben said as he brushed some dirt off his pants. "Very glad you're here, though."

"I need the fire stick thing you made," Frelati said with a huff as he deflected an attack.

"But...it's a prototype," Asben argued. "It needs to be tested."

"We'll test it now."

"I still think I should look over the mechanics of it—"

"Asben, it'll be fine. Whoa! I'll take your hand off for that one," Frelati shouted at his opponent as he began attacking more vigorously. "Get the stick, Asben!"

"Why can't we use the branch I set aflame for you?" Asben asked as he slowly removed the covering from around his invention.

Frelati backed toward him, still fighting the soldier. "Because it was small, and the fire ate away at it until it nearly burned me."

Asben held up his fire stick with a frown. "I'm not even sure it functions properly. It may not even shoot..."

Frelati grabbed the torch and hit the button. Instantly, flames shot out and engulfed the man Frelati had been fighting. He dropped his weapon, screamed, and ran for the canal, at which point the mermaids quickly dispatched of him.

"Fire," Asben finished lamely as he watched the smoke spiral up from the canal.

"I think it works," Frelati said. "Thanks!"

Then he ran off toward Diahyas.

"Line them up for me!" he shouted to her, and she lifted a row of water-trapped shadow beings to waist height.

"Ready?" Frelati asked her. She nodded with her face set tightly. "Fire!"

Out the fire shot in a great flame, and Frelati ran it along the line of shadow beings until each had vanished to nothing.

"Water and fire," he said with a chuckle. "Who knew?"

Unfortunately, it was at that point that the remaining thirty or so shadow beings realized that staying where they were meant death. As one, they all began to charge.

"Diahyas, block them!" Frelati yelled.

Using every ounce of power she had, Diahyas raised her arms and began pulling water from the Riffa Canal and the ocean to create a wall of water to block the shadow beings' path.

At the same moment, Genevia began trying to create a large wall around the city to keep the soldiers from escaping.

That's when everyone felt the ground beneath them shift. All eyes, on both sides of the battle, widened and looked around for answers. Then they began to sink, and water crawled up the edges of the city.

"To the portal!" Eorian ordered, and every one of the people with him rushed over to circle around him. "Is that everyone?"

Nods all around as water puddled around their feet.

"What about the soldiers and shadow beings?" Genevia asked.

"The wall you built over there will keep them from escaping that way, and the mermaids will take care of the rest. We've got to go, now!"

With the water at knee height and inching up faster than ever, the large group disappeared the same way they had come just before the city sank beneath the ocean.

CHAPTER 26

"Did we just sink a city?" Genevia asked in horror as they arrived back at their original location several miles outside of Cekogel.

"I'm not sure what just happened," Eorian said in all honesty.

Diahyas started crying. "I destroy everything! Never again! Never again will I use this curse I once called a gift!"

"The city was empty," Frelati tried to comfort her awkwardly. "Well, except for the soldiers and shadow beings…but we wanted to keep them there anyway."

"Those soldiers I had wrapped up in vines…they'll drown," Genevia murmured.

Frelati turned to her and rubbed her back. "The second you left, those vines would have lost the extra strength you put in them to hold the men. They could break free."

"I killed them," Diahyas said softly as she continued to cry. "And I sank the homes of so many people. Where will they live?"

"Both of you calm down," Eorian said. "This is a war we're fighting, in case you've forgotten. There will be casualties, and the only people left in that city were our enemies."

"Casualties, yes, but destroying an entire city?" Genevia asked. "What we did can't be fixed. We *sank* a *city*."

"I saw," Eorian said. "What I want to know is *how*. Yes, we unintentionally caused the destruction of a city, but like Frelati said, it was empty. It's better we know that it can happen so we can avoid doing it again in a populated area. Asben…theories?"

Asben took his glasses off, cleaned them, and replaced them on his nose before speaking. When he did, the words came hesitantly.

"I have a guess, only," he began. "From my vantage point in the middle, I had a fairly good view of everything. As such, I saw Genevia lifting the earth on the west and south sides of the city to create a wall. Simultaneously, Diahyas was drawing up water from the north and east sides of the city."

Asben held his hands out before him as if they were scales. "Genevia lifts the earth here on the one side. Diahyas pushes down with water on the other side. The sheer pressure of both was equal to a massive natural disaster felt deep below the city—essentially, an earthquake and a hurricane occurring at the same time. The foundation holding the city just above sea level crumbled..."Asben slowly let his hands sink. "There you have it."

Diahyas and Genevia looked at each other then turned away.

"I suppose I should have foreseen something along these lines happening," Asben said with a frown. "The powers each of you wield individually can be devastating; once you all start fighting together... we will need to be more aware of what each of you are doing to prevent another such incident."

"All right, we know now," Eorian said, feeling a bit scared of his own power. "We need to get our heads on straight. This isn't over yet, and we need to attack Cekogel before they catch on to us. Genevia, are you going to be all right?"

Genevia shook her head quickly.

"That's not the answer I was looking for," Eorian said on a sigh. "Frelati, please help. Take her...somewhere and try to fix it. You have an hour."

Relim, Eorian called out.

Look who has returned, the bird said sarcastically. *After I flew circle after circle and came to give you a report, what do I find? Nothing. It was so kind of you to remember to tell me about your change in plan.*

I'm sorry, Eorian said. *We had an issue down south that had to be handled quickly. Can you take another sweep for me and give me an update?*

Only if you promise you'll still be here when I return.

I'm not going anywhere.

And a dove or two...I do so love those.

Fine. Two doves.

And perhaps Lishea could rub my wings? They are quite sore from all this flying.

Just go, Relim.

Such abuse. You know, a please can go a long way in winning over a bird's favor.

Please.

He felt Relim's smug satisfaction as the bird flew off.

Eorian turned to Diahyas. "How are you?"

She merely stared at him with red-rimmed eyes from where she sat hugging her knees on the ground.

"That bad, huh?" Eorian sighed and collapsed down beside her. "All right, we have an hour. What do I need to do to get you ready to go in an hour?"

"You can do nothing," she said softly.

"Okay, then what can I say?"

"Nothing."

Eorian frowned at her. "I need you to work with me here."

"I need to go home."

"Why?"

"I cannot hurt anyone there," Diahyas said. "Everything be already under water there."

"Not the Yuen villages," Eorian replied before realizing that was not his smartest move. He quickly backtracked. "But...you know, a lot of them were thinking about coming over here or going to Tiweln. Looking for a better life or something. No need to worry about all that."

"I do not know me gift as I once thought. I feel as if me body be betraying me."

"Gotta hate that," Eorian said, once again kicking himself for yet another unhelpful response. "I'm sorry. I'm not good at this. Do you want me to find someone else you can talk to?"

Diahyas shook her head. "Sea-ena always knew what to say. I usually ignored her though."

"Sounds like me and my pa."

"What be he like...before those evil creatures messed with his mind?" Diahyas asked.

"I'll tell you all about him," Eorian said. "But I want you to show me some water tricks while I do."

"No," Diahyas said vehemently.

"Get back on the horse," Eorian said, receiving a very confused look from Diahyas. "My pa used to always say that. We have these creatures called horses that we ride, and they are quite tall. For a child, falling off of them was terrifying, but pa would say, 'Get back on the horse.' In other words, face your fear. Unfortunately, we don't have a lot of time to do that, so I need you to work with me. You play with a little water, and I promise I will answer whatever questions you may have."

"Any questions at all?" Diahyas asked with a slight gleam in her eye.

Eorian would have been worried about it had he not been so relieved to see a bit of life come back into her. "Anything."

Raef heard the reports just a few minutes after the traitors attacked. However, all he did was give orders to his soldiers to kill off as many traitors as they could before they reached the palace. That was clearly their ultimate destination. He would await them here with a few of his wraiths; the rest he would allow to play...with the understanding, of course, that they were to return to him the moment his three enemies reached the gates.

He never enjoyed the waiting. However, it was always more tolerable when the sounds of war drifted toward him. It did not take as long as he had expected before those sounds reached him through an open window. It seemed that Eorian had created a little more than a small gathering of ruffians to fight with him. That would make this a lot more satisfying.

He would have to kill all three essences this time, although his attempt to kill Genevia had proven exactly how difficult that would be. The host bodies would not pose too great a problem, but as Kiem's earth essence had stated, it would take a lot more than a simple shadow arrow to destroy a piece of the universe's creator. He would enjoy finding out exactly what it took to kill each of them.

Raef waited rather impatiently, his fingers drumming against the armrest. Soon they would be here, and activity would surround him. The sounds had been gradually increasing, and he easily followed their progress. It seemed they were coming from two directions, which made little sense for a group bent on getting into one single location.

Then Raef sat up straight, listening intently. He must be mistaken. The sound was fading, traveling to the north. Raef moved to the window and peered out. What were they doing? From his position in the castle, he couldn't see much. Surely he was mishearing something.

He strode to the door, threw it open, and addressed the small group of soldiers standing just outside. "What is happening? Have they reached the gates?"

One man shook his head. "You will be safe, your highness. They have moved on according to the last report."

"To the north?"

The man nodded.

"I suppose it does not matter which direction my men push the traitors, just so long as they leave my city," Raef mused.

"We aren't the ones doing the pushing," another soldier said.

"What?" Raef snapped.

"The enemy directed everyone north. I'm guessing they don't much like fighting in the city around civilians," the man said with a shrug.

Raef's mind began racing furiously. "Where are my wraiths?"

"The last messenger said they were with all the other soldiers."

"Why did they not return here as ordered?"

"You told them to return once the palace was under attack, but it doesn't look as if they are planning to come here."

"The landscape to the north...the wispers live there, but what else?" Raef asked.

"Well, there are quite a few towns, but they won't get to the wispers or those towns. They wouldn't be able to cross the river."

Raef's eyes widened in sudden understanding.

"They know," he muttered before loudly shouting orders to his men. "Gather whoever is left here to fight with me. We are meeting them outside the city."

Eorian was staying close, and every time Diahyas started feeling her confidence weaken, he said just the right words of encouragement to help her continue. There was a massive battle all around them. It was difficult to tell whether or not they had the upper hand. All of the essences and Frelati were close to the river. The mermaids there were fighting anyone who got close, and some of them had even come on land to fight. They were also hugely instrumental in keeping the shadow beings in check.

Diahyas gathered them up in pairs and trios with her water, Frelati fired up Asben's new weapon, and Eorian made it even more powerful by fueling it with more oxygen and directing the flame toward the shadow beings that were trapped.

Genevia had her back to them as she focused on the battle all around. She was carefully tripping the enemy with vines or mounds of earth to give her allies an upper hand. It seemed to be going fairly well.

Then darkness instantly fell.

There were shouts of fear and surprise. Most of the clanging of swords ceased since no one could be certain if they were fighting friend or foe. Not long after, though, cries of pain began to sound as the wraiths attacked, and panic ensued. Frelati lit up the fire stick to give some small bit of light, and by its glow they watched the shadow beings slip around them and begin to incapacitate their fighters. Frelati was barely managing to keep them away from their small group.

"Diahyas, surround us in water," Eorian said.

She took a deep breath and did as he asked.

"Fezam is here," Genevia said worriedly as she looked at the terror unfolding around them.

"We knew that was going to happen," Frelati said calmly. "Now you each have to do what we planned."

"Right," Eorian said as he shot high in the sky.

"I don't know how long to wait," Genevia said in a slight panic. "I can't see where Eorian is or when he'll be behind Fezam, and I don't know which direction to aim."

"Relim is signaling us, remember?" Frelati said. "Diahyas, get ready. The moment the darkness weakens, you need to trap as many shadow beings as you can."

Then the cry sounded high above and a bit to Genevia's left. She turned, focused, and slammed her foot into the ground. It began rolling straight ahead, almost as if a creature were burrowing toward her target. She heard some shouts, and the darkness flickered. A sound like a whirlwind began, and the darkness completely collapsed in time for Diahyas to see Dehga thrown forward and into the ground. The anger on his face was terrifying.

"Now, Diahyas!" Frelati shouted.

Diahyas instantly began locating the shadow beings, who had done quite a lot of damage, and surrounded each in water. Frelati began running between them and destroying each with his flame. Although Diahyas was focusing intently upon keeping each of the shadow beings trapped, she was aware of Genevia and Eorian pummeling Dehga with their respective essences.

Genevia had wrapped Dehga in thorny vines and was throwing rocks toward him while Eorian had him in the middle of a massive tornado that was taking those rocks and whipping them around viciously.

With the darkness gone, all of their soldiers began fighting again, this time with renewed energy.

Diahyas counted the remaining shadow beings. Ten left...Frelati set fire to one...nine left. A scream rent the air, breaking her concentration completely. She turned toward the sound to find Genevia crumpled on the ground, gripping her head tightly.

"Genevia!" she shouted as she rushed forward.

Frelati got there first, and he wrapped his arms around her protectively. That was when Diahyas saw a shadow being creeping toward him. She gasped and threw water toward the vicious creature, but he still managed to scrape a claw along Frelati's back. Another shout of pain filled the air as Frelati collapsed beside his wife.

"Fil! Grab the fire stick!" Eorian yelled as he continued his whirlwind around Dehga.

Diahyas saw Fil run toward the stick and snap it up. She quickly trapped the other eight shadow beings so that Fil could dispatch them.

Eorian threw Dehga up into the air and then released him to crash into the ground. As he pushed himself up, those red eyes drilled into her, and the pure fury and hatred within them was terrifying...but it was also empowering. Diahyas set her shoulders back and lifted her chin. She glanced quickly around to see how many water balls she still needed; five more shadow beings. She could handle that and help Eorian at the same time.

He started winding up his air again, and Diahyas provided a steady stream of water into the mix. She saw Eorian grin at her from behind Dehga before a look of deep concentration filled his features. Diahyas looked closely at the hurricane they had created and saw shards of ice flying around inside. Eorian had managed to cool the air enough to freeze her water. Diahyas grinned.

Before her, Genevia slowly pulled herself to her feet and added to the debris within the hurricane. It was a maelstrom in there. Diahyas could see Dehga struggling inside, fighting against the whirling particles ripping into him. He gave a tremendous shout and threw everything into darkness again. It lasted just a moment, and then the bright sunlight hit them full force.

Dehga was gone. They all looked at one another for an explanation. The fighting around them stilled.

"Fil," Eorian said tiredly. "Finish off those last few shadow beings, will you?"

Fil nodded and quickly did just that.

"Where did he go?" Diahyas asked.

Genevia quickly crouched down beside Frelati, who was taking deep, shuddering breaths, and gently settled his head into her lap.

"I assume he went back to his planet to regroup and start another fight elsewhere," she said softly before whispering lovingly to Frelati in an attempt to pull him from his wraith-induced nightmare.

"Do you surrender?" Eorian shouted to the fifty or so soldiers who remained.

Every hand went into the air.

EPILOGUE

A lot of clean-up was required after a war. The most difficult thing about it all was finding a ruler to fill the void left in Sohsena. Eorian absolutely refused to take the job, which had been offered to him in the absence of heirs and because he clearly had clout with most of the surrounding nations, but he did want a say in the person they chose. Of course, Sohsena was not the only nation that needed a ruler. The wispers were searching for someone as well. Again, Eorian refused their offer but agreed to be a mediator between them and the humans.

The elves, humans, shape-shifters, and a few nomads that had traveled over from Tiweln to aid Eorian returned home, all of them with some token of gratitude given from each of the nations allied with Eorian. The nomads received gold and jewels, the elves received samples of the different plants and some animals that were unknown to them on Tiweln, the humans and shapeshifters received some weapons and some other treasures of their choosing…in the case of Asben, that resulted in a lot of books. The Yuens were given some land in the north of Sohsena, at least for those who wished to start fresh. Those who wanted to return to Faencina were given information and tools to help make their lives a bit easier and less primitive.

Jano was slowly recovering with the help of Uratia and Finley. Frelati was also doing a lot better, and they expected him to recover even more swiftly once he was back on Tiweln and could be given some of their healing herbs. After Genevia made plans to meet up with Eorian and Diahyas at Fil and Lishea's wedding the following year, she and Frelati had returned home.

The most difficult thing, though, was helping the mermaids. Faencina was having quite a time. There had been over ten cities and towns that were now uninhabitable due to the salt content, and the rest of Faencina was not as salt-free as they would like. The scientists, along with Asben and Gallutam, were working furiously to find a way to fix the issue, but that did nothing for the thousands and thousands of misplaced mermaids. That was when Eorian remembered the sunken city. When he and Diahyas went to investigate, they discovered that more than one city had fallen beneath the ocean. The entire land mass beneath the Riffa Canal was now completely waterlogged. The mermaids stationed there had rescued several people in the aftermath. Although it was terrible that it had happened, it was the perfect place for the misplaced mermaids to settle.

After discussions with Diahyas' parents, Eorian also offered a place on Faencina to the families that had lost their homes to the water. Many of them refused, but there were several younger people that loved the idea of an adventure. After discussions with other nations, several more people were found that would stay on Faencina for at least a short time.

Eorian had delivered on almost all of his bargain. Diahyas sighed. Now her parents would make him fulfill the rest. It was not fair to him. That was why she was meeting with her parents now, though she did not expect anything to change.

She had requested to meet with them in a small room. The throne room always seemed so very overwhelming, and the distance between them seemed to make it easier for them to deny her requests. Both her mother and father were already in the small study waiting on her.

"Thank you for meeting me here," she said with true gratitude, and she received a startled smile from her father.

"We would not refuse your request," he said.

Her mother scoffed at that. "What be you wanting?"

"I..." Diahyas took a deep breath. "I request that you release Eorian from his oath. He has already fulfilled the part of the bargain that you wished for the most. There be humans here now. There be no need for you to force him to—"

"You be wishing to back out of yet another mating," her mother said angrily, her hands clenching into fists. "I shall not allow it."

"But...he doesn't deserve it!" Diahyas argued.

"He made his choice," Bailena said with flashing eyes.

Leeyan laid a calming hand on his wife's shoulder as he scrutinized his daughter curiously.

"Why be you requesting this?" he asked gently. "Would you not prefer to mate with someone you know and get along with rather than some stranger among the elite wealthy?"

Diahyas looked down sadly and bit her lip. She shook her head. "It does not matter what I prefer. He does not deserve it."

The silence around her was heavy, but she could not bring herself to look up at her parents.

"Bailena," she heard her father say softly. "You realize that we have yet to uphold our end of the deal."

"What have we not done?" she asked crossly. "We sent over our troops. Several died there."

"True," Leeyan said. "But we have not found Sea-ena."

Diahyas closed her eyes to keep the tears from falling. They had found nothing, heard nothing. She was utterly lost.

"We agreed that the mating would be postponed until Sea-ena could be there," Leeyan continued.

"She be not found at this point," Bailena argued. "We cannot postpone this indefinitely in the hopes that a mere servant be located. She be most likely dead."

"Perhaps, and perhaps she be not," Leeyan agreed. "At the very least, some time must be allowed in finding her. Two years. After that point, I say we re-evaluate, see if it still be in our best interests for these two to mate. If so, we shall proceed."

"Much can happen in two years," Bailena said crossly.

Diahyas looked up at her father in wonder, and he sent her a wink and a smile as he agreed with his wife. "Yes, quite a lot can happen."

Made in the USA
Charleston, SC
08 November 2015